The critics on Daniel Silva

'A tense, well-crafted piece of storytelling . . . Silva brings to life a tale of suspense that spirals its way to an evocative climax' *The Times*

'Silva, whose debut, *The Unlikely Spy*, put the WWII thriller back on the map, brings the genre up to date with a vengeance in an exhilarating story that roots razzle-dazzle espionage heroics in contemporary political headlines' *Kirkus*

'A literate thriller, well researched and fast-moving' *San Francisco Chronicle*

'Filled with the kind of dark passages that keep fans of spy thrillers guessing as they eagerly turn the pages . . . briskly suspenseful, tightly constructed and full of well-rounded, believable characters' *New York Times*

'A must-read' *Entertainment Weekly*

'Silva has clearly done his homework, mixing fact and fiction to delicious effect and building tension – with breathtaking double and triple turns of the plot' *People*

'Layers of depth and intrigue . . . Silva succeeds with panache' *USA Today*

Daniel Silva's first novel, *The Unlikely Spy*, was an international bestseller and was sold as a major motion picture to Twentieth Century Fox. A former journalist and television producer, Silva has covered everything from Washington politics to the conflicts of the Middle East. He has lived and worked in Cairo and now lives in the Georgetown section of Washington D.C. with his wife, NBC News Show correspondent Jamie Gangel, and their two children.

By the same author

The Unlikely Spy
The Mark of the Assassin

THE
MARCHING
SEASON

Daniel Silva

ORION

An Orion paperback
First published in Great Britain by Weidenfeld & Nicolson in 1999
This paperback edition published in 1999 by Orion Books Ltd,
Orion House, 5 Upper St Martin's Lane, London WC2H 9EA

A CIP catalogue record for this book is available
from the British Library.

ISBN: 0 75282 649 2

Typeset at The Spartan Press Ltd, Lymington, Hants
Printed and bound in Great Britain by Clays Ltd, St Ives plc.

For Ion Trewin, for friendship and faith,
and as always, for my wife Jamie,
and my children, Lily and Nicholas.

FOREWORD

The current period of violence in Northern Ireland, known as 'the Troubles,' erupted in August 1969. Broadly speaking it is a conflict between Republicans, who are predominantly Catholic and who want the North to unite with the Irish Republic, and Unionists, or Loyalists, who are predominantly Protestant and want to maintain the union between Ulster and the United Kingdom. Each side has produced a veritable alphabet soup of paramilitary groups and terrorist organizations. The most famous, of course, is the Provisional Irish Republican Army, the IRA. It has carried out hundreds of assassinations and thousands of bombings in Northern Ireland and on the British mainland. In 1984 it nearly succeeded in blowing up Margaret Thatcher and her government at a hotel in Brighton. In 1991 it fired a mortar into Downing Street. The Loyalists have their gunmen and bombers too – the UVF, the UDA, and the UFF, just to name a few – and they too have carried out appalling acts of terrorism. In fact, of the 3,500 people killed since the Troubles began, most have been Catholics.

But the violence did not begin in 1969. Catholics and Protestants have been killing each other in the north of Ireland for centuries, not decades. Historical markers can be difficult to fix, but Protestants regard 1690 as the beginning of their ascendancy in the north. It was then that William of Orange defeated King James II, a Roman Catholic, at the Battle of the Boyne. To this day Protestants celebrate William's victory over the Catholics with a series of noisy and sometimes confrontational parades. In Northern Ireland this time is known as 'the marching season.'

On May 22, 1998, the people of Northern Ireland voted to accept the Good Friday peace accords, which call for power sharing between Catholics and Protestants. But memories are long in Ulster, and neither side has been willing to declare that the civil war is truly over. Indeed, the period since the election has seen several acts of heinous terrorism, including the bombing of Omagh, which killed twenty-eight people – the bloodiest single act of terror in the history of the Troubles – and the arson fire in Ballymoney in which three Catholic children burned to death. Clearly, there are men of violence on both sides of Northern Ireland's sectarian divide – Catholic and Protestant, Republican and Unionist – who cannot forget and are not prepared to forgive. Some of those men are actively plotting to destroy the peace agreement.

It might happen something like this . . .

JANUARY

1

BELFAST
DUBLIN
LONDON

Eamonn Dillon of Sinn Fein was the first to die, and he died because he planned to stop for a pint at the Celtic Bar before heading up the Falls Road to a meeting in Andersontown. Twenty minutes before Dillon's death, a short distance to the east, his killer hurried along the pavements of Belfast city centre through a cold rain. He wore a dark green oilskin coat with a brown corduroy collar. His code name was Black Sheep.

The air smelled of sea salt and faintly of the rusting shipyards of Belfast Lough. It was just after 4 P.M. but already dark. Night falls early on a winter's night in Belfast; morning dawns slowly. The city centre was bathed in yellow sodium light, but Black Sheep knew that West Belfast, his destination, would feel like the wartime blackout.

He continued north up Great Victoria Street, past the curious fusion of old and new that makes up the face of central Belfast – the constant reminders that these few blocks have been bombed and rebuilt countless times. He passed the shining façade of the Europa, infamous for being the most bombed hotel on the planet. He passed the new opera house and wondered why anyone in Belfast would want to listen to the music of someone else's tragedy. He passed a hideous American doughnut shop filled with laughing Protestant schoolchildren in crested

5

blazers. I do this for you, he told himself. I do this so you won't have to live in an Ulster dominated by the fucking Catholics.

The larger buildings of the city receded, and the pavements slowly emptied of other pedestrians until he was quite alone. He walked for about a quarter of a mile and crossed over the M1 motorway near the towering Divis Flats. The overpass was scrawled with graffiti: VOTE SINN FEIN; BRITISH TROOPS OUT OF NORTHERN IRE-LAND; RELEASE ALL POWS. Even if Black Sheep had known nothing of the city's complex sectarian geography, which was certainly not the case, the signs were impossible to miss. He had just crossed the frontier into enemy territory – Catholic West Belfast.

The Falls spread west like a fan, narrow at its mouth near the city centre, broad to the west, beneath the shadow of Black Mountain. The Falls Road – simply 'the road' in the lexicon of Catholic West Belfast – cuts through the neighbourhood like a river, with tributaries leading into the thickets of terraced houses where British soldiers and Roman Catholics have engaged in urban guerrilla warfare for three decades. The commercial centre of the Falls is the intersection of the Springfield Road and the Grosvenor Road. There are markets, clothing shops, hardware stores, and pubs. Taxis filled with passengers shuttle up and down the street. It looks much like any other working-class neighbourhood in a British city, except the doorways are encased in black steel cages and the taxis never stray from the Falls Road because of Protestant killer squads. The dilapidated white terraces of the Ballymurphy housing estate dominate the western edge of the Falls. Ballymurphy is the ideological heartland of West Belfast, and over the years it has supplied a steady stream of recruits to the IRA. Bellicose murals stare over the Whiterock Road toward the rolling green hills of the city cemetery, where many of Ballymurphy's men are buried beneath simple headstones. To the north, across the Springfield Road, a giant army barracks and police station stands like a besieged fortress in enemy territory, which indeed it is. Strangers aren't welcome in the 'Murph,' even Catholic strangers. British soldiers don't set foot there without their giant armoured personnel carriers, called saracens – 'pigs' to the people of Ballymurphy.

Black Sheep had no intention of going anywhere near Ballymurphy. His destination was further to the east – the headquarters of Sinn Fein, the political wing of the Irish Republican Army, located at Number 51–55 Falls Road. As he moved deeper into the Falls, the spires of St Peter's Cathedral rose to his left. A trio of British soldiers drifted across the ugly asphalt square in front of the cathedral, now pausing to peer through the infrared sights of their rifles, now spinning on their heels to see if anyone was following them. *Don't speak to them*, his handlers had told him. *Don't even look at them. If you look at them, they'll know you're an outsider*. Black Sheep kept his hands in his pockets and his gaze on the pavement in front of him.

He turned into Dunville Park and sat down on a bench. Despite the rain, schoolboys played football in the weak light of the streetlights. A group of women – mothers and older sisters, by the look of them – watched carefully from the imaginary sidelines. A pair of British soldiers strode through the middle of the game, but the boys played around them as though they were invisible. Black Sheep reached in his coat pocket and withdrew his cigarettes, a ten-pack of Benson & Hedges, perfect for the perpetually tight budgets of working-class West Belfast. He lit one and returned the cigarettes to his pocket. His hand brushed against the butt of a Walther automatic.

From his vantage point on the bench the man could see the Falls Road perfectly: Sinn Fein headquarters where the target worked each day, the Celtic Bar where he drank in the late afternoon.

Dillon's speaking to a community meeting in Andersontown at five o'clock, Black Sheep's handlers had told him. *That means he's on a tight schedule. He'll leave headquarters at four-thirty and walk over to the Celtic for a quick one.*

The door of Sinn Fein headquarters swung open. For an instant the interior lights spilled onto the rainy pavement. Black Sheep spotted his target, Eamonn Dillon, the third-ranking officer of Sinn Fein, behind only Gerry Adams and Martin McGuinness, and a member of the negotiating team for the peace talks. And a dedicated family man as well, with a wife and two sons, Black Sheep thought. He pushed the image from his mind. No time for that now. One bodyguard accompanied Dillon. The door closed again, and the two men moved west along the Falls Road.

Black Sheep tossed his cigarette onto the ground, stood, and walked across the park. He climbed a short set of steps and stood at the intersection of the Falls Road and the Grosvenor Road. He pressed the button for the crossing and calmly waited for the light to turn from red to green. Dillon and his bodyguard were still about a hundred yards from the Celtic. The light changed. There were no British soldiers on the Falls Road, just the pair standing near the football match down in the park. When he reached the other side of the road Black Sheep turned and walked east, placing himself on a collision course with Dillon and the bodyguard.

He moved quickly now, head down, right hand wrapped around the butt of the Walther. He glanced up, checked Dillon's position, and looked down again. Thirty yards, thirty-five at most. He released the safety on the Walther. He thought of the Protestant children, eating doughnuts in Great Victoria Street.

8

I do this for you. I do this for God and Ulster.

He withdrew the Walther and aimed it at the body-guard, pulling the trigger twice before the man could release his own weapon from a shoulder holster beneath his raincoat. The shots struck him in the upper chest, and he collapsed onto the wet pavement.

Black Sheep swung his arm and pointed the gun at Eamonn Dillon's face. He hesitated, just for an instant. He couldn't do it, not in the face. He lowered the gun and pulled the trigger twice.

The shots pierced Dillon's heart.

He fell backward onto the pavement, one arm strewn across the bloody chest of his bodyguard. Black Sheep pressed the barrel of his Walther against the side of Dillon's head and fired one last shot.

The second act was unfolding at precisely the same moment, one hundred miles to the south, in Dublin, where a small man limped along a footpath in St Stephen's Green through a steady rain. His code name was Master. He might have been mistaken for a student at nearby Trinity College, which was his intention. He wore a tweed jacket, collar up, and corduroy trousers shiny with wear. He had the dark eyes and the unkempt beard of a devout Muslim, which he was not. In his right hand he carried a boxy briefcase, so old it smelled of damp rather than leather.

He entered Kildare Street and passed the entrance of the Shelbourne Hotel, adorned with statues of Nubian princesses and their slaves. He lowered his head as he slipped through a knot of tourists heading to tea in the Lord Mayor's Lounge.

By the time he reached Molesworth Street it was nearly impossible to pretend the briefcase hanging from his right arm was not abnormally heavy. The muscles of his shoulder burned, and he could feel dampness beneath his arms. The National Library loomed before him. He hurried inside and crossed the front entrance hall, passing a display of George Bernard Shaw's manuscripts. He switched the briefcase from his right hand to his left and approached the attendant.

'I'd like a pass for the reading room,' he said, carefully replacing his hard-edged West Belfast accent with the softer lilt of the south. The attendant handed him a pass without looking up.

Master took the stairs to the third floor, entered the famous reading room, and found an empty spot next to a fussy-looking man who smelled of mothballs and linseed oil. He opened a side flap on the briefcase, withdrew a thin volume of Gaelic poetry, and placed it softly on the leather-topped desk. He turned on the green-shaded lamp. The fussy-looking man looked up, pulled a frown, and returned to his own work.

For several minutes Master pretended to be engrossed in his poetry, yet all the while his instructions buzzed through his mind like annoying recorded announcements in a rail terminal. *The timer is set for five minutes*, his handler had said during the final briefing. *Enough time for you to get clear of the library, not enough time for security to do anything if the briefcase is discovered.*

He kept his head down, gaze fastened on the text. Every few minutes he would lift his hand and scribble a few notes in a small spiral-bound notebook. He heard soft footfalls around him, pages turning, pencils scratching, discreet sniffles and coughs, byproducts of the eternal damp of the Dublin winter. He resisted the impulse to look at them. He wanted them to remain anonymous, faceless. He had no quarrel with the Irish people, only the Irish government. He took no pleasure at the thought of shedding innocent blood.

He glanced at his wristwatch – 4:45 P.M. He reached down beneath his legs on the pretence of withdrawing a second volume of poetry, but once his hand was inside the musty old briefcase it lingered for a second or two longer, searching for the small plastic trigger that would arm the detonator. He gently threw the switch, holding it carefully between his thumb and forefinger to dampen the click. He removed his hand and placed the second volume, unopened, next to the first. He glanced at his watch, a stainless-steel analogue model with a sweep second hand, and carefully noted the time he had set the detonator.

He turned and looked at the fussy man at the next desk, who was glaring back at him as though he had been doing callisthenics. 'Can you tell me where the toilet is?' Master whispered.

'What?' the fussy-looking man said, bending his crimson ear with the end of a gnawed yellow pencil.

'The toilet,' the man repeated, slightly louder this time, though still whispering.

The man removed the pencil from his ear, frowned again, and pointed the tip toward the doorway at the far end of the room.

Master glanced at his watch as he walked across the room. Forty seconds gone. He quickened his pace, making for the doorway, but five seconds later he heard an ear-shattering sound, like a thunderclap, and felt a hot blast of air lift him from his feet and hurtle him across the great room like a dead leaf caught in an autumn gale.

In London, a tall woman wearing blue jeans, hiking boots, and a black leather jacket was picking her way through the crowded pavements along the Brompton Road. Behind her she pulled a rolling suitcase of black nylon with a retractable handle. Her code name was Dame.

The rains over Belfast and Scotland had yet to reach the

south, and the late-afternoon sky was clear and blustery: pink and orange in the west toward Notting Hill and Kensington, blue-black to the east over the City. The air was unseasonably warm and heavy. Dame walked quickly past the glittering windows of Harrods and waited with a cluster of other pedestrians at Hans Crescent.

She crossed the small street when the light changed, slicing her way through a horde of Japanese tourists bound for Harrods, and came to the Knightsbridge entrance of the Underground. She hesitated for an instant, peering down the short flight of tiled steps leading to the ticket hall. She started down the steps, pulling the bag behind her until it rolled off the first step and crashed down to the next with a heavy thud.

She had negotiated two more steps in this manner when a young man with thinning blond hair approached. He smiled flirtatiously and said, 'Please, let me help you with that.'

The accent was mid-European or Scandinavian: German or Dutch, or maybe Danish. She hesitated. Should she accept help from a stranger? Would it be more suspicious to refuse?

'Thanks a lot,' she said finally. The accent was American, flat and toneless. She had lived in New York for many months and could shed her Ulster accent at will. 'That would be great.'

He grasped the bag by the grip and lifted it.

'My God, what have you got in here, rocks?'

'Stolen gold bars, actually,' she said, and they both laughed.

He carried the bag down the steps and placed it on the ground. She took the bag by the pull handle, said, 'Thanks again,' and turned and started walking. She could feel his presence just behind her. She increased her pace, conspicuously glancing at her wristwatch, to signal she was running late. She reached the ticket lobby and found an empty automatic dispenser. She fed £3.30 into the slot and pressed the corresponding button. Her European helper appeared alongside and slipped a few coins into his machine without looking at her. He purchased a ticket for £1.10 which meant he was making a short journey, probably somewhere within central London. He collected his ticket and melted into the rush-hour crowd.

She passed through the turnstiles and took the long escalator down to the platform. A moment later she felt a breath of wind and heard the rush of the approaching train. Miraculously, there were a few empty seats. She left the bag next to the door and sat down. By the time the train reached Earl's Court, the carriage had filled with passengers, and Dame had lost sight of the bag. The train surfaced and sped through London's western suburbs. Tired commuters trickled from the train onto the wind-swept platforms of Boston Manor, Osterley, and Houn-slow East.

As the train approached the first stop at Heathrow – the platform serving Terminal Four – Dame looked at the passengers seated around her. A pair of young English businessmen who stank of prosperity, a knot of sullen German tourists, a foursome of Americans loudly debating whether London's production of *Miss Saigon* was superior to Broadway's. Dame looked away.

The plan was simple. She had been instructed to get off at Terminal Four and leave the bag behind. Before stepping from the train she would press the button on a small transmitter hidden in her coat pocket. The transmitter, disguised as a keyless remote for a Japanese luxury car, would arm the detonator. If the train continued on schedule, the bomb would explode a few seconds after it reached the platform serving terminals One, Two, and Three. The resulting damage would inconvenience travellers for months and cost hundreds of millions of pounds to repair.

The train slowed as it approached the stop for Terminal Four. The woman stood and moved to the doors as the black of the tunnel gave way to the severe light of the platform. When the doors opened she pressed the button on the transmitter, arming the bomb. She stepped onto the platform, and the doors closed behind her. She began walking quickly toward the way out. It was then that she heard pounding on the window of the train. She turned and saw one of the young English businessmen beating his fist against the glass. She couldn't hear what he was saying, but she could read his lips. *Your bag!* he was shouting. *You left your bag!*

Dame made no movement. The expression on the Englishman's face abruptly turned from mild concern to complete terror as he realized the woman had left the bag intentionally. He lunged toward the doors and tried to pry them open with his hands. Even if the man had managed to arouse attention and stop the train, nothing could be done in one minute and fifteen seconds to prevent the bomb from exploding.

Dame watched as the train slipped forward. She was turning away when, a few seconds later, the tunnel shook with an enormous blast. The train lifted from the tracks, and a wave of searing air rushed over her. Dame instinctively raised her hands to her face. Above her, the ceiling began to crumble. The concussion of the blast lifted her from her feet. She saw it all terribly clearly for an instant – the fire, crumbling cement, the human beings, like her, caught in the fiery maelstrom of the explosion.

It ended very quickly. She was not certain how she came to rest; she had lost all sense of up and down, rather like a diver too long beneath the surface. All she knew was that she was entombed in debris, and she could not breathe or feel any part of her body. She tried to speak but could utter no sound. Her mouth began filling with her own blood.

Her thoughts remained clear. She wondered how the bomb makers could have made such a mistake, and then, in the final moments before her death, she wondered whether it was really a mistake at all.

2

LONDON

Within one hour of the attacks, the London and Dublin governments launched one of the largest criminal investigations in the history of the British Isles. The British inquiry was co-ordinated directly from Downing Street, where Prime Minister Tony Blair met continuously with his key ministers and the heads of Britain's police and security services. Shortly before nine o'clock that night, the prime minister stepped from the doorway at Number Ten, into the driving rain, and stood before the reporters and cameras waiting to beam his remarks around the world. An aide tried to hold an umbrella over the prime minister's head, but he quietly nudged him away, and after a moment his hair and the shoulders of his suit jacket were soaked. He expressed his despair at the appalling loss of life – sixty-four dead at Heathrow, twenty-eight dead in Dublin, two more in Belfast – and vowed that his government would not rest until the killers were brought to justice.

In Belfast, the leaders of all the major political parties – Catholic and Protestant, Republican and Loyalist – expressed outrage. Publicly, the politicians refused to speculate on the affiliation of the terrorists until more facts became known. Privately, each side pointed fingers at the other. Everyone appealed for calm, but by midnight Catholic youths were rioting along the Falls Road, and a British army patrol came under fire on the Protestant Shankill Road.

By the early hours of the following day, investigators had made enormous progress. In London, forensic and explosive specialists concluded that the bomb had been placed in the sixth carriage of the Heathrow-bound train. The explosive material was fifty to one hundred pounds of Semtex. Shreds of material that were found around the blast zone led investigators to conclude that the bomb was probably contained in a black nylon suitcase, very likely a rolling model. At dawn, officers fanned out along the Piccadilly Line – from Heathrow in the west to Cockfosters in the northeast – and questioned morning commuters at every stop. Police received some three hundred reports of passengers carrying suitcases on a late-afternoon train, one hundred of a rolling variety.

As luck would have it, a Dutch tourist named Jacco Krajicek came forward shortly before noon and said he had helped a woman with a large rolling black nylon suitcase at Knightsbridge Underground station in the late afternoon. He provided a thorough description of her appearance and her clothing, but it was two other details that piqued the interest of investigators. The woman had operated the automatic ticket machine with the speed and confidence of a Londoner who commutes on the Underground every day, yet apparently she hadn't realized there were steps at the entrance of the Knightsbridge stop; why would she have tried to take the heavy suitcase, otherwise? She spoke with an American accent, Krajicek said, but the accent was a fake. The detective inspector who took Krajicek's call asked how he reached such a conclusion. Krajicek said he was a speech therapist and linguist who spoke several languages fluently.

With Krajicek's assistance, detectives produced a photo-kit sketch of the woman from the Underground. The sketch was sent to the Special Branch of the Royal Ulster Constabulary and the headquarters of MI5 and

MI6. Officers pored over their files and photographs of all known members of paramilitary groups, Republican and Loyalist. When no match was discovered, the photo-kit image was put into broader circulation. Police theorized that after the bombing the woman probably boarded a departing flight at Heathrow and fled the country. The photo kit was shown to ticket agents, baggage handlers, and airport security officers. Every airline that had a flight leaving Heathrow that night was given a copy. Every inch of videotape shot from every surveillance camera in the airport was viewed and viewed again. The photo kit was given to friendly intelligence services in Western Europe, along with Israel's Mossad.

At 7 P.M., the search for the woman was brought to an abrupt halt by the discovery of another body in the rubble of the train platform. The features of the face were surprisingly intact and roughly matched the photo kit provided by Krajicek. The Dutchman was brought to Heathrow to view the body. He nodded grimly and looked away. She was the woman he had helped at Knightsbridge Underground.

A similar series of events played out across the Irish Sea in Dublin. No fewer than a dozen witnesses reported seeing a bearded man with a limp carrying a large heavy briefcase into the library just before the bombing. The doorman at the Shelbourne Hotel provided a detailed description of the suspect to a pair of Garda detectives two hours after the blast.

The library attendant who had given the bearded man a pass for the reading room survived the blast with only minor cuts and bruises. He helped police pick out the suspect on a videotape shot by the library's surveillance cameras. The Garda released a photo-kit sketch and a fuzzy image made from the videotape. Copies were faxed to London. That evening, however, rescue workers once again pulled a body from the rubble that appeared to match the description of the suspect. When a pathologist removed the clothing from the corpse he discovered a heavy brace on the right knee. Detectives ordered the knee X-rayed. The pathologist discovered no injury to the knee – either to the bone, cartilage, or ligaments – that would require the support of such a heavy brace. 'I suspect the man was wearing the brace in order to *produce* a limp rather than support a damaged knee,' the pathologist said, staring down at the corpse's leg. 'And I'm also afraid that your only suspect in this case is officially quite dead.'

To the north, in Ulster, case officers from the Special Branch of the Royal Ulster Constabulary began calling on their sources and informants, from the bars and back streets of West Belfast to the lime-coloured farms around Portadown and Armagh. None turned up anything promising. An army surveillance camera had captured Eamonn Dillon's murder, and the security camera over the door of the Celtic Bar had recorded the killer's escape. Neither vantage point produced a usable image of the gunman's face. The RUC appealed for calls to the Confidential Line – a special telephone hotline where informers can provide tips to police anonymously – but none of the 450 calls produced meaningful leads. Twelve claims of responsibility were reviewed and dismissed as hoaxes. Units devoted to technical intelligence-gathering – video surveillance and electronic eavesdropping – hastily reviewed recent tapes and intercepts, searching for missed signs of an imminent attack. Their review turned up nothing.

Initially, there was a good deal of dispute about the possible perpetrators of the attacks. Was it one group or two? Was it co-ordinated or simply coincidence? Was it the work of an existing paramilitary group or a new one? Republican or Loyalist? The assassination of Eamonn

Dillon and the bombing of the National Library in Dublin suggested the terrorists were Loyalist Protestants. The bombing of the Underground suggested the terrorists were Republicans, since Loyalist paramilitaries infrequently engaged British forces and had never bombed the British mainland. Known members of the Irish Republican Army and the Protestant Ulster Volunteer Force were quietly brought in for questioning. All denied any knowledge or involvement.

At 8 P.M., the ministers and security officials gathered in the Cabinet Room at Downing Street for a briefing with the prime minister. All reluctantly admitted they had no credible evidence pointing to any group or individual. In short, they were baffled.

At 8:45 P.M. that all changed.

The telephone chirped softly in the busy newsroom at the BBC. The *Nine O'Clock News* was on the air in fifteen minutes. The executive producer planned to devote the first half of the programme to the terrorist attacks. Reporters were standing by live in Belfast, Dublin, Heathrow, and Downing Street. Because of the chaotic atmosphere in the newsroom, the telephone rang ten times before a junior production assistant named Ginger answered it.

'I'm calling to claim responsibility for the execution of Eamonn Dillon in Belfast and the bombings at Heathrow Airport and in Dublin.' Ginger took note of the voice: male; no emotion; Irish accent, West Belfast by the sound of it. 'Are you prepared to take my statement?'

'We're a little busy here, sweetheart,' Ginger said. 'I really don't have time for this right now. Nice talking to you –'

'If you hang up this telephone you'll be making the biggest mistake of your career,' the caller said. 'Now, do you want to take my statement, or would you like me to telephone ITN instead?'

'Fine,' Ginger said, twirling a red lock of hair around the gnawed tip of her forefinger.

'You have a pen?'

Ginger kept three pens on strings around her neck. 'Of course.'

'The execution of the IRA terrorist Eamonn Dillon, the bombing of the National Library in Dublin, and the bombing of the Underground at Heathrow Airport were carried out under the orders of the military council of the Ulster Freedom Brigade. The Ulster Freedom Brigade is a new Protestant paramilitary organization and is not a pseudonym for an existing organization such as the Ulster Volunteer Force or the Ulster Defence Association.'

'Hold on, let me catch up,' Ginger said calmly, scribbling furiously. The man she had nearly dismissed as a crank sounded very much like the real thing. 'All right, I've got it. Keep going.'

'The Ulster Freedom Brigade is dedicated to the preservation of the Protestant way of life in Northern Ireland and the preservation of British rule in the province. We will not stand idly by while the British government betrays its historical commitment to the Protestant people of Northern Ireland, nor will we ever permit Ulster to be annexed by the South. The Ulster Freedom Brigade will continue its campaign of armed resistance until the so-called Good Friday peace agreement is dead and buried. All those who support this betrayal of Northern Ireland's Protestant community should regard this statement as fair warning.' The man paused, then said, 'Did you get all that?'

'Yes, I think so.'

'Good,' he said, and the line went dead.

Alan Ramsey, the executive producer, was sitting at his

desk, two telephones pressed to both ears and a pile of scripts in front of him. Ginger marched across the newsroom and stood in front of him, waving her hand to get his attention. He looked up and said, 'I have Belfast on one line and Dublin on the other. This better be fucking important.'

'It is.'

'Hold on a minute,' he shouted into the mouthpieces of both receivers. He looked up at Ginger. 'Talk.'

'A man just telephoned to claim responsibility for the bombings.'

'Probably a crank.'

'I don't think so. It sounded like the real thing.'

'Have you ever *heard* the real thing?'

'No, but –'

'Then how can you be certain?'

'There was something about him,' Ginger said. 'I don't know how to put this, Alan, but he really scared the shit out of me.'

Ramsey held out his hand, and she gave him the statement. He glanced at her scrawling shorthand, frowned, and handed it back to her. 'Christ, decipher this, would you?'

She read back the statement.

Ramsey said, 'Did he have an accent?'

She nodded.

'Irish?'

'Northern Irish,' she said. 'West Belfast, I'd say.'

'How could you tell?'

'Because I was born in Belfast. We lived there until I was ten. Once you get that accent in your head it's very hard to forget.'

He looked at the large digital clock on the wall: ten minutes to air.

'How long will it take you to type that thing up?'

'About fifteen seconds.'

'You have exactly ten.'

'Right,' she said, sitting down in front of a computer.

Ramsey withdrew an electronic organizer from his coat pocket and punched in the last name of a friend from Cambridge who worked for MI5. He picked up the telephone, dialled, and drummed his fingers on the desk while he waited.

'Hello, Graham, it's Alan Ramsey. Listen, we received a rather interesting telephone call a few moments ago, and I was wondering if I could impose on our friendship.'

Ginger dropped a printout of the statement on the desk. Ramsey read it over the telephone. Then he took notes furiously for thirty seconds.

'Right, thanks very much,' he said. 'Any time I can return the favour, don't hesitate to call.'

Ramsey slammed down the phone and stood up at his desk.

'All right, listen up, everyone!' he shouted, and the newsroom fell silent. 'We have what appears to be a genuine claim of responsibility for the attacks in Belfast, Dublin, and Heathrow: a new group called the Ulster Freedom Brigade. We're leading the newscast with it. Get on the phone and get me every expert on Irish terrorism you can lay your hands on, especially *Protestant* terrorism. We have five minutes, ladies and gentlemen. If the bastard has a pulse, put him on the air.'

3

One object of the investigation was at that moment seated in his living room in Portadown watching television. The inhabitants of the Brownstown housing estate leave no doubts about where their loyalties lie. Faded Union Jacks fly over many of the houses, and the kerbs are marked with red, white, and blue stripes. Kyle Blake did not go in for displays of allegiance. Indeed, he tended to keep his political beliefs – and everything else he considered important, for that matter – quite to himself. He belonged to no Unionist organizations, attended church infrequently, and never spoke about politics in public. Still, a fair amount was known about him, or at least suspected, within the walls of Brownstown. He was a hard man, once a senior officer in the Ulster Volunteer Force, a man who had done time in the Maze for killing Catholics.

Kyle Blake watched the lead item on the *Nine O'Clock News*.

A telephone call was received a few moments ago by the BBC from a Protestant group calling itself the Ulster Freedom Brigade. The group is opposed to the Good Friday peace accords. It claimed responsibility for the attacks and vows to continue its campaign of terror until the agreement is nullified.

Kyle Blake felt no need to go on watching, so he stood in an open doorway leading out into an unkempt garden, smoking one in an endless stream of cigarettes. The air smelled of wet pastures. Blake tossed the cigarette butt into a flower bed overgrown with weeds and listened to the reaction of an expert on Northern Ireland from London's University College. He closed the door and shut off the television.

He walked into the kitchen and made a series of brief telephone calls while his wife of twenty years, Rosemary, washed the dishes from supper. She knew what her husband did – there were no secrets between them, except precise operational details of his work – and so the coded conversations over the telephone seemed perfectly normal.

'I'm going out.'

Rosemary took a scarf from the hook and tied it round his neck, looking carefully at his face, as though seeing it for the first time. He was a small man, only slightly taller than Rosemary, and chain-smoking had left him as thin as a long-distance runner. He had watchful grey eyes set deeply in his face and cadaverous cheekbones. His slight frame disguised a body of immense strength; when Rosemary took him in her arms she could feel the knotted muscles of his shoulders and back.

'Be careful,' she whispered into his ear.

Blake pulled on a coat and kissed her cheek. 'Keep the door locked, and don't wait up.'

Kyle Blake was a printer by trade, and the family's only vehicle, a small Ford van, bore the name of his Portadown shop. Reflexively, he checked the undercarriage for explosives before getting in and starting the engine. He drove through the Brownstown estate. The giant face of Billy Wright, the fanatical Protestant killer murdered by Catholic gunmen in the Maze prison, stared from the side of a terraced house. Blake kept his eyes straight ahead. He turned onto the Armagh Road and followed a British troop carrier toward central Portadown.

He switched on Radio Ulster, which was running a special bulletin on the claim of responsibility by the Ulster Freedom Brigade. The RUC had declared security alerts in sections of County Antrim and County Down. Motorists were warned to expect delays due to roadblocks. Other places have *traffic* updates on the radio, Kyle Blake thought; Ulster has security alerts. He switched off the radio, listening to the wipers beat a steady rhythm against the rain.

Kyle Blake had never been to university, but he was a student of Northern Ireland's history. He laughed when he read that the troubles of the province began in 1969; Protestants and Catholics had been killing each other in the north of County Armagh for centuries. Empires had risen and fallen, two world wars had been fought, man had gone to the moon and back, but nothing much had changed in the gentle hills and glens between the rivers Bann and Callon.

Kyle Blake could trace his roots in County Armagh back four hundred years. His ancestors had come from the Scottish Highlands during the great colonization of Ulster that began in 1609. They fought alongside Oliver Cromwell when he landed in Ulster to put down Catholic rebellions. They took part in the massacres of Catholics at Drogheda and Wexford. When Cromwell seized Catholic farmlands, Blake's ancestors planted the fields and made the land their own. In the eighteenth and nineteenth centuries, when sectarian violence raged in Armagh, members of the Blake clan joined the Peep O'Day Boys, so named because they descended on Catholic homes just before dawn. In 1795 the Blakes helped form the Orange Order.

For nearly two centuries the Orangemen of Portadown had marched to the parish church at Drumcree on the

Sunday before July 12 – the anniversary of William of Orange's victory at the Battle of the Boyne. But the previous summer – the first marching season after the peace accords – the government had acceded to the demands of the Catholics and banned the Orangemen from returning to Portadown along the largely Catholic Garvaghy Road. The stand-off ignited violence across Ulster, culminating in the deaths of three young Catholic boys, when Loyalists tossed a petrol bomb through the window of their home in Ballymoney.

Kyle Blake was no longer an Orangeman – he had left the Order years earlier, when he first became involved with Protestant paramilitaries – but the spectacle of the British army blocking the path of Loyalist marchers was too much for him. He believed that Protestants had the right to march along the Queen's highway wherever and whenever they chose. He believed that the annual parades were a legitimate expression of Protestant heritage and culture in Northern Ireland. And he believed that any infringement on the right to march was yet another concession to the fucking Taigs.

To Blake, the stand-off at Drumcree betrayed something much more ominous about the political landscape of Northern Ireland: the Protestant ascendancy in Ulster had crumbled, and the Catholics were winning.

For thirty years Blake had watched the British make concession after concession to the Catholics and the IRA, but the Good Friday accords were more than he could bear. Blake believed they could lead to only one thing: British withdrawal from Northern Ireland and union with the Irish Republic. Two previous attempts at peace in Ulster – the Sunningdale Agreement and the Anglo-Irish Agreement – had been torpedoed by Protestant intransigence. Kyle Blake had vowed to destroy the Good Friday accords too.

Last night he had taken the first step. He had engineered one of the most spectacular displays of international terrorism ever imagined, simultaneously striking at Sinn Fein, the Irish government, and the British.

The spires of St Mark's Church appeared before him, looming over the Market High Street. Blake parked outside his printshop, even though it was several blocks from his destination. He carefully checked for signs of surveillance as he walked past the shuttered shops and shop fronts.

Ironically, Blake drew his tactical inspiration not from the Protestant paramilitaries of the past but from the men who had bombed his native Portadown time and time again, the IRA. Since the onset of the current Troubles in 1969, the IRA had engaged its enemies – the British army and the Royal Ulster Constabulary – and committed spectacular acts of terrorism as well. The IRA had murdered British soldiers, assassinated Lord Mountbatten, and even tried to blow up the entire British Cabinet, yet it had maintained the image of defenders of an oppressed people.

Blake wanted to turn the sectarian politics of Northern Ireland upside down. He wanted to show the world that the Protestant way of life in Ulster was under siege. And he was willing to play the terror card to do it – harder and better than the IRA had ever dreamed.

Blake entered a small side street and stepped inside McConville's pub. The room was dark, crowded, and filled with a blue pall of cigarette smoke. Against the panelled walls were booths with high doors, each large enough for half a dozen people.

The barman behind the brass counter looked up as Blake entered. 'You hear the news, Kyle?'

Blake shook his head. 'What news?'

'There's been a claim. It's Prods. Some group calling themselves the Ulster Freedom Brigade.'

'You don't say, Jimmie.'

The barman inclined his head toward the far corner of the room. 'Gavin and Rebecca are waiting for you.'

Blake winked and sliced his way through the room. He knocked once on the door of the booth and slipped inside. Two people were seated around the small table, a large man in a black rollneck sweater and grey corduroy sports jacket and an attractive woman in a beige woollen pull-over. The man was Gavin Spencer, chief of Brigade operations. The woman was Rebecca Wells, the Brigade's intelligence chief.

Blake removed his coat and hung it on a hook on the wall. The barman appeared.

Blake said, 'Three Guinness, Jimmie.'

'If you're hungry I can run next door for some sandwiches.'

'Sandwiches would be fine.'

Blake handed the barman a £10 note; then he shut the door of the booth and sat down. They sat in silence for a moment, looking at each other. It was the first time they had dared to gather since the attacks. Each was ecstatic about the success of the operations, yet each was edgy. They realized there was no turning back now.

'How are your men?' Blake asked Gavin Spencer.

'They're ready for more,' Spencer said. He had the powerful body of a dockworker and the dishevelled air of a playwright. His black hair was shot with grey, and a thick forelock was forever falling across a pair of intense blue eyes. Like Blake, he had served in the British army and had been a member of the Ulster Volunteer Force. 'But obviously they're a wee bit concerned about the timing mechanisms on the detonators.'

Blake lit a cigarette and rubbed his eyes. It had been his

decision to sacrifice the bombers in Dublin and London by manipulating the timing mechanisms on the bombs. His reasoning was as simple as it was Machiavellian. He was nose-to-nose with the British intelligence and security establishment, one of the most ruthless and efficient in Europe. The Ulster Freedom Brigade needed to survive if it was to carry on its campaign of violence. If either bomber had fallen into the hands of the police, the Brigade would be in serious danger.

'Blame it on the bomb makers,' Blake said. 'Tell them we're new at this game. The IRA has its own engineering department, dedicated to nothing except building better bombs. But even the IRA makes mistakes. When they broke the cease-fire in '96, their first bombs malfunctioned. They were out of practice.'

'I'll tell my men,' Gavin Spencer said. 'They'll believe us once, but if it happens again they'll be suspicious. If we're going to win this fight we need men who are willing to pull the trigger and plant the bomb.'

Blake started to speak, but there was a soft knock at the door of the cubicle, and he stopped himself. The barman entered and handed Blake a bag of sandwiches.

'And what about Bates?' Blake asked, when the barman was gone.

'We may have a problem,' Rebecca Wells said.

Blake and Spencer looked at the woman. She was tall and fit, and the bulky woollen sweater could not conceal her square shoulders. Black hair fell about her face and neck, framing wide cheekbones. Her eyes were oval and the colour of an overcast winter sky. Like many women in Northern Ireland, she had become a widow too young. Her husband had worked in the intelligence section of the UVF until an IRA gunman assassinated him in West Belfast. Rebecca had been pregnant at the time. She miscarried that night. After her recovery she joined the UVF and picked up the threads of her husband's work. She quit the UVF when it agreed to a cease-fire, and a few months later she secretly joined forces with Kyle Blake.

If anyone deserved credit for the assassination of Eamonn Dillon, it was Rebecca Wells. She had patiently developed a source inside Sinn Fein headquarters on the Falls Road, a rather unattractive young woman who worked on the clerical staff. Rebecca had befriended her, taken her for drinks, introduced her to men. After several months the relationship began to bear fruit. The girl inadvertently fed Rebecca a steady stream of information of Sinn Fein and its senior officers: strategies, internal disputes, personal habits, sexual tastes, movements, and security. Rebecca gave this information to Gavin Spencer, who then planned Dillon's murder.

'The police have put together a photo-kit sketch of him,' she said. 'Every officer in the province is carrying one in his pocket. We can't move him again until things cool off.'

'Things are never going to cool off, Rebecca,' Blake said.

'The longer he stays in hiding, the better the chances are that he'll be found,' she said. 'And if he's found, we're in serious trouble.'

Blake looked at Gavin Spencer. 'Where's Bates now?'

The man in the fieldstone barn outside Hillsborough had been moved half a dozen times since the killing of Eamonn Dillon on the Falls Road. He had been permitted no radio, for fear the British army's elite intelligence eavesdropping units might pick up the sound. He had been permitted no stove, for fear the army's infrared sensors might detect any unusual source of heat. His bed was a brick-hard folding army cot with a blanket as rough as steel wool; the green oilskin jacket he had worn during the assassination served as a pillow. He survived on dry goods – biscuits, crackers, nuts – and canned meats. Cigarette smoking was permitted, though he was to be careful not to set fire to the hay. He pissed and shit in a large stockpot. The stench was unbearable at first, but gradually he grew used to it. He wanted to empty the thing, but his handlers had warned him never to set foot outside the barn, even at night.

They had left him a strange collection of books: biographies of Wolfe Tone, Eamon De Valera, and Michael Collins and a couple of battered volumes of snarling Republican poetry. There was a handwritten note stuffed in one of them: *Sun Tzu said know your enemy. Read these and learn.* But most of the time the man just lay on his cot, staring into the darkness, smoking his cigarettes, reliving those few moments on the Falls Road.

Bates heard the rattle of an engine. He rose and peered through a small window. A van clattered over the unpaved track, headlamps doused. It came to a halt in the stew of mud and gravel outside the door of the barn. Two people stepped out; the driver was large and bulky, the passenger smaller and lighter afoot. A few seconds later Bates heard a knock on the door. 'Go to the cot and lie face down,' said the voice on the other side of the door.

Bates did as he was told. He heard the sound of two people entering the barn. A moment later the same voice commanded him to sit up. The large man was seated on a stack of feed bags; the smaller figure paced behind him like a troubled conscience.

'Sorry about the smell,' Bates said uneasily. 'I smoke to cover it up. Mind?'

In the flare of a match Bates could see that both his visitors were wearing balaclavas. He touched the flame to the end of his cigarette and blew out the match, casting the barn into pitch darkness once more.

'When do I get to leave?' he said.

Before Dillon's execution, Bates had been told he would be sent out of Northern Ireland as soon as things cooled down. There were friends in an isolated patch of the Scottish Highlands, they had told him. Somewhere the security services would never find him.

'It's not safe to move you yet,' the large man said. 'The RUC have produced a photo-kit sketch of you. We need to let things cool down a wee bit more.'

Bates stood abruptly. 'Christ, I'm going mad in this hole! Can't you move me somewhere else?'

'You're safe here for now. We can't risk moving you again.'

Bates sat down, defeated. He dropped the stub of his cigarette onto the dirt floor and ground it out with his shoe. 'What about the others?' he asked. 'The agents who did Dublin and London?'

'They're in hiding as well,' the man said. 'That's all I can say.'

'Has there been a claim of responsibility yet?'

'We did it tonight. It's hell out there, roadblocks and checkpoints from County Antrim to the border. Until things loosen up we can't even think about moving you.'

Bates struck another match, illuminating the scene for an instant, the two hooded visitors, one seated, one standing, like statuary in a garden. He lit another cigarette and waved out the match.

'Is there anything we can get for you to help pass the time?'

'A girl of loose morals would be nice.'

The remark was greeted with silence.

'Lie on the cot,' the seated man said again. 'Face down.'

Charles Bates did as he was told. He heard the rustle

of the feed sacks as the large man with the tattoos on his hands rose to his feet. He heard the barn door swing open.

Then he felt something cold and hard being pressed against the base of his skull. He heard a faint click, saw a flash of brilliant light, then only darkness.

Rebecca Wells slipped the silenced Walther pistol into her coat pocket as she climbed into the van. Gavin Spencer started the engine, turned around, and drove along the pitted farm track until he reached the B177. They waited until they were clear of the farm before removing the balaclavas. Rebecca Wells stared out the window as Spencer drove expertly along the rolling, winding roadway.

'You didn't have to do that, Rebecca. I would have done it for you.'

'Are you saying I'm not good enough to handle my job?'

'No, I'm just saying that it's not right.'

'What's not right?'

'A woman killing,' Spencer said. 'It's not right.'

'And what about Dame?' Rebecca said, using the code name of the woman who had carried the suitcase bomb into the London Underground. 'She killed many more people than I did tonight, and she gave her life as well.'

'Point well taken.'

'I'm responsible for intelligence and internal security,' she said. 'Kyle wanted him dead. It was my job to make him dead.'

Spencer let it drop. He switched on the radio to help pass the time. He turned onto the A1 and headed toward Banbridge. A few moments later Rebecca groaned. 'Pull over.'

He braked to a halt on the apron of the road. Rebecca

opened the door and stumbled out into the rain. She fell to her hands and knees in the light from the headlamps and was violently sick.

4

The meeting between Prime Minister Tony Blair and President James Beckwith had been scheduled well in advance; the fact that it fell just one week after the Ulster Freedom Brigade launched its wave of terror was coincidence. In fact, both men went out of their way to portray the meeting as a routine consultation among good friends, which in most respects it was. As the prime minister arrived at the White House from Blair House, the guest quarters across the street, President Beckwith assured his visitor that the mansion had been named in his honour. The prime minister flashed his famous teeth-and-gums smile and assured President Beckwith that the next time he came to London a British landmark would be named in *his* honour.

For two hours the president and the prime minister met with their aides and assistants in the Roosevelt Room of the White House. The agenda included a wide range of issues: co-ordination of defence and foreign policy, monetary and trade policy, ethnic tension in the Balkans, the Middle East peace process, and, of course, Northern Ireland. Shortly after noon the two leaders adjourned to the Oval Office for a private lunch.

Snow drifted over the South Lawn as the two men stood at the window behind Beckwith's desk and admired the view. A large fire burned brightly in the fireplace, and a table was set before it. The president confidently took his guest by the arm and shepherded him across the room.

After a lifetime in politics, James Beckwith was comfortable with the ceremonial aspects of his job. The Washington press corps routinely said he was the best performer to occupy the Oval Office since Ronald Reagan.

Still, he was beginning to tire of it all. He had barely won re-election, trailing his opponent, Democratic Senator Andrew Sterling of Nebraska, throughout the campaign until an Arab terrorist group blew a jetliner from the sky off Long Island. Beckwith's skilful handling of the crisis – and his quick retaliatory strikes against the terrorists – had helped turn the tide.

Now he had settled comfortably into lame-duck status. The Democratic-controlled Congress had scrapped the primary goal of his second term, the construction of a national missile defence system. His agenda, such as it was, consisted of a series of minor conservative initiatives that required no congressional backing. Two members of his cabinet were being picked apart by independent counsels for financial misconduct. Every night over dinner Beckwith and his wife, Anne, talked less about politics and more about how they would spend their retirement in California. He had even granted Anne's long-time wish to take their summer vacation in the mountains of northern Italy. In years past his strategists had warned that vacationing abroad would be politically disastrous. Beckwith simply didn't care any longer. Close friends attributed the drift to the loss of his friend and chief of staff Paul Vandenberg, who apparently had shot himself to death on Roosevelt Island in the Potomac River a year earlier.

The two men sat down to lunch. Tony Blair was a notoriously fast eater – a fact included in Beckwith's briefing books – and he had devoured his grilled chicken breast and rice pilaf before Beckwith had consumed a quarter of his meal. Beckwith was famished after the morning of intense discussions, so he made the British leader sit patiently while he finished the last of his lunch.

Their relationship had soured the previous year, when Blair publicly criticized Beckwith for launching air strikes against the Sword of Gaza, the Palestinian terror group blamed for the downing of a TransAtlantic Airlines jet off Long Island. Several weeks later the Sword of Gaza retaliated by attacking the TransAtlantic ticket counter at London's Heathrow Airport, killing several Americans and British travellers. Beckwith never forgot Blair's rebuke. Known to be on a first-name basis with most of the world's leaders, Beckwith pointedly referred to Blair as 'Mr Prime Minister.' Blair responded in kind by always referring to Beckwith as 'Mr President.'

Beckwith slowly finished his lunch while Blair droned on about a 'truly fascinating' economic textbook he had read during the flight from London to Washington. Blair was a voracious reader, and Beckwith genuinely respected his powerful intellect. Christ, he thought, I barely get through my briefing books at night without falling asleep.

A steward cleared away the remains of lunch. Beckwith had tea, Blair coffee. A silence fell over the conversation. The fire crackled like small arms. Blair made a show of looking out the window toward the Washington Monument for a moment before speaking.

'I want to be very blunt with you about something, Mr President,' Blair said, turning away from the window and meeting Beckwith's pale blue gaze. 'I realize our relationship has not always been as good as it should be, but I want to ask a very serious favour of you.'

'Our relationship is not as good as it could be, Mr Prime Minister, because you publicly distanced yourself from the United States when I launched air strikes against the Sword of Gaza training bases. I needed your support then, and you were not there for me.'

A steward entered the room with dessert but, sensing the conversation had turned serious, quickly withdrew again. Blair looked down, checking his emotions, and looked up again.

'Mr President, I said what I said because I *believed* it to be the case. I thought the air strikes were heavy-handed, premature, and based on suspect evidence at best. I thought the air strikes would only increase tension and do harm to the cause of peace in the Middle East. I believe I was proven correct.'

Beckwith knew Blair was referring to the Sword of Gaza attack at Heathrow Airport. 'Mr Prime Minister, if you had concerns, you should have picked up the telephone and called me instead of running to the nearest reporter. Allies stand by each other, even when their leaders come from opposite ends of the political spectrum.'

The cold look in Blair's eyes made clear that he did not appreciate Beckwith's lecture on the fundamentals of statesmanship. He sipped his coffee as Beckwith continued.

'In fact, I suspect the Sword of Gaza chose to retaliate on British soil because your comments led them to believe they could drive a wedge between two old allies.'

Blair looked up from his coffee cup as though he had been punched. 'You're not suggesting *I'm* to blame for the attack on Heathrow.'

'Of course not, Mr Prime Minister. To engage in something like that would be unbecoming of good friends.'

Blair replaced the cup in his saucer and pushed it a few inches away. 'Mr President, I want to talk to you about Ambassador Hathaway's replacement.'

'Fair enough,' Beckwith said.

'If I may be blunt, Mr President, I've seen some of the names you're considering, and, frankly, I'm not terribly impressed.' Colour rose in Beckwith's cheeks, but Blair ploughed on. 'I was hoping for someone a bit more talented.'

Beckwith remained silent while Blair made his points. *The New York Times* had published a piece earlier that week containing the names of half a dozen candidates for the job. The names were accurate, because they had been leaked on Beckwith's orders. The list contained several large Republican donors, with a couple of professional Foreign Service officers thrown in for good measure. London was a political post by tradition, and Beckwith was under pressure from the Republican National Committee to use the short-term appointment to reward a generous benefactor.

Blair said, 'Mr President, are you aware of the American term *in your face*?'

Beckwith nodded, but his expression made clear he never used such crude street talk.

'Mr President, this group called the Ulster Freedom Brigade has launched its campaign for terror because they want to undo the steps toward peace that we've made in Northern Ireland. I want to demonstrate to these cowardly terrorists, and to the world, that they will never succeed. I want to get *in their face*, Mr President, and I need your help.'

Beckwith smiled for the first time. 'How can I help, Prime Minister?'

'You can help by appointing a superstar to be your next ambassador to London. Someone all sides can respect. A name that everyone will know. I don't want someone who's going to keep the seat warm until you leave office. I want someone who can help me achieve my goal, a permanent settlement to the conflict in Northern Ireland.'

The intensity and the honesty of the younger man's arguments were impressive. But Beckwith had been in politics long enough to know that one should never give away something for nothing.

'If I appoint a superstar to London, what do I get in return?'

Blair smiled broadly. 'You get my unequivocal support for your European trade initiative.'

'Deal,' Beckwith said, after a brief show of thought.

A steward entered the room.

Beckwith said, 'Two glasses of brandy, please.' The drinks appeared a moment later. Beckwith raised his glass. 'To good friends.'

'To good friends.'

Blair sipped the brandy with the caution of one who rarely drinks. He replaced the snifter carefully and said, 'Do you have any candidates in mind, Mr President?'

'Actually, Tony, I think I've got just the man for the job.'

5

SHELTER ISLAND, NEW YORK

For many years, little about the grand white clapboard house overlooking Dering Harbor and Shelter Island Sound had suggested that Senator Douglas Cannon owned the property. There were occasional guests requiring Secret Service protection, and sometimes there were large parties when Douglas was running for re-election and needed money. Usually, though, the house seemed like all the others along Shore Road, just a little larger and a little better cared for. After his retirement, and the death of his wife, the senator had spent more time at Cannon Point than in his sprawling Fifth Avenue apartment in Manhattan. He insisted the neighbours call him Douglas and, rather awkwardly, they complied. Cannon Point became more accessible than ever before. Sometimes, when tourists stopped to stare or take a photograph of the estate, the senator would appear on the manicured lawn, retrievers scampering at his heels, and stop to chat.

The intruders had changed all that.

Two weeks after the incident the police had allowed the senator to repair all visible reminders of the episode, thus wiping out the last of the physical evidence. An off-island contractor that no one had ever heard of – and no telephone directory seemed to list – handled the work.

Rumours about the extensive damage swept over the island. Harry Carp, the crimson-faced owner of the hardware store in the Heights, had heard there were a dozen bullet holes in the walls of the sitting room and the kitchen. Patty McLean, the checkout girl at the Mid-Island Market, heard the bloodstains in the guest cottage were so extensive that the entire floor had to be replaced and the walls repainted. Martha Creighton, the island's most prominent real estate broker, quietly predicted Cannon Point would be on the market within six months. Clearly, Martha murmured over her cappuccino at the village coffee house, the senator and his family would want to make a fresh start somewhere else.

But the senator and his daughter, Elizabeth, and his son-in-law, Michael, decided to stay on. Cannon Point, once open and accessible, assumed the air of a settlement in occupied territory. Another obscure contractor descended on the property, this time to erect a ten-foot brick and iron fence and a small clapboard gingerbread hut at the entrance for a permanent security guard. When the work was complete, a second team arrived to litter the property with cameras and motion detectors. The neighbours complained that the senator's new security measures disrupted views of Dering Harbor and the Sound. There was talk of a petition, some grumbling at a village council meeting, even a nasty letter or two in the *Shelter Island Reporter*. But by summer everyone had become used to the new fence, and no one could remember why anyone was upset about it in the first place.

'You can hardly blame them,' Martha Creighton said. 'If he wants a fucking fence, let him have a fucking fence. Hell, I'd let him build a moat if he wanted one.'

Of Michael Osbourne, little was known on the island. He was thought to be involved in business of some sort, international sales or the murky world of consulting. He usually kept to himself when he and his wife, Elizabeth, came out to the island for the weekend. When he ate breakfast at the Heights pharmacy, or stopped at the Dory for a beer, he always brought a few newspapers for protection. Attempts at polite conversation were gently rebuffed; something of grave importance always seemed to be pulling his gaze back to his newspapers. The island's female population found him attractive and forgave his coolness as a manifestation of some inner shyness. Harry Carp, known for his plain speaking, routinely referred to Michael as 'that rude sonofabitch from the city.'

The shooting had softened opinions of Michael Osbourne, even Harry Carp's. According to the rumours, he had nearly died from a gunshot wound several times that night – once on the dock at Cannon Point, once in the helicopter, once on the operating table at Stony Brook Hospital. After his release he remained inside the house for a time, but soon he could be spotted gingerly walking the grounds, his right arm in a sling beneath a battered leather bomber jacket. Sometimes he could be seen standing at the end of the dock, gazing into the Sound. Sometimes, usually in the evening, he would seem to lose himself and stay there – like Gatsby, Martha Creighton would say – until the last light was gone.

'I don't understand why the traffic is so heavy in the middle of January,' Elizabeth Osbourne said, drumming the nail of her forefinger on the leather centre armrest. They were crawling east on the Long Island Expressway, through the town of Islip, at thirty miles per hour.

Michael had been retired from the Central Intelligence Agency for a year, and time meant little to him – even time wasted in traffic. 'It's Friday night,' he said. 'It's always bad on Friday night.'

The traffic thinned as they drove east from the mid-island suburbs. The night was clear and bitterly cold; a bone-white three-quarter moon hovered just above the northern horizon. The road opened before him, and Michael pressed the accelerator. The engine roared, and after a few seconds the speedometer reluctantly rose to seventy. The exigencies of fatherhood had compelled him to trade his sleek silver Jaguar for a behemoth sport utility vehicle.

The twins, swaddled in pink and blue blankets, dozed in their car seats. Maggie, the English nanny, lay sprawled on the third seat, sleeping soundly. Elizabeth reached out in the darkness and took Michael's hand. She had returned to work that week after three months of maternity leave. While she had been away from work she had dressed in nothing but flannel shirts, baggy sweat pants, and loose-fitting khaki trousers. Now she wore the uniform of a high-priced New York lawyer: a charcoal-grey suit, a tasteful gold watch, pearl earrings. She had shed the extra weight of pregnancy by taking hour-long marches on the treadmill in the bedroom of their Fifth Avenue apartment. Beneath the crisp lines of her Calvin Klein suit, Elizabeth was slender as a fashion model. Still, the strain and fatigue of suddenly being a working mother showed. Her short ash-blonde hair was in mild disarray; her eyes were so red she had forsaken her contact lenses for tortoiseshell spectacles. Michael thought she looked like a law student crashing for exams.

'How does it feel to be back?' Michael asked.

'Like I never left. Pull over so I can have a cigarette. I can't smoke in the car with the children.'

'I don't want to make an unnecessary stop.'

'Come on, Michael!'

'I have to stop in Riverhead for gas. You can have a cigarette then. This thing gets about five miles a gallon. I'll probably have to fill up a couple of times between here and the island.'

45

'Oh, God, you're not going to start bitching about the Jaguar again?'

'I just don't understand why you got to keep your Mercedes and I'm stuck driving this beast. I feel like a soccer mom.'

'We needed a bigger car, and your mechanic got to spend more time with your Jaguar than you did.'

'I'm still not happy about it.'

'Get over it, darling.'

'If you keep talking like that, you're not going to get me in the sack tonight.'

'Don't make idle threats, Michael.'

The expressway ended at the town of Riverhead. Michael stopped at an all-night market and gas station and filled the tank. Elizabeth walked a few steps away from the pumps and smoked, stamping her feet against the concrete for warmth. She had sworn off cigarettes with the pregnancy, but two weeks after the children were born the nightmares returned, and she started smoking again to ease her nerves.

Michael raced eastward along the North Fork of Long Island, past endless fields of sod and dormant vineyards. Now and again the waters of Long Island Sound appeared on his left – black, shimmering with moonlight. He entered the village of Greenport and drove through quiet streets until he reached the landing for the North Ferry.

Elizabeth was sleeping. Michael pulled on a leather jacket and climbed out onto the deck. Whitecaps beat against the prow of the ferry, sending sea spray over the gunwales. It was bitterly cold, but the hood of the car was warm with engine heat. Michael climbed up and sat down, hands shoved into his coat pockets. Shelter Island lay before him across the Sound, blacked out except for a large summerhouse at the mouth of Dering Harbor, which burned with clean white light. Cannon Point.

When the ferry docked, Michael climbed back inside and started the engine. 'I was watching you, Michael,' Elizabeth said, without opening her eyes. 'You were thinking about it, weren't you?'

There was no point lying to her. He *was* thinking about it – the night a year earlier when a former KGB assassin, code-named October, had tried to kill them both at Cannon Point.

'Do you do it often?' she said, interpreting his silence as confirmation.

'When I'm on the ferry, looking at your father's house, I can't help it.'

'I think about it all the time,' she said distantly. 'Every morning I wake up, and I wonder if this will be the day: the day it all goes away. But it never does.'

'It takes time,' Michael said, then added, 'A lot of time.'

'Do you think he's really dead?'

'October?'

'Yes.'

'The Agency thinks so.'

'What about you?'

'I'd sleep better if a body turned up somewhere, but it won't.'

They passed through the Victorian cottages and clapboard shops of Shelter Island Heights and raced along Winthrop Road. Dering Harbor shone in the moonlight, empty except for Douglas Cannon's sloop, *Athena*, clinging to her mooring, prow turned to the wind. Michael followed Shore Road into Dering Harbor village and a moment later drew to a halt at the gate of Cannon Point.

The night security guard stepped out of the hut and shone a light over the car. Douglas was spending several thousand dollars a month on security since the assassination attempt. The Agency had offered to pay a portion of the expense, but Douglas, forever leery of the intelligence community, bore all the cost himself. Michael followed the gravel drive through the property and stopped outside the front door of the main house. The senator was waiting for them on the steps, wearing an ancient yellow sailing coat, his retrievers frolicking at his feet.

It was *The New Yorker* that first likened Douglas Cannon to Pericles. While he usually professed some mild embarrassment at the comparison, he did nothing to dispel it. He had inherited enormous wealth and decided quite early in life that the prospect of merely adding to his fortune depressed him greatly. Instead, he devoted himself to his first love, which was history. He taught at Columbia and wrote books. His vast apartment on Fifth Avenue was a gathering place for writers, artists, poets, and musicians. Elizabeth, when she was a little girl, met Jack Kerouac, Huey Newton, and a strange little man with blond hair and sunglasses named Andy. Only years later did she realize the man had been Andy Warhol.

During Watergate, Douglas realized he could no longer remain confined to the bleachers, the eternal spectator. He ran for Congress in an overwhelmingly liberal Democratic district in midtown Manhattan and entered the House as a reformer in the class of '74. Two years later he was elected to the Senate. During his four terms there he served as chairman of the Armed Services Committee, the Foreign Relations Committee, and the Select Committee on Intelligence.

Douglas was always something of an iconoclast, but since his retirement from the Senate, his dress and mannerisms had become more peculiar than ever. He wore nothing but tattered corduroy trousers, ancient boating shoes, and sweaters that, like the man himself, were beginning to show their age. He believed that cold sea air was the secret to longevity, and he was constantly giving himself bronchial infections by sailing throughout the winter and taking himself on endless treks along the frozen footpaths of the Mashomack reserve.

Elizabeth stepped out of the car, forefinger pressed to her lips, and kissed his cheek. 'Be quiet, Daddy,' she whispered. 'The children are fast asleep.'

Michael and Elizabeth had a suite of rooms overlooking the water: a master bedroom, a bathroom, and a private sitting room with a television. The bedroom next door had been converted into a makeshift nursery. Elizabeth had been superstitious about doing too much planning before the twins were born, so the spartan room contained nothing but a pair of cribs and a changing table. The walls were still pale grey and the floors bare. The senator had brought up an old wicker rocker from the veranda to add some character to the room. Maggie helped Elizabeth put the children to bed, while Michael and Douglas had a glass of Merlot downstairs by the fire. Elizabeth joined them a few minutes later.

'How are they?' Michael asked.

'They're fine. Maggie's going to sit with them a few minutes and make sure they stay down.' Elizabeth flopped down onto the couch. 'Pour me a very large glass of that wine, will you, Michael?'

Douglas said, 'How are you holding up, sweetheart?'

'I never realized just how hard this would be.' She took a long sip of the Merlot and closed her eyes as the wine flowed down her throat. 'I'd die without Maggie.'

'There's nothing wrong with that. You had a baby nurse and a nanny, and your mother didn't work.'

'She worked, Daddy! She took care of me and ran three households while you were in Washington!'

Michael murmured, 'Bad move, Douglas.'

'You know what I mean, Elizabeth. Your mother

worked, but not in an office. Frankly, I'm not at all sure mothers should work. Children need their mothers.'

'I can't believe my ears,' Elizabeth said. 'Douglas Cannon, the great liberal icon, thinks mothers should stay at home with their children and not work. Wait till the National Organization for Women gets ahold of this. My God, beneath that hopelessly liberal exterior beats the heart of a family-values conservative after all.'

'What about Michael here?' Douglas said. 'He's retired. Doesn't he help out?'

'I just play *bocci* with the rest of the boys down in the village every afternoon.'

'Michael's great with the children,' Elizabeth said. 'But forgive me for saying this – fathers can only do so much.'

'And what's that supposed to mean?' Douglas said.

The telephone rang before Elizabeth could answer.

'Saved by the proverbial bell,' Michael said.

Elizabeth picked up the receiver and said, 'Hello.' She listened intently for a moment, then said, 'Yes, he is. Hold on a moment, please.' She held out the receiver, covering the mouthpiece. 'It's for you, Daddy. It's the White House.'

'What in God's name does the White House want with me at ten o'clock on a Friday night?'

'The president wants to speak to you.'

Douglas pulled himself up, the look on his face a cross between bafflement and annoyance, and ambled across the room, wineglass in hand. He took the telephone from Elizabeth.

'This is Douglas Cannon . . . Yes, I'll hold on . . .'

He covered the mouthpiece and said, 'They're getting the sonofabitch on the line.'

Elizabeth and Michael snickered silently. The animosity between the two men was legendary in Washington. They had been the two most powerful figures on the

Senate Armed Services Committee. For several years Douglas had been the chairman and Beckwith the ranking Republican. When the GOP regained control of the Senate, the two men traded places. By the time Douglas retired, they were barely on speaking terms.

'Good evening, Mr President,' Douglas said in a jovial, parade-ground shout.

Maggie came to the top of the stairs and hissed, 'Be quiet, or you'll wake the children.'

'He's talking to the president,' Elizabeth whispered helplessly.

'Well, tell him to do it a little more quietly,' Maggie said, turning on her heel and walking back to the nursery.

'I'm just fine, Mr President,' Douglas was saying. 'What can I do for you?'

Douglas listened for a moment, saying nothing, absently running a hand through his thick grey hair.

'No, that wouldn't be a problem at all, Mr President. In fact, it would be delightful . . . Of course . . . Yes, Mr President . . . Very well, I'll see you then.'

Douglas replaced the receiver and said, 'Beckwith wants to talk.'

'What about?' Michael asked.

'He wouldn't say. He's always been like that.'

'When are you going to Washington?' Elizabeth asked.

'I'm not,' Douglas said. 'The bastard's coming to Shelter Island on Sunday morning.'

6

TAFRAOUTE, MOROCCO

Snow shimmered on the slopes of the High Atlas Mountains as the caravan of black Range Rovers rumbled along the rocky, pitted track toward the new villa at the head of the valley. The Range Rovers were identical: black with reflective smoked windows to shield the identity of the occupants. Each passenger had come to Morocco from a different embarkation point: Latin America, the United States, the Middle East, Western Europe. Each would leave just thirty-six hours later, when the conference had ended. There were few outsiders in Tafraoute this time of year – a team of climbers from New Zealand and a band of ageing hippies from Berkeley who had descended on the mountains to pray and smoke hashish – and the caravan of Range Rovers drew curious stares as it sped along the valley floor. Children in brightly coloured robes stood at the side of the track and waved excitedly as the vehicles roared past in a cloud of ginger-coloured dust. No one inside waved back.

The Society for International Development and Co-operation was a completely private organization that accepted no outside donations and no new members, except those it selected after a rigorous screening process. Nominally, it was headquartered in Geneva, in a small office with a tasteful gold plaque over an austere door which was frequently mistaken for a circumspect Swiss bank.

Despite its benevolent-sounding name the Society, as it was known to its members, was not an altruistic order. It had been formed in the years immediately following the collapse of the Soviet Union and the end of the Cold War. Its members included several current and former members of Western intelligence and security services, arms makers and weapons dealers, and also leaders of criminal enterprises such as the Russian and Sicilian mafias, South American drug cartels, and Asian crime organizations.

The Society's decision-making body was the eight-member executive council. The executive director was a former chief of the British intelligence service, the legendary 'C' of MI6. He was known simply as 'the Director' and was never referred to by his real name. An experienced field man who had cut his teeth at MI6's stations in Berlin and Moscow, the Director oversaw the Society's administration and ran its operations from his highly secure Georgian mansion in London's St John's Wood.

The creed of the Society declared that the world had become a more dangerous place in the absence of conflict between East and West. The Cold War had provided stability and clarity, the new world order turmoil and uncertainty. Great nations had grown complacent; great armies had been castrated. Therefore, the Society sought to promote constant, controlled global tension through covert operations. In doing so it also managed to earn a vast amount of money for its members and investors.

Lately, the Director had sought to expand the role and scope of the Society. He had effectively turned the organization into an intelligence service for intelligence services, an ultrasecret operations unit that could carry out a task that, for whatever reason, a legitimate service found too risky or too distasteful.

*

The Director and his staff had seen to the security arrangements. The villa sat on the rim of the small valley, surrounded by an electrified fence. The desert around the villa was a rocky no-man's-land, covered by dozens of surveillance cameras and motion detectors. Heavily armed Society security operatives, each a former member of Britain's elite SAS commando force, patrolled the grounds. Radio jammers broadcast electronic chaff to disrupt any long-range microphones. Real names were never spoken at meetings of the council, so each member was assigned a code name: Rodin, Monet, Van Gogh, Rembrandt, Rothko, Michelangelo, and Picasso.

They spent the day around the large swimming pool, relaxing in the cool dry desert air. At dusk they had drinks on the sweeping stone terrace, where gas heaters burned off the night chill, followed by a simple meal of Moroccan couscous.

At midnight the Director gavelled the proceedings to order.

For nearly an hour the Director discussed the financial state of the Society. He defended his decision to transform the organization from a mere catalyst for global instability into a full-time secret army. Yes, he had strayed from the original charter, but in a brief period he had managed to fill the Society's coffers with millions of dollars in operating capital, money that could be put to good use.

The members of the executive council broke into a round of polite boardroom applause. Seated around the table were arms merchants and defence contractors who faced dwindling markets, makers of chemical and nuclear technology who wanted to peddle their goods to the militaries of the Third World, and intelligence chiefs who faced shrinking budgets and diminishing power and influence in their capitals.

For the next hour the Director guided a round table discussion on the state of global conflict. Indeed, it seemed the world was not co-operating with them. Yes, there was the odd civil war in West Africa, the Eritreans and Ethiopians were at it again, and South America continued to be ripe for exploitation. But the Middle East peace process, though strained, had failed to break down completely. The Iranians and Americans were talking about a *rapprochement*. Even the Protestants and Catholics of Northern Ireland seemed to be putting aside their differences.

'Perhaps it's time for us to make a few investments,' the Director said in conclusion, contemplating his hands as he spoke. 'Perhaps it's time for us to plough some of our capital back into the business. I think it's incumbent on each and every one of us to look for opportunity wherever it can be found.'

Again, applause and the ring of silver utensils against glasses interrupted him. When it died away he threw open the meeting for discussion.

Rembrandt, one of the world's principal manufacturers of small arms, cleared his throat and said, 'Perhaps there's some way we can help fan the flames in Northern Ireland.'

The Director arched an eyebrow and picked at the seam of his trousers. He had been looking for a way to exploit the Irish situation but had been reluctant to involve himself in a conflict that directly involved his own country. He had dealt with Northern Ireland when he was with MI6. Like most members of the intelligence and security community, he considered the IRA a worthy opponent, a professional and disciplined guerrilla army. The Protestant paramilitaries had been something else altogether, mainly gangsters and thugs who waged a campaign of sheer terror against Catholics. But this new group, the Ulster Freedom Brigade, seemed different, and this intrigued him.

'Northern Ireland was never a terribly lucrative conflict for people in my business,' Rembrandt continued, 'simply because it was so small. What concerns me, though, is the message that the peace agreement sends to the rest of the world. If the Protestants and Catholics of Northern Ireland can learn to live in peace after four hundred years of bloodshed – well, you understand my point, Director.'

'Actually, that message has already gone forth,' said Rodin, a senior officer in the French intelligence service. 'The Basque separatist group ETA has declared a cease-fire in Spain. They say they were inspired by the peace in Northern Ireland.'

'What are you suggesting, Rembrandt?' the Director asked.

'Perhaps we could reach out to the Brigade, make an offer of assistance,' Rembrandt said. 'If the past is any guide, it is probably a very small group, with little money and only a small stock-pile of guns and explosives. If they are to continue their campaign, they'll need a sponsor.'

'Actually, I believe we may already have an opening,' said Monet.

The Director and Monet had worked together against the Palestinian guerrillas who had turned London into a terrorist playground in the 1970s. Monet was Ari Shamron, chief of operations of the Israeli intelligence service, the Mossad.

'Last month our assets in Beirut filed a report on a man named Gavin Spencer, an Ulsterman who came to Lebanon to buy guns. In fact he actually met with one of our agents who was posing as an arms dealer.'

'Did your agent sell weaponry to Spencer?' the Director wondered mildly.

'The talks are continuing, Director,' said Monet.

'Have you shared this information with your British counterparts?'

Monet shook his head.

'Perhaps you could see that a shipment of weapons finds its way into the hands of the Ulster Freedom Brigade,' the Director said to Monet. 'Perhaps you could use your contacts within the banking community to arrange financing for the package at generous terms.'

'I think that could be handled quite easily, Director,' Monet said.

'Very well,' the Director said. 'All in favour of exploring contacts with the Ulster Freedom Brigade, signify by saying aye.'

The vote was unanimous.

'Any other matters before we move on to the rest of the agenda?'

Once again it was Monet who spoke.

'If you could update us on the progress of the Ahmed Hussein case, Director.'

Ahmed Hussein was a leader of the Muslim fundamentalist group Hamas and the mastermind behind a series of bombings in Jerusalem and Tel Aviv. The Mossad wanted him dead, but Monet had not felt confident giving the assignment to a Mossad assassination team. In September of 1997 the Mossad had tried to kill a Hamas man named Khaled Meshal in Amman. The attempt failed, and two Mossad agents were arrested by Jordanian police. Rather than risk another embarrassing failure, Monet had turned to the Society to eliminate Ahmed Hussein.

'I have assigned the job to the same operative who carried out the contracts on Colin Yardley and Eric Stoltenberg after the TransAtlantic affair,' the Director said. 'He is preparing to leave for Cairo, and I expect that in a few days Ahmed Hussein will be quite dead.'

'Excellent,' Monet said. 'Our intelligence indicates that

57

the Middle East peace process cannot survive another serious blow. If the operation is a success, the Occupied Territories will explode. Arafat will have no choice but to pull out of the talks. I expect that the peace process will be only a bad memory by the end of this winter.'

There was another round of restrained applause.

'The next item on the agenda is an update on our efforts to foster conflict between India and Pakistan,' the Director said, looking down at his papers. 'The Pakistanis are having a bit of trouble with their medium-range missiles, and they've asked for our help working out the bugs.'

The meeting ended just after dawn.

The council member code-named Picasso rode in a chauffeured Range Rover across the flat rose-coloured plain separating the High Atlas Mountains from Marrakech. Picasso had entered Morocco on a false passport bearing the name Lisa Bancroft. The real passport was locked in the safe of her room at the five-star La Mamounia Hotel. Returning to the room later that morning, she punched in the code, and the safe door popped open. The passport was there, along with some cash and jewellery.

Her flight wasn't for six hours, enough time to bathe and sleep for an hour or so. Picasso removed the items from the safe, undressed, and lay down on the bed. She opened the passport and looked at the photograph.

Funny, she thought, I don't look much like Picasso.

7

The White House advance team arrived on Saturday morning and booked every available room at the Manhanset Inn, a wedding-cake Victorian hotel in the Heights overlooking Dering Harbor. Jake Ashcroft, a burned-out investment banker who had purchased the hotel with a single year's bonus, was politely asked by White House staff to keep the matter confidential. The president's visit was strictly private, they explained, and he wanted as little attention as possible. But Shelter Island is an island, after all, with an island's appetite for gossip, and by lunchtime half the place knew the president was coming to town.

By mid-afternoon Jake Ashcroft was beginning to fear it was all a nightmare. His beloved inn had been turned upside down. The award-winning dining room had been transformed into something called a 'filing centre.' The beautiful oak tables had given way to hideous rented banquet tables shrouded in white plastic. A team from the telephone company had installed fifty temporary lines. Another team had emptied the fireside lounge and turned it into a broadcast centre. Thick cable snaked through the stately halls, and a portable satellite dish stood on the front lawn.

The network news television crews arrived in the early evening, some from New York, some from Washington. Jake Ashcroft got so angry he took to his room and stayed there, sitting in a yoga posture and repeating the Serenity Prayer. The producers were bleary-eyed and

59

foul-tempered. The cameramen looked like fishermen from Greenport – beefy and bearded, with clothes that appeared to be army surplus. They played poker past midnight and drained the bar of beer.

At first light the Secret Service fanned out across the island. They established static posts at both ferry crossings and checkpoints on every road leading to Cannon Point. Sharpshooters took up positions on the roof of the old house, and bomb-sniffing German shepherds prowled the broad lawns, terrifying the squirrels and the white-tailed deer. The television crews descended on the marina at Coecles Harbor like a raiding party and rented every boat they could lay their hands on. Prices sky-rocketed overnight. The crew from CNN had to settle for a leaky twelve-foot Zodiac, for which they paid an astonishing $500. A pair of Coast Guard cutters stood watch in Shelter Island Sound. At nine-thirty the chartered bus bearing the White House press corps arrived at the Manhanset Inn. The reporters staggered into Jake Ashcroft's plundered dining room like refugees at a processing centre.

And so everything seemed to be in place shortly after 10 A.M. when the muffled *thump-thump-thump* of a helicopter rotor could be heard from the direction of Little Peconic Bay. The day had dawned overcast and damp, but by mid-morning the last of the clouds had burned away, and the east end of Long Island sparkled in the brilliant winter sun. An American flag flapped in the wind on Chequit Point. A huge banner saying WELCOME PRESI-DENT BECKWITH lay on the roof of the Shelter Island Yacht Club, so the chief executive could read it as the helicopter passed overhead. Crowds of islanders lined Shore Road, and the high school band played a spirited if disjointed rendition of 'Hail to the Chief.'

Marine One passed over Nassau Point and Great Hog Neck. It swept low over the waters of Southold Bay, then over land once more at Conkling Point. The crowd on Shore Road caught first sight of the president's helicopter as it hovered over Shelter Island Sound. The waterborne network news crews aimed their cameras at the sky and began rolling. *Marine One* floated over Dering Harbor, the beat of the rotor making ripples on the surface of the water, then set down on the lawn of Cannon Point, just beyond the bulkhead.

Douglas Cannon was waiting there, along with Elizabeth and Michael and his two retrievers. The dogs raced forward as James and Anne Beckwith disembarked from the helicopter, dressed for the country in pressed tan khakis and hunter-green English waterproof jackets.

A small group of reporters – the so-called 'tight pool' – had been allowed onto the property to witness the arrival. 'Why are you here?' shouted a leather-lunged correspondent from *ABC News*.

'We just wanted to spend some time in the country with an old friend,' the president shouted back, smiling.

'Where are you going now?'

Douglas Cannon stepped forward. 'We're going to church.'

First Lady Anne Beckwith – or Lady Anne Beckwith, as she was known among Washington's chattering classes – was visibly taken aback by the senator's remark. Like her husband, she was a borderline atheist who detested the weekly journey across Lafayette Square to St John's Episcopal Church for an hour of mouthed prayer and false reflection. But ten minutes later a makeshift motorcade was roaring along Manhanset Road toward St Mary's. Soon the two old adversaries stood shoulder to shoulder in the front pew – Beckwith in his blue blazer, Cannon in a threadbare tweed jacket with holes in the elbows – belting out 'A Mighty Fortress Is Our God.'

At noon Beckwith and Cannon decided a short sail was in order, even though it was barely 40 degrees and a 15-mile-per-hour wind was blowing across Shelter Island Sound. Much to the dismay of the Secret Service, the two men boarded *Athena* and set out.

They stayed under power through the narrow channel separating Shelter Island from the North Fork of Long Island, then pulled up the sails as *Athena* entered the open waters of Gardiners Bay. Behind them were a Coast Guard cutter, two Boston Whalers filled with Secret Service agents, and half a dozen press boats. There was one mishap; CNN's rented Zodiac took on water and sank off the rocks of Cornelius Point.

'All right, Mr President,' Douglas Cannon said. 'Now that we've given the media lots of nice pictures, why don't you tell me what the hell this is all about.'

The *Athena* was flying across Gardiners Bay toward Plum Island on a broad reach, heeling nicely on its starboard side. Cannon sat behind the wheel, Beckwith in the seating compartment behind the companionway. 'We were never the best of friends, Mr President. In fact, I think the only social event we ever attended together was my wife's funeral.'

'We were competitors when we were in the Senate,' Beckwith said. 'It was a long time ago. And drop the Mr President bullshit, Douglas. We've known each other too long for that.'

'We were never competitors, Jim. From the moment you and Anne arrived in Washington, you had your sights on the White House. I just wanted to stay in the Senate and make laws. I liked being a legislator.'

'And you were a damned good legislator. One of the best ever.'

'I appreciate that, Jim.' Cannon looked at his sails and

frowned. 'That jib is luffing a bit, Mr President. Would you mind giving that line a pull?'

Orient Point passed on the port side. The coastal foghorns blared in tribute. Plum Island lay directly off the prow. Cannon turned to the south, toward Gardiners Island, and placed the *Athena* on a gentle beam reach.

'I want you to come to work for me,' Beckwith said suddenly. 'I need you, and the country needs you.'

'What is it you want me to do?'

'I want you to go to London as my ambassador. I can't stand idly by and allow a band of Protestant thugs to derail the peace process. I need a man of stature in London right now, and so does Tony Blair.'

'Jim, I'm seventy-one years old. I'm retired, and I'm happy.'

'If the peace doesn't hold in Northern Ireland, the violence will reach levels not seen since the '70s. I don't want that on my conscience, and I don't think you do either.'

'But why me?'

'Because you're a respected and distinguished American statesman. Because you can trace your ancestry back to Northern Ireland. Because in your public statements on the conflict you have been equally tough on the IRA and the Protestant majority. Because both sides will trust you to be fair.' Beckwith hesitated a moment, looking out at the water. 'And because your president is asking you to do something for your country. That used to mean something in Washington. I think it still means something to you, Douglas. Don't make me ask twice.'

'There's something you're forgetting, Jim.'

'The assassination attempt on your son-in-law last year?'

'And my daughter. I trust a copy of Michael's memo

63

made it to the Oval Office. Michael believes one of your biggest benefactors was behind the attack on TransAtlantic Flight 002. And frankly, I believe him.'

'I did see his report,' Beckwith said, frowning. 'Michael was a fine intelligence officer, but his conclusions missed the mark. The suggestion that a man like Mitchell Elliott had something to do with the attack on that jetliner is ludicrous. If I thought he was remotely involved, I'd use every ounce of power I have to make certain he was punished. But it's simply not true, Douglas. The Sword of Gaza shot down that plane.'

'If you nominate me, the GOP money men are going to blow a fuse. London always goes to a big contributor.'

'The best thing about being a lame duck, Douglas, is that I don't have to give a fuck what the money men say any more.'

'What about the confirmation process?'

'Pardon the pun, but you'll sail through.'

'Don't sound so sure of yourself. The Senate has changed since we left. Your party sent a bunch of Young Turks there, and it seems to me that they intend to burn the place down.'

'I'll deal with the Young Turks.'

'I don't want them breaking my balls because I smoked pot a few times. I was a college professor in New York City in the '60s and '70s, for Christ's sake. Everyone smoked pot.'

'I didn't.'

'Well, that explains a lot.'

Beckwith laughed. 'I'll personally talk to the ranking Republican on Foreign Relations. He will be told in no uncertain terms that your nomination is to receive unanimous Republican support. And it will.'

Cannon made a show of careful consideration, but both men knew he had already made up his mind. 'I need time. I need to talk to Elizabeth and Michael. I have two grand-children. Moving to London at this stage of my life is not something I can do lightly.'

'Take all the time you need, Douglas.'

Cannon looked over his shoulder at the crowd of boats shadowing them across Gardiners Bay. 'I could have used that Coast Guard cutter a couple of years ago.'

'Ah, yes,' the president said. 'I read about your little disaster at sea off Montauk Light. How a sailor of your experience got caught unprepared in foul weather is beyond me.'

'It was a freak summer storm!'

'There's no such thing as a freak summer storm. You should have been watching the skies and listening to the radio. Where'd you learn to sail anyway?'

'I was monitoring the conditions. This one was a freak squall.'

'Freak squall, my ass,' the president said. 'Must have been all that pot you smoked back in the '6os.'

Both men burst out laughing.

'Maybe we should head back,' Cannon said. 'Prepare to come about, Mr President.'

'He wants me to go to London to replace Edward Hathaway as ambassador,' Cannon announced, as he came upstairs from the wine cellar, clutching a dusty bottle of Bordeaux. The president and the first lady had gone; the children were sleeping upstairs. Michael and Elizabeth were sprawled on the overstuffed couches next to the fire. Cannon opened the wine and poured out three glasses.

'What did you say to him?' Elizabeth asked.

'I told him I needed to discuss it with my family.'

Michael said, 'Why you? James Beckwith and Douglas Cannon have never been exactly the best of friends.'

Cannon repeated Beckwith's reasons. Michael said, 'Beckwith's right. You've blasted all sides for their conduct – the IRA, the Protestant paramilitaries, and the British. You also command respect because of your tenure in the Senate. That makes you a perfect man for the Court of St James's right now.'

Elizabeth frowned. 'But he's also seventy-one years old, retired, with two brand-new grandchildren. Now is not the time to go running off to London to be an ambassador.'

'You don't say no to the president,' Cannon said.

'The *president* should have taken that into consideration before he asked you,' Elizabeth said. 'Besides, London's always been a political posting. Let Beckwith send one of his big donors.'

'Blair asked Beckwith not to make a political appointment. He wants either a career diplomat or a politician of stature – like your father,' Cannon said defensively.

He drifted to the fire and stirred the embers with the poker.

'You're right, Elizabeth,' he said, staring at the flames. 'I *am* seventy-one, and I'm probably too old to take on such a demanding assignment. But my president asked me to do it, and goddammit, I *want* to do it. It's hard to be sitting on the sidelines. If I can help bring peace to Northern Ireland, it will dwarf anything I ever accomplished in Congress.'

'You sound as though you've already made up your mind, Daddy.'

'I have, but I want your blessing.'

'What about your grandchildren?'

'My grandchildren won't be able to tell the difference between me and the dogs for another six months.'

Michael said, 'There's something else you have to consider, Douglas. Less than a month ago, a new Protestant terrorist organization demonstrated its willingness and ability to attack high-profile targets.'

'I realize the job is not without risk. Frankly, I'd like to know the nature of the threat, and I'd like an assessment I can trust.'

'What are you saying, Daddy?'

'I'm saying my son-in-law used to work for the Central Intelligence Agency, penetrating terrorist groups. He knows a thing or two about this business, and he has good contacts. I'd like him to use those contacts so I'll know just what I'm up against.'

'Oh, no. I'm not going to let Michael run off and do a freelance job for you so you *both* can be in danger.'

'I'll just be a couple of days in London,' Michael said. 'Over and back.'

Elizabeth lit a cigarette and exhaled smoke sharply between her lips. 'Yeah. I remember the last time you said that.'

8

The whitewashed villa clung to the cliffs of Cape Mavros at the mouth of Panormos Bay. For five years it had been empty, except for a drunken group of young British stockbrokers who had rented the house each summer. The previous owners, an American novelist and his stunning Mexican wife, had been driven off by the eternal wind. They had entrusted the property to Stavros, the largest estate agent on the north side of Mykonos, and fled to Tuscany.

The Frenchman called Delaroche – at least Stavros assumed he was French – didn't seem to mind the wind. He had come to Mykonos the previous winter, with his right hand in a heavy bandage, and purchased the villa after a five-minute inspection. Stavros celebrated his good fortune that evening with endless rounds of wine and ouzo – in the Frenchman's honour, of course – for the patrons at the taverna in Ano Mera. From that moment on, the enigmatic Monsieur Delaroche was the most popular man on the north side of Mykonos, even though no one but Stavros had ever seen his face.

Within a few weeks of his arrival, there was a good deal of speculation on Mykonos as to just what the Frenchman did for a living. He painted like an angel, but when Stavros offered to arrange a show at a friend's gallery in Chora, the Frenchman declared that he never sold his work. He cycled like a demon, but when Kristos, the owner of the taverna in Ano Mera, tried to recruit Delaroche for the local club, the Frenchman said he preferred to ride alone. Some speculated he had been born to wealth, but he did all the repairs on his villa himself, and he was known as a frugal customer in the village shops. He had no visitors, threw no parties, and took no women, even though many of the Mykonos girls would gladly have volunteered their services. His days had a clockwork regularity about them. He rode his Italian racing bike, he painted his paintings, he cared for his windswept villa. Most days, at dusk, he could be seen sitting on the rocks at Linos, staring at the sea. It was there, according to myth, that Poseidon had destroyed Ajax the Lesser for the rape of Cassandra.

Delaroche had spent the day on Syros painting. That evening, as the sun set into the sea, he returned to Mykonos by ferry. He stood on the foredeck, smoking a cigarette, as the boat entered Korfos Bay and docked at Chora. He waited until everyone had left the boat before disembarking.

He had purchased a used Volvo station wagon for days when it was too cold and rainy to cycle. The Volvo was waiting in a deserted lot at the ferry terminal. Delaroche opened the rear door and placed his things in the back compartment: a large flat case containing his canvases and his palette, a smaller case with his paints and his brushes. He climbed inside and started the engine.

The drive northward to Cape Mavros took only a few minutes; Mykonos is a small island, about ten miles by six miles, and there was little traffic on the road, because of the season. The moonscape terrain passed through the yellow cone of the headlights – treeless, barren, the rough features smoothed over by thousands of years of human habitation.

Delaroche pulled into the gravel drive outside the villa and climbed out. He had to lean hard on the door to close it in the wind. Whitecaps glowed on Panormos Bay and the Ionian Sea beyond. Delaroche followed the short walkway to the front door and shoved his key in the lock. Before opening the door, he withdrew a Beretta automatic pistol from the shoulder holster beneath his leather jacket. The alarm chirped softly as he stepped inside. He disarmed the system, switched on the lights, and moved through the entire villa, room by room, until he felt certain no one was there.

He was hungry after painting all day, so he went into the kitchen and made supper: an omelette of onions, mushrooms, and cheese, a plate of Parma ham, roasted Greek peppers, and bread fried in olive oil and garlic.

He carried his food to the rustic wooden dining table. He switched on his laptop computer, logged onto the Internet, and read newspapers while he ate. It was quiet except for the wind rattling the windows overlooking the sea.

When he was finished reading he checked his E-mail. There was one message, but when he called it up on his screen it appeared as a meaningless series of characters. He typed in his password, and the gibberish turned to clear text. Delaroche finished eating his supper while he studied the dossier of the next man he would kill.

Jean-Paul Delaroche had lived in France most of his life, but he was not French at all. Code-named October, Delaroche had been an assassin for the KGB. He had lived and operated exclusively in Western Europe and the Middle East, and his mission had been simple: to create chaos within NATO by inflaming tension within the borders of its member nations. When the Soviet Union collapsed, men like Delaroche weren't absorbed by the

KGB's more presentable successor, the Foreign Intelligence Service; he went into private practice and quickly became the world's most sought-after contract killer. Now, he worked for just one person, a man he knew only as the Director. For his services he was paid $1 million a year.

Sea fog hung over the cliffs the following day as Delaroche rode a small Italian motor scooter along the narrow lane above Panormos Bay. He took lunch at the taverna in Ano Mera: fish, rice, bread, and salad, with olive oil and wedges of hard-boiled egg. After lunch he walked through the village to the fruit market. He purchased several melons and placed them in a large paper sack, which he held between his legs as he rode to a deserted patch of track in the barren hills above Merdias Bay.

Delaroche stopped the motor scooter next to an outcrop of rock. He took a melon from the bag and placed it on a ledge of the rock, so it was approximately level with his own head. Next, he removed three more melons and placed them along the pathway about twenty yards apart. The Beretta hung in a shoulder holster beneath his left arm. He drove about two hundred metres down the path, stopped, and turned around. He reached inside his coat pocket and pulled on a pair of black leather gloves. A year earlier, during his last assignment, the man he had been hired to kill had shot him through the right hand. It was the only time Delaroche had failed to fulfil the terms of a contract. The shooting had left an ugly puckered scar. He could do many things to alter his appearance – grow a beard, wear sunglasses and a hat, colour his hair – but he could do nothing about the scar except conceal it.

Suddenly, he opened the bike's throttle full and raced along the track, dust flying in a plume behind him. He expertly manoeuvred his way through the obstacles. He reached beneath his left arm, drew the gun, and levelled it at the approaching target. As he swept past he fired three times.

Delaroche stopped, turned around, and went back to inspect the melon.

None of the three shots had hit its mark.

Delaroche swore softly beneath his breath and replayed the whole thing in his mind, trying to determine why he had missed. He looked down at his hands. He had never worn gloves and didn't like the way they felt; they robbed his gun hand of sensitivity, and it was difficult to feel the trigger against his forefinger. He removed the gloves, holstered the Beretta, sped down the track to the starting point, and turned around.

He opened the bike's throttle again and weaved in and out of the melons at speed. He drew the Beretta and fired as he passed the target. The melon disintegrated in a flash of bright yellow.

Delaroche sped away.

Ahmed Hussein was residing in a squat four-storey apartment house in Ma'adi, a dusty suburb along the Nile a few miles south of downtown Cairo. Hussein was short, less than five and a half feet tall, and small of frame. His hair was cut close to the scalp, his beard piously unkempt. He took all his meals and received all his visitors inside the flat, venturing outside only to go to the mosque across the street five times each day to pray. Sometimes he stopped in the coffee house next to the mosque for tea, but usually his troop of amateur security men insisted he return directly to the flat. Sometimes they all piled into a dark blue Fiat for the short trip to the mosque; sometimes they walked. It was all in the dossier.

Delaroche began his journey to Cairo three days later, on an overcast windless morning. He took coffee on his terrace above Cape Mavros, a flat sea all around him, and then drove the Volvo into Chora and left it in a parking lot. He could have flown directly to Athens, but he decided to take a ferry to Paros and fly on from there. He was in no rush, and he wanted to watch his tail for signs of surveillance. As the boat cleared Korfos Bay and passed the small island of Delos, he strolled the decks and examined the faces of the other passengers, committing them to memory.

In Paros, Delaroche took a taxi from the waterfront to the airport. He dawdled at a telephone kiosk, a newsagent, and a café, all the while checking the faces around him. He boarded the flight to Athens; no one from the ferry was among those on board. Delaroche sat back and enjoyed the short flight, watching the grey-green winter sea passing below his window.

He spent the afternoon in Athens, touring the ancient sites, and in the evening boarded a flight for Rome. He checked into a small hotel off the Via Veneto under the name Karel van der Stadt and began speaking fractured English with a Dutch accent.

Rome was cold and damp, but he was hungry, so he hurried through the drizzle to a good restaurant he knew on the Via Borghese. The waiters brought red wine and endless appetizers: tomato and mozzarella, roasted eggplant and peppers marinated in olive oil and spices, omelette and Parma ham. When the appetizers ended the waiter appeared and said simply, 'Meat or fish?' Delaroche ate sea bass and boiled potatoes.

After dinner he went back to his hotel. He sat down at the small writing table and switched on his notebook computer. He logged onto the Internet and downloaded an encrypted file. He typed in his password, and once again the gibberish turned to clear text. The new file was an updated watch report on Ahmed Hussein's activities in

Cairo. Delaroche had worked for a professional intelligence service, and he knew good fieldwork when he saw it. Hussein was under the surveillance of a top-notch service in Cairo, most likely the Mossad.

In the morning, Delaroche took a taxi to Leonardo da Vinci Airport and boarded an early afternoon Egypt Air flight to Cairo. He checked into a small Egyptian-owned hotel in downtown Cairo and changed into lighter clothes. He took a taxi to Ma'adi in the late afternoon. The driver raced along the Corniche, dodging cyclists and donkey carts, as the setting sun turned the Nile into a ribbon of gold.

By dusk, Delaroche was taking sweet tea and pastries in the coffee house across from Ahmed Hussein's flat. The muezzin sounded the evening call to prayer, and the faithful streamed toward the mosque. Ahmed Hussein was among them, surrounded by his motley troupe of bodyguards. Delaroche watched Hussein carefully. He ordered more tea and pictured how he would kill him tomorrow.

The following day, Delaroche took lunch on the sun-drenched terrace café at the Nile Hilton. He spotted the blond man in the sunglasses, sitting alone among the tourists and rich Egyptians with a large bottle of Stella beer and a half-empty glass. A thin black attaché case rested on the chair next to him.

Delaroche walked to the table. 'Mind if I join you?' he asked, in Dutch-accented English.

'Actually, I was just leaving,' the man said, and stood up.

Delaroche sat down and ordered lunch.

He placed the attaché on the ground next to his feet.

After lunch, Delaroche stole a motor scooter. It was parked outside the Nile Hilton, in the madness of Tahrir

Square, and it took him a matter of seconds to pick the ignition lock and fire the engine. It was dark blue, coated in a fine layer of Cairo's powderlike dust, and seemed to be in good working order. There was even a helmet with a dark visor.

Delaroche drove south through the Garden City section of Cairo – past the fortified American embassy, past dilapidated villas, sad reminders of a grander time. The contents of the attaché case, a Beretta 9-millimetre automatic and silencer, were now in a holster beneath his left arm. He sped through a narrow alley, past the back of the old Shepherd's Hotel, turned onto the Corniche, and raced south along the Nile.

He arrived in Ma'adi before sunset. He waited about two hundred yards from the mosque, purchasing flatbread and limes from a peasant boy on the street corner, head covered with the helmet. The amplified voice of the muezzin sounded, and the call to prayer echoed over the neighbourhood.

God is most great.
I testify that there is no god but God.
I testify that Muhammad is the Prophet of God.
Come to prayer.
Come to success.
God is most great.
There is no god but God.

Delaroche saw Ahmed Hussein emerge from his apartment house, surrounded by his bodyguards. He crossed the street and entered the mosque. Delaroche gave the boy a few crumpled piastres for the bread and limes, climbed on the motor scooter, and started the engine.

According to the reports, Ahmed Hussein always stayed in the mosque at least ten minutes. Delaroche drove half a block and stopped at a kiosk. He leisurely purchased a pack of Egyptian cigarettes, some candy, and razors. He placed these items in the larger bag containing the bread and limes.

The faithful were beginning to trickle out of the mosque.

Delaroche started the engine.

Ahmed Hussein and his bodyguards emerged from the mosque into the rose-coloured dusk.

Delaroche opened the throttle, and the motorbike leapt forward. He raced along the dusty street, dodging pedestrians and slow-moving cars, just the way he had practised on the track above Merdias Bay, and brought the bike to a sliding stop in front of the mosque. The bodyguards, sensing trouble, tried to close ranks around their man.

Delaroche reached inside his coat and withdrew the Beretta.

He levelled it at Hussein, taking aim at his face; then he lowered the gun a few inches and pulled the trigger rapidly three times. All three shots struck Ahmed Hussein in the chest.

Two of the four bodyguards were pulling weapons from beneath their garments. Delaroche shot one through the heart and the other through the throat. The last two bodyguards threw themselves to the ground next to the bodies. Delaroche gunned the engine and raced away.

He melted into the teeming slums of south Cairo, ditched the motorbike in an alleyway, and dropped the Beretta down a sewer. Two hours later he boarded an Alitalia flight to Rome.

9

LONDON

'How long will you be staying in the United Kingdom?' the officer in the passport control booth asked rapture-lessly.

'Just a day.'

Michael Osbourne handed over his passport, which bore his real name because the Agency had taken back his false passports upon his retirement – at least the ones they knew about. Over the years several friendly intelligence services had also granted him passports out of professional courtesy. He could travel as a Spaniard, an Italian, an Israeli, or a Frenchman. He even had obtained an Egyptian passport from an asset inside that country's intelligence service, which permitted him to enter certain Middle Eastern countries as a fellow Arab rather than an outsider. None of those intelligence services had asked for their passports after Michael's departure from the secret world. They were locked in Douglas Cannon's safe on Shelter Island.

The inspection of his passport was taking longer than usual. Obviously, it had been flagged by the British security services. The last time Michael was in England he had been caught in the middle of the Sword of Gaza's attack at Heathrow Airport. He had also conducted an unauthorized meeting with a man named Ivan Drozdov – a KGB defector under the care of MI6 – who was murdered later that afternoon.

'Where are you staying in the United Kingdom?' the

officer asked tonelessly, reading from the small computer screen in front of him.

'In London,' Michael said.

The officer looked up. 'Where in London, Mr Osbourne?'

Michael gave the officer the address of a hotel in Knightsbridge, which he dutifully wrote down. Michael knew the officer would give the address to his supervisor, and the supervisor would give it to Britain's internal Security Service, MI5.

'Do you have a reservation at your hotel, Mr Osbourne?'

'Yes, I do.'

'Is it in your name?'

'Yes.'

The officer handed back the passport. 'Enjoy your stay.'

Michael picked up his slender garment bag, passed through customs, and entered the arrival hall. He had telephoned his old London car service from the plane. He scanned the waiting crowd, looking for his driver and, instinctively, any sign of surveillance: a familiar face, a figure that seemed somehow out of place, a set of eyes watching him.

He spotted a small limousine driver in a dark suit holding a cardboard sign that said MR STAFFORD. Michael crossed the hall and said, 'Let's go.'

'Take your bag, sir?'

'No, thanks.'

Michael slumped down in the back seat of the Rover sedan as it crawled through the thick morning traffic toward the West End. The motorway had given way to the Edwardian façades of the hotels along the Cromwell Road. Michael knew London all too well; he had lived in a flat in

Chelsea for more than ten years, when he was working in the field. Most CIA officers stationed abroad work from embassies, with diplomatic jobs for cover. But Michael had worked in counterterrorism, recruiting and running agents in the terrorist playgrounds of Europe and the Middle East. An assignment like that was next to impossible under diplomatic cover, so Michael had operated as an NOC, which in the lexicon of the Agency meant he had 'nonofficial cover.' He posed as a salesman for a company that designed computer systems for businesses. The company was a CIA front, but the job permitted Michael to travel throughout Europe and the Middle East without suspicion.

Michael's control officer, Adrian Carter, used to say that if there ever was a man born and bred to spy it was Michael Osbourne. His father had worked for the OSS during the war and then entered the clandestine service of its successor, the CIA. Michael and his mother, Alexandra, followed him from posting to posting – Rome, Beirut, Athens, Belgrade, and Madrid – with short tours at Headquarters in between. While his father was running Russian spies, Michael and his mother absorbed languages and cultures. Michael's dark skin and hair allowed him to pass for an Italian or a Spaniard or even a certain type of Lebanese Arab. He used to test himself in markets and cafés, to see how long he could go without being recognized as an outsider. He spoke Italian with a Roman accent and Spanish like a native of Madrid. He struggled a bit with Greek but mastered Arabic so thoroughly the shopkeepers in Beirut's *soukh* assumed he was Lebanese and didn't cheat him.

The car arrived at the hotel. Michael paid off the driver and got out. It was a small hotel, with no doorman and no concierge – just a pretty Polish girl behind an oak desk

79

with keys hanging on pegs behind her. He checked in and asked for a 2 P.M. wake-up call.

Retirement had not robbed Michael of a healthy professional paranoia. For five minutes he inspected the room, turning over lamps, opening closet doors, tearing apart the telephone and then carefully reassembling it. He had performed the same ritual in a thousand hotel rooms in a hundred different cities. Only once had he ever found a bug – a Soviet-made museum piece crudely attached to the telephone of a hotel room in Damascus.

His search turned up nothing. He turned on the television and watched the morning news on the BBC.

> Northern Ireland Secretary Mo Mowlam has vowed that the new Protestant paramilitary group, the Ulster Freedom Brigade, will never be allowed to destroy the Good Friday accords. She has called on the chief constable of the RUC, Ronnie Flanagan, to redouble his efforts to capture the leaders of the terrorist group.

Michael shut off the television and closed his eyes, still dressed in the clothes he had worn on the flight. He slept fitfully, wrestling with his blanket, sweating in his clothing, until the telephone screamed. For an instant he thought he had been transported behind the Iron Curtain, but it was only the flaxen Polish girl at the front desk, gently informing him it was two o'clock.

He ordered coffee, showered, and dressed in jeans, bucks, black turtleneck sweater, and blue blazer. He hung the DO NOT DISTURB sign on the doorknob and left a telltale in the jamb.

Outside, the sky was the colour of gunpowder, and cold wind bent the trees in Hyde Park. He turned up the collar of his overcoat, knotted the scarf at his throat, and he started walking, first along Knightsbridge, then the

Brompton Road. He spotted the first watcher: balding, mid-forties, leather jacket, stubble on his chin. Anonymous, ordinary, unthreatening, perfect for pavement work.

He ate an omelette in a French café on the Brompton Road and read the *Evening Standard*. A leader of the Muslim fundamentalist group Hamas had been assassinated in Egypt. Michael read the article once, then read it a second time, and thought about it some more as he walked to Harrods. The balding watcher was gone, and a new one was in his place – same model but wearing a forest-green Barbour coat instead of a leather jacket. He entered Harrods, paid an obligatory visit to the shrine to Dodi and Diana, and then took the escalator up. The man in the Barbour jacket followed him. He purchased a Scottish sweater for Douglas and a pair of earrings for Elizabeth. He went downstairs again and meandered through the food hall. A new watcher was trailing him; a rather attractive young woman in jeans, combat-style boots, and a tan quilted jacket.

Night had fallen, and with it came a windblown rain. He left the Harrods bag at the desk of his hotel and flagged down a taxi. For the next hour and a half he moved restlessly about the West End – by taxi, Underground, and bus – through Belgravia, Mayfair, Westminster, and finally Sloane Square. He walked south until he reached Chelsea Embankment.

He stood in the rain, looking at the lights of Chelsea Bridge. It had been more than ten years since the night Sarah Randolph was shot on this spot, but the image of her death played out in his thoughts as if it were on videotape. He saw her, walking toward him, long skirt dancing across buckskin boots, the Embankment shining with river mist. Then the man appeared, the black-haired man with brilliant blue eyes and a silenced automatic – the

KGB assassin Michael knew only as October, the same man who had tried to murder Michael and Elizabeth on Shelter Island. Michael closed his eyes as Sarah's exploding face flashed through his thoughts. The Agency had assured him that October was dead, but now, after reading the account of the assassination of Ahmed Hussein in Cairo, he was not so certain.

'I think I'm being followed,' Michael said, standing in the window overlooking Eaton Place.

'You *are* being followed,' Graham Seymour said. 'The Department flagged your passport. You were a very naughty boy the last time you paid a visit to our fair island. We picked you up this morning at Heathrow.'

Michael accepted a tumbler of Scotch from Graham and sat down in the wing chair next to the fire. Graham Seymour opened an ebony cigarette box on the coffee table and took out two Dunhills, one for himself and one for Michael. They sat in silence, two old chums who have told each other every story they know and are content just to sit in each other's presence. Vivaldi played softly on Graham's elaborate German sound system. Graham closed his grey eyes and savoured his cigarette and whisky.

Graham Seymour worked for the counterterrorism division of MI5. Like Michael, he had been a child prodigy. His father had worked closely with John Masterman in the Double Cross operation of MI5 during the war, capturing German spies and playing them back against their masters at the Abwehr in Berlin. He had stayed on with MI5 after the war and worked against the Russians. Harold Seymour was a legend, and his son was forever bumping into his memory at Headquarters and running across his exploits in old case files. Michael understood the pressure this placed on Graham, because he had experienced the same thing in the Agency. The two men had developed a friendship when Michael was based in London. They had shared information from time to time and watched each other's back. Still, friendships have well-defined limits in the intelligence business, and Michael maintained a healthy professional mistrust of Graham Seymour. He knew Graham would stab him in the back if MI5 ordered him to do so.

'Is it all right for you to be seen with a leper like me?' Michael asked.

'Dinner with an old friend, darling. No harm in that. Besides, I plan to feed them some good gossip about the inner workings of Langley.'

'I haven't set foot in Langley in over a year.'

'No one ever *really* retires from this business. The Department hounded my father till the day he died. Every time something special came up they sent a couple of nice men round to sit at the feet of the great Harold.'

Michael raised his glass and said, 'To the great Harold.'

'Here, here.' Graham drank some of the whisky. 'So how is retirement anyway?'

'It sucks.'

'Really?'

'Yes, really,' Michael said. 'It was all right for a while, especially when I was recovering, but after a while I started to go stir crazy. I tried to write my book, then decided writing one's memoirs at forty-eight was an exercise in extreme self-absorption. So I read other people's books, I potter, and I take long walks in Manhattan.'

'What about the children?' Graham asked this question with the scepticism of a man who had elevated child-lessness to a religion. 'What's it like being a father for the first time at your age?'

'What the hell do you mean by *your* age?'

'I mean, you're forty-eight years old, love. The first time you try to play a set of tennis with your children you may very well drop dead of a coronary.'

'It's marvellous,' Michael said. 'It's the best thing I've ever done.'

'But?' Graham wondered.

'But I'm cooped up in the apartment with the children all day, and I'm beginning to go a bit insane.'

'So what are you planning to do with the rest of your life?'

'Develop a drinking problem. More Scotch, please.'

'Absolutely,' Graham said. He made a vast show of snatching up the bottle with his long hands and dumping an inch of the whisky into Michael's glass. Graham had a deftness about him, a shocking uncontrived grace even in the simplest gesture. Michael thought he was a little too pretty for a spy: the half-closed grey eyes that projected bored insolence, the narrow features that would have been attractive on a woman's face. He was an artist at heart, a gifted pianist who could have made his living on the concert stage instead of the secret stage, had he chosen to do so. Michael assumed it was his father's wartime heroics – 'his bloody wonderful war,' Graham snarled once after too much Bordeaux – that drove Graham into intelligence work.

Graham said, 'So when the senator asked you to do a little freelance work on the Ulster Freedom Brigade –'

'I didn't exactly stomp my feet and resist.'

'Did Elizabeth see through your little game?'

'Elizabeth sees through everything. She's a lawyer, remember? And a damned good one. She would have made an excellent intelligence officer, too.' Michael hesitated for a moment. 'So what can you tell me about the Ulster Freedom Brigade?'

'Precious little, I'm afraid.' Graham hesitated. 'Usual

rules for the game, right, Michael? Any information I give you is for your background purposes only. You may not share it with any member of your former service – or any other service, for that matter.'

Michael raised his right hand and said, 'Scout's honour.'

Graham spoke for twenty minutes without interruption. The British intelligence and security organizations were not certain whether the Ulster Freedom Brigade had five members or five hundred. Hundreds of known members of Protestant paramilitary organizations had been interrogated, and none had provided a single useful lead. The sophistication of the attacks suggested the group had expertise and serious financial backing. There was also evidence to suggest that its leaders would go to extraordinary lengths to safeguard internal security. Charlie Bates, a Protestant suspected in the murder of Eamonn Dillon, had been discovered shot to death in a barn outside Hillsborough in County Armagh, and the bombers in Dublin and London had both died in the explosions – a fact that had not been made public.

'This is Northern Ireland, not West Beirut,' Graham said. 'The Northern Irish aren't suicide bombers. It's simply not part of the fabric of the conflict.'

'So the leaders of the Ulster Freedom Brigade recruit action agents with no known paramilitary connections and then make certain they die so no one is left behind to talk.'

'That would appear to be the case,' Graham said.

'So what is this Ulster Freedom Brigade trying to accomplish?'

'If we take them at their word, they're out to destroy the peace process. If we judge them by their actions they are not going to be content to just kill off a few ordinary Catholics, like their Protestant brethren in the Loyalist Volunteer Force. They've demonstrated their willingness to attack high-profile soft targets and shed innocent blood.'

'It looks to me as though they're out to punish *all* parties to the peace process.'

'Exactly,' Graham said. 'The Irish government, the British government, Sinn Fein. And I think the leaders of the Protestant parties who signed the agreement had better watch their backs as well.'

'What about the Americans?'

'Your Senator George Mitchell brokered the Good Friday agreement, and the Protestant hard-liners have never been too fond of the Americans. They think you've clearly sided with the Catholics and want the North to be united with the Irish Republic.'

'So the American ambassador to London would have to consider himself a potential target.'

'The Ulster Freedom Brigade has demonstrated quite clearly that they have the will and the expertise to carry out spectacular acts of terrorism. Given their accomplishments thus far, taking out an American ambassador would seem to be a reasonable proposition.'

An hour later they met Graham's wife, Helen, at a French restaurant called Marcello's in Covent Garden. Helen wore black: a tight-fitting black sweater, a short black skirt, black stockings, black shoes with impossibly thick heels. She went through phases like a teenage girl. The last time Michael was in London, Helen had been in the midst of her Mediterranean period – she had dressed like a Greek peasant and cooked only with olive oil. After a long absence from the workforce she had recently taken a job as art director for a successful publishing house. Her new job came with a coveted space in the company car park. She had commandeered Graham's BMW and insisted on driving to work each morning, listening to her ghastly alternative rock CDs and screaming at her mother over her mobile phone, even though the trip would take half the time by tube. She was the kind of wife who turned heads at Personnel. Graham indulged her because she was beautiful and because she was gifted. She possessed a fire for life that the Service had long ago extinguished in him. He wore her like a loud tie.

Helen was already seated at a table next to the window, drinking Sancerre. She rose, kissed Michael's cheek, and held him tightly for a moment. 'God, it's marvellous to see you, Michael.'

Marcello appeared, all smiles and *bonhomie*, and poured wine for Michael and Graham.

'Don't bother looking at the menu,' Helen said, 'because I've already ordered for you.'

Graham and Michael quietly closed their menus and surrendered them without protest. Helen's return to the workforce had left her no time to pursue her great passion, which was cooking. Unfortunately, her talent ended at the doorway to her £50,000 modern Scandinavian kitchen. Now, she and Graham ate only in restaurants. Michael noticed that Graham was beginning to put on weight.

Helen spoke of her own work because she knew Michael and Graham could not speak of theirs. 'I'm trying to finish the cover for a new thriller,' Helen said. 'Some beastly American who writes about serial killers. How many different ways can you illustrate a serial killer? I produce a cover, we send it across the Atlantic, and the agent in New York rejects it. So bloody frustrating sometimes.' She looked at Michael, and her bright green eyes turned suddenly serious. 'My God, I'm being such a crashing bore. How's Elizabeth?'

Michael looked at Graham. He gave a nearly imperceptible nod. Graham routinely flouted the regulations of the Security Service by telling Helen too much about his work.

'Some days are better than others,' Michael said. 'But overall she's doing fine. We've turned the apartment and the Shelter Island house into fortresses. It helps her sleep better at night. And then there are the children. Between her work and the twins, she has little time to dwell on the past.'

'Did she really kill that German woman – oh, God, Graham, what was her name again?'

'Astrid Vogel,' Graham put in.

'Did she really do it with a bow and arrow?'

Michael nodded.

'My God,' Helen murmured. 'What happened?'

'Astrid Vogel followed her into the guest cottage, where you and Graham stayed a couple of years ago. Elizabeth hid in the bedroom closet. One of her old bows was there. She was a champion archer when she was a girl, just like her father. She did what she had to do to survive.'

'What happened to the other assassin, this October fellow?'

'The Agency received reports through channels it trusted that October is dead, that he had been killed by the men who hired him to kill me because he had failed.'

'Do you believe it?' Helen asked.

'I thought it was remotely possible once,' Michael said. 'But now I don't believe it at all. In fact, I'm almost certain October is alive and working again. This assassination in Cairo –'

'Ahmed Hussein,' Graham put in, for Helen's benefit.

'I've read the eyewitness accounts carefully. I can't explain it, but it just feels like him.'

'Didn't October always shoot his victims in the face?'

'He did, but if he's supposed to be dead, it makes sense that he would have to alter his signature.'

'What do you plan to do?' Graham asked.

'I'm booked on the first flight to Cairo tomorrow morning.'

10

CAIRO

Michael arrived in Cairo early the following afternoon. As in Britain, he entered the country on his true passport and was granted a two-week tourist visa. He sliced his way through the madness of the airport arrival lounge – past Bedouins with all their worldly possessions crammed inside wilting cardboard boxes, past a bleating cluster of goats – and waited twenty minutes at the taxi stand for a rattletrap Lada sedan. He smoked cigarettes to cover the stench of exhaust pouring into the back seat.

Michael found Cairo intolerably hot in summer, but the winters were remarkably pleasant. The air was warm and soft, and a desert wind chased puffy white clouds around an azure sky. The road from the airport was jammed with poor Egyptians trying to take some pleasure in the good weather. Entire families sprawled in the grassy median around picnic lunches. The taxi driver spoke to Michael in English, but Michael wanted to see whether his skills had atrophied, so he answered him in rapid Arabic. He told the driver he was a Lebanese businessman, living in London, who had fled Beirut during the war. For half an hour they talked of Beirut in the old days, Michael in flawless Beirut-accented Arabic, the driver in the accent of his Nile Delta village.

Michael was bored with the Nile Hilton – and sick of the turmoil of Tahrir Square – so he took a room at the Inter-Continental, a sandstone-coloured edifice looming over the Corniche that, like all newer buildings in Cairo, bore the scars of dust and diesel fumes. He lay by the rooftop pool, drinking warm Egyptian beer, his mind flowing from one thought to the next, until the sun vanished into the western desert and the evening call to prayer started up – first one muezzin, a very long way off, then another, and another, until a thousand recorded voices screamed in concert. He forced himself out of his chaise longue and went to the railing overlooking the river. A few faithful drifted toward the mosques, but mostly Cairo continued to churn beneath him.

At five o'clock he went to his room, showered, and dressed. He took a taxi a short distance up the river to a restaurant called Paprika, next to the towering head-quarters of the state-run Egyptian television network. Paprika was the equivalent of Joe Allen in New York, a place where actors and writers came to be seen by each other and by Egyptians wealthy enough to afford the rather mediocre food. One side of the restaurant over-looked the parking lot of Egyptian television. Those were the most coveted tables in the restaurant, because some-times patrons caught a glimpse of an actor or celebrity or senior government official.

Michael had reserved a table on the unfashionable side of the restaurant. He drank bottled water and watched the sun setting over the Nile and thought of the first agent he had ever recruited, a Syrian intelligence officer based in London who had a taste for English girls and good champagne. The Agency suspected the Syrian was siphon-ing some of his operating funds to support his habits. Michael approached the officer, threatened to expose him to his superiors in Damascus, and coerced him into becoming a paid spy for the CIA. The agent provided valuable intelligence on Syrian support for several differ-ent terrorist groups, Arab and European. Two years after his recruitment he provided his most valuable piece of information. A PLO terror cell had set up shop in Frankfurt, where it was planning to bomb a nightclub frequented by American servicemen. Michael passed the information to Headquarters, and Headquarters tipped off the West German police, who arrested the Palestinians. The Syrian was paid $100,000 for the information, and Michael was awarded the Distinguished Intelligence Medal during a secret ceremony. The medal had to be locked away in a file cabinet at Headquarters.

Yousef Hafez entered the restaurant. Unlike the Syrian, Hafez had come to the Agency voluntarily rather than through coercion. He had the fleshy good looks of an ageing film star: black hair gone to grey, square features gone soft with twenty extra pounds, deep fissures around his eyes when he smiled. Hafez was a colonel in the Mukhabarat, the Egyptian intelligence service, and his job was to combat Egypt's Islamic fundamentalist rebels, the al-Gama'at Ismalyya. He had personally captured and tortured several of its leaders. Cairo Station had recruited Hafez, but he refused to work with Cairo-based officers because their movements were monitored so closely by his own service. Michael had been assigned to the case. Hafez had provided a steady stream of information on the state of the Islamic revolt in Egypt and the movement of Egyptian terrorists around the globe. In return he was paid handsomely – money that helped defray the costs of his relentless womanizing. Hafez liked younger women, and they liked him. He believed he was doing nothing to endanger his country, and therefore he felt no guilt.

He spoke to Michael in Arabic – loudly enough so that the diners at surrounding tables could hear him – and Michael followed suit. He asked Michael what brought him to town, and Michael said business interests in Cairo and Alexandria. The restaurant buzzed for a moment, as a famous Egyptian actress climbed out of her car and walked inside the television building.

'Why Paprika?' Michael asked. 'I thought Arabesque was your favourite restaurant.'

'It is, but I'm meeting someone here when we've finished.'

'What's her name?'

'Calls herself Cassandra. Comes from a Greek family in Alexandria. She's the most gorgeous creature I've ever seen. She plays a minor character in an Egyptian television drama, a little bitch who's always causing trouble – within the confines of our strict Islamic morals, of course.' The waiter came over to the table. 'I'm going to have some whisky before we eat. What about you, Michael?'

'Beer, please.'

'One Johnnie Walker Black on the rocks, one Stella.'

The waiter vanished. Michael said, 'How old is she?'

'Twenty-two,' Hafez said proudly.

The drinks came. Hafez raised his Johnnie Walker. 'Cheers.'

Michael drank his beer and lit one of the Silk Cut cigarettes he had purchased at Heathrow. Hafez was the Muslim equivalent of a lapsed Catholic. He had no quarrel with his religion, and its rituals and ceremonies provided him the comfort of a childhood blanket. But he ignored anything in the Koran that got in the way of his enjoyment of worldly things. He also worked most Fridays, the Muslim sabbath, because his job required that he monitor the sermons of Egypt's more radical sheikhs.

'Does she know what you do for a living?'

'I tell her I import Mercedes automobiles into Egypt, which accounts for my well-appointed love nest on Zamalek.' He nodded toward the river. Zamalek was a long, slender island, removed from the madness of central Cairo, filled with expensive shops and restaurants and fashionable apartment houses. If Hafez was keeping a mistress on Zamalek – a television actress, no less – he had blackmailed his new case officer into a significant increase in salary. 'Ah, there she is now.'

Michael turned discreetly toward the door of the restaurant. A woman who looked remarkably like Sophia Loren walked through the door on the arm of a young man with oiled hair and sunglasses.

They ordered dinner. Hafez sent a bottle of expensive French champagne to Sophia Loren's table. Michael was paying; he always paid. 'You don't mind, do you, Michael?' Hafez asked.

'Of course not.'

'So, what brings you to Cairo, besides a chance to have dinner with a debauched old friend?'

'The murder of Ahmed Hussein.'

Hafez tilted his head slightly, as if to say, these things happen.

Michael said, 'Were the Egyptian security services involved in his murder?'

'Absolutely not,' Hafez said. 'We don't engage in such behaviour.'

Michael rolled his eyes and said, 'Do you know who was behind the assassination?'

'The Israelis, of course.'

'How can you be so sure?'

'Because we were watching the Israelis watching Hussein.'

'Back up,' Michael said. 'Start at the beginning.'

'Two weeks ago an Israeli team arrived in Cairo on various European passports and set up a static observation post in a flat in Ma'adi. We set up a static post in the flat across the street.'

'How do you know they were Israelis?'

'Please, Michael, give us a little credit. Oh, they could

pass as Egyptians, but they were definitely Israelis. They used to be good, the Mossad. But now they sometimes act like a bunch of bumbling amateurs. In the old days they could attract the best – every spy a prince, and all that bullshit. Now, the bright boys want to make money and talk on their mobile phones in Ben Yehuda Street. Let me tell you, Michael, if Moses had these people spying for him, the Jews would never have made it out of Sinai.'

'You've made your point, Yousef. Go on.'

'They were clearly watching Hussein – monitoring his movements, photographic surveillance, audio coverage, the usual. We took the opportunity to engage in a little countersurveillance. As a result we have a nice photo album of six Mossad agents: four men, two women. Interested?'

'Talk to your real case officer.'

'I also have a videotape of Hussein's death.'

'What?'

'You heard me,' Hafez said. 'Every time he set foot outside his flat, we rolled the video cameras. We were rolling when the gunman on the motorcycle killed him on the steps of the mosque.'

'Jesus Christ.'

'I have a copy of the tape in my briefcase.'

'I want to see it.'

'You can have the fucking thing, Michael. No charge.'

'I want to see it now.'

'Please, Michael,' Hafez said. 'The tape's not going to disappear. Besides, I'm famished, and the veal here is excellent.'

Forty-five minutes later, they entered the Egyptian television building: Michael, Hafez, and Cassandra. She escorted them to the newsroom and showed them into a small edit room. Hafez dug the videocassette from his briefcase and loaded it into a playback deck. Cassandra stepped out and closed the door, leaving behind the scent of sandalwood oil. Hafez smoked until the edit room felt like a gas chamber and Michael begged him to stop. Michael watched the tape three times at normal speed and three more in slow motion. He pushed the eject button and clutched the tape in his hand.

Hafez said, 'He's damned good with a gun, that fellow. Not many people in the world could make that shot and get away.'

'He's extremely good with a gun.'

'Do you know who he is?'

'Unfortunately, I think I do.'

11

BELFAST

The Ulster Unionist Party is headquartered in a four-storey building at Number 3 Glengall Street, near the Europa Hotel and the Grand Opera House. Because of its location – on the western edge of the city centre near the Falls Road – the UUP headquarters was a frequent target of the IRA attacks throughout the Troubles. But the IRA was abiding by the cease-fire for now, and so the man in the silver Vauxhall sedan felt little apprehension as he headed toward Glengall Street through the early morning rain.

Ian Morris was one of four vice presidents of the Ulster Unionist Council, the party's central committee. He had Ulster Loyalism in his blood. His great-grandfather had earned his fortune in linen during the industrial boom in Belfast in the nineteenth century and built a large estate in the Forthriver Valley overlooking the slums of West Belfast. In 1912, when the original Ulster Volunteer Force formed to fight Irish Home Rule, Morris's ancestor allowed guns and supplies to be hidden in the stables and wooded gardens of the estate.

Morris had no financial concerns as a young man – his great-grandfather's fortune provided him with a comfortable income – and he had planned a career in academia after graduating from Cambridge. But the Troubles got its hooks into him, the way it had so many men of his generation on both sides of Ulster's religious divide, and he turned to violence instead. He joined the Ulster

Volunteer Force and spent five years in the Maze prison for bombing a Catholic pub on the Broadway. In prison he had decided to turn away from the gun and the bomb and campaign for peace.

Now, there was little about his demeanour to suggest that Ian Morris had ever been a part of Northern Ireland's terrorist underworld. His home in the Castlereagh section of East Belfast was a sanctuary of books. He spoke Latin, Greek, and Irish – unusual for a Protestant, since most considered Irish the language of Catholics. As he drove along the Castlereagh Road through the steady rain, Mozart's Piano Concerto in D minor, performed by Alfred Brendel, played softly from the Vauxhall's sound system.

He turned into May Street and passed Belfast City Hall at Donegall Square.

At Brunswick Street a van in front of him appeared to stall.

Morris gave a short, polite beep of his horn, but the van remained stationary. He had a staff meeting at nine and he was running late. He pressed the horn a second time, but the van still did not move.

Morris shut off the Mozart. Ahead of him he saw the offside door open and a leather-jacketed man emerge. Morris let down his window, but the man in the leather jacket stepped directly in front of the Vauxhall and withdrew a large-calibre pistol.

Shortly before noon the newsroom of the *Belfast Telegraph* was in bedlam. The staff of Northern Ireland's most important newspaper was putting together extensive coverage of the assassination of Ian Morris: a main story, a sidebar on Morris's career with the Ulster Unionist Party and the UVF, and an analysis of the state of the peace process. All that was missing was a claim of responsibility.

At 12:05 P.M. a telephone on the news desk rattled. A junior news editor called Clarke answered it. '*Telegraph* newsroom,' Clarke shouted over the din.

'Pay attention, because I'm only going to say this once,' the caller said. Male, calm, authoritative, Clarke noted. 'This is a representative of the Ulster Freedom Brigade. A Brigade officer, under orders from the Brigade military council, carried out the assassination of Ian Morris earlier today. The Ulster Unionists have betrayed the Protestant people of Northern Ireland by supporting the Good Friday accords. The Ulster Freedom Brigade will continue its campaign until the Good Friday agreement is nullified.' The caller paused, then said, 'Did you get that?'

'Got it.'

'Good,' the voice said, and the line went dead.

Clarke stood at his desk and shouted, 'We have a claim for Ian Morris!'

'Who is it?' came a shout from somewhere in the newsroom.

'Ulster Freedom Brigade,' Clarke said. 'My God, it's Prods killing Prods.'

12

Elizabeth met Michael outside the British Airways terminal at Kennedy Airport. His body ached from travel – three very long flights in three days – and for the first time in many weeks he could feel the pulling of the scar tissue in his chest. His mouth was sour from too many cigarettes and too much airline coffee. When Elizabeth flung her arms about his body, he gave her only a brief kiss below her ear. He was really too tired to drive, but he feared inactivity more. He placed his bag into the rear storage compartment, next to half a dozen packages of diapers and a case of Similac, and climbed behind the wheel.

'You look like you got some sun, Michael,' Elizabeth said, as Michael entered the Van Wyck Expressway. Michael switched on the radio, turning the dial from Elizabeth's adult contemporary rock station to WCBS, so he could listen to the traffic updates. 'Must have been quite a warm spell in London while you were there.'

'I wasn't in London the entire time.'

'Oh, really,' she said. 'Where the hell were you?'

'I stopped in Cairo for a day.'

'You *stopped* in Cairo for a day? What the hell does Cairo have to do with Northern Ireland?'

'Nothing,' he said. 'I needed to see an old friend about something.'

'What?'

Michael hesitated.

'You don't work for them any more, so you can't hide

behind their regulations,' she said icily. 'I'd like to know why you went to Cairo.'

'Can we talk about this later?' he said. This was code for I-don't-want-to-quarrel-in-front-of-the-nanny, who was in the back seat with the children.

'You have that look, Michael. That look you used to have when you came home from the field and couldn't tell me where you'd been or what you'd been doing.'

'I'm going to tell you everything. Just not now.'

'Well, I'm glad you're back, darling,' Elizabeth said, looking away again. 'You look wonderful, by the way. You always did look nice with a tan.'

Douglas was already asleep when they reached the island. Elizabeth and the nanny put the children down. Michael went to their bedroom and unpacked. His hair smelled of Cairo – diesel, dust, and woodsmoke – so he showered. When he came back into the bedroom, Elizabeth was seated at her dressing table, pulling earrings from her ears and rings from her fingers. He remembered a time when she would sit at her dressing table for an hour, taking pleasure in her appearance and her ability to make it more perfect. Now she worked quickly and without joy, like an assembly-line worker. Since his retirement Michael did nothing quickly. Haste in others mystified him.

'Why did you go to Cairo?' Elizabeth said, violently brushing her hair.

'Because a leader of Hamas was assassinated there a couple of days ago.'

'Ahmed Hussein,' she said. 'I read about it in the *Times*.'

'There was something about the way the job was carried out that intrigued me, so I went and knocked on a few old doors.'

He told her of his meeting with Yousef Hafez. He told

her of the Mossad team and the Egyptian countersurveillance. Then he told her about the videotape.

'I want to see it,' she said.

'A man gets shot to death, Elizabeth; it's not make-believe.'

'I've seen people shot before.'

He inserted the tape into the VCR. A street scene appeared on the screen, robed men streaming from a mosque. A few seconds later a motorcycle roared into the frame at high speed. The motorcyclist stopped suddenly at the steps of the mosque, and his arm swung up. He fired several times, the silenced handgun emitting no discernible sound. The shots struck a small bearded man, turning his white robe crimson with blood. The man on the motorcycle fired twice more, shooting a second man in the chest and a third through the throat. The engine roared again, and the gunman vanished into traffic. Michael stopped the tape.

'Jesus Christ,' Elizabeth said softly.

'I think it may be him,' Michael said. 'I think it's October.'

'How can you tell?'

'I've seen him move. I've seen him handle a gun. The way his arm swings before he fires – it's very distinctive.'

'He's wearing a helmet, so you can't see his face. The tape proves nothing.'

'Maybe, maybe not.'

Michael rewound the tape. Ahmed Hussein was alive again. The motorcycle swept into the frame and skidded to a stop. The assassin's arm swung up. Michael froze the image of the killer levelling his gun at his first victim, arm straight out from his side. Then he walked to the closet, opened the doors, and took down a small box from the top shelf. He opened the box and pulled out a gun.

'What the hell is that?'

'It's his gun,' Michael said. 'The one he dropped in the water off the dock that night. It's a Beretta 9-millimetre competition pistol. I'm not sure, but I think it's the same kind of gun used by the killer in Cairo.'

'That's still hardly conclusive evidence,' Elizabeth said.

'He dropped the gun because I shot him in the hand.' Michael tapped the television screen. 'His right hand, the hand we can see holding the gun.'

'What's your point, Michael?'

'I shot him with a high-powered Browning automatic. The round probably tore through his hand, broke bones, left an ugly scar. If I find a scar on that hand, I'll be certain it's him.'

'It's awfully far away to see something as small as a scar.'

'The Agency has computers capable of bringing out the smallest detail in videotape images. I want to run this tape through those computers and see if there's anything there.'

Elizabeth stood up and switched off the television. 'So what if that's him. So what if he's still alive and killing people again. What difference does it make to us?'

'I just want to know.'

'He can't hurt us. You and your friends at the Agency turned this place into a fortress. And don't pretend that driver you hired for me in New York isn't CIA.'

'He's not from the Agency,' Michael said. 'He used to do some work for us from time to time.'

'Does he carry a gun?'

'What difference does it make?'

'Answer me. Does he carry a gun?'

'Yes. He carries a gun because I asked him to carry a gun.'

'Jesus Christ,' Elizabeth said, and turned off the light.

She climbed into bed and pulled the comforter beneath her chin. Michael lay next to her.

'It's over, Michael. It's done.'

'It's not over as long as I know he's alive.'

'I almost lost you. I held you in my arms and prayed for you not to die after he shot you. I watched your blood running out of you. I don't want to go through that again.'

Michael kissed her mouth, but her lips did not respond. He rolled over and closed his eyes. A match flared, and a moment later he smelled the smoke of Elizabeth's cigarette.

'It's her, isn't it. It's Sarah Randolph. It's been more than ten years, and you're still obsessed with her.'

'No, I'm not.'

'You're obsessed with avenging her death.'

'This has nothing to do with Sarah. It has to do with us. He tried to kill us too.'

'You're a lousy liar, Michael.' She crushed out her cigarette in an ashtray on the bedside table and exhaled the last smoke sharply between her lips. 'How you ever managed to function as a spy is beyond me.'

The bedroom windows faced north and west, over Shelter Island Sound and Dering Harbor, so it was nearly eight o'clock the following morning when they woke with the weak winter dawn.

The children were already awake, and one of them – Michael was not certain which one – was crying. Elizabeth sat up, tore away her bedding, and swung her feet to the floor. She had slept poorly, troubled by nightmares, and her eyes were puffy and dark. She walked out of the room without speaking and went downstairs.

He lay in bed for several minutes, listening to her coo at the children. After a moment he rose and went into the small sitting room attached to the bedroom. Douglas had left a vacuum thermos of coffee on the table with a folded copy of *The New York Times*. It was a weekend tradition at

Cannon Point; Douglas always rose first and made coffee for everyone else in the house.

Michael poured coffee and opened the newspaper. The West Bank had exploded in violence over the assassination of Ahmed Hussein. The Israeli government was threatening to send troops into Palestinian-controlled areas. The peace process was in critical condition. In Northern Ireland, a Protestant leader had been assassinated in Belfast. The Ulster Freedom Brigade had claimed responsibility.

Half an hour later Michael found himself trudging along a frozen path through the Mashomack nature reserve. Douglas led the way along a narrow footpath threaded through bare trees. He was a tall, broad man, poorly designed for hiking, yet he nimbly negotiated the slippery trail.

The previous night's storm had moved out to sea. A white sun shone in a sky streaked with cirrus clouds. It was intensely cold, and after a few minutes Michael felt as though his lungs were filled with shattered glass. Winter had drained all colour from the landscape. They came upon half a dozen white-tailed deer, standing on their hind legs, stripping bark from the trees.

'Isn't it fantastic,' Douglas said. He grew annoyed when Michael didn't concur. Michael found little beauty in nature; a secluded piazza in Venice gave him more pleasure than a Long Island bay. Woods and water bored him. People intrigued him because he mistrusted them, and he could outwit them if they threatened him.

Michael told his father-in-law about the Ulster Freedom Brigade as they walked the stony shore of Smith Cove. Douglas Cannon was a professional listener. He allowed Michael to speak uninterrupted for fifteen minutes; then he peppered him with questions for ten more.

'I want a straight answer from you, Michael. Will I be in any physical danger if I accept this job?'

'The Ulster Freedom Brigade has shown its intentions very clearly. They want to punish every party to the peace accords. One major party remains – the Americans. Neither side, Republican or Loyalist, has ever intentionally killed an American, but the rules have changed.'

'Twenty years in Washington, and never once did I get a straight answer from a goddamned spook.'

Even Michael had to laugh. 'It's not an exact science. Intelligence estimates involve a good deal of conjecture and guesswork, based on available evidence.'

'Sometimes I think pulling petals from a daisy would be just as effective.'

Douglas stopped walking and turned to face the water. His face had turned crimson with the cold and wind. Smith Cove was the colour of nickel. A half-empty ferry fought the strong current racing through the narrow channel between the southern tip of Shelter Island and North Haven Peninsula.

'Damn me for saying this, but I *do* want one more chance in the spotlight,' Douglas said. 'I could help make history, and that's pretty seductive for an old professor like me. Even if it means working for a stupid sonofabitch like Jim Beckwith.'

'Elizabeth is going to be furious.'

'I'll deal with Elizabeth.'

'Yeah, but I have to live with her.'

'She's just like her mother, Michael. You never knew Eileen, but if you had, you'd understand where Elizabeth gets her stubbornness and her strength. If it hadn't been for Eileen, I would never have had the courage to leave Columbia and run for Congress.'

Douglas kicked at the stones with the toe of his wellington boot.

'You have a phone?'

Michael reached inside his coat pocket and handed Douglas a cellular telephone. Douglas dialled the president's office directly and left a message with Beckwith's personal secretary. They retraced their course, leaving the sunlight of Smith Cove for the cold shadows of the woods. Five minutes later the telephone chirped. Douglas, who was forever grappling with the complexities of modern communications, thrust the phone at Michael and said, 'Answer this damn thing, will you?'

Michael punched a button on the keypad and said, 'Osbourne.'

'Good morning, Michael,' said President James Beckwith. 'I can't tell you how good it was to see you again last weekend. I'm pleased that you've made such a remarkable recovery. I just wish I could get you back at Langley where you belong.'

Michael resisted the impulse to warn the president that they were speaking on an insecure cell phone.

'Has your father-in-law reached a decision?'

'He has, Mr President.'

'Good news, I hope.'

'I'll let him tell you.'

Michael handed the phone to Douglas and walked up the path a short distance, so Douglas could speak to the president alone.

Douglas flew to Washington that evening. He had told Elizabeth of his decision after returning from the Mashomack reserve. She absorbed the news with stoic restraint and gave him a cool congratulatory kiss on the cheek, reserving her anger for Michael, because he had failed to talk Douglas out of accepting the assignment. Michael accompanied Douglas to Washington for the ceremony. The two men stayed in Michael and Elizabeth's old red-brick Federal on N Street and went to the White House the following morning.

Douglas and Beckwith met in the Oval Office, drinking tea in wing chairs before a fire. Michael had wanted to wait outside, but the president insisted he join them. He sat down on one of the couches, a little apart from the others, and studied his hands while they talked. For five minutes Douglas made the obligatory noises about loyalty and the honour of serving one's country. The president talked about the importance of the US–British relationship and about the situation in Northern Ireland.

At ten-thirty the two men stepped through the french doors into the Rose Garden. It was a warm winter's day in Washington, the sun bright, the air soft, and the two men strode to the podium side by side wearing suit jackets but no overcoats.

'Today, I am proud to nominate former Senator Douglas Cannon of New York to be our next ambassador to the Court of St James's in London,' Beckwith said matter-of-factly. 'Douglas Cannon served the great state of New York, and the American people, brilliantly in both the House and the Senate. And I know first-hand he possesses the intellect, the strength, and the grace to represent this nation's interests in an important foreign capital such as London.'

Beckwith turned and shook Douglas's hand as the small audience broke into applause. He held out his hand to the podium, and Douglas moved to the microphones.

'There will be many important issues in London, issues of trade and defence, but none more important now than helping the government of Prime Minister Blair to bring a lasting peace to Northern Ireland.'

Douglas paused for a moment, looking past the audience directly into the television cameras.

'I have one thing to say to the men of violence, to those

who wish to undo the Good Friday accords. The days of the gun and the bomb and the balaclava are over. The people of Northern Ireland have spoken. Your day is done.' He paused a moment. 'Mr President, I look forward to serving you in London.'

13

'You hear the news this afternoon?' Kyle Blake asked, as he sat down in his usual booth at McConville's pub.

'I did indeed,' Gavin Spencer said. 'The man has a big mouth.'

'Can we get to him?' Blake said, to no one in particular.

'If we can get to Eamonn Dillon, we can get to an American ambassador,' Gavin Spencer said. 'But does it serve our purposes?'

'The Americans haven't paid a price for their support of the Good Friday accords,' Blake said. 'If we're able to assassinate the American ambassador, everyone in the States will know who we are and what we're about. Remember, we're not trying to win a battlefield victory, we're trying to win publicity for our cause. If we kill Douglas Cannon, the entire American media will be forced to tell the story of Ulster from the Protestant perspective. It's like a reflex action. That's what they do. It worked for the IRA, and it worked for the PLO. But can it really be done?'

'We can do it any number of ways,' Spencer said. 'We need just one thing: we need to know when and where. We need intelligence on his movements, his where-abouts. We have to choose our opportunity carefully, or it won't work.'

Blake and Spencer looked at Rebecca Wells.

Blake said, 'Can you get us the kind of information we'll need?'

'Without question,' Rebecca said. 'I'll need to go to London. I'll need a flat, some money, and most of all plenty of time. Information like this doesn't come overnight.'

Blake took a long pull from his Guinness while he thought it all through. After a moment he looked up at Rebecca. 'I want you to set up shop in London as soon as possible. I'll get you the money in the morning.'

He turned to Gavin.

'Start preparing your team. They're not to be told the target until it's absolutely necessary. And tread softly, both of you. Tread very softly.'

FEBRUARY

14

'How was London?' Adrian Carter asked.

They had entered Central Park at Ninetieth Street and Fifth Avenue and were walking the cinder and dirt footpath on the levee surrounding the reservoir. Freezing wind stirred the leafless tree limbs above their heads. Near the banks of the reservoir the water had frozen, but a short distance from shore, in a patch of mercury-coloured water, a flotilla of ducks bobbed like tiny vessels at anchor.

'How did you know I was in London?' Michael asked.

'Because British Intelligence sent me a polite note asking if your visit was business or pleasure. I told them you were retired, so it was surely pleasure. Was I right?'

'Depends on your definition of pleasure,' Michael said, and Carter laughed mildly.

Adrian Carter was the chief of the CIA's Counterterrorism Center and had served as Michael's control officer when Michael was working in the field. Even now they moved as though they were meeting behind enemy lines. Carter walked like a man wrestling with an eternally guilty conscience, shoulders hunched, hands thrust deep into his pockets. His large droopy eyes gave him the appearance of perpetual fatigue, yet they flickered constantly around the trees and the reservoir and across the faces of the joggers foolish enough to brave the biting cold. He wore an ugly woollen ski hat that robbed him of any physical authority. His pudgy down jacket created a floating effect, so he seemed to be blowing along the footpath with the wind. Strangers tended to underestimate Carter, which he had used to his advantage throughout his career, both in the field and in the bureaucratic trenches at Headquarters. He was a brilliant linguist – he dreamed in half a dozen languages – and he had lost count of the countries where he had operated.

'So what the hell *were* you doing in London?' Carter asked.

Michael told him.

Carter said, 'Pick up anything interesting?'

Michael told Carter what he had learned during his meeting with Graham Seymour without divulging the source. Typically, Carter didn't indicate whether any of the information was news to him. He was like that, even with Michael. The office wits in the CTC used to say that Carter would rather face torture than volunteer where he had eaten lunch.

'And what brings *you* to New York?' Michael asked.

'Some business at New York Station.' Carter stopped speaking as a pair of joggers – a young woman and an older man – pounded past. 'A little housekeeping that needed to be done in person. And I wanted to see you.'

'Why?'

'Jesus Christ, Michael, we've known each other twenty years,' Carter said, with the amiable irritation that in him passed for anger. 'I didn't think there was anything wrong with dropping by for a chat while I was in town.'

'So why are we walking in the park in 20-degree weather?'

'I have an aversion to closed, unswept rooms.'

They reached the clock in the old pumping station at the southern end of the reservoir. A group of tourists speaking German with Viennese accents were posing for pictures. Michael and Carter turned reflexively, like a pair of synchronized swimmers, and crossed a wooden footbridge. A moment later they were walking along the Park Drive, behind the Metropolitan Museum.

'That was awfully nice of the Senate to send Douglas off to London with a unanimous confirmation vote,' Carter said.

'He was surprised. He thought that at least one of his old Republican adversaries would want to spoil the party.'

Carter put his gloved hands to his mouth and exhaled heavily to warm his face, which had gone crimson with the cold. Carter was a habitual golfer, and winters depressed him.

'But you didn't come here to discuss Douglas, did you, Adrian?'

Carter removed his hand from his face and said, 'Actually, I was wondering when you were going to come back to work. I need you in the CTC.'

'Why do you need me all of a sudden?'

'Because you're one of those rare birds who can move effortlessly between Headquarters and the field. For very selfish reasons I want you back on my team.'

'Sorry, Adrian, but I'm out, and I intend to stay out. Life's good.'

'You're bored out of your mind. And if you tell me otherwise, you're a liar.'

Michael stopped and turned to face Carter, anger on his face. 'How dare you fucking come here and –'

'All right,' Carter said. 'Perhaps my choice of words was inappropriate, but what the hell *have* you been doing with yourself all these months?'

'I've been taking care of my family, spending time with my children, and trying to act like a normal human being for the first time in my adult life.'

'Any job prospects?'

'Not really.'

'Do you ever intend to go back to work?'

'I'm not sure,' Michael said. 'I have no *real* job experience, because the company I worked for was a CIA front. And I'm barred from telling a potential employer what I really did for a living.'

'Why not come home?'

'Because it didn't feel much like home the last time I visited.'

'Let's put all that behind us and start over again.'

'Did you learn that line in one of those employee management seminars at Personnel?'

Carter stopped walking. 'The Director is coming to New York tonight. Your presence has been requested at dinner.'

'I have plans.'

'Michael, the Director of the Central Intelligence Agency would like to have dinner with you. Surely you can put aside your arrogance and make a little time in your busy schedule.'

'I'm sorry, Adrian, but you're wasting your time, and so is the Director. I'm just not interested. It was good seeing you, though. Give my love to Christine and the children.'

Michael turned and started walking.

'If you want out so badly, why did you go to Cairo?' Carter said. 'You went to Cairo because you think October is still alive. And frankly, so do I.'

Michael turned around.

Carter said, 'I guess I finally got your attention.'

Monica Tyler had reserved a private room at Picholin on West Sixty-fourth Street near the park. When Michael entered the restaurant, Carter was sitting alone at the end of the bar, nursing a glass of white wine. He wore a double-breasted blue suit, while Michael wore jeans and a black blazer. They greeted each other without speaking and without shaking hands. Michael gave his overcoat to the coatroom girl, and the two men followed the glossy hostess through the restaurant.

The private dining room in Picholin is actually the wine room, dark and cool, with hundreds of bottles lying in stained-oak, floor-to-ceiling racks. Monica Tyler sat alone, bathed in the gentle glow of the recessed lighting, a file spread before her. She closed the file and put away her gold-rimmed reading glasses as Michael and Carter entered the room.

'Michael, so good to see you again,' she said. She remained seated and held out her right hand at a strange angle so that Michael wasn't certain whether he was expected to shake it or kiss it.

It was Monica Tyler who had hastened Michael's departure from the Agency by ordering an internal investigation into his conduct in the TransAtlantic affair. She had been the executive director then, but six months later, President Beckwith had nominated her to be the director. Beckwith had entered that phase of any two-term presidency when the most important item on his agenda was securing his place in history. He believed nominating Monica Tyler to be the first woman to head the CIA would help. The Agency had survived novices before, Michael thought, and the Agency would survive Monica Tyler.

Monica ordered a bottle of Pouilly Fuissé without looking at the wine list. She had used the room for important meetings when she worked on Wall Street. She assured Michael that their conversation was utterly private. They made small talk about Washington politics and benign Agency gossip while deciding what to order. Monica and Carter spoke in front of Michael the way parents sometimes speak in front of children – he was no longer a member of the secret fraternity and therefore not to be entirely trusted.

'Adrian tells me he failed to convince you to return to the Agency,' Monica said abruptly. 'That's why I'm here. Adrian wants you back in the CTC, and I want to help Adrian get what he wants.'

Adrian wants you back, Michael thought. *But what about you, Monica?*

She had turned her body to Michael and settled her unfaltering gaze on him. Somewhere during her ascent, Monica Tyler had learned to use her eyes as a weapon. They were liquid and blue and changed instantly with her mood. When she was interested her eyes became translucent and fastened on her subject with therapeutic intensity. When she was annoyed – or, worse yet, bored – her pupils froze over and her gaze turned unreflecting. When she was angry her eyes flickered about her victim like searchlights, scanning for a kill zone.

Monica had had no experience in Intelligence when she came to Langley, but Michael and everyone else at Headquarters quickly learned that underestimating Monica could be fatal. She was a prodigious reader with a powerful intellect and a spy's flawless memory. She was also a gifted liar who had never been saddled with a cumbersome moral compass. She controlled the circumstances around her like a seasoned professional field officer. The rituals of secrecy fitted Monica as well as her tailored Chanel suit.

'Frankly, I understand why you chose to leave in the first place,' she said, placing an elbow on the table and a hand beneath her chin. 'You were angry with me because I had suspended you. But I revoked that suspension and removed all references to it from your service record.'

'Am I supposed to be grateful, Monica?'

'No, just professional.'

Monica paused as the first course was presented. She pushed her salad away from her a few inches, signalling she had no intention of eating. Carter kept his head down and devoured a plate of grilled octopus.

'I wanted out because you let me down and the Agency let me down,' Michael said.

'An intelligence service has rules, and officers and agents must live by those rules,' Monica said. 'I shouldn't have to explain this to you, Michael. You grew up in the Agency. You knew the rules when you signed up.'

'What's the job?'

'Now that's more like it.'

'I haven't agreed to anything yet,' Michael said quickly. 'But I'll hear what you have to say.'

'The president has ordered us to create a special task force on Northern Irish terrorism.'

'Why would I want to come back and get involved in Northern Ireland? Ulster is a British problem and a British matter. We're just spectators.'

'We're not asking you to come out of retirement and penetrate the Ulster Freedom Brigade, Michael,' Carter said.

'That's what I do, Adrian.'

'No, Michael, that's what you *used* to do,' Monica said. 'Why the sudden push inside the Agency on Northern Ireland? Ulster's never been a high priority at Langley.'

'The president considers the peace agreement in Northern Ireland one of the crowning foreign policy achievements of his presidency,' Monica said. 'But he also understands, as we do, that the agreement could unravel in a heartbeat. What he needs from the Agency is information and assessment. He needs to know when to step in and lean on the parties and when to sit back and do nothing. He needs to know when a public statement might be helpful and when it would be better to keep his mouth shut.'

'What do you want from me?'

'It's what James Beckwith wants – not what I want. And what the president wants is for *you* to lead the task force.'

'Why me?'

'Because you're an experienced counterterrorism officer, and you have some experience with the terrain. You also know how Headquarters works and how to negotiate the bureaucracy. You have a powerful ally in Adrian' – she hesitated a moment – 'and in me. There's one other thing. Your father-in-law is going to be the next ambassador to the Court of St James's.'

'I live in New York now,' Michael said. 'Elizabeth left the firm in Washington and she's practising law in Manhattan.'

'You can work from New York Station a couple of days a week and take the shuttle to Washington the rest of the time. The Agency will pay for your travel for the duration of the special task force. After that, we'll have to discuss other arrangements.'

Monica picked up her fork and impaled a few leaves of lettuce.

'And then, of course, there's the issue of October,' she said. 'Adrian has been working that front.'

Carter pushed away his empty plate and wiped his mouth. 'The assassination of Ahmed Hussein in Cairo didn't smell right to us from the beginning. We suspected the Israelis were involved, but they denied it publicly, and they denied it privately to us. So we started calling on contacts, knocking on doors. You know the drill.' Carter spoke as though he were describing the events of a very dull weekend at home. 'We have a source inside the Mossad. He told us Ari Shamron, the Mossad chief, ordered the killing and personally oversaw the operation to make certain there were no fuckups.'

Monica Tyler looked up sharply from her salad. She detested coarse language and had outlawed cursing in all senior staff meetings. She dabbed at her lips with the corner of her napkin.

'The source said Shamron went outside the Mossad for the shooter,' Carter said. 'A high-priced assassin, a contract killer. He said Shamron paid for the job with funds raised from private sources.'

'Did he have a description of the assassin?'

'No.'

'Geographic location?'

'Europe or the Middle East. Maybe the Mediterranean.'

'I've seen a videotape of the assassination.'

'I beg your pardon?' Adrian asked.

Michael told Adrian of his meeting with Yousef Hafez.

'You think the gunman was October?' Carter asked.

'I've seen him move, and I've seen him use a gun,' Michael said. 'It could very well be the same man, but it's difficult to say. I may be able to prove it, though.'

'How?'

'I shot him through his hand that night on Shelter Island,' Michael said. 'His right hand. His gun hand. During the assassination of Ahmed Hussein the gunman wasn't wearing gloves. If I can spot a scar on the hand, I'll know it's October.'

'Where's the tape?' Carter said.

'I have it.'

The waiter knocked, entered the room, and cleared away the remains of the first course.

When he was gone again, Monica said, 'If you return to the Agency, I'm prepared to expand your portfolio. You will be the head of the Northern Ireland task force, and you will also be given the assignment of tracking and arresting October, if he truly is alive. Now, do we have a deal, Michael?'

'I need to speak to Elizabeth first,' he said. 'I'll give you an answer in the morning.'

'You're a case officer who's been trained to persuade men to betray their country,' Monica said, smiling pleasantly. 'I'm sure you'll have no trouble convincing your wife that this is the right decision.'

Adrian Carter laughed and said, 'You don't know Elizabeth.'

After dinner Michael wanted to walk. The apartment was directly across Central Park, on Fifth Avenue, but even Michael, a former CIA field officer trained in the martial arts, knew it was best to avoid the park at night. He went south on Central Park West, rounded Columbus Circle, and walked past the stinking horse-drawn carriages along Central Park South.

It started to snow as he headed uptown on Fifth Avenue, along the cobblestone sidewalk bordering the park. He was dreading the conversation he was about to have with Elizabeth; she would be furious, and rightly so. He had made her a promise after October and Astrid Vogel had tried to kill them – that he would leave the Agency and never return – and now he was going to break that promise.

He sat down on a bench and looked up at the lights burning in the window of their apartment. He thought of the day he and Elizabeth had first met, a sweltering afternoon on the Chesapeake Bay aboard the sailboat of a mutual friend, six months after the murder of Sarah Randolph. The Agency had determined that Michael's cover was hopelessly blown; he had been pulled from the field in London and given a tedious desk job at Langley. He was miserable in his work and still devastated by Sarah's death. He never even looked at other women. Then he was introduced to Elizabeth Cannon – the beautiful, accomplished daughter of the famous senior senator from New York – and for the first time since that night on the Chelsea Embankment, Michael actually felt the shadow of Sarah Randolph receding.

They made love to each other that night, and afterward Michael lied to her about what he did for a living. In fact, he lied to her about his work for months. It was only when they discussed marriage for the first time that he was forced to tell her the truth: that he worked for the CIA running penetration agents against terrorist groups, and that a woman he had loved desperately had been murdered before his eyes. Elizabeth slapped his face and told him she never wanted to see him again. Michael thought he had lost her for ever.

Their relationship never quite recovered from those first lies. Elizabeth equated Michael's work with other women because of Sarah. Each time he went away, she reacted as if he had betrayed her. When he returned home from the field she would unconsciously search his body for the marks of other lovers. The day he left the Agency had been the happiest day of her life. Now it was all going to start again.

Michael crossed the street and stepped beneath the awning over the doorway to his building, slipped past the doorman, and took the elevator to a private foyer on the fourteenth floor.

He found Elizabeth where he had left her two hours earlier, sprawled on the couch beneath a large window overlooking the park, surrounded by piles of manila folders. The ashtray on the floor was filled with half-smoked cigarettes. She was defending a Staten Island tugboat company that was being prosecuted by the federal government for allegedly causing an oil spill off New Jersey. The case was going to trial in two weeks – her first trial since returning to the firm. She was working too many hours, drinking too much coffee, and smoking too much. Michael kissed her on the forehead and removed the smouldering cigarette from her fingertips. Elizabeth glanced at him over her reading glasses, then returned her gaze to the yellow legal pad where she was making notes in her looping, sprawling hand. Absently, she reached out for her pack of cigarettes and lit another.

'You're smoking too much,' Michael said.

'I'll quit when you do,' she said, without looking up from her work. 'How was dinner?'

'Dinner was fine.'

'What did they want?'

'They want me to come back. They have a job for me.'

'What did you tell them?'

'That I wanted to talk to you first.'

'That sounds to me like you want to take it.'

She dropped her legal pad on the floor and removed her reading glasses. She was exhausted and tense, a lethal combination. Michael, looking into her eyes, suddenly lost the will to continue, but Elizabeth pressed him.

'What's the job?'

'They want me to head a special task force on Northern Ireland.'

'Why you?'

'I've worked in Northern Ireland, and I've worked at Headquarters. Monica and Adrian think that's the perfect combination for the job.'

'Monica tried to have you thrown out of the Agency a year ago, and your great friend Adrian did precious little to stop her. Why the sudden turnaround?'

'She says all is forgiven.'

'And you obviously want to accept their offer. Otherwise you would have turned them down on the spot.'

'Yes, I want to take it.'

'Jesus Christ!' She crushed out her cigarette and lit another. 'Why, Michael? I thought you were done with the Agency. I thought you wanted to move on with your life.'

'So did I.'

'Then why are you letting them drag you back in?'

'Because I miss working! I miss getting up in the morning and having someplace to go.'

'So get a job, if you want. It's been a year since you were shot. You're fully recovered now.'

'There aren't a lot of companies looking for employees with skills like mine.'

'So do some volunteer work. We don't need money.'

'We don't need money because *you* have a job. An important job.'

'And you want to have an important job too.'

'Yeah, I think helping to bring peace to Northern Ireland would be a fulfilling and rewarding experience.'

'I hate to burst your bubble, but the people of Northern Ireland have been killing each other for a very long time. They'll make peace or make war regardless of what the CIA thinks about it.'

'There *is* something else,' Michael said. 'Your father is about to become the potential target of terrorists, and I want to make certain nothing happens to him.'

'How very noble and selfless of you!' Her eyes flashed. 'How dare you drag my father into this? If you want to go back to the Agency, at least have the decency not to use my father as a crutch.'

'I miss it, Elizabeth,' he said gently. 'It's what I do. I don't know how to do anything else. I don't know how to *be* anything else.'

'God, that's pathetic. Sometimes I feel sorry for you. I hate this part of you, Michael. I hate the secrets and the lying. But if I stand in your way – if I put my foot down and say no – then you'll resent me, and I won't be able to stand that.'

'I won't resent you.'

'Have you forgotten you have two infant children sleeping down the hall?'

'Most fathers with young children also manage to hold down a job.'

She said nothing.

'Monica says I can work from New York Station a couple of days a week and take the shuttle back and forth the other days.'

'You two seem to have everything all worked out. When would your new best friend like you to start?'

'Your father's going to be sworn in at the State Department the day after tomorrow. The president wants him in London right away. I thought I would spend a few hours at Headquarters and get settled in.'

Elizabeth stood up and stalked across the room. 'Well, congratulations, Michael. Forgive me if I don't crack open a bottle of champagne.'

15

Douglas Cannon was sworn in as the American ambassador to the Court of St James's during a ceremony on the
seventh floor of the State Department. Secretary of State
Martin Claridge administered the oath, which was the
same as the oath for president. Douglas swore to 'preserve,
protect, and defend the Constitution of the United States,'
and two hundred hastily invited guests burst into applause.

The ceremonial room at the State Department leads
onto a large balcony looking south over the Washington
Mall and the Potomac River. The skies were clear and the
temperature mild after the brutal cold snap, so after the
ceremony most of the guests fled the overheated room for
the fresh air outside. The Washington Monument and the
Lincoln Memorial shone in the bright sunlight. Michael
stood apart from the crowd, drinking coffee from a dainty
china cup and smoking a cigarette for protection. What do
you do? is the second line of most conversations in
Washington, and Michael wasn't in the mood to tell lies.

He watched Elizabeth, moving effortlessly through the
crowd. She hated growing up in a political family, but it
had given her the skills to work a room like an incumbent
president. She bantered easily with the secretary of state,
several members of Congress, and even a few reporters.
Michael was filled with admiration. He had been trained
to blend in, to move unseen, to search constantly for

trouble. Receptions made him nervous. He sliced his way through the crowd until he arrived at Elizabeth's side.

'I have to go now,' he said, kissing her cheek.

'When will you be home?'

'I'll try to make the seven o'clock shuttle.'

One of her old law partners spotted Elizabeth and drew her into conversation. Michael walked away through the brilliant light. He glanced once more at Elizabeth, but she had donned her sunglasses, and Michael couldn't tell whether she was looking at him or her old friend from the firm. Elizabeth had good tradecraft. He had always thought she would have made an excellent spy.

Michael crossed Memorial Bridge and drove north along the George Washington Memorial Parkway. The river shimmered below him. Bare tree limbs moved in the wind. He had the sensation of driving through a flickering tunnel of light. In the old days, before he had sold his Jaguar, driving back and forth from their home in Georgetown to Headquarters was the favourite part of his day. It wasn't quite the same in a rented Ford Taurus.

He turned into the main entrance of the CIA, stopped at the bulletproof guard shack, and gave the Special Protective Services officer his name; since he no longer had an Agency identification card he handed over his New York driver's licence. The officer checked the name against a list. He provided a pink pass for the dashboard – the choice of colour always mystified Michael – and directions to the visitors' lot.

Walking through the white marble entrance hall, Michael had the sensation of floating through a room from childhood. Everything seemed a little smaller and a little dirtier than he remembered. He walked over the Agency seal set in the floor. He glanced at the statue of Bill Donovan – the founder of the CIA's predecessor, the wartime Office of Strategic Services – and at the wall of stars for CIA officers who had been killed in the line of duty.

He walked to the guard desk, next to a series of high-tech security turnstiles, and presented himself to the morning duty officer. The guard dialled Adrian Carter's line and murmured a few words into the receiver. Then he hung up and, eyeing Michael suspiciously, told him to have a seat on one of the padded black benches in the entrance hall. A trio of pretty girls wearing jeans and sweatshirts clattered past and slipped through the turn-stiles. The new CIA, Michael thought: the children's crusade. What would Wild Bill Donovan think of this place? Suddenly, he felt very old.

Carter smiled uncharacteristically ten minutes later as he approached from the other side of the security barri-cade.

'Well, well, well, the prodigal son returneth,' Carter said. 'Let him in, Sam. He's a troublemaker, but he's relatively harmless.'

'What the hell took you so long?' Michael said.

'I was stuck on the phone with Monica. She wants an assessment on the situation in Northern Ireland by tomorrow.'

'Jesus Christ, Adrian, I haven't even been to my desk yet.'

'First things first, Michael.'

'What?'

'Office of Personnel, of course.'

Carter deposited Michael at Personnel, and for three hours he endured the ritual hazing required to re-enter the secret world. He promised that he had no intention of betraying secrets to a foreign power. That he did not abuse alcohol or take illegal drugs. That he was not a homosexual or sexual deviant of any kind. That he did not have debts he could not pay. That he was not experiencing marital problems – other than the problems caused by my return to the Agency, he thought. Having signed and initialled all the necessary documents, he was photographed and given a new identification card with a chain to wear around his neck while inside headquarters. He suffered through the inane lecture about not displaying the badge in public. He was also given a computer log-in and a security clearance so he could retrieve classified documents from the Agency's computerized file system.

The Counterterrorism Center had moved during Michael's absence, from cramped quarters on the sixth floor of the old headquarters building to a sprawling expanse of white cubicles in the South Tower. To Michael, entering the vast room that morning, it looked like the claims department of an insurance conglomerate. The CTC had been established during the Reagan administration to counteract a wave of terrorist attacks against Americans and US interests overseas. In the lexicon of Langley it was designated a 'Center' because it drew on the personnel and resources of both the clandestine and the analytical sides of the CIA. It also included staff from other government agencies, such as the Drug Enforcement Administration, the Justice Department, the Coast Guard, and the Federal Aviation Administration. Even the CIA's arch rival, the FBI, played a major role in the CTC, something that would have been condemned as heresy in the days of Michael's father.

Carter was practising his putt on the carpet of his spacious office and didn't see Michael arrive. The rest of the staff rose to greet him. There was Alan, a bookish FBI accountant who tracked the secret flow of money through the world's most discreet and dirty banks. There was Stephen, alias Eurotrash, who monitored the moribund leftist terror groups of Western Europe. There was Blaze, a giant from New Mexico who spoke ten different Indian dialects and Spanish with dozens of regional accents. His targets were the guerrilla movements and terrorist groups of Latin America. As usual he was dressed like a Peruvian peasant, in a loose-fitting shirt and leather sandals. He considered himself a modern samurai, a true warrior poet; he had once tried to teach Michael how to kill with an American Express card. Michael unconsciously braced himself as he put out his hand to Blaze and watched it disappear inside his enormous paw.

Carter came out of his office, a putter in one hand and a batch of files in the other.

'Where do I sit?' Michael said.

'Corner of Osama bin Laden and Carlos the Jackal.'

'What the hell are you talking about?'

'This place is so big now we had to create addresses for the staff to find each other.' Carter pointed to small blue signs attached to the tops of the cubicles. 'We had a little fun with the street names.'

He led Michael down Abu Nidal Boulevard, a long pathway between the cubicles, and turned right on Osama bin Laden Street. He stopped when he reached a windowless cubicle at Carlos the Jackal Avenue. The desk was stacked with old files, and someone had pinched his computer monitor.

'You're supposed to get a new one by the end of the day,' Carter said.

'That means next month if we're lucky.'

'I'll get someone to clean up those files. You need to get to work. Cynthia will get you started.'

Cynthia was Cynthia Martin, a flaxen angel of British birth and the Center's lead officer on Northern Irish terrorism. She had studied social movements at the

London School of Economics and taught briefly at Georgetown before joining the Agency. She had forgotten more about the IRA than Michael would ever know. Northern Ireland was her turf. If anyone should be heading the task force, it was Cynthia Martin.

She looked at Michael's chaotic desk and frowned.

'Why don't we do this at my place.'

She led Michael into her cubicle and sat down.

'Listen, Michael, I'm not going to pretend that I'm not pissed off about this.' Cynthia was known for her bluntness and sharp tongue. Michael was surprised she had waited until they were in her cubicle to let him have it. 'I should have been given the Irish task force, not someone who hasn't set foot in the Center in a year.'

'Nice to see you again too, Cynthia.'

'This place is still a boys' club, despite the fact the director's a woman. And even though I have an American passport, the Seventh Floor still thinks of me as that British bitch.'

'Are you finished?'

'Yes, I'm finished. I just had to get that off my chest.' She smiled and said, 'How the hell are you anyway?'

'I'm fine.'

'And your wounds?'

'All healed.

'Do you blame me for being upset?'

'Of course not. You have a right to be angry.' Michael paused, then said, 'Adrian has given me the authority to organize the task force any way I see fit. I need a strong deputy.'

'Are you offering me the job?'

Michael nodded.

'Then I suppose I accept.'

He put out his hand, and Cynthia took it.

'Welcome aboard, Cynthia.'

'Thank you, Michael. Right, we have a lot of ground to cover, so let's get started.'

Four hours later Adrian Carter poked his head inside Cynthia's cubicle. 'I have something you need to see.'

Michael followed Carter into his office. Carter closed the door and handed Michael a large manila envelope.

'What's this?'

'Office of Technical Services has been working on that video of Ahmed Hussein's assassination,' Carter said. 'They've used a computer to enhance the image.'

Michael opened the envelope and pulled out a large photograph of a hand holding a gun. On the back of the hand, between the wrist and the first knuckles, was a puckered scar.

'It's him, Adrian. Goddammit, it's him.'

'We've alerted Interpol and friendly services around the world. OTS is using the images we have to produce a computerized full-face portrait. As you know, the images are all partially obscured. We really don't know what he looks like. OTS wants you to fill in the blanks.'

'I've never had a great look at his face,' Michael said, 'but I have a general idea.'

'Get your butt down to OTS and give them a hand. I want this thing in circulation as quickly as possible.'

Michael stared at the scarred hand in the photograph.

'If he wants to work, he has to move,' Carter said. 'And if he tries to move we'll be on his ass.'

Michael smiled and handed Carter the photograph.

Carter said, 'Glad you accepted my invitation to come back?'

'Fuck, yes.'

Michael missed the seven o'clock shuttle by five minutes. He called the apartment in New York to tell Elizabeth he would be late, but there was no answer, so he left a message and drank a beer in the airport bar until his flight was called.

On the plane he stared out the window while images of Northern Ireland played out in his mind. He had spent much of the day cloistered in Cynthia Martin's cubicle, studying the paramilitary organizations of Ulster.

It was possible that any one of the existing Protestant groups had carried out the attacks and used the pseudonym Ulster Freedom Brigade to deflect suspicion. It was also possible that the Ulster Freedom Brigade was a new group consisting of members with no previous paramilitary experience. Michael had another theory: the Ulster Freedom Brigade was a small, highly organized, and experienced group of Protestant hard-liners who had defected from the mainstream organizations because of the cease-fire. The trio of attacks was too professional and too successful to be the work of inexperienced operatives. The leaders were obviously ruthless and would go to great lengths to protect the security of the organization, demonstrated by the fact that all three terrorists who took part in the attacks were now dead. Identifying its members was going to be difficult if not impossible.

Michael had spent most of the day reviewing the dossiers of every known member of those paramilitary organizations. Their faces flashed before him now: prison mug shots, intelligence surveillance photographs, artist sketches.

One other face flashed before him: the blurry, incomplete image of October. Michael had suspected he was alive. Now he had proof, the photographs of a scarred hand. Still, he knew the chances of catching him were small. All he could do was put out the alert and hope for another break.

Michael ordered a beer from the flight attendant. He

telephoned the apartment again, but there was still no answer. He usually spoke to Elizabeth several times a day because she called home constantly to check on the children. Today, they had not spoken since Douglas's swearing-in ceremony. He had been back at work just one day, but already he could sense a distance between them. He felt guilty, but he also felt a contentment – a sense of purpose; indeed, a sense of excitement – that he had not felt in many months. He hated to admit it, but the Agency seemed like home. Sometimes it was a dysfunctional home, with quarrelling adults and incorrigible children, but it was home nonetheless.

He found Elizabeth lying in bed, surrounded by paper. He kissed her neck, but she rubbed the spot as though it itched. He undressed, made a sandwich, and climbed into bed next to her.

'I'd ask you how your day was,' she said, 'but I know you couldn't tell me anyway.'

'It felt good to be back to work,' he said, and immediately regretted it.

'Your children are fine, by the way.'

He placed the sandwich on the nightstand and removed Elizabeth's legal pad from her grasp.

'How long is this going to last?' he asked.

'How long is *what* going to last?'

'You know what, Elizabeth. I want to know how long you're going to treat me like a pariah.'

'I can't pretend that I'm happy about this, Michael. I can't pretend that I'm not overwhelmed by my job and the children, and now my husband is commuting to Washington.' She lit a cigarette, snapping the lighter with too much force. 'I hate that place. I hate what it does to you. I hate what it does to *us*.'

'Your father presents his credentials to the Queen next

week in London. I need to go to London for a couple of days. Why don't you come with me so we can spend some time together?'

'Because I can't go jetting off to London just now,' she snapped. 'I have a trial coming up. I have children. *You* have children, in case you've forgotten.'

'Of course I haven't forgotten.'

'You just went to London. Why do you have to go back so soon?'

'I need to renew some old contacts.'

'In London?'

'No, in Belfast.'

16

LONDON

The official residence of the American ambassador to Great Britain is Winfield House, a red-brick Georgian mansion located on twelve acres in the middle of Regent's Park. Barbara Hutton, the heiress to the Woolworth fortune, built the house in 1934, when she came to London with her husband, the Danish aristocrat Count Haugwitz-Reventlow. She divorced the count in 1938 and returned home to the United States, where she married Cary Grant. After the war she sold Winfield House to the US government for the sum of $1, and Ambassador Winthrop Aldrich took up residence there in 1955.

Douglas Cannon had stayed at Winfield House twice before, during official trips to London, yet, settling in that first day, he was again overwhelmed by its elegance and size. As he surveyed the grand, airy rooms of the ground floor, he found it hard to believe that Barbara Hutton had built Winfield House as a private home.

When Michael arrived two days later, Douglas shepherded him from one vast room to the next, showing off the furnishings and decorations as though he had selected and paid for each himself. His favourite room was the Green Room, a large light-splashed space overlooking the side garden, with hand-painted Chinese wallpaper meticulously pillaged from the walls of an Irish castle. There, he could sit next to the fire, beneath the giant Chippendale mirrors, and watch peacocks and rabbits wandering through the dells and willows of the garden.

The enormous house was so quiet that, on the morning of Douglas's credentialling ceremony, Michael awakened to the distant toll of Big Ben. As he dressed in white tie and tails in the window of his upstairs guest room, he watched a red fox stalking a white swan across the half-lit lawn.

They rode to the embassy in Douglas's official car, escorted by a team of Special Branch bodyguards. Shortly before eleven o'clock, Grosvenor Square was filled with the clatter of horses. Michael looked out and spotted the marshal of the diplomatic corps, arriving in the first of three carriages. The embassy staff broke into applause as Douglas stepped out of the lift and made his way through a gauntlet of marine guards.

Douglas rode in the first carriage, next to the marshal. Michael rode in the third with three senior staff members. One of them was the CIA London Station chief, David Wheaton. Wheaton was an unabashed Anglophile; with his morning coat and head of oiled grey hair, he looked as though he were auditioning for a part in *Brideshead Revisited*. Wheaton had never made a secret of the fact that he detested Michael. A hundred years ago Wheaton had worked for Michael's father, recruiting Russian spies. Michael's father believed Wheaton lacked the social skills and street smarts to be a good agent-runner and gave him a devastating fitness report that nearly derailed his career.

The Agency decided to give Wheaton another chance; men like Wheaton, men with the right pedigree, the right education, and the right rabbis, were always given a second chance. He was packed off to southern Africa to be the chief of station in Luanda. Six months later he was stopped at a police checkpoint on his way to a meeting with an agent. In the glove box was his 'black book' – the names, contact procedures, and pay schedules for every CIA asset in Angola. Wheaton was declared persona non grata and an entire network of agents was arrested, tortured, and executed. The loss of fourteen men never seemed to weigh too heavily on Wheaton's conscience. In his own report on the disaster, he faulted his agents for failing to hold up under interrogation.

The Agency finally pulled Wheaton from the clandestine service and assigned him to the Soviet desk at Headquarters, where he thrived in the backbiting, pipe-smoking bureaucracy. London was a victory lap for an altogether unremarkable – and sometimes disastrous – career. He ran the station as though it were his private fiefdom. Michael had heard rumblings of a rebellion in the ranks. The Agency abbreviation for chief of station is COS, but among the officers in London, COS stood for 'COckSucker.'

'Well, if it isn't the hero of Heathrow,' Wheaton said, as Michael climbed into the carriage and sat down on the wooden seat. During the now infamous attack at Heathrow, Michael had subdued one gunman and killed another. The Agency awarded him a citation for bravery and Wheaton had never forgiven him for it.

'How have you been, David?'

'I thought you retired.'

'I did, but I missed you, so I came back.'

'We need to talk.'

'I'm looking forward to it.'

'I'm certain you are.'

Tourists and pedestrians gawked as the carriages moved through the thick midday traffic from Grosvenor Square to Park Lane, around Hyde Park Corner, and down Constitution Hill. They seemed disappointed it was only a group of middle-aged diplomats and not some exciting member of the Royal Family.

As the carriages drew inside the gates of Buckingham Palace, a small band – the same band that accompanies the Changing of the Guard – burst into a spirited rendition of 'Yankee Doodle Dandy.' Douglas stepped from his carriage and was greeted by the Queen's private secretary and the Foreign Office chief of protocol.

They ushered him inside the palace, up the grand staircase, and through a series of gilded rooms that made Winfield House seem like a fixer-upper. Michael and the senior embassy staff followed a few paces behind. Finally, they came to a set of double doors. They waited for a moment until somewhere a secret signal was flashed and the doors drew back.

Queen Elizabeth II stood in the middle of a cavernous room. She wore a dark blue suit with the ever-present handbag dangling from her wrist. The permanent under-secretary at the Foreign Office, Sir Patrick Wright, waited at her side. Douglas walked the length of the room, a little too quickly, and bowed correctly before her. He held out the envelope containing his credentials and recited the prescribed line: 'I have the honour, Your Majesty, to present the letter of recall of my predecessor and my letter of credential.' Queen Elizabeth took the envelope and casually handed it to Sir Patrick without looking at the contents.

'I'm so pleased President Beckwith had the foresight and good sense to appoint someone of your stature to London at a time like this,' the Queen said. 'If I may speak bluntly, Ambassador Cannon, I don't understand why your presidents usually appoint their political supporters to London rather than professionals like you.'

'Well, Your Majesty, I'm not a professional either. I'm a politician at heart. To my knowledge there's only been one professional Foreign Service officer to serve as ambassador in London: Raymond Seitz, who represented President Bush.'

'He was a lovely man,' the Queen said. 'But we look forward to working with you. You're very experienced when it comes to international affairs. If I recall correctly, you were the chairman of that committee in the Senate – oh, Patrick, help me –'

'The Senate Foreign Relations Committee,' Sir Patrick put in.

'Yes, I was.'

'Well, the situation in Northern Ireland is very tense now, and we need the support of your government if we are going to see this peace process through to its conclusion.'

'I look forward to being your partner, Your Majesty.'

'As do I,' she said.

Douglas could sense the Queen was restless; the conversation had reached its natural conclusion.

'May I present the senior members of my staff, Your Majesty?'

The Queen nodded. The doors opened and ten diplomats strode into the room. Douglas introduced each of them. When he described Wheaton as his political liaison officer, the Queen eyed Douglas dubiously.

Douglas said, 'I'm a widower, Your Majesty. My wife died several years ago. My daughter couldn't be here with me today, but may I introduce you to my son-in-law, Michael Osbourne?'

She nodded, and Michael entered the room. A look of recognition flashed in Queen Elizabeth's eyes. She leaned close to him and said softly, 'Aren't you the one who was involved in that business at Heathrow Airport last year?'

Michael nodded. 'Yes, Your Majesty, but –'

'You don't have to worry, Mr Osbourne,' the Queen whispered conspiratorially. 'You'd be surprised the things they tell me. I assure you I can be trusted with a secret.'

Michael smiled. 'I'm sure that's true, Your Majesty.'

'If the day ever comes that you put this business behind you, I'd like to honour you properly for what you did that day. Your actions saved countless lives. I'm sorry we haven't had a chance to meet until now.'

'We have a deal, Your Majesty.'

'We do indeed.'

Michael stepped back and stood next to the embassy staff. He looked at Wheaton and smiled, but Wheaton grimaced slightly, as though he had just swallowed his cuff link.

They retraced their path through Buckingham Palace. Wheaton appeared at Michael's side and grabbed the back of his elbow. Wheaton was a tennis player; he had a powerful right hand from squeezing a tennis ball to relieve the anxiety of command. Michael resisted the impulse to pull away. Wheaton was a bully, probably because he had been bullied himself.

'I want to go on the record with you, Michael,' Wheaton said pleasantly. Wheaton was always going 'on the record' and 'off the record,' which Michael thought was absurd for an intelligence officer. 'I think your little day trip to Belfast is a lousy goddamn idea.'

'Do you really think it's appropriate to use language like that in here, David?'

'Fuck you, Michael,' he whispered.

Michael pulled his elbow from Wheaton's grasp.

'Kevin Maguire is no longer your asset,' Wheaton said. Michael shot Wheaton a glance of disapproval for committing the death-penalty offence of speaking an agent's name aloud in an unsecured room. Wheaton regarded intelligence work as a game to be played and won.

Conducting a *sotto voce* discussion of an agent while strolling the rooms of Buckingham Palace fitted in nicely with his own image of himself. 'If you want him debriefed for the purposes of the task force, his control officer from London Station should handle it.'

'Harbinger was my agent,' Michael said, using Maguire's code name. 'I recruited him and I ran him. I was the one who coaxed him into giving us information that saved countless lives. I'm going to meet with him.'

'Now is not the time for taking a stroll down memory lane, especially not in a town like Belfast. Why don't you brief Harbinger's control officer on what you need? He can go in and make the meeting.'

'Because I want to do it myself.'

'Michael, I know we've had our disagreements, but I offer this counsel very sincerely. You're a desk man now, not a field officer. You're forty-eight years old, and you were nearly killed a year ago. Even the best of us would lose a step. Let me send my man in to meet with Harbinger.'

'I haven't lost a step,' Michael said. 'And as for Northern Ireland, it hasn't changed in four hundred years. I think I'll be able to take care of myself while I'm there.'

They stepped outside into the bright sunlight of the courtyard.

Wheaton said, 'Harbinger wants to use your old procedures for the meeting. If he doesn't decide to make a meeting in two days, he wants you out of Belfast. You read me?'

'I read you, David.'

'And if you fuck this up, I'll have your ass.'

17

BELFAST

Flights for Northern Ireland depart from a separate section of Heathrow's Terminal One, where passengers negotiate a gauntlet of security before boarding. Michael posed as a travel writer doing a piece for a magazine about the beauties of the Ulster countryside. During the flight he read guidebooks and maps. The English businessman seated next to him asked if Michael had been to Belfast before. Michael smiled stupidly and said it was his first time. The plane passed Liverpool and headed over the Irish Sea. The pilot announced that they had just left the airspace of the United Kingdom and would be touching down in Belfast in twenty-five minutes. Michael laughed to himself; even the British had trouble remembering Northern Ireland is actually part of the United Kingdom.

The plane descended through broken cloud. Northern Ireland is rather like a vast farm interrupted by a couple of large cities, Belfast and Londonderry, and hundreds of small towns, villages, and hamlets. The countryside is carved into thousands of square plots – some emerald, some the colour of limes and olives, some fallow and brown. To the east, where the waters of Belfast Lough opened onto the Irish Sea, Michael glimpsed the castle at Carrickfergus. Belfast lay at the foot of Black Mountain, straddling the lough. Once it had been a thriving linen and shipbuilding centre – the *Titanic* was built in the shipyards of Belfast – but now it looked like any other British industrial city fallen on hard times, a low smoking labyrinth of red-brick terraces.

The plane touched down at Aldergrove Airport. Michael dawdled in the arrival lounge for a while to see if he could spot any surveillance. He bought tea in a café and browsed in the gift shop. One wall was covered with books on the conflict. There were brightly coloured souvenir shirts and hats that perversely shouted NORTH-ERN IRELAND! as if it were Cannes or Jamaica.

The wind nearly tore Michael's coat from his body as he stepped outside. He passed the taxi stand and boarded an Ulster Bus coach for the city centre. Belfast conjures images of civil conflict, of gunsmoke and cordite, but the first smell that greeted Michael was the stench of manure. The bus passed through a checkpoint, where a pair of RUC officers were tearing apart a van. Fifteen minutes later it reached the city centre.

Downtown Belfast is a charmless place – cold and neat, too new in some spots, too old in others. It was bombed countless times by the IRA, twenty-two times alone on July 21, 1972, Bloody Friday. Northern Ireland was the one place on earth that made Michael uncomfortable. There was a viciousness, an incoherence and medieval quality to the violence, that unsettled him. It was one of the few cities where Michael struggled with language. He could speak Italian, Spanish, French, Arabic, reasonable Hebrew, passable German, and even a bit of Russian, but English spoken with the hard-edged accent of West Belfast bewildered him. And Gaelic, which many Catholics speak fluently, was meaningless gibberish to Michael: it sounded to him like a shovel blade plunging into gravel. Still, he found the people remarkably friendly, especially to outsiders, quick to buy you a drink or offer you a cigarette, with a black sense of humour derived from living in a world gone mad.

He checked into his room at the Europa Hotel and spent ten minutes searching for bugs. He managed to sleep but was awakened by a siren and a recorded voice telling him to evacuate the hotel immediately. He telephoned the front desk, and the girl cheerfully informed him it was only a test. He ordered coffee from room service, showered and dressed, and went downstairs. He had ordered a rental car from the concierge. It was waiting outside in the small circular drive, a bright red Ford Escort. Michael went back inside the hotel and asked the concierge if the rental company had something in a more subtle colour.

'I'm afraid that's all they have now, sir.'

Michael got in the car and drove north along Great Victoria Street. He turned into a small side street, pulled over, and climbed out. He opened the hood and loosened wires until the engine stopped. He closed the hood, removed the keys from the ignition, and walked back to the Europa. He informed the concierge the Escort had broken down and told him where he could find it.

Twenty minutes later a new car arrived, a Vauxhall, dark blue.

Kevin Maguire, code name Harbinger, had used a dozen different rendezvous sequences over the years, but he had asked to use his original pattern tonight, three sites scattered around Belfast city centre at one-hour intervals. Both men were to proceed to the first site. If either spotted surveillance or felt uncomfortable for any reason, they would try again at the second. If the second was no good they would try the third. If the third site was bad, they would call it a night and try to make the meeting the next evening at three new sites.

Michael drove toward the first site: the Donegall Quay, near the Queen Elizabeth Bridge, over the River Lagan.

He knew the streets of Belfast well, and for twenty minutes he engaged in a standard SDR, the Agency abbreviation for a surveillance detection run. He weaved his way through the streets of the city centre, checking his tail constantly. He went to Donegall Quay, intending to make the meeting, but there was no sign of Maguire, so Michael drove on without stopping. It was not like Maguire to pass on a meeting; he was a seasoned professional terrorist, not the kind of agent to see danger when it wasn't there.

Kevin Maguire had grown up in the Ballymurphy housing estates during the 1970s, the son of an unemployed shipyard worker and a seamstress. At night he had gone into the streets with the other boys and fought the British army and the RUC with stones and petrol bombs. Once he had shown Michael a childhood photograph, a ragamuffin with cropped hair, a leather jacket, and a necklace of spent shell casings. He had been something of a hero in the Ballymurphy because he was expert at upending army saracens with empty beer barrels. Like most Catholics in West Belfast he admired and feared the men of the IRA – admired them because they protected the population from the Protestant killer squads of the UVF and the UDA, feared them because they kneecapped or brutally beat anyone that stepped out of line. Maguire's father had been kneecapped for selling stolen goods door-to-door to supplement the family's monthly payment from the dole.

Maguire had been a member of Na Fianna Eirean – a sort of Republican boy scouts – and his father had insisted he stay in despite the kneecapping. When he was twenty-two he volunteered for the IRA. He took the IRA's secret oath during a ceremony in the living room of his parents' house in the Ballymurphy. Maguire never would forget the look on his father's face, the strange mixture of pride and humiliation that his son was now a member of the organization that had taken his legs. He was assigned to the Belfast Brigade and eventually became part of an elite active service unit in Britain. Maguire developed good contacts inside the Army Council, the IRA's military command, and the IRA's Belfast Intelligence Unit, which proved invaluable when he crossed over and became a spy.

The event that pushed Maguire into betrayal was the IRA bombing of a Remembrance Day parade at Enniskillen, County Fermanagh, on November 8, 1987. Eleven people were killed and sixty-three wounded when a massive bomb exploded with no warning. The IRA tried to defuse public outrage over the massacre by saying it was a mistake. Maguire knew the truth; he had been part of the unit that carried out the attack.

Maguire was furious with the Army Council for attacking a 'soft' civilian target. He privately vowed he would prevent the IRA from carrying out similar attacks in the future. His hatred and mistrust of the British ruled out working for British Intelligence or the RUC's Special Branch, so on his next trip to London he contacted the CIA. Michael was sent to Belfast to establish contact with him. Maguire refused to take money – 'your thirty pieces of silver,' as he called it – and despite the fact he was an IRA terrorist, Michael came to regard him as a decent man.

The CIA and their British counterparts have an implicit agreement: the Agency does not 'collect' on British soil, meaning it does not attempt to penetrate the IRA or recruit assets inside British Intelligence. After Michael had established contact with Maguire, the Agency went to the British. MI5 was dubious at first, but it agreed to allow Michael to continue meeting with Maguire as long as it received the intelligence simultaneously with Langley.

Over the next several years, Maguire fed Michael a steady stream of information on IRA operations, giving the Agency and the British a window on the high command of the organization. Maguire became the most important IRA informer in the history of the conflict. When Michael was pulled from the field, a new American case officer was assigned to Maguire, a man named Jack Buchanan from London Station. Michael had not seen or spoken to Maguire since.

Michael drove south on the Ormeau Road. The second rendezvous point was the Botanic Gardens, at the intersection of the Stranmills Road and the University Road. Once again, Michael felt confident he was not being followed. But once again Maguire didn't make the rendezvous.

The last site was a rugby pitch in a section of Belfast known as Newtownbreda, and it was there, an hour later, that Michael found Kevin Maguire, standing beneath a goal.

'Why did you pass on the first two?' Michael asked, as Maguire climbed in and closed the door.

'Nothing I could see – just bad vibes.' Maguire lit a cigarette. He looked more like a coffee-house revolutionary than the real thing. He wore a dark raincoat, black sweater, and black jeans. Belfast had aged Maguire since Michael had seen him last. His short-cropped black hair was shot with grey, and there were lines around his eyes. He wore fashionable European glasses now, round metal-rimmed spectacles, too small for his face.

'Where'd you get the car?' Maguire asked.

'The concierge at the Europa. I pulled the engine cables on the first one, and they sent this twenty minutes later. It's clean.'

'I don't talk in closed rooms or cars, or have you forgotten everything since they brought you inside?'

'I haven't forgotten. Where do you want to go?'

'How about the mountain, just like the old days? Pull over so I can get us some beer.'

Michael drove north through Belfast, then followed a narrow road up the side of Black Mountain. The rain had ended by the time he pulled into a lay-by and killed the engine. They climbed out and sat on the hood of the Vauxhall, drinking warm beer, listening to the ticking of the engine. Belfast spread below them. Clouds lay over the city like a silk scarf thrown over a lampshade. It was a dark city at night. Yellow sodium light burned in the city centre, but in the west, in the Falls, the Shankill, and the Ardoyne, it looked like a blackout. Maguire usually felt at peace in this place – he had lost his virginity here, as had half the boys of the Ballymurphy – but tonight he was on edge. He was smoking too much, gulping his lager, sweating in spite of the cold.

He talked. He told Michael old stories. He talked about growing up in the Ballymurphy, about fighting the Brits and torching their 'pigs.' He told Michael about making love on Black Mountain for the first time. 'Her name was Catherine, a Catholic girl. I was so guilty I went to confession the next day and spilled my guts to Father Seamus,' he said. 'I spilled my guts to Father Seamus quite a few other times over the years, every time I popped a British soldier or an RUC man, every time I planted a bomb in a city centre or London.'

He told Michael about an affair that he had had with a Protestant girl from the Shankill just before he joined the IRA. She became pregnant, and both sets of parents forbade them to ever see each other again.

'We knew it was for the best,' he said. 'We would have been outcasts in both communities. We would have had to leave Northern Ireland, live in fucking England or emigrate to America. She had the baby, a boy. I've never seen him.' He paused. 'You know, Michael, I never planted a bomb in the Shankill.'

'Because you were afraid you might kill your own son.'

'Yeah, because I was afraid I might kill my son, a son I've never seen.' He pulled the top off another beer. 'I don't know what the fuck we've been doing here for the last thirty years. I don't know what it was for. I've given twenty years of my life to the IRA, twenty years to the fucking cause. I'm forty-five years old. I've no wife. I've no real family. And for what? A deal that could have been reached a dozen times since '69?'

'It was the best the IRA could hope for,' Michael said. 'There's nothing wrong with compromise.'

'And now Gerry Adams has a wonderful idea,' Maguire said, ignoring Michael. 'He wants to turn the Falls into a tourist area. Start up a bed-and-breakfast or two. Can you imagine it? Come and see the streets where the Prods and the Micks fought an ugly little war for three decades. Jesus fucking Christ, but I never thought I'd live to see the day! Three thousand dead so we can make the travel section of *The New York Times*.'

He finished his beer and threw the empty can down the side of the mountain.

'The thing you Americans don't understand is that there'll never be peace here. We may stop slaughtering each other for a while, but nothing's ever going to change in this place. Nothing's going to change.' He tossed his cigarette over the edge of the hillside and watched the ember disappear into the darkness. 'Anyway, you didn't come all the way here to listen to me babble about politics and the failures of the Irish Republican Army.'

'No, I didn't. I want to know who killed Eamonn Dillon.'

'So does the fucking IRA.'

'What do you know?'

'We suspect Dillon had been targeted for assassination for a very long time.'

'Why?'

'As soon as Dillon was killed, the boys from the Intelligence Unit went to work. They suspected someone inside Sinn Fein had betrayed him because the killer appeared at precisely the right spot at precisely the right time. It was possible the Loyalists followed him around the Falls, watched him, but not very likely. It's difficult for them to operate in a place like the Falls without being identified, and Dillon was careful about his routine.'

'So what happened?'

'IRA Intelligence turned Sinn Fein headquarters upside down. They searched every square inch of the place for transmitters and miniature video cameras. They scared the shit out of the staff and the volunteers, and it paid off.'

'What did they find?'

'One of the volunteers, a girl named Kathleen who answered the phones, had been carrying on a friendship with a Protestant girl.'

'Did the girl have a name?'

'Called herself Stella. Kathleen thought there was nothing wrong with her friendship with Stella because of the peace agreement. The IRA leaned on her in a very big way. She acknowledged that she had told Stella things about the Sinn Fein leadership, including Eamonn Dillon.'

'Is Kathleen still with us?'

'Barely,' Maguire said. 'Dillon was beloved inside the IRA. He was a member of the Belfast Brigade in the '70s. He served under Gerry Adams. He spent ten years in the Maze on a weapons charge. The IRA was ready to put a bullet in the back of her head, but Gerry Adams intervened and saved her life.'

'I assume Kathleen gave the IRA a description of Stella?'

'Tall, attractive, black hair, grey eyes, good cheekbones, square jawline. Unfortunately, that's all the IRA has to work with. Stella was a real pro and damned careful. She never met Kathleen in a place with Sinn Fein surveillance cameras.'

'What does the IRA know about the Ulster Freedom Brigade?'

'Fuck all,' Maguire said. 'But I'll tell you this. The IRA isn't going to sit on its hands for ever. If the security forces don't get this thing under control, and soon, this fucking place is going to blow sky high.'

Michael dropped Maguire at the intersection of Divis Street and the Millfield Road. He climbed out and melted back into the Falls without looking back. Michael drove the few blocks to the Europa and left the car with the valet. Maguire hadn't given him much, but it was a start. The Ulster Freedom Brigade appeared to have a sophisticated intelligence apparatus, and one of their operatives was a tall woman with black hair and grey eyes. He also felt very good about himself; after a long time on the sidelines he had gone into the field and carried off a successful clandestine meeting with an agent. He was anxious to get back to London so he could get the information to Headquarters.

It was late, but he was hungry and too edgy to stay in his hotel room. The girl at the reception desk sent him to a restaurant called Arthur's, just off Great Victoria Street. He sat at a small table near the door with his guidebooks for protection. He ate Irish beef and potatoes smothered in cream and cheese, washed down by a half bottle of decent claret. It was eleven o'clock when he stepped outside again. A cold wind was howling through the city centre.

He walked north along Great Victoria Street, toward the Europa. Ahead of him was a girl, clattering toward him along the pavement, hands pushed deeply into the pockets of a black leather coat, a handbag over her shoulder. He had seen her somewhere in the Europa – in the bar, maybe, or pushing a cleaning cart down a hall. She looked straight ahead. The Belfast stare, he thought. No one in this town ever seemed to look at anyone, least of all on the empty pavements of the city centre late at night.

When the girl was about twenty feet in front of him, she appeared to stumble over a grate in the pavement. She fell heavily, spilling the contents of her handbag. Michael moved forward quickly and knelt beside her.

'Are you all right?' he asked.

'Yeah,' the girl said. 'Just a wee spill – nothing serious.'

She sat up and began picking up her things.

'Let me help you,' Michael said.

'It's not necessary,' she said. 'I'll be fine.'

Michael heard a car accelerate on Great Victoria Street. He turned around and spotted a medium-sized Nissan speeding toward him, headlights doused. It was then that he felt something hard pressing against the small of his back.

'Get in the fucking car, Mr Osbourne,' the girl said calmly, 'or I'll put a bullet through your spine, so help me God.'

The car skidded to a halt next to the kerb, and the rear door flew open. Seated in the back were two men. Both wore balaclavas. One of them jumped out, pushed Michael into the car, and then climbed in next to him. The car accelerated rapidly, leaving the girl behind.

When they were clear of the city centre, the two men forced Michael to the floor and began beating him with their fists and the butts of their guns. He wrapped his arms around his head and face, trying to shield himself from the blows, but it was no good. He saw flashing lights, heard ringing in his ears, and blacked out.

18

COUNTY ARMAGH, NORTHERN IRELAND

Michael came awake suddenly. He had no idea how long he had been unconscious. They had moved him into the boot of the car. He opened his eyes but saw nothing but blackness; they had placed a sack of black cloth over his head. He closed his eyes again and took stock of his injuries. The men who had assaulted him were not the kind of professionals who could beat a man half to death without leaving a mark. Michael's face felt bruised and swollen, and he could taste dried blood around his mouth. He couldn't breathe through his nose, and his skull hurt in a dozen different places. Several ribs were broken, so even a shallow breath caused excruciating pain. His abdomen ached, and his groin was swollen.

Because of the hood, the rest of Michael's senses were suddenly alive. He could hear everything taking place in the car: the groan of springs in the seats, the music on the car radio, the hard edges of spoken Gaelic. They could have been talking about the weather or where they planned to dump his body, and Michael wouldn't have known the difference.

For several minutes the car travelled at speed over a smooth road. Michael knew it was raining, because he could feel the hiss of wet asphalt beneath him. After a while – twenty minutes, Michael guessed – the car made a 90-degree turn. Their speed decreased, and the surface of the road deteriorated. The terrain turned hilly. Every pothole, every bend in the road, every incline sent waves of pain from his scalp to his groin. Michael tried to think about something, anything, besides the pain.

He thought about Elizabeth, about home. It would be early evening in New York. She was probably giving the children one last bottle before bed. For an instant he felt like a complete idiot, that he had traded an idyllic life with Elizabeth for a kidnapping and beating in Northern Ireland. But it was defeatist, so he drove it from his mind.

For the first time in many years, Michael thought of his mother. He supposed it was because at least part of him suspected he might not make it out of Northern Ireland alive. His memories of her were more like those of an old lover than of a mother: afternoons in Roman cafés, strolls along Mediterranean beaches, dinners in Grecian tavernas, a moonlight pilgrimage to the Acropolis. Sometimes his father would be gone for weeks at a time with no word. When he did come home he could say nothing of his work or where he had been. She punished him by speaking only Italian, a language that bewildered him. She also punished him by bringing strange men to her bed – a fact she never hid from Michael. She used to tease Michael that his real father was a rich Sicilian landowner, which accounted for Michael's olive skin, nearly black hair, and long narrow nose. Michael was never certain whether she was joking. The shared secret of her adultery created a mystical bond between them. She died of breast cancer when Michael was eighteen. Michael's father knew his wife and son had kept secrets from him; the old deceiver had been deceived. For a year after Alexandra's death, Michael and his father barely spoke.

Michael wondered what had happened to Kevin Maguire. The penalty for betraying the IRA was swift and harsh: severe torture and a bullet in the back of the head. Then he thought, did Maguire betray the IRA or did he betray me? He replayed the events of the evening. The two cars from the Europa, the red Escort and the blue Vauxhall. The two rendezvous sights Maguire had missed, the embankment on the River Lagan and the Botanic Gardens. He thought about Maguire himself – the chain-smoking, the sweating, the long journey down old roads. Had Maguire been jittery because he feared he was being watched? Or was he feeling guilty because he was setting up his old case officer?

They turned from the roadway onto an unpaved pitted track. The car bounced and rocked from side to side. Michael groaned involuntarily when a burst of pain from his broken ribs tore through his side like a knifepoint.

'Don't worry, Mr Osbourne,' a voice called out from inside the car. 'We'll be there in a few minutes.'

Five minutes later the car drew to a stop. The boot opened, and Michael felt a gust of wet wind. Two of the men took hold of his arms and pulled him out. Suddenly he was standing upright. He could feel the rain hammering on his head wounds despite the hood. He tried to take a step, but his knees buckled. His captors caught him before he hit the ground. Michael draped one arm around each of them, and they carried him into a stone cottage. They passed through a series of rooms and doorways, Michael's feet dragging along the floorboards. A moment later he was placed in a hard straight-backed chair.

'When you hear the door close, Mr Osbourne, you may remove the hood. There's warm water and a washcloth. Clean yourself up. You have a visitor.'

Michael removed the hood; it was stiff with dried blood. He squinted in the harsh light. The room was bare except for a table and two chairs. The peeling floral wallpaper reminded him of the guest cottage at Cannon Point. On the table was a white enamel basin filled with water. Next to the basin was a cloth and a small shaving mirror. There was a peephole in the door so they could watch him.

Michael inspected his face in the mirror. His eyes were bruised and nearly swollen shut. There was a deep cut in the soft tissue above his left eye that needed stitches. His lips were puffy and split, and there was a large abrasion across his right cheek. His hair was matted with blood. There was a reason they had given him a mirror. The IRA had studied the art of interrogation well; they wanted him to feel weak, inferior, and ugly. The British and the RUC Special Branch had used those same techniques on the IRA for three decades.

Michael carefully removed his coat and pulled up the sleeves of his sweater. He soaked the cloth in the warm water and went to work on his face, gently wiping away blood from his eyes, his mouth, and his nose. He leaned his head over the basin and washed the blood from his hair. He carefully ran a comb through his hair and looked at the mirror again. His features were still hideously distorted, but he had managed to removed most of the blood.

A fist hammered on the door.

'Put the hood back on,' the voice said.

Michael remained still.

'I said put the fucking hood on.'

'It's covered with blood,' Michael said. 'I want a clean one.'

He heard footsteps outside the door and angry shouts in Gaelic. A few seconds later the door burst open and a man wearing a balaclava strode into the room. He grabbed the bloody hood and pulled it roughly over Michael's head.

'The next time I tell you to put the hood on, you put the fucking thing on,' he said. 'You understand me?'

Michael said nothing. The door closed, and he was alone again. They had imposed their will on him, but he had won a small victory. They left him sitting that way, wearing a hood that stank of his own blood, for twenty minutes. He could hear voices in the house, and somewhere a long way off he thought he heard a scream. Finally, he heard the door open and close again. A man had entered the room. Michael could hear him breathing and he could smell him: cigarettes, hair tonic, a breath of a woman's cologne that reminded him of Sarah. The man settled into the remaining chair. He must have been a large man, because the chair crackled beneath his weight.

'You can remove the hood now, Mr Osbourne.'

The voice was confident and naturally rich in timbre, a leader's voice. Michael removed the hood, placed it on the table, and looked directly into the eyes of the person seated across the table. He was a man of blunt edges – a broad flat forehead, heavy cheekbones, the flattened nose of a pugilist. The cleft in his square chin looked as though it had been chipped away with a hatchet. He wore a white dress shirt and tie, charcoal-grey trousers, and a matching waistcoat. The bright blue eyes burned with light and intelligence. For some reason he was smiling.

Michael recognized the face from Cynthia Martin's files at Headquarters: a prison photograph from the Maze, where the man had spent several years in the '80s.

'Jesus Christ! I told my men to give you a wee hiding, but it looks as though they gave you a real pasting instead. Sorry, but sometimes the lads get a little carried away.'

Michael said nothing.

'Your name is Michael Osbourne, and you work for the Central Intelligence Agency in Langley, Virginia. Several years ago you recruited an agent inside the Irish Republican Army named Kevin Maguire. You ran Maguire in a joint operation with MI5. When you returned to Virginia you handed Maguire to another case officer, a man named

Buchanan. Don't bother to deny any of this, Mr Osbourne. We don't have the time, and I mean you no harm.'

Michael said nothing. The man was right; he could deny everything, say it was all a mistake, but it would only prolong his captivity, and it might lead to another beating.

'Do you know who I am, Mr Osbourne?'

Michael nodded.

'Humour me,' he said, lighting two cigarettes, keeping one for himself and handing one to Michael. After a moment a pall of smoke hung between them.'

'Your name is Seamus Devlin.'

'Do you know what I do?'

'You're the head of IRA Intelligence.'

There was a sharp knock at the door and a few murmured words in Gaelic.

Devlin said, 'Turn around and face the wall.'

The door opened, and Michael heard someone enter the room and place an object on the table. The door closed again.

'You can turn around now,' Devlin said.

The object that had been laid on the table was a tray with a pot of tea, two chipped enamel mugs, and a small pitcher of milk. Devlin poured tea for both of them.

'I hope you've learned a valuable lesson tonight, Mr Osbourne. I hope you've learned that you can't penetrate this army and get away with it. You think we're just a bunch of stupid Taigs? A bunch of dumb Micks from the bogs? The IRA has been fighting the British government for nearly a hundred years on this island. We've picked up a thing or two about the intelligence business along the way.'

Michael drank his tea and remained silent.

'By the way, if it makes you feel any better, it was Buchanan who led us to Maguire, not you. The IRA has a special unit that follows volunteers suspected of treason.

The unit is so secret I'm the only one who knows the identities of the members. I had Maguire followed in London last year, and we saw him meeting with Buchanan.'

That piece of news didn't make Michael feel any better. 'Why grab me?' he said.

'Because I want to tell you something.' Devlin leaned across the table with his dockworker's hands beneath his chin. 'The CIA, and the British services are trying to track down the members of the Ulster Freedom Brigade. I think the IRA can be of help. After all, it's in our interests too that this violence be brought under control quickly.'

'What do you have?'

'A weapons cache in the Sperrin Mountains,' Devlin said. 'It's not ours, and we don't think it belongs to one of the other Protestant paramilitaries.'

'Where in the Sperrin Mountains?'

'A farmhouse outside the village of Cranagh.' Devlin handed Michael a slip of paper with a crudely drawn map showing the location of the farm.

Michael said, 'What have you seen?'

'Trucks coming and going, crates being unloaded, the usual.'

'People?'

'A couple of lads seem to live there full time. They patrol the fields around the house regularly. Well armed, I might add.'

'Does the IRA still have the farm under watch?'

'We pulled back. We don't have the equipment to do it right.'

'Why give this to me? Why not give it to the British or the RUC?'

'Because I don't trust them, and I never will. Remember, there are some elements within the RUC and British intelligence who have co-operated with the Protestant paramilitaries over the years. I want these Protestant bastards stopped before they drag us into a full-scale war again, and I don't trust the British and the RUC to do the job alone.' Devlin crushed out his cigarette. He looked at Michael and smiled again. 'Now, was that worth a couple of cuts and scrapes?'

'Fuck you, Devlin,' Michael said.

Devlin burst out laughing. 'You're free to go now. Put on your coat. I want to show you something before you leave.'

Michael followed Devlin through the house. The air smelled of frying bacon. Devlin led him through a sitting room into a kitchen with copper pots hanging above the stove. It might have been something out of an Irish country magazine, if not for the half-dozen men seated around the table, glaring at Michael through the slits in their balaclavas.

'You'll need this,' Devlin said, taking a wool cap from the rack next to the door and placing it carefully on Michael's swollen scalp. 'A dirty night out tonight, I'm afraid.'

Michael followed Devlin along a muddy footpath. It was so dark he might as well have been wearing the hood again. He could see the outline of Devlin's wrestler's physique in front of him, marching along the path, and he felt himself strangely drawn to him. When they reached the barn, Devlin hammered on the door and murmured something in Gaelic. Then he pulled open the door and led Michael inside.

It took Michael a few seconds to realize that the man tied to the chair was Kevin Maguire. He was naked and shivering with cold and terror. He had been beaten savagely. His face was horribly distorted, and blood flowed from a dozen different cuts – above his eyes, on his cheeks, around his mouth. Both eyes were swollen shut. There were wounds on every part of his body: contusions, abrasions, lacerations from being whipped with a belt, burns from cigarettes being ground into his skin. He was sitting in his own excrement. Three men in balaclavas stood guard around him.

'This is what we do to touts in the IRA, Mr Osbourne,' Devlin said. 'Remember this the next time you try to convince one of our men to betray the IRA and his people.'

Maguire said, 'Michael, is that you?'

Michael moved forward carefully, slipping between Maguire's tormentors and kneeling at his side. He knew there was nothing he could say, so he just wiped some of the blood from his eyes and laid a hand gently on his shoulder.

'I'm sorry, Kevin,' Michael said, his voice hoarse with emotion. 'My God, I'm so sorry!'

'It's not your fault, Michael,' Maguire whispered. He paused for a moment because the effort required to speak caused him more pain. 'It's this place. I told you. Nothing's going to change here. Nothing's ever going to change in this place.'

Devlin stepped forward and took Michael's arm, pulling him away. He walked Michael back outside. 'That's the real world in there,' Devlin said. 'I didn't kill Kevin Maguire. You killed him.'

Michael spun and punched Devlin. The blow landed high on his left cheekbone and sent him sprawling into the mud. Devlin just laughed and rubbed his face. A pair of men came running out of the house. Devlin waved them away.

'Not bad. Not bad at all.'

'Get him a priest,' Michael said, breathing hard. 'Let

him have his last confession. Then put a bullet in him. He's suffered enough.'

'He'll get his priest,' Devlin said, still rubbing his face. 'And I'm afraid he'll get his bullet too. But remember one thing. If you and your British mates don't stop the Ulster Freedom Brigade, this place will blow. If that happens, don't try to penetrate us, because the fucking tout will end up just like Maguire.'

They drove for a very long time. Michael tried to keep track of the turns so he might find the farm again, but after a while he just closed his eyes and tried to rest. Finally, the car stopped. Someone hammered on the boot and said, 'Is your fucking hood on?'

'Yes,' Michael answered. He had no strength left for mental games, and he wanted to be away from them. Two men lifted him out and laid him in the wet grass bordering the roadway. A moment later they placed something next to him.

'Leave the hood on until you can't hear the car engine any more.'

Michael sat up as they drove off. He ripped away his hood, hoping to catch a glimpse of the identification number, but they had doused the lights. Then he turned to see what they had placed next to him and found himself staring into the lifeless face of Kevin Maguire.

19

'They obviously followed you to the meeting,' Wheaton said, with the certainty of a man who never permitted the facts to get in the way of his theory, especially if it resolved things in his favour.

'I engaged in a thorough SDR, totally by the book,' Michael said. 'I was clean. They followed Maguire to the meeting, not me. That's why he passed on the first two sites – because he suspected he was being watched. I only wish he'd had the good sense to trust his instincts. He'd still be alive.'

Michael was sitting at a table in the small private kitchen of Winfield House. It was early evening, nearly twenty-four hours since the IRA had snatched him from the streets of Belfast. They had dumped him outside the village of Dromara. Michael had had no choice but to leave Maguire's body by the roadside and get as far away as he could as quickly as possible. He had walked to Banbridge, a Protestant town southeast of Portadown, and flagged down a delivery truck. He told the driver he had been robbed and beaten and that his car had been stolen. The driver was bound for Belfast but said he would be willing to take Michael to the RUC station in Banbridge to file a report. Michael said he would prefer to get back to his hotel in Belfast and file a report there. After arriving at the Europa in Belfast, Michael awakened Wheaton in London. Wheaton made the necessary calls to his British counterparts and arranged for an

RAF helicopter to collect Michael from Aldergrove Airport.

'You haven't been operational in the field for a long time, Michael,' Wheaton said. 'Maybe you missed something.'

'You're suggesting that I got Kevin Maguire killed?'

'You're the only case officer that was there.'

'I remember how to spot surveillance. I remember the perameters for making a meeting or passing on one. Devlin said they'd known Maguire was working for us for months.'

'Seamus Devlin is not exactly a source I trust.'

'He knew Buchanan's name.'

'Maguire probably gave it to him under torture.'

Michael knew it was impossible to win this argument. Jack Buchanan worked for London Station. He was one of Wheaton's men, and Wheaton would go to the mat to protect him.

'Obviously one of you fucked up, and fucked up badly,' Wheaton said. 'We've lost one of our most valuable assets, our British cousins are in a tizzy, and you're lucky to be alive.'

'What about Devlin's information?'

'It's all been passed on to Headquarters and MI5, in accordance with our original arrangement to the Maguire matter. Obviously, we can't put a site under watch in Northern Ireland. The British will have to make that decision, and they need to weigh it against other operational priorities. Quite frankly, it's out of our hands at this point.'

'That information cost the life of my agent.'

'Maguire wasn't *your* agent. He was *our* agent, the British and ours. We ran him jointly, and we shared in the take, remember? We're all upset he was blown.'

'I don't want to lose an opportunity to crack the Ulster

Freedom Brigade because we're jittery about the way we got the information.'

'You must admit the whole thing was a bit unorthodox. What if the information from Devlin is smoke?'

'Why would the IRA do that?'

'To murder a few British intelligence officers and SAS men. We give the information to the British, the British put a team in place, and the IRA sneaks up on them in the middle of the night and slits their throats.'

'The IRA is abiding by the cease-fire and the peace accords. They have no reason to set up the British.'

'I still don't trust them.'

'The information is good. We need to act on it quickly.'

'It's a *British* matter, Michael, and therefore it's a *British* decision. If I try to lean on them they won't like it, just as we wouldn't like it if the roles were reversed.'

'So let me do it quietly.'

'Graham Seymour?'

Michael nodded. Wheaton made a show of careful deliberation.

'All right, arrange a meeting with him tomorrow, then get the fuck out of here. I want you stateside.' Wheaton paused a moment and examined Michael's face. 'It's probably better that you stay here another day anyway. I wouldn't want your wife to see you like this.'

Michael went to bed early but couldn't sleep. Each time he closed his eyes the whole thing played out inside his head: the beating in the back of the car, Devlin's Cheshire-cat smile, Maguire's dead eyes. He pictured his agent, strapped to the chair, beaten beyond recognition, beaten until there was nothing left of his face. Twice he stumbled into the bathroom and was violently sick.

He remembered Devlin's words.

I didn't kill Kevin Maguire . . . You killed him.

His body ached every place they had hit him. No position was comfortable enough to sleep. Whenever he felt sorry for himself he thought of Maguire and his miserable, humiliating death.

Michael took pills for the pain and finally pills to make him sleep. He dreamed about it all night, except in his dreams it was Michael who beat Kevin Maguire and Michael who put a bullet in the back of his head.

'That's some eye,' Graham Seymour said, the following morning.

'Beautiful, isn't it?'

Michael put his sunglasses back on even though the skies were overcast. They were walking side by side along a footpath on Parliament Hill in Hampstead Heath. Michael needed to rest, so they sat down on a bench. To their left, Highgate Hill rose into the mist. In front of them, beyond the Heath, spread central London. Michael could make out the dome of St Paul's Cathedral in the distance. Children flew colourful kites around them as they spoke.

'I still can't believe you actually punched Seamus Devlin.'

'Neither can I, but goddammit, it felt good.'

'Do you know how many people would love to smack him one?'

'I suspect it would be a long line.'

'A *very* long line, darling. Did it hurt?'

'Him or me?'

'You,' Graham said, reflexively rubbing one long bony hand with the other.

'A little.'

'I'm sorry about Maguire.'

'He was a damned good agent.' Michael lit a cigarette. The smoke grabbed at the back of his throat, and when he coughed he clutched his broken ribs in pain. 'What's the thinking inside Thames House? Are you going to put the site under watch?'

'The top floor is a bit incredulous, to be honest,' Graham said. 'They're also quite miffed over the loss of Maguire.'

'Wheaton thinks it's a trap – that the IRA wants to kill a few intelligence officers.'

'Wheaton *would* think that. That's the way he'd do it.'

'I think the information is good,' Michael said. 'Devlin knew we would be sceptical. That's why he met face-to-face, to show us he was serious.'

'You're probably right,' Graham said. 'I'll try to push things along quietly from the inside. In fact, I may pop over to Ulster and handle it myself. I need a break from Helen. She's entered a new phase, retro punk. She's spiked her hair, and she listens to nothing but the Clash and the Sex Pistols.'

'This too shall pass,' Michael pronounced solemnly.

'I know, but I'm just afraid the next one will be something worse.'

Michael laughed for the first time in many days.

At Cannon Point, Elizabeth laid a pair of large quilts on the floor of the bedroom. She placed the children on the quilts, first Jake, then Liza, and surrounded them with stuffed animals, squeeze toys, and rattles. For twenty minutes she lay on the floor between them, playing, and making the same silly cooing sounds that drove her mad before she had children. She sat down on the end of the bed and just watched them. She had forced herself to abandon her trial preparations and focus on nothing but the children for the entire weekend. It had been wonderful; that morning she had taken the children for a long walk along the Shore Road, then to lunch at her favourite restaurant in Sag Harbor. It would have been perfect, except for the fact that her husband and her father were both in London.

She marvelled at how different the children were already. Liza was like her mother: outgoing, social, talkative in her own way, eager to please others. Jake was just the opposite. Jake lived in his head. Liza was already trying to tell everyone what she was thinking. Jake was private. He kept secrets. He's four months old, she thought, and he's already just like his father and his grandfather. *If he becomes a spy I think I'll shoot myself.*

Then she thought of the way she had been treating Michael, and she immediately felt guilty. She had no right to resent Michael for accepting the Northern Ireland task-force job. In fact, she had come to the conclusion that it had been foolish of her to allow him to leave the Agency in the first place. He was right. It *was* an important job, and for some reason it seemed to make him happy.

Elizabeth looked at the children. Liza was chattering at a tiny stuffed dog, but Jake lay on his back, gazing upward through the window, lost in his own secret world. Michael was what he was, and there was no use trying to change him. Once, she had loved him for it.

She thought of Michael in Belfast, and a chill ran over her. She wondered what he was doing – whether he had gone to dangerous places. She would never get used to the idea of his leaving home and going into the field. Such a silly term, she thought: *the field*, as if it were some sort of pleasant meadow where nothing bad ever happened. When he was away she had a constant ball of anxiety in her abdomen. At night she slept with a light burning and the television playing softly. It wasn't necessarily that she feared for his safety; she had seen Michael in action before, and she knew he could take care of himself. The anxiety came from the knowledge that Michael became a different

173

man when he was away. When he came home he always seemed a bit like a stranger. He lived a different life when he was in the field, and sometimes Elizabeth wondered whether she was a part of it.

She saw headlights on the Shore Road. She went to the window and watched as a car stopped at the security gate. The guard waved the car into the compound without telephoning the house first, which meant the driver was Michael.

'Maggie?' Elizabeth called.

Maggie came into the room. 'Yes, Elizabeth?'

'Michael's home. Can you watch the children for a minute?'

'Of course.'

Elizabeth ran down the stairs. She grabbed a coat from the hook in the entrance hall and wrapped it around her shoulders as she hurried across the drive toward the car.

She threw her arms around him and said, 'I've missed you, Michael. I'm so sorry about everything. Please forgive me.'

'For what?' he said, kissing her forehead softly.

'For being such a horse's ass.'

She squeezed him, and Michael groaned. She pushed him away, a puzzled look on her face, and pulled him into a patch of light leaking from a window.

'Oh, my God. What happened to you?'

20

One week after Michael Osbourne's departure from London, a silver Jaguar slipped into the drive of the Georgian mansion in St John's Wood. In the back seat sat the Director. He was a small man, narrow of head and hips, with sandstone hair gone to grey and eyes the colour of sea water in winter. He lived alone with a boy from the Society for protection and a girl called Daphne, who served as a receptionist and tended to his personal needs. His driver, a former member of the elite Special Air Service commandos, climbed out and opened the rear door.

Daphne stood outside the entranceway, shielded from the driving rain by a large black umbrella. She always looked as though she had just returned from a holiday in the tropics. She was six feet tall with skin the colour of caramel and brown hair streaked with blonde that fell about her throat and shoulders.

She stepped forward and escorted the Director into the entrance hall, carefully holding the umbrella aloft to make certain he remained perfectly dry. The Director was prone to recurring bronchial infection; for him the damp of an English winter was the equivalent of walking across a minefield without a grid.

'Picasso is on the secure line from Washington,' Daphne said. The Director had spent thousands of pounds on speech therapy to eliminate the lilt of Jamaica from her accent. Now she had the voice of a BBC newsreader. 'Will you take the call now, or shall I ring her back?'

'Now is fine.'

He walked straight to his study, pressed the blinking green button on the telephone, and picked up the receiver. He listened for several minutes, murmured a few words, and listened again.

'Everything all right, petal?' Daphne asked, after the Director had replaced the receiver.

'We need to go to Mykonos in the morning,' he said. 'I'm afraid Monsieur Delaroche is in rather serious trouble.'

It still felt very much like winter in London, but it was mild and sunny when the Island Air turboprop carrying the Director and Daphne touched down on Mykonos early the following afternoon. They checked into a hotel room in Chora and strolled along the waterfront in Little Venice until they found the café. Delaroche sat at a table overlooking the harbour. He wore khaki shorts and a sleeveless boater shirt. His fingers were red and black with paint. The Director shook his hand as though he were searching for a pulse; then he pulled the white cotton handkerchief from the breast pocket of his jacket and dabbed at his palm.

'Any signs of the opposition?' the Director asked mildly.

Delaroche shook his head.

'Why don't we adjourn to your villa,' the Director said. 'I do like what you've done with the place.'

Delaroche drove them in his battered Volvo station wagon to Cape Mavros. His canvases and easel rattled in the rear storage compartment. The Director sat in the front seat, clutching the armrest as Delaroche sped over the narrow rolling road. Daphne lay sprawled over the back seat, the breeze from the open window tossing her hair.

Delaroche served supper on the terrace. When they had finished, Daphne excused herself and lay on a chaise out of earshot.

'I commend you on your work in the Ahmed Hussein case,' the Director said, raising his glass of wine.

Delaroche did not return the gesture. He took no pleasure from the act of killing, only a sense of accomplishment from carrying out his assignment in a professional manner. Delaroche did not consider himself a murderer; he was an assassin. The men who ordered the killings were the real murderers. Delaroche was just the weapon.

'The contractors are quite pleased,' the Director said. His voice was as dry as dead leaves. 'Hussein's death has provoked exactly the response they had hoped. It has, however, left us with a bit of a security issue where you are concerned.'

The back of Delaroche's neck turned suddenly hot with a rush of anxiety. Throughout his career he had obsessively guarded his personal security. Most people in his line of work regularly had plastic surgery to change their appearance. Delaroche dealt with it another way: only a handful of people who knew what he really did for a living had ever seen his face. The only photographs made of him were the pictures in his false passports, and Delaroche had slightly altered his appearance in each one to make them useless to police and intelligence services. When he passed through airports or train terminals he always wore a hat and sunglasses to hide his face from surveillance cameras. Still, he was aware of the fact that the CIA knew of his existence and had compiled a rather extensive dossier on his killings over the years.

'What kind of security issue?' Delaroche asked.

'The CIA has issued an alert to Interpol and all friendly intelligence services. You've been placed on an international watch list. Every passport control officer and border policeman in Europe has one of these.'

The Director withdrew a folded piece of paper from the breast pocket of his jacket and handed it to Delaroche. Delaroche unfolded the paper and found himself staring at a composite sketch of his own face. It was remarkably lifelike; obviously it had been produced by a sophisticated computer.

'I thought they believed I was dead.'

'So did I, but obviously they now assume you are very much alive.' The Director paused to light a cigarette. 'You didn't shoot Ahmed Hussein in the face, did you?'

Delaroche shook his head slowly and tapped his forefinger against his chest. Delaroche had but one professional vanity – over the years he had killed most of his victims with three gunshots to the face. He supposed he had done it because he had wanted his enemies to know he existed. Delaroche had only two things in his life, his art and his trade. He left his paintings unsigned for reasons of security, and those he sold were sold anonymously. He had chosen to leave a signature on his killings.

'Who's behind this?' Delaroche said.

'Your old friend, Michael Osbourne.'

'Osbourne? I thought he retired.'

'He was brought out of retirement recently to lead a special CIA task force on Northern Ireland. It seems Osbourne has some expertise in that area as well.'

Delaroche handed the composite back to the Director. 'What do you have in mind?'

'It seems to me we have two options. If we do nothing, I'm afraid your ability to work has been seriously diminished. If you cannot travel, you cannot work. And if your face is known to policemen around the world, you cannot travel.'

'Option number two?'

'We give you a new face and a new place to live.'

Delaroche looked out at the sea. He knew he had no choice but to endure plastic surgery and change his appearance. If he could not work, the Director would terminate their relationship. He would lose the protection of the Society and lose the ability to earn a living. He would have to spend the rest of his life looking over his shoulder, wondering which day his enemies would come for him. Delaroche, more than anything, wanted security, and that meant accepting the Director's offer.

'You have someone who can do the work?'

'A Frenchman named Maurice Leroux.'

'Is he trustworthy?'

'Absolutely,' the Director said. 'You can't leave Greece until the surgery is done. Therefore, Leroux will have to come here. I'll rent a flat in Athens where he can do the work. You can recuperate there until the scars have healed.'

'What about the villa?'

'I'll keep it for the time being. I need a venue for the spring meeting of the executive council. This will do nicely.'

Delaroche looked around him. The isolated house on the north side of Mykonos had given him everything he needed: privacy, security, excellent subjects for his work, challenging terrain for his cycling. He did not want to leave it – just as he had not wanted to leave his last home, on the Breton coast, in France – but there was no choice.

'We'll need to find you a new place to live,' the Director said. 'Do you have a preference?'

Delaroche thought for a moment. 'Amsterdam.'

'Do you speak Dutch?'

'Not much, but it won't take long.'

'Very well,' the Director said. 'Amsterdam it is.'

Stavros the estate agent arranged for a caretaker. Delaroche told him he would be away for a long time but that a friend might use the villa from time to time. Stavros offered to take Delaroche to the taverna for a farewell meal; Delaroche politely declined.

He spent his last day on Mykonos painting: the square in Ano Mera, the terrace of his villa, the rocks at Linos. He worked from first light until dusk, until his right hand, the hand that had been wounded, began to ache.

He sat on the terrace and drank wine until the setting sun painted his whitewashed villa a shade of raw sienna that Delaroche could never hope to duplicate on canvas.

He went inside and set several logs ablaze in the fireplace. Then he went through the villa, room by room, cabinet by cabinet, drawer by drawer, and burned anything that suggested he ever had existed.

'It's a shame we have to spoil such a beautiful face,' Maurice Leroux said the following day. They were seated before a large, harshly-lit mirror in the Athens flat the Director had rented for Delaroche's surgery and recovery.

Leroux continued, gently probing Delaroche's cheekbone with the tip of his thin forefinger.

'You're not French,' he pronounced solemnly, as though he believed this might be hard news for a fellow Frenchman to take. 'One learns a great deal about ethnicity and ancestry in this line of work. I'd say you're a Slav of some sort, perhaps even a Russian.'

Delaroche said nothing while Leroux continued with his lecture.

'I can see it here, in the broad cheekbones, in the flat forehead, and in the angular jawline. And look here, look at your eyes. They're virtually almond-shaped and brilliant blue. No, no, you may have a French name, but I'm afraid there is Slavic blood coursing through your veins. Very fine Slavic blood, however.'

Delaroche looked at Leroux's reflection in the mirror. He was a weak man with a large nose, a receding chin, and a ridiculous hairpiece that was far too black. Leroux was touching Delaroche's face again. He had the hands of an old woman – pale, soft, shot with thick blue veins – but they stank of a young man's aftershave.

'Sometimes it's possible to make a man more attractive through plastic surgery. I worked on a Palestinian a few years ago, a man called Muhammad Awad.'

Delaroche flinched at the mention of Awad's name. Leroux had committed the ultimate sin for a man in his line of work, revealing the identity of a previous client.

'He's dead now, but he was quite beautiful when I'd finished with him,' Leroux continued. 'In your case I think the reverse is going to be true. I'm afraid we're going to be forced to make you less attractive in order to alter your appearance. Are you at peace with that prospect, monsieur?'

Leroux was an ugly man to whom appearances mattered a great deal. Delaroche was an attractive man to whom appearances mattered very little. He knew some women found him attractive – beautiful, in some cases – but he had never cared much how he looked. He was concerned with only one thing. His face had become a threat to him, and he would deal with it the way he dealt with all threats – by eliminating it.

'Do what you have to do,' Delaroche said.

'Very well,' Leroux replied. 'You have a face of angles and sharp edges. Those angles will be turned into curves and the edges dulled. I intend to shave a portion of your cheekbones to make them smoother and rounder. I'll inject collagen into the tissue of your cheeks to make your face heavier. You have a very thin chin. I'll make it squarer and thicker. Your nose is a masterpiece, but I'm afraid it must go. I'll flatten it and make it wider between the eyes. As for the eyes, there's nothing I can do except change their colour with contact lenses.'

'Will it work?' Delaroche asked.

'When I'm finished, even you won't recognize your face.' He hesitated. 'Are you sure you want to go through with this?'

Delaroche nodded.

'Very well,' Leroux said. 'But I feel a bit like that idiot who took a hammer to the Pietà.'

He removed a pen from his pocket and began making marks on Delaroche's face.

21

Preston McDaniels was a career Foreign Service officer attached to the public affairs section of the American embassy in London. He was forty-five, trim, and presentable, if not conventionally attractive. He was also a lifelong bachelor who had dated few women, which had led to persistent speculation among colleagues that he was homosexual. Preston McDaniels was not a homosexual; he simply had never had a way with women. Until recently.

It was six o'clock in the evening, and McDaniels was packing away his things and tidying up his small office. He stood in his window and looked out on Grosvenor Square. He had fought hard to get to London after years of brutal postings in places like Lagos, Mexico City, Cairo, and Islamabad. He had never been happier. He loved the theatre, the museums, the shopping, the interesting places to go on weekends. He had a smart flat in South Kensington and came to work each morning by tube. His job was still rather dull – he issued routine press releases, prepared daily summaries from the British press on issues of interest to the ambassador, and co-ordinated press coverage of the ambassador's public events – but living in London made it all seem somehow exciting.

He grabbed a stack of files from his desk and placed them in his leather briefcase. He removed his mackintosh from the hook behind the door and went out. He stopped in the bathroom and looked himself over in the mirror.

Sometimes he wondered what she saw in him. He tried

to arrange his hair to conceal the bald spot but only managed to make things worse. She said she liked balding men, said they looked smarter, more mature. She's too young for me, he thought, too young and far too pretty. But he couldn't help himself. For the first time in his life he was in an exciting sexual relationship. He couldn't stop now.

Outside it was raining, and darkness had fallen on Grosvenor Square. He put up an umbrella against the rain and picked his way along the crowded pavements to the restaurant on Park Lane. He stood outside the restaurant and watched her through the window for a moment. She was tall and fit, with rich black hair, an oval face, and grey eyes. Her white blouse could not conceal her large, rounded breasts. She was a wonderful lover; she seemed to know his every fantasy. Each afternoon at work he stared at the clock, anticipating the moment he could see her again.

McDaniels went inside the restaurant and sat down at a table in the bar. When she spotted him she winked and mouthed the words, 'I'll be there in a minute.'

She brought him a glass of white wine a moment later. He touched her hand as she placed the glass on the table.

'I've missed you terribly, darling.'

'I thought you'd never come,' she said. 'But I can't talk long – Ricardo's having a complete psychotic episode tonight. If he sees me talking to you he'll sack me.'

'You're just being friendly to a regular customer.'

She smiled seductively and said, 'Very friendly.'

'I need to see you.'

'I'm off at ten.'

'I can't wait that long.'

'I'm afraid you have no choice.'

She winked and walked away. McDaniels drank his wine and watched her as she moved from table to table, taking

orders, delivering food, and interacting with the custo-
mers. She was the kind of woman that men noticed. She
was too attractive and too talented to be waiting tables. He
knew she would find her own place in the world eventually, and then she would leave him.

McDaniels finished his wine, left a £10 note on the
table, and went out. He realized it was too much money
for a single glass of wine. She'll get the idea I think she's a
whore, he thought. He considered going back inside and
leaving less money, but he knew that would look even
more peculiar. McDaniels walked away, thinking that if
she ever left him he might very well kill himself.

McDaniels took his time going home. The rain eased up,
so he walked, enjoying the city and the floating sensation
from the wine and spending even a few minutes with
Rachel. He had never felt anything like obsession before,
but he knew it must feel something like this. It was
beginning to affect his work. He was drifting off in
meetings, losing his train of thought in mid-sentence.
People were beginning to talk, to ask questions. He didn't
care, really. He had lived without the love of a woman his
entire life. He was going to enjoy the sensation while it
lasted.

He ate supper in a pub off the Brompton Road. He read
the newspapers, and for a few minutes Rachel managed
not to intrude on his thoughts. But after a while she was
there again, like a pleasant piece of music running round
his head. He imagined her in bed, her mouth open in
pleasure, her eyes closed. Then the silly fantasies took
over: the wedding ceremony in an English country
church, the cottage in the Cotswolds, the children. It was
a ludicrous image, but he enjoyed the idea of it. He had
fallen hopelessly in love, but Rachel didn't seem like the
marrying kind. She wanted to write. She cherished her

freedom – her intellectual freedom and her sexual freedom. The first time he mentioned marriage she would probably run as fast as she could.

McDaniels drifted through the quiet side streets of South Kensington. He had a pleasant two-bedroom flat on the first floor of a Georgian terraced house. He let himself in and flipped through the afternoon post. He took a long shower and changed into a pair of khaki trousers and a cotton pullover.

He used the spare bedroom as a study. He watched the *Nine O'Clock News* while he worked his way through a stack of papers from the office. Ambassador Cannon had a busy day tomorrow: a meeting with the foreign secretary, a luncheon with a group of British business leaders, an interview with a reporter from *The Times*. When he finished he placed his papers in a manila file folder and placed the folder back in his briefcase.

Shortly before ten-thirty the intercom buzzed softly. McDaniels pressed the button and said playfully, 'Who's there?'

'It's me, darling,' she said. 'Were you expecting one of your other lovers?'

It was a little game they played: joked about other lovers, feigned jealousy. It was amazing how quickly their relationship had progressed.

'You're the only woman I've ever had in my entire life.'

'Liar.'

'Hang up and I'll buzz you in.'

He smoothed his hair while he waited for her to arrive. He heard footsteps outside in the hall, but he didn't want to appear over eager to see her, so he waited for her to knock. When he pulled back the door she stepped into his arms and kissed him on the mouth. Her lips parted and her silken tongue slid over his. She pulled away slightly and said, 'I've been waiting to do that all night.'

Preston McDaniels smiled. 'How did I get so lucky to find someone like you?'

'I'm the lucky one.'

'Can I get you something to drink?'

'Actually, I have a very serious problem, and you're the only one who can help me.'

She took his hand and led him to the bedroom, unbuttoning her blouse as she moved. She pushed him down on the end of the bed and pulled his face to her breasts.

'Oh, my God,' he groaned.

'Hurry, darling,' she said. 'Please hurry.'

Rebecca Wells awakened at three o'clock in the morning. She lay very still for several minutes, listening to McDaniels's breathing. He was a heavy sleeper naturally, and he had made love to her twice tonight. She sat up, eased her way out of bed, and crossed the floor. Her blouse lay on the floor where she had left it. She scooped it up, let herself out, and softly closed the door.

She pulled on the blouse as she crossed the hall and entered his study. She closed that door too and sat down at the desk. The briefcase was on the floor, unlocked. She opened it and picked through the contents until she found what she was looking for: the folder containing details of Ambassador Douglas Cannon's schedule for the following day.

She took a notepad from his desk and began scribbling furiously. It was all there – the time of each meeting, the method of transportation, the route. She finished copying the schedule and quickly flipped through the rest of the papers to see if there was anything interesting. When she was done she returned the file to its place in the briefcase and switched off the light.

She slipped into the hallway and entered the bathroom.

She closed the door and turned on the light. She threw water on her face and stared at her reflection in the mirror.

She had made a promise to herself when the IRA killed Ronnie: she would never marry, and she would never take another man to their bed. She had thought it was going to be a difficult vow to keep, but the hatred that filled her heart after his death left no room for any other emotion, especially love for another man. A few men from Portadown had tried to pursue her, but she had pushed them all away. Inside the Brigade, the men knew better than to waste their time.

She thought of Preston McDaniels inside her body and wanted to vomit. She told herself it was for an important cause, the future of the Protestant way of life in Northern Ireland. In a way she almost felt sorry for McDaniels. He was a decent man, kind and gentle, but he had fallen for the oldest trick in the book – the honey trap. Tonight he had said he was in love with her. She dreaded what would happen to him when, inevitably, he learned that she had betrayed him.

She drank a glass of water and flushed the toilet; then she shut off the light and slipped back into bed.

'I thought you'd never come back,' McDaniels said softly.

She nearly screamed, but she managed to keep her composure. 'I was just a little thirsty.'

'Bring any for me?'

'Sorry, darling.'

'Actually, there's something else I want.'

He rolled on top of her.

'You,' he said.

'Can you?'

He pulled her hand to his groin.

'Well, well,' she said. 'We should do something about that.'

He thrust deeply into her body.

Rebecca Wells closed her eyes and thought of her dead husband.

22

THE SPERRIN MOUNTAINS, NORTHERN IRELAND

Shortly after Northern Ireland exploded into violence in 1969, British Intelligence decided that the best way to combat terrorism was to track the movements of individual terrorists. Known members of paramilitary organizations are routinely followed and monitored by British Intelligence and by E4, the special surveillance unit of the Royal Ulster Constabulary. Sightings and movements are fed into a computer at army intelligence headquarters in Belfast. If a terrorist suddenly vanishes from a watch list, the computer automatically raises a red flag; the security forces assume he is probably involved in an operation.

Surveillance of such magnitude requires thousands of officers and advanced technology. Trouble spots, like the Falls Road in Belfast, are covered by a multitude of video cameras. The army maintains a post atop the towering Divis Flats. During the day, soldiers scan the streets with high-powered binoculars, looking for known members of the IRA; at night they search with infrared night-vision glasses. The security services place tracking devices in cars. They place listening devices and miniature video cameras in homes, pubs, automobiles, and hay sheds. They monitor telephones. They have even planted bugs in individual weapons to track their movements throughout the province. Sophisticated intelligence aircraft patrol the skies, looking for human activity at night where there should be none. Small pilotless drones perform low-level reconnaissance. Sensors are hidden in trees to detect human movement.

But despite all the high-tech equipment, much of the monitoring must be done the old-fashioned way, the man-on-man surveillance. It is dangerous work, sometimes deadly. Undercover officers routinely patrol the Falls Road area of Belfast. They hide in attics and on rooftops for days on subsistence rations, photographing their quarry. In the countryside they hide in holes, behind bushes, atop trees. In the lexicon of Northern Ireland intelligence, this practice is known as 'digging in.' It was the method chosen to monitor the tumbledown farm-house outside the village of Cranagh in the Sperrin Mountains.

Graham Seymour arrived from London on the sixth day of the operation. For their static post they had chosen a clump of gorse, surrounded by a stand of tall beech trees, on a hillside about half a mile from the house. A pair of E4 officers handled the technical equipment: long-lens and infrared cameras, long-range directional microphones. They worked as quietly as altar boys and looked as young. They playfully introduced themselves as Marks and Sparks.

Over the years the IRA had ambushed and killed dozens of intelligence officers on surveillance; even though the targets were suspected Loyalists they took no chances. Two commandos from the elite Special Air Service, the SAS, formed a protective perimeter around Graham and Marks and Sparks. They wore camouflage gear and blacked out their faces with greasepaint. Twice, Graham nearly tripped over them while relieving himself in the gorse. He longed for a cigarette, but smoking wasn't allowed. After three days of eating nothing but special high-calorie sludge he was desperate for even Helen's appalling cooking. At night, sleeping on the damp, freezing hillside, he silently cursed Michael Osbourne's name.

It was clear something wasn't right about the farmhouse in the small glen below them. A pair of brothers called Dalton owned it. They tended a small flock of scrawny sheep and a few dozen chickens. Each day, once in the morning and again at dusk, they slowly walked the edge of their land, as if looking for signs of trouble.

They received their first visitor on the tenth night.

He arrived in a small Nissan sedan. Marks and Sparks fired away rapidly with their infrared cameras, while Graham peered down toward the farmhouse through night-vision binoculars. He saw a tall, powerfully built man with a head of unruly hair, carrying a tennis bag over his right shoulder.

'What do you think?' Graham asked no one in particular.

'He's trying to make it look light,' Marks said, 'but the shoulder strap is straining.'

'He's definitely not carrying rackets and balls in that thing,' said Sparks.

Graham picked up a small radio and contacted the RUC station in Cookstown, fifteen miles to the southeast.

'We have company. Stand by for further instructions.'

The visitor remained inside the farmhouse for twenty minutes. Marks and Sparks tried to eavesdrop on the activity inside the house, but all they could hear was Bach blaring from a tinny hi-fi.

'You recognize the piece?' Marks asked.

'Concerto Number Five in D major,' Sparks said.

'Lovely, isn't it?'

'Quite.'

Graham was peering into the glen through infrared binoculars.

'He's leaving,' he said.

'Short stay for this time of night,' Marks said.

'Maybe he had to relieve himself,' Sparks said.

'I'd say he probably relieved himself of a few weapons,' Marks said. 'That bag looks a bit lighter now, don't you think?'

Graham picked up the radio again and raised Cookstown.

'The subject is heading east toward Mount Hamilton. Make it look like a routine stop. Plant a report on the radio of a security alert in the area. Send a few good guys through there so he doesn't feel like we're singling him out. I'll be down in a few minutes.'

The man in the Nissan sedan was Gavin Spencer, the operations chief of the Ulster Freedom Brigade, and the tennis bag – now empty and lying on the seat next to him – had contained a shipment of Israeli-made Uzi machine guns from an arms dealer in the Middle East. The weapons were to be used for the assassination of Ambassador Douglas Cannon. For now they were hidden inside a stone wall in the cellar of the farmhouse.

Gavin Spencer had selected his team and briefed them on their mission. Rebecca Wells had gained access to the ambassador's schedule in London and was filing regular reports. All they needed now was the right moment, the moment when Cannon was most vulnerable. They would get only one chance. If they made a mistake – if they failed – the British and the Americans would tighten security even further, and they would never be able to get close to him again.

Spencer sped along the winding B47, through the darkened village of Mount Hamilton and then back onto the open roadway. A wave of relief passed over him. The weapons were out of his car and safely inside the walls of the farmhouse. If they had been discovered in his possession he would have been given a one-way ticket to the Maze. He pressed the accelerator, and the Nissan responded, rising and falling over the rolling roadway. He switched on the radio, hoping to find some music, but a news bulletin on Ulster radio caught his attention. A security alert had been declared in the Sperrin Mountains between Omagh and Cookstown.

Three miles later he spotted the blue flashing lights of an RUC patrol car and the bulky outline of two army troop carriers. An RUC officer stood in the middle of the road, waving his flashlight for Spencer to pull to the side. Spencer stopped and rolled down his window.

'Security alert in the area tonight, sir,' the RUC man said. 'Mind if I ask where you're heading tonight?'

'Home to Portadown,' Spencer said.

'What brings you up here?'

'Visiting a friend.'

'Where's the friend?'

'Cranagh.'

'May I see your driver's licence, sir?'

Spencer handed it over. A second car braked to a halt behind him. Spencer could hear another officer asking the driver the same questions he had been asked. The RUC man looked over the licence and handed it back to Spencer.

'All right, sir,' he said. 'We're just going to have a look inside your car. Mind stepping out, sir?'

Spencer got out. The RUC man climbed in and pulled the car behind the troop carriers. A moment later the second car disappeared behind the troop trucks. The motorist was a squat, powerfully built man with short-cropped hair and a greying moustache. He stood next to Spencer with his hands in the pockets of his leather jacket.

'What the fuck's this all about?' he said.

'They said it's a security alert.'

'Fuckin' IRA, no doubt.'

'Suppose so,' Spencer said.

The man lit a cigarette and gave one to Spencer. It started to rain. Gavin Spencer smoked and tried to appear as calm as possible while the RUC and the army tore apart his car.

Graham Seymour stood behind the army truck while a team of soldiers and police officers searched the Nissan. They used a portable imager to peer beneath the seat covers for hidden weapons. They tested for residue from explosives. They searched beneath the undercarriage and beneath the hood. They unscrewed the door panels and looked beneath the carpeting. They opened the boot and picked through the contents.

After ten minutes one of the RUC men gestured silently for Seymour to come over. Inside the spare tyre, wrapped in a greasy rag, they had discovered a few suspicious-looking papers.

Graham borrowed the officer's flashlight and shone it on the papers. He flipped through them quickly, committing as many of the details as he could to memory, and handed them back to the officer.

'Place them where you found them,' he said. 'Exactly the way you found them.'

The RUC man nodded and did as he was told.

'Hide a tracking beacon in the car and let him go,' Graham said. 'And then get me back to Belfast as fast as you fucking can. We've got a rather serious problem, I'm afraid.'

23

It was seven o'clock in the evening when Michael Osbourne stepped outside the CIA's New York Station in the World Trade Center and flagged down a taxi. It had been nearly two weeks since his return from London, and he was beginning to settle comfortably into the routine of his new life inside the Agency. He usually worked three days a week in Washington and two in New York. Counterintelligence was wrapping up its inquiry into the death of Kevin Maguire, and Michael was confident his version of events would be accepted: Kevin Maguire was under suspicion by the IRA before Michael's trip to Belfast, and his death, while unfortunate, was not Michael's fault.

The taxi crawled uptown through snarled traffic. Michael thought of Northern Ireland – of the dim lights of Belfast below the Black Mountains, of Kevin Maguire's broken body strapped to a chair. He rolled down the window and felt the cold air on his face. Sometimes he went a few minutes without thinking of Maguire, but at night, or when he was alone, Maguire's ravaged face always intruded. Michael was anxious for the information Maguire and Devlin had given him to bear fruit; if the Ulster Freedom Brigade was destroyed, Maguire's death would not be meaningless.

The taxi driver was an Arab with the untrimmed beard of a devout Muslim. Michael gave him an address on Madison

Avenue, five blocks from the apartment. He paid off the taxi and walked the crowded sidewalks, stopping to gaze into store windows, checking his tail constantly. It was the nagging fear: that one day an old enemy would appear and take his revenge. He thought of his father, searching his car for bombs, tearing apart telephones, and checking his tail for physical surveillance until the day he died. The secrecy was like a disease, the anxiety like an old and trusted friend. Michael was resigned to the fact it would never leave him – the assassin called October had seen to that.

He walked west to Fifth Avenue, then turned right and headed uptown. The business of intelligence required remarkable patience, but Michael was beginning to grow restless when it came to October. Each morning he scanned the cables, hoping to catch some glimpse of him on a watch list – a sighting in an airport or a train terminal – but nothing had appeared. As more time elapsed, the trail would grow colder.

Michael entered his building and took the elevator up to the apartment. Elizabeth was already home. She kissed his cheek and handed him a glass of white wine.

'Your face is beginning to look almost normal again,' she said.

'Is that a good thing or a bad thing?'

She kissed his mouth. 'Definitely a good thing. How are you feeling?'

He looked at her quizzically. 'What the hell's gotten into you?'

'Nothing, sweetheart, I'm just happy to see you.'

'It's good to see you too. How was your day?'

'Not bad,' she said. 'I spent the day preparing my main witness for testifying in court.'

'Is he going to hold up?'

'Actually, I'm afraid he's going to get killed under cross.'

'Are the children still awake?'

'They're going down now.'

'I want to see them.'

'Michael, if you wake them up, so help me God –'

Michael walked into the nursery and leaned over the cribs. The children slept end to end, head to head, so they could see each other through the slats. He stood there for a long time, listening to them breathing softly. For a few minutes he felt peace, a sense of contentment he had not known in a long time. Then the anxiety crept up on him again, the fear that his enemies might harm him or his children. He heard the telephone ringing. He kissed each of them and went out.

In the living room Elizabeth held out the telephone to him.

'It's Adrian,' she said.

Michael took the phone from her hand. 'Yeah?'

He listened for a few minutes without speaking, then murmured, 'Jesus Christ.'

He hung up the telephone.

'What's wrong?' Elizabeth said.

'I have to go to London.'

'When?'

Michael checked his watch. 'I can make a flight tonight if I hurry.'

Elizabeth looked carefully at him. 'Michael, I've never seen you like this before. What's wrong?'

Early the next morning, as the British Airways jet carrying Michael Osbourne neared Heathrow Airport, Kyle Blake and Gavin Spencer walked side by side along the Market High Street of Portadown. The sky was turning grey-blue in the east with the coming dawn. Streetlights still burned. The air smelled of farmland and baking bread. Spencer moved with the long loose-limbed walk of a man with few cares, which was not the case that morning. Kyle Blake, a head shorter and several inches narrower, had the economy of movement of a battery-powered toy. Spencer spoke for a long time, constantly pushing his forelock of thick black hair from his forehead. Blake listened intensely, lighting one cigarette after the next.

'Maybe your eyes are playing tricks on you,' Kyle Blake said, when he finally spoke. 'Maybe they were telling you the truth. Maybe it *was* just a routine security alert.'

'They gave the car a thorough going-over,' Spencer said. 'And they took their fuckin' time about it.'

'Anything missing?'

Spencer shook his head.

'Anything there that shouldn't be there?'

'I searched the fuckin' thing from end to end. I didn't find anything, but that doesn't mean much. Those bugs are so small, they could put one in my pocket and I wouldn't know it.'

Kyle walked in silence for a moment. Gavin Spencer was a smart man and a gifted operations chief. He was not the kind to see a threat that wasn't there.

'If you're right – if they were after you – that means they're watching the farmhouse.'

'Aye,' Spencer said. 'And I just hid the first shipment of Uzis there. I need those guns to do the job on the ambassador. I can kill Eamonn Dillon with a handgun, but if I'm going to assassinate an American ambassador, I need considerably more firepower.'

'What's the status of the team?'

'The last man leaves for England tonight on the Liverpool ferry. By tomorrow evening I'll have four of my best lads in London, waiting for the order to strike. But I need those guns, Kyle.'

'So we'll get the guns.

'But the farmhouse is under watch.'

'So we'll take out the watchers,' Blake said.

'Those men are probably protected by the SAS. I don't know about you, but I'm not in the mood to tangle with the fuckin' SAS right now.'

'We know they're out there somewhere. All we need to do is find them.' Blake stopped walking and fixed a hard stare on Spencer. 'Besides, if the bloody IRA can take on the SAS, so can we.'

'They're British soldiers, Kyle. We were British soldiers once, remember?'

'We're not on the same side any more,' Blake said harshly. 'If the British want to play games, we'll play fuckin' games.'

24

'It appears as though you have a leak somewhere in this building,' Graham Seymour said.

They were seated around a table in a soundproof glass-enclosed cubicle in the CIA section of the embassy: Michael, Graham, Wheaton, and Douglas. When Graham spoke, Wheaton flinched, as though he had been threatened with a punch, and began squeezing his tennis ball. He was a man permanently prepared to take offence, and there was something in Graham's tone – in his bored insolent gaze – that Wheaton had never liked.

'What makes you so certain the leak came from *this* building?' Wheaton said. 'Maybe the leak came from your side. Special Branch provides protection for the ambassador. We give them the schedule days in advance.'

'I suppose anything's *possible*,' Graham said.

'Why didn't you photograph the documents?' Wheaton said.

'Because there wasn't time,' Graham replied. 'I made the decision that he was worth more to us in the field than in custody. We had a quick look round, planted a tracking device on his car, and let him run.'

'Who is *he*?' Michael asked.

Graham opened a secure briefcase and passed out several photographs of a large man with a thick head of black hair – one police mug shot and several grainy surveillance pictures.

'His name is Gavin Spencer,' Graham said. 'He used to

be a rather senior man in the Ulster Volunteer Force. He was arrested once on a weapons charge, but the case was dismissed. He's a hard-liner. He quit the UVF at the outset of the peace process, because he was opposed to it.'

'Where is he now?' Wheaton said.

'He lives in Portadown. He went there after we stopped him.'

Douglas Cannon said, 'What do we do now, gentle-men?'

'We find the source of the leak,' Wheaton said. 'We determine whether the leaker is committing an act of treason or if there is something else involved. And then we plug it.'

Michael stood up and paced slowly around the small cubicle. 'How many people in the embassy know the ambassador's schedule in advance?' he said finally.

'Depends on the day, but usually at least twenty,' Wheaton said.

'And how many of those are men?'

'Slightly more than half,' Wheaton said, irritation creeping into his voice. 'Why?'

'Because of something Kevin Maguire told me before he died. He said when IRA Intelligence investigated the murder of Eamonn Dillon, they determined there had been a leak from within Sinn Fein headquarters. A young girl, a secretary, had befriended a Protestant woman and inadvertently leaked details of Dillon's schedule to her.'

'What did the girl look like?' Graham asked.

'Early thirties, attractive, black hair, fair skin, grey eyes.'

A smile crept over Michael's face. Graham said, 'I've seen that look before. What are you thinking, Michael?'

'That from adversity comes opportunity.'

It was five-thirty that afternoon when the phone on Preston McDaniels's desk purred softly. For an instant

McDaniels considered not answering it; he was anxious to get to the restaurant so he could see Rachel. His voice mail would answer, and he could deal with it first thing in the morning. But the embassy had been buzzing with rumours all day – rumours of some sort of security problem, of staff being hauled before a panel of inquisitors on the top floor. McDaniels knew the bloodhounds of the media had a way of picking up the scent of rumours like that. Reluctantly, he reached down and snatched the receiver from its cradle.

'McDaniels here.'

'This is David Wheaton,' said the voice on the other end of the line. He did not bother identifying himself further; everyone in the embassy knew that Wheaton was the CIA's London Station chief. 'I was wondering if we could have a word in private.'

'Actually, I was just leaving. Is it something that could hold till the morning?'

'It's important. Mind coming upstairs right away?'

Wheaton hung up without waiting for an answer. There was something about the tone in his voice that disturbed McDaniels. He'd never liked Wheaton, but he knew it wasn't wise to cross him. McDaniels left his office, walked down the hall, and took the lift upstairs.

When he entered the room he found three men seated along one side of a long rectangular table: Wheaton, Ambassador Cannon's son-in-law, Michael Osbourne, and a bored-looking Englishman. There was one empty seat opposite them. Wheaton jabbed the tip of his gold pen at the seat without speaking, and McDaniels sat down.

'I'm not going to beat around the bush,' Wheaton said. 'It appears there's a leak somewhere within the embassy concerning the ambassador's schedule. We want to find that leak.'

'What does that have to do with me?'

'You're one of the people within the embassy who knows the ambassador's schedule in advance.'

'That's right,' McDaniels snapped. 'And if you're asking whether I've ever breached confidentiality, the answer is an unequivocal no.'

'Have you ever given anyone outside the embassy a copy of the ambassador's schedule?'

'Absolutely not.'

'Have you ever discussed it with a reporter?'

'When it's a public event, yes.'

'Have you ever given a reporter details, such as the route the ambassador might take to a meeting or the method of transportation?'

'Of course not,' McDaniels snapped. 'Besides, most reporters wouldn't give a hoot about a detail like that.'

Michael Osbourne was flipping through a file.

'You're not married,' he said, looking up from the file.

'No, I'm not,' McDaniels said. 'And why are you here?'

'We'll ask the questions, if you don't mind,' Wheaton said.

'Are you seeing anyone?' Michael asked.

'I am, actually.'

'How long have you been seeing her?'

'A couple of weeks.'

'What's her name?'

'Her name is Rachel. Would you mind telling me what this is –'

'Rachel what?'

'Rachel Archer.'

'Where does she live?'

'Earl's Court.'

'Have you ever been to her flat?'

'No.'

'Has she ever been to yours?'

'That's none of your business.'

'If it concerns security, it *is* our business, I'm afraid,' Michael said. 'Now, please answer the question, Mr McDaniels. Has Rachel Archer ever been to your flat?'

'Yes.'

'How many times?'

'Several times.'

'How many times?'

'I don't know – eight times, ten, perhaps.'

'Do you ever bring a copy of the ambassador's schedule home with you?'

'Yes, I do,' McDaniels said. 'But I'm very careful. It's never out of my possession.'

'Has Rachel Archer ever been in your flat when you've brought home a copy of the ambassador's schedule?'

'Yes, she has.'

'Have you ever shown her the schedule?'

'No. I've already told you that I've never done that.'

'Is Rachel Archer in her early thirties, with black hair, fair skin, and grey eyes?'

Preston McDaniels turned ashen. 'My God,' he said. 'What have I done?'

When the evening began it was Michael's idea. Wheaton at first went on the record in opposition, but by the end of that long night – after the teleconferences with Langley, after the tense meetings with the mandarins of MI5 and MI6, after the terse exchanges with Downing Street and the White House – Wheaton had claimed the idea as his own.

There were two issues to be resolved. Should they do it? And if they did, who would run the show? The first question was answered rather quickly. The second question was more difficult because it involved turf, and in the world of intelligence, turf is protected at all costs, often better than secrets. It was an American security issue dealing with the American ambassador. But Northern Ireland was a British matter, and the operation would take place on British soil. After an hour of strained negotiation, the two sides reached an agreement. The British would provide the street talent – the watchers and the technical surveillance artists – and when the time came they would provide the muscle. The Americans would run Preston McDaniels and provide the material for his briefcase – after close consultation with the British, of course.

The fight within the Agency was just as bitter. The Counterterrorism Center had broken the case, and Adrian Carter wanted Michael to run the American end of things. Wheaton dug in his heels. In an acid cable to Headquarters he argued it was a London operation, requiring close co-operation from the host services, and London Station should take over the case from the CTC. Monica Tyler retreated to her office in the rarefied atmosphere of the Seventh Floor to contemplate her decision. Wheaton rallied old friends and old enemies to his cause. In the end she chose Wheaton, arguing that Michael had just returned to the Agency from a long absence and couldn't be expected to be operationally sharp. It would be Wheaton's show with Michael remaining in London in a supporting role.

Preston McDaniels went operational that night. From Wheaton's desk in the CIA station he telephoned Ristorante Ricardo on Park Lane and asked to speak to Rachel Archer. An Italian-accented voice informed McDaniels she was busy – 'It's the dinner rush now, you know' – but McDaniels said it was urgent, and a moment later she came on the line. The conversation lasted precisely thirty-two seconds; Michael and Wheaton timed it to make certain and listened to it a dozen times, searching for God knows what. McDaniels said he couldn't stop by for a drink because he was working late. The woman expressed mild disappointment over the sound of crashing dishes and Ricardo Ferrari screaming obscenities in Italian. McDaniels asked if he could see her later. The woman said she would stop by after work and rang off.

The recording was beamed by satellite to Langley and sent the old-fashioned way – by motorbike courier – to MI5 and MI6. A linguist on the staff of MI5 concluded her English accent was a fake. The woman was almost certainly from Northern Ireland, he argued. Probably from outside Belfast.

Wheaton wasn't sure he trusted McDaniels. He insisted on full coverage, audio and visual, of every move he made. MI5 descended on his South Kensington flat and placed cameras and microphones in every room. Only the bedroom was exempted; Michael thought audio coverage would suffice, and Wheaton reluctantly agreed. A pair of MI5 watchers, an older man and a pretty girl, was dispatched to Ristorante Ricardo. By chance their quarry waited on them. She recommended the veal special and they pronounced it divine. The second team, for the sake of operational security, ordered spaghetti carbonara and chicken Milanese.

For their base camp, MI5 hastily procured a large furnished flat in Evelyn Gardens, a short distance from McDaniels. Michael and Wheaton, when they arrived late that night, were greeted by the stink of cigarettes and takeaway curry. In the drawing room half a dozen worried technicians fretted over their receivers and their video monitors. Bored watchers stared at a flickering television, watching a dreadful BBC documentary on the migratory patterns of grey whales. Graham Seymour sat at the piano, playing softly.

So thoroughly was McDaniels's flat bugged that when the woman known as Rachel Archer arrived the buzzer sounded like a hotel fire alarm. 'Show time,' Wheaton announced, and they gathered around the video monitors – all except for Graham, who remained at the piano, playing the final notes of 'Clair de Lune.'

Any lingering doubts about how Preston McDaniels would hold up were put to rest by the long kiss he gave her at the doorway. He fixed them drinks – white wine for her, a very large whisky for himself – and they sat on the couch in the drawing room, chatting in full view of one of the concealed video cameras. They began to kiss, and for an instant Michael feared she was going to make love to him on the couch, but McDaniels stopped her and led her to the bedroom. Michael thought there was something of Sarah in her and wondered whether there was something of McDaniels in him.

'We need a code name,' Wheaton said, trying to think of something else, anything else, besides the sounds emanating from the monitors. 'We don't have a code name.'

'My father worked on a similar operation during the war,' Graham said, his fingers flickering lightly over the keyboard. 'MI5 fed Double Cross material to a female German spy through an American naval officer.'

'What was the code name?'

'I believe it was Kettledrum.'

'Kettledrum,' Wheaton repeated. 'Nice ring to it. Kettledrum it is.'

'How did it turn out?' Michael asked.

Graham stopped playing and looked up.

'We won, darling.'

It was an MI5 technician named Rodney who saw it first and awakened the rest of the team. Wheaton had claimed the only bedroom for himself. Michael slept on the couch; Graham dozed fitfully in an overstuffed wing chair like a restless passenger on a transatlantic flight. Heavy-eyed, they crowded around the bank of video monitors and watched as the woman sat down at the desk in McDaniels's study and began softly rifling the contents of his briefcase.

'Well, ladies and gentlemen, looks like we just cracked the Ulster Freedom Brigade,' Wheaton said. 'Congratulations, Michael. You're buying dinner tonight.'

Preston McDaniels lay awake in bed, his back to the door. He had tried to sleep but couldn't, so he just remained very still, until he heard her slip from the bed and leave the room. He imagined her in his study, picking through his papers. He was overcome by wave after wave of conflicting emotions. He was embarrassed that he had been so easily taken in, humiliated that Wheaton and Michael Osbourne had made him a pawn in their game. More than anything else, he felt betrayed.

For a few moments, while she was making love to him, McDaniels imagined that she really did have feelings for him regardless of her motives. He would cut a deal, he thought. He would arrange things so they could be together when it was all over.

He heard the door open. He closed his eyes. He felt her body settle next to his. He wanted to roll over and take her in his arms, pull her body down on his, feel her legs around him. But he just lay there, pretending to sleep, wondering what he would do without her when it was all over.

25

'It's called Hartley,' Graham Seymour said, late that morning in Wheaton's office. 'It's located here, along the north Norfolk coast.' He tapped at the large Ordnance Survey map with the tip of his pen. 'It has several hundred acres of grounds for walking and riding, and of course the beach is nearby. In short, it's the perfect sort of place for an American ambassador to spend a quiet weekend in the country.'

'Who owns it?' Michael asked.

'A friend of the Intelligence Service.'

'A close friend?'

'Did his bit during the war and a few odd jobs during the '50s and '60s, but nothing heavy.'

'Anything public that could link him to British Intelligence?'

'Absolutely not,' Graham said. 'The Ulster Freedom Brigade would have no way of knowing that the ambassador's host was connected to the Service.'

Wheaton said, 'What are you thinking, Michael?'

'That Douglas wants to spend a weekend outside London in the English countryside, a *private* weekend with minimal security at the house of an old friend. We put it on his schedule and feed it to the woman through McDaniels. With a bit of luck the Ulster Freedom Brigade will bite.'

'And we'll have an SAS team waiting for them,' Graham said. 'The scenario has one other important benefit: there will be no possibility of civilian casualties, because of the remote location.'

'Arresting people isn't really the specialty of the SAS,' Wheaton said. 'If we go through with this, and the Ulster Freedom Brigade takes the bait, a lot of blood is going to be spilled.' He looked first at Graham, who remained silent, and then at Michael.

'Better their blood than Douglas's,' Michael said. 'I recommend we do it.'

'I need to run it up the food chain,' Wheaton said. 'The White House and the State Department are going to need to sign off on this one. It might take a few hours.'

'What about the woman?' Michael said.

'We followed her this morning when she left McDaniels's flat,' Graham said. 'She was telling McDaniels the truth. She's living in a flat in Earl's Court. Moved in a couple of weeks ago. We have a team watching the flat.'

'Where is she now?'

'It appears she's sleeping.'

'I'm glad someone's getting some sleep around here,' Wheaton said.

He picked up his secure phone and dialled Monica Tyler's office at Langley.

'This is all your idea, isn't it?' Preston McDaniels said. 'You're a real sonofabitch. Anyone can see that.'

They were seated on a bench overlooking the Serpentine in Hyde Park. Wind moved in the willow trees and made ripples on the surface of the lake. Clouds, heavy with coming rain, floated above them. Michael tried to spot Graham's watchers. Was it the man tossing bread crumbs to the ducks? The woman on the next bench reading Josephine Hart? Perhaps the lanky blond boy in the dark blue anorak doing tai chi on the lawn?

Twenty minutes earlier, Michael had shown McDaniels

the videotape of his lover sneaking into his study and picking through the contents of his briefcase. McDaniels had nearly become physically ill. He had demanded fresh air, so they had walked in silence, across Mayfair and along the footpaths of Hyde Park, until they had reached the lake. McDaniels was trembling; Michael could almost feel the park bench vibrating with his shaking. He remembered how he had felt when he learned Sarah Randolph had been working for the KGB. He had wanted to hate her but could not. He suspected Preston McDaniels felt precisely the same way about the woman he knew as Rachel Archer.

'Did you get any sleep?' he asked mildly.

'Of course not.' The wind gusted, lifting his grey hair and exposing his bald spot. He self-consciously coaxed it back into place. 'How could I sleep knowing that you bastards were probably listening to my every breath?'

Michael did not want to dispel McDaniels of the notion that they were watching his every move and listening to his every utterance. He lit a cigarette and offered one to McDaniels.

'Vile habit,' McDaniels snorted, and waved his hand. He glared at Michael as though he were an untouchable.

Michael didn't mind; it was good for McDaniels to feel superior for a moment, even over something so trivial.

'How long?' he said. 'How long do I have to do this?'

'Not long,' Michael said casually, as though McDaniels had asked how long it might be before the next train arrived.

'My God, why can't I get a straight answer from you people about anything?'

'Because there are very few straight answers in this line of work.'

'It's your line of work, not mine.' McDaniels waved his hand violently. 'Jesus Christ! Put that thing out, will you!'

Michael tossed the cigarette onto the pavement.

'Who is she?' McDaniels asked. 'What is she?'

'As far as you're concerned she's Rachel Archer, a starving playwright who's working as a waitress at Ristorante Ricardo.'

'Dammit, I want to know! I have to know! I need to know that this whole ugly business might come to some good.'

Michael could not argue with the logic of McDaniels's request. Often, agent-running is about motivation, and if Preston McDaniels was going to get through the operation, he needed encouragement.

'We don't know her real name,' Michael said. 'Not yet, anyway. We're working on it. She's a member of the Ulster Freedom Brigade. They're planning to assassinate my father-in-law. She was using you to gain access to his schedule and find the best time to make their attempt.'

'My God, how could she? She's such a wonderful —'

'She's not the person you think she is.'

'How could I have been such a fool?' McDaniels was staring somewhere into the middle distance. 'I knew she was too young for me. That she was too pretty. But I allowed myself to actually believe that she had fallen in love with me.'

'No one's blaming you,' Michael lied.

'So what happens when it's all over?'

'You go on with your job as if nothing happened.'

'How can I?'

'It will be easier than you think,' Michael said.

'And what about her, whoever she is?'

'We don't know yet,' Michael said.

'Yes, you do. You know everything. You're setting her up, aren't you?'

Michael stood abruptly, signalling that it was time to leave. McDaniels remained seated.

'How long?' he said. 'How long until this is over?'
'I don't know.'
'How long?' he repeated.
'Not long.'

Later that afternoon Michael sat in Wheaton's office, reviewing the new addition to Ambassador Douglas Cannon's schedule, a private visit the following weekend to the home of a friend in the Norfolk countryside. At the ambassador's request, security for the visit would be extremely light, a two-man Special Branch team with no American support. Michael finished reading it and handed it across the desk to Wheaton.

'Think they'll bite?' Wheaton asked.
'They should.'
'How's our boy holding up under the strain?'
'McDaniels?'
Wheaton nodded.
'As well as you might expect.'
'Meaning?'
'Meaning we don't have a lot of time.'
'Then this had better work.'
Wheaton handed the paper back to Michael.
'Put it in his briefcase and send it home with him tonight.'

It was just after four o'clock the next morning when Rebecca Wells rose from Preston McDaniels's bed and let herself into his study. She sat down at the desk, quietly opened the briefcase, and withdrew a sheaf of papers. Attached to the ambassador's usual schedule of official events was a note about a private weekend in the Norfolk countryside.

Rebecca could feel her heart hammering inside her chest as she read the memo.

It was perfect: a remote location, with plenty of advance notice for planning purposes. She took her time copying down the details. She didn't want to make a mistake.

When she had finished she felt a fierce pride. She had done her job well, just as she had done in Belfast. Eamonn Dillon was dead because of the information she had provided for Kyle Blake and Gavin Spencer, and soon Ambassador Douglas Cannon would be dead too.

She turned off the light and went back to bed.

At the base camp in Evelyn Gardens, Michael Osbourne and Graham Seymour stood before the video monitors, watching her. They watched as she carefully recorded the details of the memo concerning the ambassador's trip to Norfolk. They could sense her excitement at the discovery. When she turned off the light and left the room, Graham turned to Michael and said, 'Think she took the bait?'

'Hook, line, and sinker.'

The following day they watched her. They went with her to the dreary café outside Earl's Court Underground where she had tea and a bun for breakfast. They listened when she telephoned Ricardo Ferrari at the restaurant and told him she had a family emergency, an aunt who had been taken ill in Newcastle; she needed a couple of days off, four at the most. Ricardo screamed a series of obscenities at her, first in Italian, then in heavily accented English. But he won the affection of Graham Seymour's listeners when he said, 'Take care of your poor aunt. There's nothing more important than family. When you're ready to come back, you come back.'

Then they listened as she telephoned Preston Mc-Daniels at his desk at the embassy and told him she would be going away for a few days. They held their breath when McDaniels asked to see her for a few minutes before she left. They breathed a sigh of relief when she told him there wasn't time.

And when she boarded a train for Liverpool, they let her run.

Preston McDaniels replaced the receiver and sat at his desk. A secretary who spotted him through the open door at that moment told Michael later that poor Preston looked as though he had just been told of a death. He jumped up suddenly, announced he needed to run an errand, and said he would be back in fifteen minutes. He took his raincoat from its hanger and rushed out of the embassy, across Grosvenor Square, toward the Park.

He knew they were following him, Wheaton and Osbourne and the rest of them; he could feel it. He wanted to be rid of them. He wanted to never see them again. What would they do? Would they grab him? Snatch him off the streets? Bundle him into a car? He had read his fair share of spy novels. How would the hero get away from the villains in a spy novel? He would get lost in a crowd.

When he reached Park Lane he hurried north toward Marble Arch. He ducked into the Underground station, slipped through the turnstiles, and walked quickly along the connecting passageway to the platform.

A train was arriving as he reached the platform. He stepped into the carriage and stood near the doors. At the next stop, Bond Street, he stepped out of the train, crossed to the opposite platform, and boarded another train back to Marble Arch. At Marble Arch he performed the same manoeuvre, and a moment later he was heading east across London, feeling quite alone.

Graham Seymour rang Michael from MI5 headquarters.

'I'm afraid your man has vanished.'

'What do you mean?'

'I mean we lost him,' Graham said. 'He lost us, actually. He performed quite a routine on the Underground. He's not half bad.'

'Where?'

'Central Line between Marble Arch and Bond Street.'

'Dammit. What are you doing about it?'

'Well, we're trying to find him, aren't we, darling.'

'Call me if you hear anything.'

'Right.'

At Tottenham Court Road, Preston McDaniels left the Central Line train and walked through the connecting passageway to the Northern line. How fitting, he thought; the dreaded Northern Line. Antiquated, wheezing, clattering, the Northern Line was forever breaking down at the height of the rush hour. To those forced to endure its fickle moods, it was the Misery Line. The Black Line. It was perfect, Preston thought. The London tabloids would have a field day with this.

What was it Michael Osbourne had said? *You go on with your life as if nothing had happened.* But how could he? He felt the platform begin to vibrate. He turned and peered into the darkness of the tunnel and saw the faint light of the approaching train.

He thought of her, beneath his body, her back arched to him, and then he pictured her in his study, stealing his secrets. He heard her voice on the telephone. *I'm afraid I'm going to have to go away for a few days . . . No, I'm sorry, Preston, but I can't see you just now . . .*

Preston McDaniels looked at his watch. They would be worried about him by now, wondering where he had gone. There was a staff meeting in ten minutes. He was going to miss it.

217

The train burst from the tunnel with a rush of hot air and swept into the station. Preston McDaniels took one step closer to the edge of the platform. Then he leapt onto the track.

26

PORTADOWN
LONDON
COUNTY TYRONE

The following evening Rebecca Wells was back in Porta-down, sitting in a booth in McConville's pub. Gavin Spencer entered first, followed five minutes later by Kyle Blake. The pub was crowded. Rebecca Wells spoke quietly beneath the din, briefing Blake and Spencer on what she had discovered in the briefcase of the American.

'When does Cannon arrive?' Blake asked simply.

'Next Saturday,' Rebecca said.

'And how long does he stay?'

'One night, the Saturday. Then he returns to London early Sunday afternoon.'

'That gives us five days.' Blake turned to Gavin Spencer. 'Can you pull it off in that amount of time?'

Spencer nodded. 'We just need the weapons. If we can get our hands on the guns, Ambassador Douglas Cannon is a dead man.'

Kyle Blake thought it over a moment, rubbing the ink and nicotine stains on his fingers. Then he looked up at Spencer and said, 'So we'll get the guns.'

'Are you sure, Kyle?'

'You're not losing your nerve, are you?'

'Maybe we should wait a wee bit. Let things cool down.'

'We don't have time to wait, Gavin. Every week that goes by is a victory for the supporters of the accords. Either we destroy the peace agreement now or we're stuck with it for ever. And it's not just this generation that will pay the price. It's our children, our grandchildren. I can't live with that.'

Blake stood up abruptly and zipped up his jacket.

'Get those guns, Gavin, or I'll find someone who will.'

As the three leaders of the Ulster Freedom Brigade were departing McConville's pub, Graham Seymour was arriving at the American embassy. Wheaton's office felt like the command bunker of an army in retreat. The suicide of Preston McDaniels had ignited a firestorm in Washington, and Wheaton had been on the telephone for most of the past twenty-four hours, trying unsuccessfully to put it out. The State Department was furious with the Agency for their handling of the affair; indeed, Douglas Cannon had been placed in the unenviable position of secretly protesting the actions of his own son-in-law. President Beckwith had summoned Monica Tyler to the White House and read her the riot act. Monica had taken out her anger on Wheaton and Michael.

'Please tell us you have some good news,' Michael said, as Graham sat down.

'Actually, I do,' Graham said. 'Scotland Yard's decided to play ball. Later this evening they'll put out a statement that the suicide at Tottenham Court Road was an escaped mental patient. The Northern Line is notorious for that sort of thing. There's a psychiatric hospital south of the river.'

'Thank God,' Wheaton said.

Michael felt himself relax slightly. The suicide needed to be kept secret if the operation was to continue. If the Ulster Freedom Brigade learned McDaniels had jumped in front of a Northern Line train, they might very well conclude the information they had stolen from him was tainted.

Graham said, 'How will you cover up things here?'

'Fortunately, McDaniels has no family to speak of,' Wheaton said. 'State has reluctantly given us some latitude. As far as the cover story goes, McDaniels had to return to Washington for two weeks. If the woman calls here looking for him, she'll be given that story and a personal message from McDaniels.'

'The woman has a name, by the way,' Graham said. 'E4 picked her up when she arrived in Belfast early this morning. Her real name is Rebecca Wells. Her husband was Ronnie Wells, a member of the Ulster Volunteer Force intelligence section who was murdered by the IRA in '92. It looks as though Rebecca has picked up the threads of her husband's work.'

'And the RUC is giving her room to run?' Michael asked.

'They followed her to Portadown in order to establish her identity, but that's as far as it goes,' Graham said. 'As of right now she's running free.'

'Is the SAS on board?'

'I'm meeting with them at their headquarters in Hereford tomorrow to brief them. You're both welcome to attend. Strange lot, the SAS. I think you might actually enjoy it.'

Wheaton stood up and rubbed his red, swollen eyes.

'Gentlemen, the ball is in the court of the Ulster Freedom Brigade.' He pulled on his suit jacket over his wrinkled shirt and headed for the door. 'I don't know about either of you, but I need some sleep. Don't bother me unless it's urgent.'

The first night had been clear and calm and bitterly cold. Kyle Blake and Gavin Spencer decided to wait; one more night would make no difference, and the forecast looked promising. The second night was perfect: thick cloud cover to weaken the infrared glasses of the SAS men, wind and rain to help cover the sound of their approach. Kyle Blake approved, and Spencer dispatched two of his best men to do the job. One was a British army veteran who had done time abroad as a mercenary. The other was a former UDA gunman, the same lad who had killed Ian Morris. Spencer had code-named the first Yeats and the second Wilde. He sent them into the field a few hours after sundown and instructed them to attack an hour or so before dawn – just like the Peep O'Day Boys.

The farmhouse stood in the basin of a small glen. Around the farm were several acres of cleared pasture-lands, but beyond the fence line rose hills covered with dense trees. It was on one of these hillsides, the one directly east of the farmhouse, where the E4 and SAS men had established their watch post. On the second night, the hillside lay beneath a blanket of low, thick cloud.

Yeats and Wilde wore black. They used coal dust to darken their pale Ulster complexions. They approached from the east, through the thick pine, up and down the rolling terrain, moving just a few feet each minute. Sometimes they lay very still for several minutes at a time, bodies pressed to the sodden earth, peering at their quarry through night-vision binoculars. When they had closed to within a quarter of a mile they separated, Yeats moving off to the north, Wilde to the south.

By 4 A.M. both men were exhausted, soaked to the skin, and bitterly cold. Yeats had been trained by the British army and was better prepared, mentally and physically, for a night on a freezing hillside. Wilde was not; he had grown up in the Shankill of West Belfast, and his experience had been on the streets, not in the field. In the final moments before the attack, he wondered whether he could go forward. Hypothermia had set in; his hands and feet were numb, yet no longer felt the cold. He was shivering violently, and he feared he wouldn't be able to fire his gun when the time came.

At 5 A.M. both gunmen were in position. Yeats, lying on his stomach behind a large tree, watched the SAS man. He was sitting in a blind, covered with sprigs of bush and small tree limbs. Yeats took out his gun, a Walther 9-millimetre semi-automatic with a silencer fitted into the barrel. Wilde carried the same weapon. Both men knew they were going to be heavily outgunned by their opponents. If they were to survive the encounter, they would have to make their first shots count.

Yeats rose to one knee suddenly and began firing. The silenced Walther made almost no sound. The first shots struck the SAS man in the torso with a dull thud and knocked him backward. By the sound of it the SAS man was wearing a vest, which meant he was almost certainly still alive.

Yeats scrambled to his feet and rushed forward through the darkness. When he was a few feet away the SAS man sat up suddenly and fired. His weapon was silenced too, and the only sound it made was a faint metallic clicking.

Yeats threw himself to the ground, and the shots sailed harmlessly over his head, splintering trees. Yeats rolled and came to rest on his stomach, arms outstretched, the Walther in his hands. He took aim and squeezed the trigger twice rapidly, just as the army had taught him. The shots struck the SAS man in the face. He fell to the ground, dead.

Yeats rushed forward, tore the automatic rifle from the grasp of the dead SAS man, and rushed to the spot where he knew the E4 men were hiding.

Wilde had an easier time of things. The SAS man that he was assigned to kill had reacted to the sound of bodies rustling the heather. He rose, pivoted quickly in several directions, then ran to the assistance of his comrade.

Wilde stepped from behind a tree as the SAS man moved past him. He levelled the gun at the back of his head and fired. The soldier's arms opened wide and he fell forward. Wilde grabbed the dead man's gun and raced forward, following Yeats through the trees.

The two E4 men – Marks and Sparks – were hidden in their blind, concealed by camouflage tarpaulins, tree limbs, and undergrowth. Marks was just coming awake. Yeats shot him several times through his sleeping bag. Sparks, who was on duty, was reaching for a small automatic. Wilde shot him through the heart.

It was just after five o'clock as Gavin Spencer sped through the village of Cranagh, then along the narrow B-road toward the farmhouse. He pulled into the muddy drive and shut down the engine. He walked to the back of the house through the darkness, picking his way through broken crates and old rusting farm equipment. He spotted them a moment later, descending the hillside in the rain. Spencer stood in the yard, hands in his pockets, as the two men crossed the pasture. For a moment he would have done anything to trade places with them; then he saw their wet, soiled clothing and the haunted look in their eyes, and he knew there was nothing to celebrate.

'It's done,' the one called Wilde said simply.

'How many?' Spencer asked.

'Four.'

Yeats tossed a rifle toward Spencer in the darkness. Spencer deftly pulled his hands from his pockets and caught the rifle before it struck him in the chest.

'There's a souvenir for you,' Yeats said. 'The rifle of a dead SAS man.'

Spencer pulled back the slider on the weapon, chambering a round.

'Anything left in this one?'

'He never got off a fuckin' shot,' Wilde said.

'Get in the car,' Spencer told them. 'I'll be along in a minute.'

Spencer carried the gun across the yard and let himself into the house. Sam Dalton, the older of the two brothers, was sitting at the kitchen table, drinking tea and smoking nervously. He wore blue jogging trousers, moccasins, and a woollen pullover. His face was unshaven, his eyes heavy with sleep.

'What the fuck's going on out there, Gavin?' he said.

'We eliminated your friends on the hillside. You've any more of that?' he said, nodding at the tea.

Dalton ignored Spencer's request. 'Eliminated them?' he said, his eyes suddenly wide. 'And what happens when it's discovered that you've eliminated them? I said I'd hide a few guns and a wee bit of Semtex for you, Gavin. You didn't tell me you were going to bring down the Special Branch and the British army on top of my fuckin' head.'

'You've nothing to worry about, Sam,' Spencer said. 'I'm taking all of it tonight. Even if the Branch and the army break down the door, there'll be nothing for them to find.'

'All of it?' Sam Dalton asked incredulously.

'All of it,' Spencer replied. 'Where's your brother?'

Dalton looked up at the ceiling and said, 'Upstairs sleeping.'

'Start pulling out the guns and the Semtex. I want a word with Sleeping Beauty. I'll be down in a minute.'

Sam Dalton nodded and went downstairs into the cellar. Gavin Spencer went upstairs and found Christopher Dalton asleep in his bed, mouth open, snoring softly. Spencer withdrew a silenced Walther automatic pistol from his coat pocket, leaned down, and slipped the barrel into the sleeping man's mouth. Christopher Dalton gagged and awakened with a jolt, eyes wide. Spencer pulled the trigger; blood and brain tissue exploded onto the pillow and the bedding. Spencer put the gun away and walked out of the room, leaving Christopher Dalton's twitching body on the bed.

'Where's Chris?' Dalton asked, when Spencer arrived in the cellar.

'Still sleeping,' Spencer said. 'I didn't have the heart to wake him.'

Dalton finished packing the guns and the explosives. When he was finished, three canvas duffels lay side by side on the floor. He was kneeling, zipping up the last of the bags, when Spencer pressed the barrel of the captured SAS automatic against the back of his head.

'Gavin, no,' he pleaded. 'Please, Gavin.'

'Don't worry, Sam. You're going to a better place than this.'

Spencer pulled the trigger.

At 6 a.m. the telephone rang on Michael's bedside table in the guest bedroom at Winfield House. He rolled over and snatched the receiver before it could ring a second time. It was Graham Seymour, telephoning from his home in Belgravia.

'Get dressed. I'll pick you up in half an hour.'

Graham hung up abruptly. Michael showered and dressed quickly. Twenty minutes later a chauffeured Rover pulled into the drive at Winfield House. Michael got in next to Graham Seymour.

Graham handed him coffee in a paper cup. He looked like a man who had been awakened with bad news. His eyes were red-rimmed, his shave was patchy and obviously hurried. As the car sped through the dawn light of Regent's Park, Graham quietly described what had happened overnight at the farmhouse in the Sperrin Mountains.

'Jesus Christ,' Michael said softly.

The car raced along the Outer Circle, then east a short distance on the Euston Road before heading south on Tottenham Court Road. Michael clutched the armrest as the driver weaved in and out of the early-morning traffic.

'Mind telling me where we're going?' Michael asked.

'I thought I'd surprise you.'

'I detest surprises.'

'I know,' Graham said, managing a brief smile.

Five minutes later they were speeding along Whitehall. The car drew to a halt at the iron gates guarding the entrance of Downing Street. Graham identified himself to the security officer, and the gates opened. The car moved forward, coming to a stop in front of the world's most famous doorway. Michael looked at Graham.

'Come along, darling,' Graham said. 'Mustn't keep the great man waiting.'

They entered Number Ten and walked along the front corridor and up the famous staircase, hung with the portraits of Tony Blair's predecessors. An aide showed them into the prime minister's study. Blair was seated behind a disorderly desk wearing a shirt and tie. A breakfast tray was untouched.

'When I approved Operation Kettledrum, gentlemen, I didn't expect it would come at a price like this,' Blair said, without waiting for introductions. 'My God, two E4 officers and two SAS men dead.'

Michael and Graham remained silent, waiting for the prime minister to continue.

'The whole of Northern Ireland is going to awaken to this news in a few minutes, and when it does the Catholic community is going to react strongly.'

Graham cleared his throat. 'Prime Minister, I assure you –'

'I've heard your assurances, gentlemen, but what I want now are results. If the peace process is to survive, we must get the gun out of Irish politics – decommission the paramilitaries. And in this atmosphere, the IRA are never going to give up their weapons.'

'If I may speak, Prime Minister?' Michael said.

Blair nodded briskly. 'Please do.'

'The fact that the Ulster Freedom Brigade engaged in an action like this suggests to me they've taken the bait. They are planning to assassinate Ambassador Cannon in Norfolk. And if they proceed they will be dealt a devastating blow.'

'Why not arrest Gavin Spencer and this Rebecca Wells woman now? Surely that would deal the Ulster Freedom Brigade a serious blow as well. And it would show the Catholics that we *are* doing something to stop these murderous thugs.'

'The RUC doesn't have the kind of evidence necessary to produce an airtight case against Spencer,' Graham said. 'And as for Rebecca Wells, she's more valuable to us in the field than she would be behind bars.'

Blair began shuffling papers, a sign the meeting had concluded.

'I'm going to allow this to continue,' he said, then paused for a moment. 'Despite what my critics say about me, I don't often engage in hyperbole. But if this group isn't stopped, the peace process will be destroyed, truly. Good morning, gentlemen.'

27

Hartley Hall stood two miles from the North Sea, just southeast of the town of Cromer. A Norman aristocrat built the first manor house on the site in the thirteenth century. Beneath the present structure, in the labyrinth of cellars and passages, were the original medieval arches and doorways. In 1625, a wealthy merchant from Norwich named Robert Hartley built a Jacobean mansion atop the Norman manor house. To create a barrier between his home and the storms of the North Sea, he planted several thousand trees in the sandy soil along the northern edge of his land, even though he knew it would be generations before the trees reached maturity. The result was the North Wood, two hundred acres of firs, Scots pines, maples, sycamores, and beeches. Ambassador Cannon marvelled at the trees as his small motorcade passed through the dark grove. A moment later, Hartley Hall floated into view.

Robert Hartley's descendant, Sir Nicholas Hartley, stepped out of the south porch as the cars pulled into the gravel drive. He was a large man with a barrel chest and a thick forelock of sandy-grey hair. A pair of setters scampered at his feet. Douglas climbed out of the second car and walked a few steps across the drive with his right arm extended. The two men shook hands as though Douglas owned the manor house down the road and had been coming to Hartley Hall for fifty years.

Hartley suggested a brief walk, even though it was not

quite 40 degrees and the dusk was fading rapidly. He had no job and few interests other than chronicling the history of his ancestral home, and he lectured Douglas intensely as they moved about the grounds. A pair of Special Branch men trailed softly behind them, followed by the dogs.

They admired the Jacobean south front, which had been designed and built by the Norfolk master mason Robert Lyminge. They meandered past the wisteria-covered east wing, with its large traceried windows and Flemish gables. They gazed upon the magnificent orangery, a large interior greenhouse overlooking the parterre where potted orange and lime trees were stored during the cold months. Beyond the walled garden lay the deer park, which once supported a herd of three hundred. They walked south along a footpath, past the stables and a terrace of servants' cottages. The five-hundred-year-old St Margaret's Church stood atop a small promontory, a silhouette against the blue-black twilight. Around it lay the remains of a fifteenth-century village that had been abandoned after an outbreak of plague.

By the time the two men reached the south front again, the last of the dusk was gone. Light shone through the mullion-and-transom windows, illuminating small patches of the gravel drive. They passed through the rusticated door and entered the great hall. Douglas admired the fifteenth-century English stained glass, the portraits of Hartley's ancestors, and the oak writing table beneath the window. He ingratiated himself with his host by being the first American visitor to correctly identify the table as Flemish Renaissance.

They passed through the dining room, with its sweeping rococo plasterwork, and into the drawing room. They stood in the centre of the room, necks craned at the original plasterwork ceiling, staring at the rich array of roses, orange blossoms, grapes, pears, and pomegranates.

'This panel is devoted to game birds found locally here along the Norfolk coast,' Hartley said, aiming his long arm like a rifle. 'As you can see, there are partridges, pheasant, plover, and woodcock.'

'It's just magnificent,' Douglas said.

'But you must be exhausted, and I could go on all evening,' Hartley said. 'Let me show you to your room. You can freshen up and relax for a few minutes before dinner.'

They ascended the central staircase and followed the corridor past a series of closed doors. Hartley showed Douglas into the Chinese bedroom. There was an eighteenth-century four-poster bed and a brightly-coloured knotted Exeter carpet. At the foot of the bed were a Japanese black lacquer cabinet and a single carved Chippendale chair.

A man was seated in the chair, his back to the door. He stood as Hartley and Douglas entered the room. For an instant Douglas had the sensation of staring at his own reflection in a fogged glass. His mouth actually fell open as he held out his hand toward the other man and waited for him to take it. The man just stood there, smiling slightly, clearly enjoying the effect of his presence. He was precisely the same height and stature as Douglas, and his thinning grey-white hair had been cut and styled in a similar fashion. His skin had the same open-air quality: ruddy cheeks, leathery complexion, large pores. The features were slightly different – the eyes a bit narrower – but the effect was overwhelming.

The door to the dressing room opened and Michael stepped into the room, followed by Graham Seymour. Michael noticed the look on his father-in-law's face and burst out laughing.

'Ambassador Douglas Cannon,' he said, 'I'd like you to meet Ambassador Douglas Cannon.'

Douglas shook his head and said, 'I'll be goddamned.'

Rebecca Wells spent the afternoon bird-watching. She had been in Norfolk for three days, living in a small caravan on the beach outside Sheringham. She had toured the coastline from Hunstanton in the west to Cromer in the east, walking the Peddars Way and the Norfolk Coast Path with her field glasses and her cameras, photographing the rich variety of local birds – plover and curlew, redshank and partridge. She had never been to Norfolk, and for a little while each day she actually seemed to forget the reason she had come. It was a magical place of salt marshes, tidal creeks, mudflats, and beaches that seemed to stretch to the horizon – flat, desolate, starkly beautiful.

Late that afternoon she entered the Great North Wood adjacent to Hartley Hall. She knew from her guidebooks that the Hartley family had turned over the wood to the government thirty years ago. Now it was a nature reserve and campsite. She walked along a sandy footpath, soft with pine needles and fallen sprigs of fir, and settled herself into a blind.

She pretended to be photographing a flock of migrating Brent geese. Her real target was Hartley Hall, which stood just south of the wood, across a meadow dead with winter. The ambassador was scheduled to arrive at four o'clock. She reached the blind at 3:45 P.M.; she didn't want to linger too long needlessly. The sun dropped below the horizon, and the air turned bitterly cold. The western sky was streaked with watercolour hues of purple and orange. The sea wind came up and stirred the trees. She rubbed her face with her ragwool gloves for warmth.

At 4:05 she heard cars passing along the road through the wood. A moment later they emerged from the shadows and sped along Hartley's private access road. A man emerged from the grand porch as the small motorcade pulled into the drive. Rebecca Wells raised her field glasses to her eyes. She watched as Douglas Cannon climbed out of the back of the limousine and shook the other man's hand. For several minutes they toured the grounds of Hartley Hall. Rebecca Wells watched them carefully.

When they had completed their circuit of the house and vanished inside, she stood and packed away her camera and field glasses into a nylon rucksack. She followed the trail through the woods, back to the car park where she had left her hired Vauxhall, and drove along the narrow coast road back to her caravan on the beach.

It was quite dark by now, the campsite nearly empty, just a family of transient travellers and a group of Danish teenagers who were backpacking across Norfolk. The four members of her team were spread throughout other campsites along the coast. The tide was going out, and the air had the sharp tang of the mudflats and marshes. Rebecca let herself into the caravan and switched on the portable electric heater. She lit the propane stove, boiled water, and made a pot of Nescafé. She filled a thermos bottle with the coffee and poured the remainder into a ceramic mug. She drank the coffee as she walked along the beach.

It was odd, she thought, but for the first time in a very long while she felt a strange sense of peace. It was this place, she thought: this beautiful, mystical place. She thought how strange it was to pass through a village and see no signs of sectarian conflict: no Union Jacks and Tricolours, no warlike murals or political slogans scrawled on the walls, no fortresslike police stations. Her entire life had been consumed by the conflict. Her father had been involved in the Protestant paramilitaries, and she had married a man from the UVF. She had been raised to hate and distrust Catholics. In Portadown, the conflict was everywhere; there was no escaping it. To be Protestant in Portadown had given her life a sense of purpose. She felt her place in history. The rituals of hatred, the cycles of killing and revenge, had provided a macabre sense of order to things.

She thought about what would happen after the assassination. Kyle Blake had provided her with money, a false passport, and a place to lie low in Paris. She knew she would have to remain in hiding for months, if not years. She might never be able to return to Portadown.

She finished the last of her coffee, watching the waves breaking over the beach, phosphorescent in the moon-light. I want to go somewhere like this, she thought. I wish I could stay here for ever.

She walked back to the caravan through the darkness, let herself inside, and switched on her laptop computer. Using a cellular modem, she connected to her Internet server and composed a brief E-mail message.

I'M HAVING A MARVELLOUS TIME HERE IN NORFOLK. THE WEATHER IS COLD BUT QUITE BEAUTIFUL. TODAY, I SPOTTED SEVERAL RARE SPECIES OF BIRDS. I PLAN TO REMAIN HERE FOR A FEW MORE DAYS.

She sent the message and switched off the computer. She picked up the thermos of coffee and a packet of cigarettes. She had a very long drive ahead of her tonight. She let herself out of the caravan and climbed into the Vauxhall. A moment later she was speeding along the A148 towards King's Lynn, the first leg of her journey to the western coast of Scotland.

'His real name is Oliver Taylor,' Graham Seymour said to Douglas. 'But I'd like you to forget you ever heard it. He's a watcher by trade, aren't you, Oliver? One of the best actually.'

'The resemblance is remarkable,' Douglas said, astonished.

'Oliver trains new recruits for the most part now, but we still put him out in the field now and again when we need a real pro. In fact, he spent a little time following the lovely Rebecca Wells, didn't you, Oliver?'

Taylor nodded.

'Come this way if you would, Ambassador Cannon,' Graham said. 'I'd like to show you a few things.'

Graham led Douglas and Michael into a room filled with electronic equipment and video monitors. A pair of technicians acknowledged the presence of the three men and then carried on with their work.

'This is the electronic nerve centre of the operation,' Graham said. 'The grounds have been littered with infrared surveillance cameras, motion detectors, and heat sensors. When the Ulster Freedom Brigade make their move, we'll know about it here first.'

'How do you know they'll try?' Douglas asked.

'Because Rebecca Wells is in Norfolk,' Graham said. 'She's been here for about three days. She's staying in a caravan out on the beach a couple of miles away. She was in the North Wood a few minutes ago when you arrived. She knows you're here.'

'Actually, she's just left the campsite, sir,' one of the technicians said.

'Where's she headed?'

'West on the coast road.'

'What about the caravan?' Michael asked.

'Still in the campsite, sir.'

Graham said, 'These men are our scythes, Ambassador Cannon. Let me introduce you to our blunt instruments.'

The Special Air Service is the elite unit of the British armed forces and one of the world's most respected military organizations. Based in Hereford, about 140 miles northwest of London, it has one active regiment, 22 SAS, and about 550 members. The SAS is an insertion force, designed to operate behind enemy lines. It is divided into four operational squadrons, each with a different specialty: airborne, amphibious, mountain, and assault vehicles. The unit demonstrated its antiterrorist prowess in May 1980, when it successfully ended the siege of the Iranian embassy in London before a worldwide television audience. SAS recruiters seek out soldiers of above-average intelligence who demonstrate the ability to improvise and to act alone. SAS soldiers are notorious for egotism, brashness, and sarcasm, and therefore the SAS is mistrusted by much of the British military establishment. The organization's motto is 'Who dares, wins.' True to form, SAS men deliberately mutilate their own creed, sacrilegiously proclaiming, 'Who cares who wins.'

The eight men in the large games room didn't look much like any soldiers Douglas had ever seen. They had shaggy hair or no hair at all and a few wore drooping moustaches. Two were playing billiards; two more were engaged in a noisy flailing game of table tennis. The rest lay around a wide-screen television, watching a video – *The Double Life of Veronique* – and occasionally pleading for quiet. The billiards game and the ping-pong match fell quiet as the SAS noticed that Douglas was in the room.

'When the Ulster Freedom Brigade makes its move, these men will be waiting for them,' Graham said. 'I can assure you it will all be over very quickly. These gentlemen know what happened to their colleagues in County Tyrone the other night. The SAS is a small unit. As you might expect, they're anxious to make amends.'

'I can understand that,' Douglas said. 'But if it is possible to avoid needless bloodshed –'

'They will do their very best to take the terrorists alive,'

Michael said. 'It depends on how the Ulster Freedom Brigade react once they discover they're walking into a trap.'

'Time to get you out of here, Ambassador Cannon,' Graham said. 'You've done your bit. I'm afraid the ride home isn't going to be quite as scenic as the journey here.'

Michael and Douglas parted in the great hall. As they shook hands, Douglas put an arm on his son-in-law's shoulder and said, 'Take care of yourself, Michael.'

Graham led Douglas through the house to a service entrance. A panelled van waited outside the door, engine idling. The name of a local catering service was stencilled on the side. Douglas climbed in and sat down in a special chair that had been anchored in the rear storage compartment. He winked. Graham closed the rear doors, and the van sped away.

Early the following morning, Rebecca Wells stood on the beach at Ardnacross Bay on the western coast of Scotland. It was misty, bitterly cold, and still quite dark, even though it was an hour after sunrise. She walked along the narrow rocky beach, smoking a cigarette, drinking the last of the Nescafé she had made more than twelve hours earlier. She was exhausted, running on nerves and adrenaline. The morning was windless, the water flat and calm. Beyond the bay lay Kilbrannan Sound. To the southwest, across the North Channel, was the Antrim coast of Northern Ireland.

Twenty more minutes passed. Rebecca was beginning to grow nervous about whether the boat would come. It would be a Zodiac, Kyle Blake had said, lowered from the side of a Protestant-owned freighter bound from Londonderry. On board would be a member of the Brigade with a duffel bag of guns for the assault on Hartley Hall.

Another ten minutes passed, while Rebecca considered

whether she should abort. The sky had lightened, and the first morning traffic was moving on the road behind the beach. Only then did she hear the putter of a small engine echoing across the flat water. A moment later, a tiny Zodiac broke through the fog on the bay.

As the boat drew closer to shore, Rebecca studied the man seated in the stern, tiller in hand. It was Gavin Spencer. He raised the propeller, and the Zodiac grounded itself on the beach. Rebecca rushed forward and pulled on the bowline.

'What in God's name are you doing here?' she asked.

'I wanted to be a part of it.'

'Does Kyle know?'

'He'll know soon enough, won't he?' Spencer stepped out of the Zodiac and lifted the duffel from the prow. 'Help me get this thing off the beach.'

Together, they dragged the Zodiac off the beach and hid it in the gorse-covered dunes. Spencer walked back to the beach and shouldered the duffel bag. Rebecca led him to the Vauxhall.

He studied her face. 'When's the last time you slept?'

'I can't remember.'

'I'll drive.'

She tossed Spencer the keys. He placed the duffel in the trunk, then climbed behind the wheel and started the engine; he was shuddering with the cold. He switched the heater on full, and a moment later the inside of the Vauxhall felt like a sauna. They stopped in the village of Ballochgair and bought tea and bacon sandwiches from a roadside café. Spencer devoured three of the sandwiches and slowly savoured the tea.

'Tell me about it,' he said, and for fifteen minutes Rebecca described the topography of the Norfolk coast and the layout of Hartley Hall. She was exhausted. She spoke automatically, as if reciting from memory without conscious thought. It was silly for Gavin Spencer to be here – he was a strategist, not a gunman – but she was glad he had come.

Rebecca closed her eyes as he asked more questions. She did her best to answer, but she felt her voice growing weaker as the car sped through desolate moorland and the Carradale Forest. The stifling warmth from the heater sapped the last of her strength. She fell asleep – the deepest sleep she had had in a very long time – and didn't wake again until they were racing along the Norfolk coast.

28

By all appearances it was a typical winter's day at Hartley Hall. The weather was clear and bright, and air fresh with the scent of the sea. After lunch they drove to Cley in Douglas Cannon's official car and walked the sands of Blakeney Point, bundled in their overcoats and wool hats. The North Sea sparkled in the brilliant sunlight. The Special Branch bodyguards walked quietly behind them while Nicholas Hartley's retrievers terrorized the terns and Brent geese. Rain moved over the Norfolk coast at dusk. By the time the dinner guests began arriving, the storm had matured into a fully-fledged North Sea winter gale.

It was just after 10 P.M. when Gavin Spencer slipped from the blind in the North Wood and hurried through the trees back to the beach. He opened the boot of the Vauxhall and removed the canvas duffel. He carried the bag across the campsite and rapped on the door of the caravan.

Rebecca Wells parted the curtains in the window next to the door and peered out. She opened the door, and Spencer climbed into the caravan. The wind blew the door shut behind him. The tiny space was crowded with the members of his unit. Spencer had personally selected the team, and he knew each of the men well: James Fletcher, Alex Craig, Lennie West, and Edward Mills.

The air was thick with cigarette smoke and the smell of

nervous men who had been sleeping in tents for two days. Fletcher and Craig sat at the small galley table, West and Mills on the edge of the bed, faces unshaven, hair dishevelled. Rebecca was making tea.

Spencer placed the duffel on the floor and ripped open the zipper. He removed the Uzi submachine guns one by one and passed them to the men, followed by ammunition clips. A moment later the caravan was filled with the sound of metal on metal as the team shoved the clips into their Uzis and worked the sliders. Spencer took the last weapon and tossed the empty duffel onto the bed.

'Where's mine?' Rebecca said.

'What are you talking about?'

'My gun,' she said. 'Where is it?'

'You've no training for this sort of thing, Rebecca,' Spencer said softly. 'Your work is done.'

She slammed the teapot onto the table. 'You can make your own bloody tea then, can't you.'

Spencer moved forward and put a hand on her shoulder. 'Now's not the time for this,' he said softly. 'I put our chances of success at one in two at best. A couple of these lads might not make it home again. Don't you think you owe it to them to keep your head in the game?'

She nodded.

'All right, then. Let's get down to business, shall we?'

Rebecca opened the cabinet above the stove and took down a large folded piece of paper. She spread it on the table, revealing a detailed map of Hartley Hall and the surrounding grounds. Spencer let Rebecca handle the briefing.

'There are several entrances to the manor house,' she said. 'The main entrance, of course, is here' – she tapped the diagram with her fingertip – 'at the south porch. There are also entrances here in the orangery, here and here on the east wing, and the main service entrance here. Each night I circled the house and took note of where lights were burning. The night of the ambassador's arrival, I noticed a light burning in a bedroom for the first time here, on the first floor. I suspect Cannon is sleeping there.'

Spencer stepped forward and took over. 'I want to overwhelm them. I want to create confusion. We approach separately and enter the house simultaneously at 4 A.M. I'll go in the front. James will enter through the orangery. Alex and Lennie will enter through the east wing, and Edward will go through the service entrance. Some of us will meet resistance. Some of us won't. As soon as you're inside, head straight upstairs to the guest bedroom. And the first one to arrive puts a bullet in the ambassador. Any questions?'

The dinner guests began leaving just after midnight, though they were not dinner guests at all but a collection of MI5 watchers and desk officers, actors in the illusion of Operation Kettledrum. When the last had gone, the two Special Branch bodyguards went off duty and two new officers came on. One made a cursory tour of the grounds, dressed in foul-weather gear like a North Sea fisherman. The light burned in the Chinese bedroom until 1 A.M., when Michael slipped into the chamber and doused it.

The members of the SAS team had slowly filtered into position outside the house. One lay in wait in the walled garden, another in the deer park. A third lay in the parterre, and a fourth in the cemetery next to St Margaret's Church. The rest took up positions throughout the ground floor of the house.

Each soldier wore infrared night-vision glasses and a miniature radio with an earpiece that would allow him to communicate with the nerve centre inside the manor. Each carried the standard-issue SAS compact submachine gun, the HK MP5, as well as a Herstal 5.7-millimetre handgun for backup. The Herstal is regarded as one of the world's most powerful handguns. It fires two-gram bullets at a muzzle speed of 650 metres per second and is capable of penetrating forty-eight layers of laminated Kevlar, the substance used in protective body armour, from two hundred metres away. Michael carried the CIA's standard-issue handgun, a high-powered Browning 9-millimetre with a fifteen-shot clip. Graham Seymour was unarmed.

The two men waited in the control room, upstairs in the first-floor guest bedroom. The weather was playing havoc with the electronic sensing equipment. The motion detectors were sounding constantly because of the twisting of the trees and shrubbery. The high-powered directional microphones were overwhelmed with the roar of the wind and the hammering of the rain. Only the infrared video cameras were functioning properly.

At 3:30 A.M., MI5 field agents stationed in the campsites around Hartley reported movement by the members of the assassination squad. The field agents did not follow the terrorists. Instead, they allowed them to proceed unhindered toward the estate.

At 3:55 A.M., camera operators on the top floor of Hartley Hall briefly spotted two gunmen moving into position, one in the trees bordering the deer park, a second creeping across the ruins of the village toward St Margaret's Church.

At precisely 3:58 A.M., James Fletcher rose from his hiding place in the parterre and moved quickly along the gravel footpath toward the orangery. Before joining the Brigade, Fletcher had been a member of the Ulster Defence Association, a violent Protestant paramilitary organization. Indeed, he had been one of the group's most prolific assassins, with half a dozen confirmed kills of IRA gunmen. He had broken with the UDA when it agreed to a cease-fire during the peace negotiations. When Gavin Spencer approached him about joining a new group, the Ulster Freedom Brigade, he had accepted without hesitation. Fletcher was virulently anti-Catholic and believed Ulster should be a Protestant province for Protestant people. He also desperately wanted to be the one to murder the ambassador, so he went into action two minutes early, disobeying Spencer's order to wait until four o'clock.

Fletcher wore a balaclava, a black jumpsuit, and rubber-soled black athletic shoes. As he padded along the footpath, the gravel crunched softly beneath his feet. He reached the french doors and tried the latch; it was locked. He took a half step back and rammed the butt of the Uzi through the pane nearest the latch. Shards of glass rained down on the stone floor.

He was reaching through the empty pane when he heard footfalls on the gravel behind him. He removed his hand and placed it on the Uzi. He was about to spin around and fire when an English-accented voice said, 'Drop the gun and put your hands on your head. There's a good lad.'

Fletcher quickly calculated the odds of winning the encounter with the man standing behind him. If he was Special Branch, Fletcher almost certainly possessed more firepower, though the Special Branch protective officers were notoriously good marksmen. He was wearing body armour beneath his jumpsuit and he could survive almost anything but a head shot. He also knew that if he was arrested he would probably spend his remaining years in an English jail.

James Fletcher dropped suddenly into a crouch and pivoted, raising his gun to the firing position. He saw the man only for an instant, but he realized at once that he was not Special Branch. He was SAS, which meant they had all walked straight into a trap, the same trap the IRA had walked into several times with disastrous results.

Fletcher also realized that he had just made a fatal miscalculation.

The soldier's gun made no sound other than a dull clicking. He knew it had fired, though, because he could see the muzzle flash. The rounds shredded his jumpsuit and pierced his body armour, shattering his spine and ripping a gaping hole in the muscle of his heart. He fell backward, crashing through the french doors, and collapsed onto the floor of the orangery.

The SAS man appeared before him a few seconds later. He bent over Fletcher and brusquely grabbed his throat, searching for a pulse. Then he snatched up the Uzi and moved away as James Fletcher died.

Edward Mills heard the sound of shattering glass as he raced across the ruins surrounding St Margaret's Church. He still had the lean, lightly muscled physique that had made him a champion cross-country runner at school, and he scampered easily across the piles of stones and low walls of the ruins. Like Fletcher he wore a black jumpsuit and a balaclava. Ahead, framed in the glow from Hartley Hall, stood St Margaret's, looming over the graveyard. Mills raced along an ancient footpath leading from the village to the back of the church.

He had never done anything like this in his life, yet he felt surprisingly calm. He was a member of the Orange Order – his father had been the standard-bearer for his lodge in Portadown, and so had his grandfather – but he had avoided the paramilitaries until the previous summer. It was then that the army and the RUC had prevented the Orange Order from marching along the Catholic Garvaghy Road in Portadown. Like most Orangemen, Mills believed he had an absolute right to march along the Queen's highway any time he pleased, regardless of what the Catholics might think. To protest the blockade he had remained in the fields around Drumcree church for six weeks. Gavin Spencer approached Mills there, in the sloppy makeshift campsite at Drumcree, and asked him to join the Ulster Freedom Brigade.

Now he sprinted across the old graveyard, picking his way through headstones and crosses. He was nearing the lych-gate, running effortlessly, when he felt a sharp pain in his left shin. His legs became entangled, and he crashed heavily to the ground, face down. He tried to regain his footing, but a second later a man leapt onto his back, hit him twice on the back of the head, and clasped a gloved hand around his mouth. Mills felt himself losing consciousness.

'If you so much as twitch or grunt, I'll put a bullet in the back of your head,' the man said, and by the calm tone of voice Edward Mills knew the threat was not idle. He also felt the sickening realization that they had walked straight into a trap. The man tried to pull the Uzi from his grasp. Foolishly, Mills resisted. The man drove an elbow into the back of his head, and a second later Edward Mills blacked out.

Alex Craig and Lennie West raced across the flat, open grass of the deer park toward the east wing of Hartley Hall. The two men were veterans of the UVF, and they had worked together many times before. They moved silently, side by side, guns at the ready. They reached the end of the deer park and arrived at the gravel approach to the east wing. Behind them, a male voice called out, 'Stop, drop your weapons, and place your hands on your heads!'

Craig and West froze, but their hands remained wrapped around their Uzis.

'Drop the guns, now!' the voice repeated.

Camping on the beach near Blakeney before the operation, Craig and West had decided that if there was trouble they would rather fight than be taken into custody. They looked at each other.

'Looks like we've been set up,' Craig whispered. 'For God and Ulster, eh, Lennie?'

West nodded and said, 'I'll take the one behind us.'

'Right.'

West fell to the ground, rolled over, and started firing blindly in the darkness. Alex Craig fell to his stomach and fired wildly at the east wing, shattering glass. A second later he saw the reply in one of the shattered windows, a muzzle flash of a silenced submachine gun.

West saw the same thing, low in the deep grass of the deer park, but it was too late. A burst of rounds obliterated his head in a flash of blood and brain tissue.

Craig had no idea what had happened to his comrade. He turned his fire on the gunman in the window, but a second appeared, and then a third. He realized that West's gun had fallen silent. He turned and saw a headless corpse lying next to him on the gravel.

He emptied the first clip, shoved another into the Uzi, and started firing again. A few seconds later the gunman inside the mansion found his mark, as did the man behind him in the deer park. Craig's body was torn apart by gunfire. His final shots, fired by a spasm in his dying hands, shattered the magnificent clock in the cupola of the east wing, freezing the hands at 4:01.

Gavin Spencer, sprinting across the gravel drive toward the south porch, heard the intense firefight in the deer park. For an instant he considered turning away and heading back to the sanctuary of the North Wood. He had no idea what had just happened to any of his men.

Had they penetrated the manor? Had the Special Branch bodyguards stopped them?

He paused for a moment, mind racing, breath ragged. He listened for more gunfire but heard nothing except wind and rain. He started running again. He passed between the ornate columns of the south porch and leaned against the door.

Again, Spencer paused to listen. The gunfire seemed to have stopped for good. The door was locked. He took a step back and opened fire, closing his eyes against the shower of splintered wood. He drove his foot against the door, and it crashed open. Spencer stepped into the entrance hall and paused, Uzi at the ready.

A figure appeared in the doorway to the great hall: tall, broad shoulders, helmet, and night-vision glasses. SAS, Spencer thought, no question. He spun around and took aim with the Uzi. The SAS man tried to fire his own weapon, but it jammed. He reached for a handgun, holstered beneath his armpit, but Spencer fired a burst from his Uzi.

The gunfire blew the soldier off his feet. Spencer moved forward and snatched the handgun from the holster. He crossed the great hall and started up the staircase.

The radio operator in the command centre said calmly, 'Base to Alpha 534, base to Alpha 534, can you hear me? Repeat, can you hear me?'

He turned around and looked at Michael.

'He's off the air, Mr Osbourne. I think we have a terrorist loose in the house.'

'Where's the closest SAS man?'

'Still in the east wing.'

Michael removed the Browning automatic from his coat pocket. He pulled the slider, chambering the first round.

'Get him up here, now!'

*

Michael slipped through the doorway, into the darkened corridor, and closed the door behind him. He heard Gavin Spencer, clambering up the central staircase, and crouched, holding the Browning with both hands, arms extended. A few seconds later he spotted Spencer, mounting the last flight of stairs.

'Drop the gun, now!' Michael yelled.

Gavin Spencer turned and levelled his Uzi in Michael's direction. Michael fired two shots. The first sailed past Spencer and shattered one of the classical busts along the staircase. The second hit Spencer in the left shoulder and drove him back.

Spencer kept hold of the Uzi and fired a burst along the corridor. Michael, armed only with the Browning and with nowhere to take cover, was no match for a terrorist with an Uzi. He turned the knob of the door behind him and dived back into the command centre.

He slammed the door and locked it.

'Get down!'

Graham Seymour and the other officers in the room hit the floor as Gavin Spencer, standing outside in the corridor, fired through the wall and the door.

Each bedroom on the wing was connected to the adjoining room by a communicating doorway. Michael ran to the doorway and entered the next room. He repeated the move twice more, until he found himself in the Chinese bedroom.

Outside, in the corridor, he could hear Spencer, breathing heavily, obviously in pain. Michael crossed the room and leaned against the wall next to the doorway.

Spencer fired a short burst from the Uzi, splintering the door, and kicked it open. As he stepped into the room, Michael struck him in the side of the head with the butt of his Browning.

Spencer buckled but did not fall.

Michael hit him a second time.

Spencer fell to the floor, and the Uzi tumbled from his grasp.

Michael leapt on top of him, clutching Spencer's throat with one hand and holding the Browning to his head with the other. Outside in the corridor he could hear the clatter of the approaching SAS men.

'Don't move a fucking muscle,' Michael said.

Spencer tried to throw him off. Michael pressed the barrel of the Browning into the wound in Spencer's shoulder. Spencer screamed in pain and lay still.

Two SAS men arrived in the room, guns trained on Spencer. Graham Seymour arrived a few seconds later. Michael ripped the balaclava from Spencer's head. He smiled as he recognized the face.

'Oh, my goodness,' Michael said, looking at Graham. 'Look who we have here.'

'Gavin, darling,' Graham said lazily. 'So glad you could drop by.'

Rebecca Wells watched it all unfold from the blind in the North Wood. The gunfire had ended, and the night was filled with the sound of distant sirens. The first police cars raced along the entrance road, followed by a pair of ambulances. The men had walked straight into a trap, and it was her fault.

She tried to control her anger and think clearly. The British had certainly been watching them the entire time. There were probably agents in the campsite, agents who had followed her as she reconnoitred Hartley Hall. She understood that she had few options now. If she went back to the caravan or tried to hide in the North Wood, she would be arrested.

She had three hours before first light – three hours to

get as far from the Norfolk coast as possible. The Vauxhall was no good; it was back at the caravan, almost certainly being watched by the police.

If she was to escape Norfolk, she had only one choice. She had to walk.

She picked up her rucksack. Inside was her money, her maps, and her Walther automatic. Norwich lay twenty miles to the south. She could be there by midday. She could purchase a change of clothing, check into a hotel to clean herself up, buy hair dye at a chemist, and change her appearance. From Norwich she could take a bus further south to Harwich, where there was a large European ferry terminal. She could take an overnight ferry to Holland and be on the continent by morning.

She removed the gun from her rucksack, pulled on her hood, and started walking.

MARCH

29

Amsterdam was a city Delaroche loved, but not even Amsterdam, with its gabled houses and picturesque canals, could lift him from the grey fog of depression that had settled over him that winter. He had taken a flat in a house overlooking a small canal running between the Herengracht and the Singel. The rooms were large and airy, with vaulted windows and french doors that opened onto the water, but Delaroche kept the blinds drawn except when he was working.

The flat was bare except for his easels and his bed and a large chair near the french doors where he sat and read late into most evenings. Two bicycles were propped against the wall in the entrance hall, an Italian racer, which he used for long rides in the flat Dutch countryside, and a German-made mountain bike for the cobblestones and bricks of central Amsterdam. He refused to keep them in the lockup outside the house as the rest of the tenants did; there was a huge black market for stolen bicycles in Amsterdam, even for the rickety one-speed coasters that most people rode. His mountain bike would not have survived more than a few minutes.

Uncharacteristically, he had grown obsessed with his own face. Several times each day he would go into the bathroom and stare at his reflection in the glass. He had never been a vain man, but he hated what he saw now, because it offended his artistic sense of proportion and symmetry. Each day he made a pencil sketch of his face to document the slow healing process. At night, lying alone in his bed, he toyed with the collagen implants in his cheeks.

Finally, the incisions healed and the swelling went down, and his features settled into a boring, rather ugly stew. Leroux, the plastic surgeon, had been right; Delaroche did not recognize himself any more. Only the eyes were the same, sharp and distinct, but they were now surrounded by dullness and mediocrity.

The security requirements of his trade had prevented Delaroche from painting his own face, but shortly after coming to Amsterdam he produced an intensely personal work of self-portraiture – a hideous man staring into a mirror and seeing a beautiful reflection staring back at him. The reflection was Delaroche before surgery. He had to work from memory because he had no photographs of his old face. He kept the work for a few days, leaning against the wall of his studio, but paranoia eventually won out, and he shredded the canvas and burned it in the fireplace.

Some nights, when he was bored or restless, Delaroche went to the nightclubs around the Leidseplein. Before, he had avoided bars and nightclubs because he tended to attract too much attention from women. Now he could sit for hours without being bothered.

That morning he rose early and made coffee. He showered and dressed in jeans and a woollen sweater. He logged onto the computer, checked his E-mail, and read newspapers on-line until the German girl in his bed stirred.

He had forgotten her name – something like Ingrid, maybe Eva. She had childbearing hips and heavy breasts. She had dyed her hair black to appear more sophisticated. Now, in the grey morning light, Delaroche could see she was a child, twenty at most. There was something of Astrid Vogel in her awkwardness. He felt angry with himself. He had seduced her for the challenge of it – like making a steep ascent on his bike at the end of a long ride – and now he just wanted her to leave.

She rose and wrapped her body in a sheet.

'Coffee?' she asked.

'In the kitchen,' he said, without looking up from his computer screen.

She drank her coffee German style, with lots of heavy cream. She smoked one of Delaroche's cigarettes and eyed him silently as he read.

'I have to go to Paris now,' he said.

'Take me with you.'

'No.'

He spoke quietly but firmly. Once, when he used that tone of voice, a girl like her might have been nervous or anxious to leave his presence, but she just stared at him over her coffee cup and smiled. He suspected it was his face.

'I'm not finished with you,' she said.

'There isn't time.'

She pouted playfully.

'When am I going to see you again?'

'You're not.'

'Come on,' she said. 'You're interesting, strange. I want to know more about you.'

'No, you don't,' he said, shutting off the computer.

She kissed him and padded away. Her clothes were strewn across the floor: ripped black jeans, a flannel lumberjack shirt, a black concert T-shirt with the name of a rock band that Delaroche had never heard of. When she finished dressing she stood before him and said, 'Are you sure you won't take me to Paris?'

'Quite sure,' he said resolutely, but there was something

about her that he liked. He said gently, 'I'll be back tomorrow evening. Come at nine o'clock. I'll make you dinner.'

'I don't want dinner,' she said. 'I want you.'

Delaroche shook his head. 'I'm too old for you.'

'You're not too old. Your body is wonderful, and you have an interesting face.'

'Interesting?'

'Yes, interesting.'

She looked around the room at the canvases leaning against the walls.

'Are you going to Paris to work?' she asked.

'Yes.'

Delaroche took a taxi to Amsterdam's Centraal Station and purchased a first-class ticket on the morning train to Paris. He bought newspapers at a gift shop in the terminal and read them as the train raced through the flat Dutch countryside into Belgium.

The news that morning intrigued him. During the night a Protestant paramilitary group from Northern Ireland had tried to assassinate the American ambassador to Britain while he was spending the weekend at a country house in Norfolk. According to the newspapers, Special Branch agents had killed three members of the group and arrested two others. The alleged leader of the Ulster Freedom Brigade, a man named Kyle Blake, had been arrested in Portadown. Police were looking for a woman connected to the group.

Delaroche folded the newspaper and looked out the window. He suspected Michael Osbourne, the ambassador's son-in-law, was somehow involved in the incident. The Director had told him in Mykonos that Osbourne had been brought back to the CIA to deal with Northern Ireland.

The train drew into the Gare du Nord in Paris in the early afternoon. Delaroche collected his small grip from the luggage rack. He passed through the station quickly and caught a taxi outside. He was staying at a small hotel on the rue de Rivoli overlooking the Tuileries Gardens. He told the driver to drop him a few blocks away, on the rue Saint-Honoré, and he walked the rest of the way.

He checked into the hotel as a Dutchman and spoke accented French to the desk clerk. They gave him a garret room on the top floor with a fine view of the gardens and the Seine bridges.

He slipped a clip into his Beretta pistol and went out.

Dr Maurice Leroux, cosmetic surgeon, kept an office in a fashionable building on the avenue Victor Hugo, near the Arc de Triomphe. Delaroche, without giving his name, confirmed by telephone that the doctor was in that day. He told the receptionist he would be around later to see him and hung up abruptly.

He sat in the window table of a café across the street and waited for Leroux to come out. Shortly before five o'clock Leroux emerged. He wore a grey cashmere overcoat, and he seemed to be the last man in Paris to actually sport a beret. He walked quickly and appeared pleased with himself. Delaroche left money on the table and went out.

Leroux walked to the Arc de Triomphe, then circled the Place Charles de Gaulle and strolled down the avenue des Champs-Élysées. He entered Fouquet's restaurant and was greeted by a middle-aged woman. Delaroche recognized her; she was a minor actress who played bit roles on French television dramas.

The maître d' showed Leroux and the ageing actress into the club side of the restaurant. Delaroche took a small table on the public side, where he could see the door. He ordered a hash of potatoes and ground meat and drank a half bottle of decent Bordeaux. When there still was no sign of Leroux, he ordered cheese and *café au lait*.

It was nearly two hours before Leroux and his companion left the restaurant. Delaroche watched them through the glass. It was windy, and Leroux turned up the collar of his cashmere coat dramatically. He gave the actress a theatrical kiss and touched her cheek, as if admiring his work. He helped her into a car. Then he purchased newspapers and magazines from a kiosk and started walking through the buzzing evening crowds along the Champs-Élysées.

Delaroche paid his bill and went after him.

Maurice Leroux was a walker. With his newspapers tucked beneath his arm, he walked along the Champs-Élysées to the Place de la Concorde. He had no reason to suspect he was being followed, and therefore tailing him was very easy. Delaroche had only to keep pace with him along the busy sidewalks. The cut of his expensive coat, and the farcical beret, made him easy to spot among the crowds. He crossed the Seine at the Pont de la Concorde and walked for a long time on the Boulevard Saint-Germain. Delaroche lit a cigarette and smoked as he walked.

Leroux entered a café bistro near the church of Saint-Germain-des-Prés and sat down at the bar. Delaroche entered a moment later and sat at a small table near the door. Leroux drank wine and chatted with the barman. A pretty girl ignored his flirting.

After half an hour Leroux left the bar, by now thoroughly drunk. This pleased Delaroche, because it would make his task easier. Leroux teetered along the Boulevard Saint-Germain through the light rain and entered a small side street near the Mabillon metro station.

He stopped at the entrance of an apartment building

and punched in the security code. Delaroche slipped in the door behind him before it could close. They entered the lift together, an old-fashioned cage threaded through the middle of the staircase. Leroux punched the fifth floor, Delaroche the sixth. Delaroche chatted about the miserable weather in Parisian-accented French. Leroux grunted something unintelligible. Clearly, he did not recognize his patient.

Leroux got off at his floor. As the lift rose, Delaroche peered through the grille and watched Leroux enter his apartment. He stepped out of the lift on the sixth floor and walked down one flight of stairs. He knocked gently on Leroux's door.

The doctor answered a moment later, face perplexed, and said, 'Can I help you?'

'Yes,' Delaroche said, and he punched Leroux in the throat with a knifelike fist. The blow left Leroux doubled over in agony, speechless, gasping for air. Delaroche closed the door.

'Who are you?' Leroux rasped. 'What do you want?'

'I'm the one whose face you took a hammer to.'

He realized it was Delaroche.

'Dear God,' he whispered.

Delaroche removed the silenced Beretta pistol from his coat.

Leroux began to tremble violently. 'I can be trusted,' he said. 'I've done many men like you.'

'No, you haven't,' Delaroche said, and he shot him twice through the heart.

Delaroche arrived back in Amsterdam early the following afternoon. He returned to his flat by taxi and packed a blue nylon backpack with his painting kit: two small canvases, paints, a Polaroid camera, a portable easel, and the Beretta pistol. He rode his mountain bike along the cobblestone streets to a spot on the Keizersgracht where there was a good bridge with lights on the arches that came on after dark.

He locked his bike and walked around the bridge for some time until he found a perspective he liked, with houseboats in the foreground and a trio of magnificent gabled houses in the background. He removed his camera from the backpack and made several Polaroid photographs of the scene, first in black and white, so he could see the essential forms and lines of the setting, then in colour.

He set to work, painting quickly, instinctively, racing to capture the fleeting twilight before darkness took hold. When the lights flickered into life on the bridge he set down his brush and simply watched. He studied the reflection of the lights on the smooth surface of the canal for a long time. He waited for the painting to cast its spell – waited for the image of Maurice Leroux's dead eyes to evaporate from his mind – but neither happened.

A long water taxi slid past. The reflection of the lights dissolved with its wake. Delaroche packed away his things. He rode along the Keizersgracht, gingerly holding the canvas in his right hand. In any other city he might have drawn stares with such a pose, but not in Amsterdam.

Delaroche crossed the Keizersgracht at Ree Straat, then pedalled slowly along the Prinsengracht, until the old houseboat appeared before him. He chained his bicycle to a lamppost, leaned the canvas against the front tyre, and hopped onto the deck.

The *Krista* was forty-five feet long, with a wheelhouse aft, a slender prow, and a row of portholes along the gunwale. The green and white paint was flaking with neglect. The hatch at the top of the companionway was secured with a heavy padlock. Delaroche still had the key. He unlocked the hatch and stepped down the companionway into the salon, which was dark except for the soft glow of the yellow streetlamps leaking through the dirty skylights.

The boat had been Astrid Vogel's. They had lived here together the previous winter, after Delaroche had hired her to assist him with a series of particularly difficult assassinations. He could imagine her now, her long body bumping about in the cramped spaces of the houseboat. He looked at the bed and thought of making love to her with rain drumming on the skylight. Astrid had nightmares; she used to pummel him in her sleep. Once, she awakened after a bad dream, surprised to find Delaroche in her bed. She nearly shot him before he could wrench the gun from her hand.

Delaroche had not been back to the *Krista* since then. He spent several minutes rifling cabinets and drawers, looking for any trace of himself he might have left behind. He found nothing. There was nothing of Astrid either, just some appalling clothing and a few well-thumbed books. Astrid was used to living in hiding. She had been a member of the Red Army Faction and had spent many years in places like Beirut and Tripoli and Damascus. She knew how to come and go without leaving tracks.

Delaroche's obsessive independence made him incapable of loving another, but he had cared for Astrid and, more important, he had trusted her. She was the only woman who knew the truth about him. He could relax around her. They had planned to go to the Caribbean when the job was done – to live together in something approaching a marriage – but Michael Osbourne's wife had killed her on Shelter Island.

Delaroche climbed the companionway and locked the hatch behind him. He mounted his bike and pedalled toward his apartment through the lamplight. Delaroche killed for two reasons: because he was hired to kill or to protect himself. Maurice Leroux fell into the second category. He had never killed out of anger, nor had he ever killed for revenge. He believed the blood lust for revenge was the most destructive of emotions. He also thought it was unbecoming of a professional of his stature. But now, cycling through the streets of a strange city, with a face he did not recognize, Delaroche was overcome by a desire to kill Michael Osbourne.

He saw the German girl waiting on the front steps of the house. He crossed the Herengracht to the opposite side and waited. He had no desire to see her again. Finally, she scribbled a note and shoved it beneath the door before storming off along the canal. Delaroche scooped up the note as he entered the foyer – *You are a fucking bastard! Please call. Love, Eva* – and pushed his bicycle into the flat.

He entered his studio and dropped the unfinished painting on a stack of other incomplete works. He hated it suddenly; it seemed contrived, unimaginative, tiresome. He stripped off his coat and placed a large blank canvas on his easel. He had painted her once, but the work, like the rest of his possessions, had been destroyed in Mykonos. He stood there in the half light, thinking about it for a long time, trying to remember her face. There was a Byzantine quality about it, he remembered: wide cheek-bones, a large mobile mouth, liquid blue eyes set slightly too far apart. The face of a woman from another time and place.

He switched on the harsh halogen lamps suspended from the ceiling and started to work. He discarded one canvas because he did not like the pose and a second because the structure of her facial bones was all wrong. The third canvas felt right from the moment he started to work on it. He painted his most enduring visual memory of her – Astrid, leaning on a rusting wrought-iron railing on a hotel balcony in Cairo, wearing only a man's gallabiah unbuttoned to her stomach, the setting sun shining through the thin white cotton, revealing the soft lines of her back and her upturned breast.

He worked through the night until morning. He had polluted his body with coffee and wine and cigarettes. When it was finished he could not sleep because he had a headache. He carried the canvas to his room and propped it up at the foot of his bed. Finally, some time before noon, he fell into a restless sleep.

30

Michael Osbourne was forced to remain in London for three days after the Hartley Hall affair, dealing with the real enemy of any servant of the secret world: the bureaucracy. He had spent two days giving lengthy statements to the authorities. He had helped Wheaton clean up the mess of Preston McDaniels's suicide. He had worked with Special Branch to tighten security around Douglas. He had attended a memorial service for the two SAS officers slain in the Sperrin Mountains of Northern Ireland.

His last day in London was spent in a soundproof cell deep in the catacombs of Thames House, enduring a ritual debriefing by the mandarins of MI5. When it was over he stalked Millbank in the rain for twenty minutes, searching for a taxi, because Wheaton had commandeered Michael's staff car on a dubious pretext. Finally, he retreated to Pimlico Underground and took the tube. London, a city he loved, suddenly seemed dreary and oppressive to him. He knew it was time to go home.

Graham appeared in the drive of Winfield House the following morning to take Michael to Heathrow, this time in a Jaguar instead of his department Rover.

'We have to make a stop on the way to the airport,' Graham said, as Michael climbed into the back seat next to him. 'Nothing serious, darling. Just a couple of loose ends to tie up.'

The car left Regent's Park and headed south along Baker Street. Graham changed the subject.

'You see this?' he said, pointing to an article in that morning's *Times* about the mysterious murder of a prominent French plastic surgeon.

'I glanced at it,' Michael said. 'What about it?'

'He was a naughty boy.'

'What do you mean?'

'We've always suspected he was earning a little extra cash by fixing the faces of bad guys,' Graham said. 'The good doctor made several house calls to exotic places like Tripoli and Damascus. We asked the French to keep a watch on him, and as usual they basically told us to fuck off.'

Michael read the article; it was two paragraphs, with only the barest details. Maurice Leroux was shot to death in his apartment in the Sixth Arrondissement of Paris. Paris police were investigating.

'What kind of gun did the killer use?'

'Nine-millimetre.'

The Jaguar sped south along Park Lane, then crossed Green Park along Constitution Hill. A moment later it passed through the gates of Buckingham Palace.

Michael glanced at Graham. 'Never a dull moment with you, is there?'

'I wouldn't have it any other way.'

'It's so nice to see you again, Mr Osbourne,' Queen Elizabeth said, as they entered a palace drawing room. 'Please sit down.'

Michael sat down. Tea was served, and her aides and assistants withdrew. Graham Seymour waited outside in the anteroom.

'I want to thank you for the fine work you did in dealing with the menace of the Ulster Freedom Brigade,' the Queen said. 'The people of Northern Ireland owe you a tremendous debt. Indeed, so does the whole of Great Britain.'

'Thank you, Your Majesty,' Michael said politely.

'I was very sorry to hear about your agent, the one who was killed in Northern Ireland.' She paused a moment, face perplexed, and glanced at the ceiling. 'Oh, good heavens, I can't remember the poor man's name.'

'Kevin Maguire,' Michael said.

'Ah, yes, Harbinger,' the Queen said, using Maguire's code name. 'Such a frightful business that was. I was relieved to hear you weren't seriously hurt. But I know losing an agent like Harbinger in such a horrible way must have affected you deeply.'

'Kevin Maguire wasn't perfect, but there are countless people who are alive today because of him. It took a tremendous amount of courage for him to betray the IRA, and in the end he paid with his life.'

'What are your plans now that the Protestant threat appears to have been neutralized? Do you plan to stay with the CIA or vanish back into retirement?'

'I'm not sure yet,' Michael said. 'Right now I'd just like to go home and see my wife and children. I've been away for a long time.'

'I'm not sure I could be married to someone in your line of work.'

Michael smiled. 'It takes a very special kind of woman.'

'So your wife is supportive?'

'I wouldn't go that far, Your Majesty.'

'I suppose you have to do what makes you happy,' the Queen said. 'And if working for the CIA makes you happy, I'm sure she'll understand. It's certainly important work. You should be very proud of what you've accomplished here.'

'Thank you, Your Majesty. I am proud.'

'Well, since it appears you're going to remain inside the CIA for the time being, I suppose we'll have to do this in private.'

'Do what, Your Majesty?' Michael asked.

'Your honorary knighthood.'

'You're joking.'

She smiled mischievously and said, 'I never joke about something as important as this.'

She opened a small rectangular case and showed Michael the medal of the Honorary Knighthood of the British Empire.

'It's beautiful,' he said. 'I'm honoured and very flattered.'

'You should be.'

'Do I have to kneel?'

'Don't be silly,' she said. 'Just finish your tea and tell me what it felt like to capture Gavin Spencer.'

'You mean I just had sex with a real knight?' Elizabeth said.

'I'm afraid so.'

'I think you're my first.'

'I'd better be.'

'So what did you two chat about besides Northern Ireland?'

'We talked about you.'

'Oh, please.'

'We did.'

'What about me?'

'She wanted to know whether I was going to stay with the Agency or vanish back into retirement, as she put it.'

'And what did you tell her?'

'I told her I didn't know.'

'Such a coward.'

'Watch it. I'm a knight, remember?'

'So what's the answer?'

'For one of the first times in my career with the Agency, I feel I actually accomplished something. It feels good.'

'So you want to stay on?'

'I want to hear what Monica has to say before I make any final decisions. And I want to hear what you have to say.'

'Michael, you know how I feel. But I also need you to be happy. It's strange, but listening to you for the last hour, you've seemed happier than you have in months.'

'So what are you saying?'

'I'm saying that I wish working somewhere other than the Central Intelligence Agency could make you happy. But if it's what you want, and you're going to be content, then I want you to stay.'

She crushed out her cigarette, untied her robe, and rolled on top of him, pressing her breasts against his warm skin. 'Just make me one promise,' she said. 'If you really think October is still alive, let someone else go after him.'

'He murdered Sarah, and he tried to kill us both.'

'That's why someone else should handle the case. Recuse yourself, Michael. Let Adrian give the job to someone else, someone with no personal stake.' She hesitated a moment. 'Someone who's not out for revenge.'

'What makes you think I'm out for revenge?'

'Come on, Michael. Don't be dishonest with yourself or me. You want him dead, and I don't blame you. But revenge is a dangerous game. Didn't you learn anything while you were in Northern Ireland?'

Michael turned away. She took his face in her hands and pulled him back.

'Don't be angry with me – I just don't want anything to happen to you.' She kissed him gently. 'Take the advice of your lawyer on this one. It's over. Let it go.'

31

The Executive Council for the Society for International Development and Co-operation convened its spring meeting on the island of Mykonos on the first Friday of March. Delaroche's vacant villa on the cliffs of Cape Mavros served as the site for the gathering. It was too small to accommodate anyone but the Director, his bodyguards, and Daphne, so the other council members and their entourages took refuge in the hotels and guest-houses of Chora. At sundown they trickled across the island – the intelligence chiefs and arms merchants, the businessmen and organized crime figures – in a caravan of black Range Rovers.

The Director and his staff had seen to the security arrangements. There were heavily armed guards around the grounds and a high-speed motorboat on Panormos Bay filled with former amphibious troops from the SAS. The villa had been thoroughly swept for bugs, and radio jammers broadcast electronic chaff to disrupt long-range microphones.

They had cocktails on Delaroche's fine stone terrace overlooking the sea and a meal of traditional Greek food. At midnight the Director gavelled the proceedings to order.

For the first hour the executive council dealt with routine house-keeping matters. As always the council members addressed each other by their code names:

Rodin, Monet, Van Gogh, Rembrandt, Rothko, Michelangelo, and Picasso. The Director turned his attention to Society operations now under way in North Korea, Pakistan, Afghanistan, Kosovo, and, finally, Northern Ireland.

'In February, Monet saw to it that a shipment of Uzi submachine guns reached the hands of the Ulster Freedom Brigade,' the Director said. 'Those guns were used in the attempted assassination of Ambassador Douglas Cannon. Unfortunately, they seemed to do no good. The ambassador survived the attack, but the Ulster Freedom Brigade did not. Most of its members are either dead or in custody. So, for now, our involvement in Northern Ireland is terminated.'

The Director recognized Rodin, the operations chief of the French intelligence service. 'If we wish to renew our involvement in Northern Ireland, there might be an opportunity sitting in Paris,' Rodin said.

The Director raised one eyebrow and said, 'Continue, please.'

'As you know, one member of the team involved in the assassination attempt in Norfolk managed to escape,' Rodin said. 'A woman named Rebecca Wells. I happen to know she is hiding in Paris with a British mercenary named Roderick Campbell. I also know she has sworn to even the score after the incident in Norfolk. She is trying to find an assassin capable of killing the American ambassador.'

The Director lit a cigarette, clearly intrigued.

'Perhaps we should make direct contact with Rebecca Wells and offer assistance,' Rodin said.

The Director made a show of careful deliberation. Ultimately, the decision would be made by the executive council, not by him, but his opinion would hold considerable weight with the other members. After a moment, he said, 'I doubt Miss Wells could afford our services.'

'I agree,' said Rodin. 'The work would have to be *pro bono*. As you say, it would be an investment.'

The Director turned to Picasso, who appeared uneasy.

'For obvious reasons, I cannot support an operation like the one suggested,' Picasso said. 'Support for a Protestant paramilitary group is one thing, direct involvement in the murder of an American diplomat is quite another.'

'I understand you're in a difficult position, Picasso,' the Director said. 'But you knew from the outset that some of the actions taken by this organization might conflict with your own narrow self-interests. Indeed, that is the spirit of co-operation embodied by the Society.'

'I understand, Director.'

'And if the executive council gives its blessing to this operation, you must do nothing to prevent it from succeeding.'

'You have my word, Director.'

'Very well,' the Director said, looking about the room. 'All in favour, signify by saying aye.'

The meeting broke up just after dawn. One by one the members of the executive council left the villa and headed back across Mykonos to Chora. Picasso remained behind to have a private word with the Director.

'The Hartley Hall affair –' the Director said distantly, watching the sun appear on the horizon. 'It was a trap, wasn't it, Picasso?'

'It was a major victory for our service. It will make it more difficult for our detractors to say that we have lost our way in the post-Cold War world.' Picasso paused, then added carefully, 'I thought results like that were the goal of this organization.'

'Indeed.' The Director smiled briefly. 'You were well within your rights to act against the Ulster Freedom Brigade in order to further your own interests. But now the Society has decided to help the Brigade carry out a specific task – the assassination of Ambassador Cannon – and you must do nothing to prevent it from going forward.'

'I understand, Director.'

'In fact, there is one thing you can do to help.'

'What's that?'

'I intend to give the assignment to October,' the Director said. 'Michael Osbourne seems to have made it his crusade to find October and destroy him.'

'He has good reason.'

'Because of the Sarah Randolph affair?'

'Yes.'

The Director looked disappointed. 'Osbourne seems like such a talented officer,' he said. 'This fixation with avenging the past boggles the mind. When will this fellow get it through his head that it was nothing personal, just business?'

'Not any time soon, I'm afraid.'

'It's come to my attention that Osbourne is in charge of the search for October.'

'That's true, Director.'

'Perhaps it would be best for all concerned if he were given other responsibilities. Surely, an officer of such obvious talent could be better utilized elsewhere.'

'I couldn't agree more.'

The Director cleared his throat gently. 'Or perhaps it would be best if Osbourne was out of the way completely. He got quite close to us during the TransAtlantic affair. Too close for my comfort.'

'I would have no objections, Director.'

'Very well,' he said. 'It's done.'

Daphne wanted sun, and the Director reluctantly agreed to spend the rest of the day on Mykonos before returning to London. She lay on the terrace, her long body exposed to the sun. He never tired of watching her. The Director had long ago lost the ability to make love to a woman – he suspected it was the secrecy, the years of lying and dissembling, that had left him impotent – so he admired Daphne as one might admire a fine painting or sculpture. She was his most treasured possession.

He was naturally a restless man, despite his placid demeanour, and by the early afternoon he had had as much sun and sea air as he could endure. Besides, he was an operations man at heart, and he was anxious to get to work. They left at sundown and drove across Mykonos to the airport. That evening, after the Director's plane had left the island, a series of explosions ripped through the whitewashed villa on the cliffs of Cape Mavros.

Stavros, the estate agent, was the first to arrive. He telephoned the fire department from his cellular phone and watched as flames engulfed the villa. Monsieur Delaroche had given him a Paris number. He dialled the number, prepared to break the news to his client – that his beloved home above Panormos Bay was gone.

The telephone rang once, and a recorded voice came on the line. Stavros spoke a little French, enough to know that the number had been disconnected. He punched the button and severed the connection.

He watched as the firefighters vainly tried to put out the flames. He drove back to Ano Mera and went to the taverna. The usual crowd was there, drinking wine and eating olives and bread. Stavros told the story.

'There was always something funny about this man Delaroche,' Stavros said, when he had finished. He pulled his face into a smirk and stared into a cloudy glass of ouzo. 'I knew this the moment I set eyes on him.'

32

PARIS

Rebecca Wells was living in Montparnasse, in a drab apartment building a few blocks from the train terminal. Since her flight from Norfolk, she had stayed in the appalling flat most of the time, staring at French television programmes she couldn't comprehend. Sometimes, she listened to news from home on the radio. The Brigade had been crushed, and she was to blame.

She needed to get out. She picked herself off the couch and moved to the window. Grey, as usual: cold, dreary. Even Ulster was better than Paris in March. She went to the bathroom and looked into the mirror. A stranger stared back at her. Her rich black hair had been wrecked by the peroxide she had used in Norwich. Her skin was yellow from too little air and too many cigarettes. The skin beneath her eyes appeared bruised.

She pulled on a leather jacket and paused outside the bedroom door, listening to the clang of dumbbells. She knocked, and the clanging stopped. Roderick Campbell opened the door and stood there, shirtless, his lean body shining with sweat. Campbell was a Scot who had served in the British army, then put himself about as a mercenary and gunrunner in Africa and South America. He had cropped black hair, a goatee, and tattoos over his chest and arms. A naked whore lay on his bed, toying with one of his guns.

'I'm going out,' she said. 'I need some air.'

'Watch your back,' he said. He spoke with the soft brogue of his native Highlands. 'Want some company?'

'No, thanks.'

He held out a gun. 'Take this.'

The lift was broken again, so she took the stairs down to the street. God, but she was glad to be out of the place! She was angry with Kyle Blake for sending her to a man like Campbell. But things could be worse, she thought. She could be in jail or dead like the rest of them. The cold felt good, and she walked for a long time. Occasionally, she paused by a shop front and glanced behind her. She was confident she was not being followed.

For the first time in many days she felt genuine hunger. She went into a small café and, using her abysmal French, ordered an omelette with cheese and a *café crème*. She lit a cigarette and looked out the window. She wondered if it would always be like this – living in strange cities, surrounded by people she did not know.

She wanted to finish what they had started; she wanted Ambassador Douglas Cannon dead. She knew the Ulster Freedom Brigade was no longer capable of handling the job; effectively, there was no more Ulster Freedom Brigade. If the ambassador was going to be killed, someone else would have to do it. She had turned to Roderick Campbell for help. He knew the kind of men she needed: men who killed for a living, men who killed for no other reason but money.

When the waiter brought the food, Rebecca ate quickly. She could not remember the last time she had eaten real food. She finished the omelette and washed down some baguette with the coffee. The waiter reappeared and seemed astonished that her plate was empty.

'I was very hungry,' she said self-consciously.

She paid her bill and went out. Pulling her coat tightly to her throat, she walked the quiet streets of Montparnasse. A moment later she heard a car behind her. She stopped at a public phone and pretended to dial a number while she looked at the car: a black Citroën sedan, two men in front, one in back. Maybe French police. Maybe French intelligence, she thought. Maybe friends of Roderick. Maybe nothing.

She walked faster. She was suddenly sweating in spite of the cold. The driver of the Citroën pressed the accelerator, and the engine note grew louder. My God, she thought, they're going to run me over! She turned her head as the car swept past and braked to a halt a few yards ahead of her.

The rear passenger-side door opened. The man in the back leaned over and said, 'Good afternoon, Miss Wells.'

She was stunned. She stopped walking and looked at him. He had oiled blond hair, swept straight back from his forehead, and pale sunburned skin. 'Get in the car, please. I'm afraid it isn't safe for us to be talking on the street.'

He had the accent of an educated Englishman.

'Who are you?' she asked.

'We're not the authorities, if that's what you think,' he said. 'In fact, we're quite the opposite.'

'What do you want?'

'Actually, this has to do with what *you* want.'

She hesitated.

'Please, we haven't much time,' the blond man said, holding out a pale hand. 'And don't worry, Miss Wells. If we wanted to kill you, you'd already be dead.'

From Montparnasse they drove across Paris to an apartment building in the Fifth Arrondissement, on the rue Tournefort overlooking the Place de la Contrescarpe. The blond man disappeared in the Citroën. A balding man with a florid face relieved her of Roderick's gun and escorted her into a flat that had the air of a seldom-used pied-à-terre. The furnishings were masculine and comfortable: black informal couches and chairs grouped around a glass coffee table; teak bookshelves with histories, biographies, and thrillers by American and English writers. The remaining portions of the walls were bare, with faint outlines where framed paintings had once hung. The man closed the door and punched a six-digit code into a keypad, presumably arming the security system. Wordlessly, he held out his hand and led her into the bedroom.

The room was dark, except for a patch near the window, which was illuminated by rainy light leaking through the partially open blind. A moment after the door closed, a man spoke from the darkness. His voice was dry and precise, the voice of a man who did not like to repeat himself.

'It has come to our attention that you are looking for someone capable of assassinating the American ambassador in London,' the man said. 'I think we can be of assistance.'

'Who are you?'

'That's none of your affair. I *can* assure you that we are perfectly capable of carrying out a task like the one you have in mind. And with much less mess than that affair at Hartley Hall.'

Rebecca trembled with anger, which the man in the shadows seemed to detect.

'I'm afraid you were duped in Norfolk, Miss Wells,' he said. 'You walked straight into a trap engineered by the Central Intelligence Agency and MI5. The man who ran the operation was the ambassador's son-in-law, who happens to work for the CIA. His name is Michael Osbourne. Do you wish me to continue?'

She nodded.

'If you accept our offer of assistance, we will waive our

usual fee. Let me assure you that normally it is quite steep for a job like this – I suspect well beyond the means of an organization such as the Ulster Freedom Brigade.'

'You're willing to do it for nothing?' Rebecca asked incredulously.

'That's right.'

'And what do you want from me?'

'At the appropriate time, you will claim responsibility for the act.'

'Nothing more?'

'Nothing more.'

'And when it's over?'

'You'll have no further obligation, except under no circumstances are you ever to discuss our partnership with you. If you do discuss our arrangements, we reserve the right to take punitive measures.'

He paused for a moment to allow his warning to take hold.

'You may find it difficult to move about when this is all over,' he said. 'If you wish, we can provide services that will help you remain at large. We can provide you with false travel documents. We can help you alter your appearance. We have contacts with certain governments who are willing to protect fugitives in exchange for money or favours. Once again, we would be willing to supply these services to you at no charge.'

'Why?' she asked. 'Why are you willing to do this for nothing?'

'We are not a philanthropic organization, Miss Wells. We are willing to work with you because we have mutual interests.' A lighter flared, revealing a portion of his face for an instant before the room was in darkness again: silver hair, pale skin, a hard mouth, wintry eyes. 'I'm afraid it's no longer safe for you to remain in Paris,' he said. 'The French authorities are aware of your existence here.'

She felt as if iced water had been poured down the back of her neck. The thought of being arrested, of being sent back to Britain in chains, made her physically sick.

'You need to leave France at once,' he said. 'I propose Bahrain. The head of the security forces is an old colleague of mine. You'll be safe, and there are worse places to be than the Persian Gulf in March. The weather is quite glorious this time of year.'

'I'm not interested in spending the rest of my days lying next to a pool in Bahrain.'

'What are you trying to say, Miss Wells?'

'That I want to be a part of it,' she said. 'I'll accept your help, but I want to be there to watch the man die.'

'Are you trained?'

'Yes,' she said.

'Have you ever killed?'

She thought of the night two months earlier – the barn in County Armagh – when she had shot Charlie Bates. 'Yes,' she said evenly. 'I've killed.'

'The man I have in mind for the assignment prefers to work alone,' the man said, 'but I suspect he will see the wisdom of taking on a partner for this contract.'

'When do I leave?'

'Tonight.'

'I'd like to go back to the flat, pick up a few things.'

'I'm afraid that's not possible.'

'What about Roderick? What's he going to think if I disappear without explanation?'

'Let us worry about Roderick Campbell.'

The blond man drove the Citroën back to Montparnasse and parked outside Roderick Campbell's apartment building. He got out and crossed the street. He had stolen the woman's keys. He opened the main door on the ground level and walked up the stairs to the apartment.

Removing the high-powered Herstal automatic from the waistband of his jeans, he opened the door and quietly slipped inside.

33

AMSTERDAM

The forecast for the Dutch coast was decent for March, so Delaroche mounted his Italian road bike early that morning and pedalled south. He wore long black cycling shorts and a white cotton turtleneck beneath his bright yellow jersey, tight enough to avoid flapping in the wind, loose enough to conceal the Beretta automatic beneath his left armpit. He headed south toward Leiden through the Bloembollenstreek, the largest flower-producing region in Holland, his powerful legs pumping effortlessly through fields already ablaze with colour.

For a time his eyes took in the Dutch countryside – the dykes and the canals, the windmills and the fields of flowers – but after a while the face of Maurice Leroux appeared in his thoughts. He had come to Delaroche in a dream the previous night, standing before him, white as a snowdrift, two holes in his chest, still wearing the foolish beret.

I can be trusted. I've done many men like you.

Delaroche entered Leiden and had lunch at an outdoor café on the edge of the Rhine. Here, just a few miles from its mouth on the North Sea, the river was narrow and slow-moving, quite unlike the mountain whitewater near its birthplace high in the Alps or the wide industrial giant of the German plain. Delaroche ordered coffee and a sandwich of ham and cheese.

The inability to purge his subconscious of Leroux's image unnerved him. Usually, he suffered only a brief period of uneasiness after a killing. But it had been a week since he had killed Leroux, and he still saw his face floating through his mind.

He thought of the man called Vladimir. Delaroche had been taken from his mother at birth and given to the KGB to raise. Vladimir had been his entire world. He had trained him in languages and tradecraft. He had tried to teach him something about life before teaching him how to kill. Vladimir had warned him that it would happen eventually. *One day you will take a life and that man will follow you*, Vladimir had said. *He will take his meals with you, share your bed. When that happens, it is time for you to leave the trade, because a man who sees ghosts can no longer behave like a professional.*

Delaroche paid his bill and left the café. The weather worsened as he moved toward the North Sea. The sky grew overcast and the air turned colder. He fought a stiff headwind all the way to Haarlem.

Perhaps Vladimir had been right. Perhaps it was time for him to get out of the game before the game caught up with him. He could move back to the Mediterranean, and he could spend the days riding his bicycles and painting his paintings and drinking his wine on his terrace overlooking the sea, and to hell with Vladimir and to hell with his father, and to hell with the Director and everyone else who had forced this life on him. Perhaps he could find a woman – a woman like Astrid Vogel, a woman with enough dangerous secrets of her own that she could be trusted with his.

He had wanted to leave once before but with Astrid gone, there hadn't been much point, and the Director had made him a generous offer that was too good to turn down. The Director paid him a tremendous amount of money and provided Delaroche with protection from his enemies. If he left the Society, Delaroche would be on his own. He would have to see to his own security or find a new guardian.

He entered Haarlem and crossed the River Spaarne. Amsterdam was fifteen miles away, a good ride along the banks of the Noordzeekanaal. The wind was at Delaroche's back, the road smooth and flat, so it took him little more than half an hour to reach the city.

He took his time making his way to the Herengracht. He entered his flat and checked his telltales to make certain no one had been there in his absence. There was another hastily scrawled note from the German girl. *I want to see you again you cocksucker! Eva.*

He switched on his computer and logged onto the Internet. He had one E-mail message. He opened it and typed in his code name. The message was from the Director; he wanted to meet Delaroche the following day in Amsterdam in the Vondelpark.

Delaroche sent back a message saying he would be there.

The following morning Delaroche meandered through the stalls of the Albert Cuypmarkt in the Eastern Canal Ring. He meticulously checked his tail as he strolled past baskets laden with fruit, fish from the North Sea, Dutch cheeses, and freshly cut flowers. Satisfied he wasn't being followed, he walked from the market to the Vondelpark, the sprawling public gardens near Amsterdam's Museum Quarter. He spotted the Director, seated on a park bench overlooking a duck pond, the tall Jamaican girl next to him.

The Director had not seen Delaroche since the plastic surgery in Athens. Delaroche did not enjoy games or other amusements – the isolation and secrecy of his life had robbed him of any opportunity to develop a true sense of humour – but he decided to play a prank to test the effectiveness of Maurice Leroux's work on his face.

He placed a cigarette into his mouth and put on his sunglasses. He approached the Director and, speaking in Dutch, asked him for a light. The Director handed Delaroche a heavy silver lighter. Delaroche lit the cigarette and handed the lighter back to the Director. '*Dank u,*' Delaroche said. The Director nodded distantly as he placed the lighter back in his coat pocket.

Delaroche walked away along the footpath. He returned a few moments later and sat next to the Director, eating a pear he had purchased in the Albert Cuypmarkt, saying nothing. The Director and the girl walked away and sat down on another bench. Delaroche eyed them curiously for a moment; then he stood too and joined them on the next bench.

The Director frowned. 'I say, do you mind –'

'I believe you wanted to see me,' Delaroche said, removing his sunglasses.

'Dear God,' the Director murmured. 'Is that really you?'

'I'm afraid so.'

'You're quite hideous. No wonder you killed the poor bastard.'

'I have a contract for you.'

The Director's eyes flickered back and forth as the two men moved in tandem along the footpath through the Vondelpark. He had started as a field man – he had parachuted into France with the SOE during the war and run agents in Berlin against the Russians – and his survival instincts were still sharp.

'Have you been following the situation in Northern Ireland?' the Director asked.

'I read the newspapers.'

'Then you know that a Protestant terrorist group called the Ulster Freedom Brigade tried and failed to murder the

American ambassador to the Court of St James's, Douglas Cannon.'

Delaroche nodded. 'I read about it, yes.'

'What you don't know is that the assassination team walked straight into a trap engineered by MI5 and the CIA. The CIA officer in charge of the American end of things was an old friend of yours.'

Delaroche glared at the Director. 'Osbourne?'

The Director nodded. 'Needless to say, the Ulster Freedom Brigade would like both the ambassador and his son-in-law dead, and we've agreed to do the job for them.'

'To what end?'

'The Brigade would like to destroy the peace process and, frankly, so would we. It's bad for business. In less than two weeks' time, on St Patrick's Day, President Beckwith is holding a meeting of Northern Irish leaders at the White House. Douglas Cannon will be there.'

'You know this for certain?'

'I have an impeccable source. The Americans are good at protecting their ambassadors abroad, but at home it's quite another story. Cannon will be lightly guarded, if at all. A professional of your skill should have no difficulty fulfilling the terms of the contract.'

'Do I have a choice?'

'Let me remind you that I pay you a tremendous amount of money and provide protection for you,' the Director said coldly. 'In return, you kill for me. It's a simple arrangement.'

The Director had always behaved rather like a befuddled old don in Delaroche's presence, but clearly he was a man who would use whatever means at his disposal to achieve his ends.

'Actually, I would have thought you'd be thrilled at the opportunity to engage your old enemy,' the Director said.

'Why would you assume that?'

'Because of Astrid Vogel. I'm astonished that you haven't killed Osbourne on your own already.'

'I didn't kill him because I wasn't hired to kill him,' Delaroche said. 'I'm an assassin, not a murderer.'

'Some people might see that as a distinction without a difference, but I understand your point and I respect you for it. However, Osbourne continues to be a serious threat to your security. I'd sleep better if he were no longer with us.'

Delaroche stopped walking and turned to face the Director.

'Two weeks is not much time – especially for a job in the United States.'

'It's certainly enough time for you.'

Delaroche nodded. 'I'll do it.'

'Brilliant,' the Director said. 'Now that you've agreed to take on the contract, there's a catch. I'd like you to work with a partner.'

'I don't work with people I don't know.'

'I understand, but I'm asking you to make an exception in this case.'

'Who is he?'

'*She*, actually. Her name is Rebecca Wells. She's the woman who survived the Ulster Freedom Brigade's attempt to assassinate Douglas Cannon in England.'

'She's an amateur,' Delaroche said.

'She's a seasoned operative, and she's been blooded. For political reasons, we believe it's important for her to take part in the operation. I'm sure you'll enjoy the opportunity to work with her.'

'And if I refuse?'

'Then I'm afraid you'll forfeit your salary and the protection I provide you.'

'Where is she?'

The Director pointed down the gravel footpath. 'Walk that way about a hundred yards. You'll find her seated on a bench: blonde hair, reading a copy of *Die Welt*. I'll begin preparing the dossiers and arranging your transport to America. Remain here in Amsterdam until I contact you.'

And with that the Director turned and melted into the fog drifting over the Vondelpark.

Delaroche purchased a small map of central Amsterdam from a tourist booth in the park. He sat down on the bench next to the one where Rebecca Wells was dutifully pretending to read the previous day's edition of *Die Welt*. He was less interested in the woman than in what was going on around her. For twenty minutes he scanned faces, looking for signs of physical surveillance. She appeared to be alone, but he wanted to make certain. He circled a spot on the map and walked over to her. 'Meet me here in exactly two hours,' he said, handing her the folded map. 'Keep moving, and don't arrive a minute early.'

The spot Delaroche had circled on the map was the National Monument in Dam Square. Rebecca Wells remained in Vondelpark for more than half an hour, wandering through the gardens and past the winding lakes. Once, she doubled back expertly and forced Delaroche to lunge into a public toilet for cover.

From the park she walked to the Van Gogh Museum. She purchased a pass from the ticket window at the main entrance and went in. Delaroche followed her easily through the crowded museum. Van Gogh had been one of his earliest influences; he became distracted by one of his favourite works, *Crows in the Wheatfield*, and lost track of her. He found her a moment later, lingering before *The Bedroom at Arles*. Something about the colourful canvas,

Van Gogh's celebration of domestic peace, seemed to intrigue her.

She left the museum, wandered through the Albert Cuypmarkt, and walked along the Singel until she reached the Amstel River. There, she jumped suddenly onto a passing tram. Delaroche flagged down a taxi and followed her.

She took the tram to the Leidseplein and walked to an outdoor café near the American Hotel, where she had coffee and a pastry. Delaroche watched her from a café on the other side of the canal. She paid her bill and stood up, but instead of walking away along the sidewalk, she ducked inside the café.

Delaroche quickly crossed the canal. In Dutch, he asked the waiter if he had seen his girlfriend – an Irishwoman, a bleached blonde. The waiter nodded toward the toilet. Delaroche knocked on the door. There was no answer, so he opened it; the woman was gone. He peered through the kitchen and saw that there was a service entrance leading out into a narrow alley. He walked through the kitchen, ignoring the protests of the chefs, and entered the alley. There was no sign of her.

He took a tram to Dam Square and found her seated next to one of the lions at the foot of the National Monument. She looked at her watch and smiled. 'Where have you been?' she said. 'I was worried about you.'

'You're not being followed,' Delaroche said, sitting down next to her, 'but you move like an amateur.'

'I lost you – didn't I?'

'I'm one man on foot. Anyone can lose one man on foot.'

'Listen to me, you bastard. I'm from Portadown, Northern Ireland. Don't fuck with me. I'm cold, I'm tired, and I've had enough of this shit. The old man said you'd give me a place to stay. Let's go.'

*

They walked in silence along the Prinsengracht until they reached the *Krista*. Delaroche hopped down onto the aft deck and held out his hand for Rebecca to follow. She remained on the pavement, staring at him as if he were mad. 'If you think I'm going to live on a fucking barge –'

'It's not a barge,' he said. 'Take my hand. I'll show you.'

She boarded the houseboat without his help and watched him open the padlock on the hatch over the companionway. She followed him down into the salon and looked around at the comfortable furnishings.

'Is this your boat?' she asked.

'It belongs to a friend of mine.'

She tried the switch on one of the lamps, but nothing happened. Delaroche went back onto the deck, removed the boat's power cable, and plugged it into a public outlet on the sidewalk. An instant later, *Krista*'s salon burned with warm light.

'Do you have any money?' Delaroche asked, as he came back down the companionway.

'The old man gave me some,' she said. 'Who is he, by the way?'

'He's called the Director.'

'The director of what?'

'The director of the organization that is helping you kill the ambassador.'

'What's it called?'

Delaroche remained silent.

'You don't know what it's called?'

'I know,' he said.

'Do you know who belongs to it?'

'I've made it my business to find out.'

She walked through the salon and sat down on the edge of Astrid's bed. Delaroche switched on the small heater.

'Do you have a name?' she asked.

'Sometimes,' he said.

'What should I call you?'

'You can stay here until we leave for America,' Delaroche said, ignoring her question. 'You'll need clean clothes and food. I'll bring some things for you later this afternoon. Do you smoke?'

She nodded.

Delaroche tossed her a packet of cigarettes. 'I'll bring you more.'

'Thank you.'

'Do you have any other languages?'

'No,' she said.

Delaroche exhaled sharply and shook his head.

'I didn't need other languages to operate in Northern Ireland.'

'This isn't Northern Ireland,' he said. 'Can you do anything about that accent?'

'What's wrong with my accent?'

'You might as well hang an Orange sash across your chest.'

'I can speak like an Englishwoman.'

'Please do,' he said, and with that he pounded up the companionway and closed the hatch behind him.

34

One week after the Director's meeting with Delaroche in Amsterdam, Michael Osbourne returned to the Counter-terrorism Center for the first time since leaving London. He punched in his code at the secure door and stepped inside. Carter was sitting at his desk, hunched over a stack of memos, clearly irritated. He looked up at Michael and frowned. 'Well, well, Sir Michael has decided to grace us with his presence,' Carter said.

'It's an honorary knighthood. Your Majesty will do just fine.'

Carter smiled. 'Welcome home. We missed you. Every-thing all right?'

'Couldn't be better.'

'You have ten minutes to get read-in. Then I need to see you and Cynthia in my office.'

'Fine. I'll see you in half an hour.'

Michael walked down Abu Nidal Boulevard to his cubicle. One of the Center's wits had hung a large Union Jack over the cubicle wall, and 'God Save the Queen' issued softly from a small tape player.

'Very funny,' Michael called out, to no one in particular.

Blaze and Eurotrash appeared, followed by Cynthia Martin and Gigabyte. 'We just wanted to dress the place up a little bit for you, Sir Michael,' Blaze said. 'You know, make it feel a little less like Langley and a little more like home.'

'That was very thoughtful of you.'

Blaze, Eurotrash, and Gigabyte drifted away, singing a throaty rendition of 'He is an Englishman.' Cynthia remained behind and sat down in the chair facing Michael's desk. 'Congratulations, Michael. You pulled off quite a coup.'

'Thank you. I appreciate that.'

'Secretly, I think I was hoping you'd fall flat on your face. Nothing personal, you understand.'

'At least that's honest.'

'Honesty has always been something of an affliction with me.'

Michael smiled. 'My father-in-law's coming to Washington a couple of days before the White House conference on Northern Ireland starts. He wants to spend some time with his grandchildren and see some old friends on the Hill. We're having a small dinner party the night before the conference. Why don't you join us? I know Douglas would value your opinion.'

'I'd love to.'

Michael scribbled his address on a slip of paper and handed it to her.

'Seven o'clock,' he said.

'I'll be there,' Cynthia said, folding the paper. 'See you in Carter's office.'

Michael sat down, switched on his computer, and read the overnight cables. An RUC patrol had discovered a car filled with 200lb of Semtex in County Antrim outside Belfast. A Republican splinter group called the Real IRA was thought to be responsible. Michael closed the cable and opened another. A Catholic man had been shot dead near Banbridge in County Down. The RUC suspected that the Loyalist Volunteer Force, an ultra-violent Protestant extremist group, was responsible. Michael opened the next cable. The Portadown lodge of the Orange Order had filed the proposed route for its annual parade. Once again it was demanding the right to march along the Garvaghy Road. This summer's marching season promised to be as confrontational as the last.

He logged off the computer and walked into Carter's office. Cynthia was already there.

'I hope you two don't plan on having a life for the next forty-eight hours,' Carter said.

'Our life is the Agency, Adrian,' Michael said.

'I just got off the phone with Bill Bristol.'

'Are we supposed to be impressed because you spoke with the president's national security adviser?'

'Would you shut the fuck up for one minute and let me finish?'

Cynthia Martin smiled and looked down at her notebook.

Carter said, 'Beckwith has a bug up his ass about the Northern Ireland conference. It seems his poll numbers are down, and he wants to use the peace process to shore up his approval rating.'

'Isn't that nice,' Michael said. 'How can we be of service?'

'By making sure he's fully prepared for the conference. He needs a complete picture of the situation on the ground in Ulster. He needs background and intelligence to know how far he can push the Loyalists and the Nationalists to move things along. He needs to know whether we think a presidential trip to Northern Ireland is a good idea, given the climate.'

'When?' Michael asked.

'You and Cynthia are briefing Bristol at the White House the day after tomorrow.'

'Oh, good, I thought it was going to be something unreasonable.'

'If you two don't think you can handle it –'

'We can handle it.'

'I thought so.'

Michael and Cynthia stood up. Carter said, 'Hold on a minute, Michael.'

'You guys want to talk about me behind my back?' Cynthia asked.

'How'd you guess?' Adrian said.

Cynthia scowled at Carter and went out.

Carter said, 'Don't make any plans for lunch.'

The CIA dining room is on the seventh floor, behind a heavy metal door that looks as though it might lead to the boiler room. It used to be called the executive dining room until Personnel discovered that the junior staff found the name offensive. The Agency got rid of the word 'executive' and opened the restaurant to all employees. Technically, workers from the loading dock could come to the seventh floor and eat lunch with deputy directors and division chiefs. Still, most staff preferred the massive basement cafeteria, affectionately known as 'the swill pit,' where they could gossip without fear of being overheard by superiors.

Monica Tyler sat at a table next to the window overlooking the thick trees along the Potomac. Her two ever-present factotums, known derisively as Tweedledum and Tweedledee, sat next to her, each clutching a leather folder as though they contained lost secrets of the ancient world. The tables around them were empty; Monica Tyler had a way of creating vacant space around herself, rather like a psychopath with a fistful of dynamite.

Monica remained seated as Michael and Carter entered the room and sat down. A waitress brought menus and order cards. Guests in the dining room did not give their orders verbally; instead, they had to meticulously fill out a small form and total their own bill. The Agency wits joked that the forms were collected at the end of each day and sent to Personnel for psychological evaluation. Carter sought vainly to engage Monica in small talk while he struggled with the complex order form. Michael knew the meal would be billed to the Director's office, so he selected the most expensive items on the menu: shrimp cocktail, broiled crab cakes, and *crème brûlée* for dessert. Tweedledee filled out Monica's form for her.

'Now that you've managed to neutralize the Ulster Freedom Brigade,' Monica began suddenly, 'we think it's time that you leave the Northern Ireland task force and move on to something more productive.'

Michael looked at Carter, who shrugged. 'Who's we?' Michael asked.

Monica looked up from her salad as though she found the question impertinent. 'The Seventh Floor, of course.'

'Actually, I was hoping I could spend more time working on the October case,' Michael said.

'Actually, I intend to remove you from the October case altogether.'

Michael pushed away his plate of half-eaten shrimp and laid his napkin on the table. 'Part of our agreement about my return to the Agency was that I would be allowed to spend part of my time searching for him. Why are you trying to back out of our agreement?'

'To be honest with you, Michael, Adrian thought that allowing you to pursue October might be enough to entice you back to the Center. But I never thought much of the idea, and I still don't. Once again, you've proven yourself to be an effective officer, and I would be derelict if I permitted you to continue to work on a case that is unlikely to bear fruit.'

'But it *has* borne fruit, Monica. I've proven October is still alive and still working as an assassin and terrorist.'

'No, Michael, you didn't prove he's alive. You *theorize*

that he is still alive, based on an enhancement of a photograph of a hand. That is quite a long way from ironclad proof.'

'We rarely deal with ironclad proof in this business, Monica.'

'Don't lecture me, Michael.'

They fell silent as the waitress appeared and cleared away the first course.

'We've sent an alert to Interpol,' Monica resumed. 'We've given warnings to our allies. There is little else that can be done. At this point, it is a law enforcement matter, and this is not a law enforcement agency.'

'I disagree,' Michael said.

'On which point?'

'You know which point.'

Monica's acolytes stirred in their seats restlessly. Carter picked at a loose thread in the tablecloth. Nothing infuriated Monica Tyler more than being challenged by someone below her on the Agency food chain.

'Someone hired October to assassinate Ahmed Hussein,' Michael said. 'Someone is providing him with protection, travel documents, money. We need to find out who's sponsoring him. That's intelligence work, Monica, not law enforcement.'

'Once again, Michael, you're assuming October was the man in Cairo. It could have been an Israeli intelligence officer. It could have been a rival member of Hamas. It could have been a PLO assassin.'

'It could have been a Peking duck, but it wasn't. It was October.'

'I disagree.' She smiled to demonstrate that she had borrowed Michael's words intentionally. Her eyes flickered about him, as if searching for the best place to insert her dagger.

Michael yielded. 'What do you have in mind for me?'

'The Middle East peace process is on life support,' she said. 'Hamas is planting bombs in Jerusalem, and we've received indications the Sword of Gaza is about to go operational in Europe. In all likelihood, that means they will target Americans. I want you to finish the preparations for the White House conference on Northern Ireland, and then I want you back on the Sword of Gaza.'

'What if I'm not interested?'

'Then I'm afraid your return to the Central Intelligence Agency, though highly successful, will be rather brief.'

Morton Dunne was to the Agency as 'Q' was to Bond's Secret Service. The deputy chief of the Office of Technical Services, Dunne was the maker of exploding pens and high-frequency microphone transmitters that could be hidden in a belt buckle. He was an MIT-trained electrical engineer who could have earned five times his government salary in the private sector. He chose the Agency because the paraphernalia of espionage had always intrigued him. In his spare time he maintained the antique spy cameras and weapons housed in the Agency's makeshift museum. He was also one of the world's top designers of experimental kites. On weekends he could be found on the Ellipse, flying his creations around the Washington Monument. Once he placed a high-resolution miniature camera aboard a kite and photographed every square inch of the White House South Lawn.

'You have authorization for this, I assume,' Dunne said, seated in front of a large computer monitor. He was prototype MIT – thin, pale as a cave dweller, with wire-rimmed glasses that were forever slipping down the bridge of his narrow nose. 'I can't do this without authorization from your chief.'

'I'll bring you the chit later this afternoon, but I need the photos now.'

Dunne laid his hands on the keyboard. 'What was his name?'

'October. The one we did last month for the Interpol alert.'

'Oh, yeah, I remember,' Dunne said, his fingers rattling over the keyboard. A moment later the face of October appeared on the screen. 'What do you want me to do?'

'I think he may have undergone plastic surgery to change his face,' Michael said. 'I'm almost certain the work was done by a Frenchman named Maurice Leroux.'

'Dr Leroux could have done any number of things to alter his appearance.'

'Can you show me a few?' Michael asked. 'Can you give me a complete series? Change the hair, give him a beard, the works.'

'It's going to take a while.'

'I'll wait.'

'Sit over there,' Dunne said. 'And for God's sake, Osbourne, don't touch anything.'

It was just after midnight when Monica Tyler's chauffeured car arrived at the Harbor Place complex on the waterfront in Georgetown. Her bodyguard opened the door and shadowed her through the lobby into the elevator. He walked her to the door of her apartment and remained there as she went inside.

She ran water in her oversized bath and undressed. It was nearly morning in London. The Director was a notorious early riser; she knew he would be at his desk in a few minutes. She slipped into the bath and relaxed in the warm water. When she was finished, she wrapped herself in a thick white robe.

She went into the living room and sat down behind the mahogany desk. There were three telephones: an eight-line standard phone, an internal phone for Langley, and a special secure phone that permitted her to conduct conversations without fear of eavesdroppers. She looked at the antique gold desk clock, a gift from her old firm on Wall Street: 12:45 A.M.

Monica thought of the circumstances – the coincidences, political alliances, and serendipity – that had brought her to the top of the Central Intelligence Agency. She had graduated second in her class at Yale Law, but instead of heading off to a big firm she added an MBA from Harvard to her résumé and went to Wall Street to make money. There she met Ronald Clark, a Republican fund-raiser and wise man who drifted in and out of Washington each time the Republicans controlled the White House. Monica followed Clark to the Treasury, Commerce, State, and Defense. When President Beckwith appointed Clark to be Director of Central Intelligence, Monica became the executive director, the second most powerful position in the CIA. When Clark decided to retire, Monica lobbied for the top job, and Beckwith gave it to her.

Ronald Clark left her a CIA in disarray. A series of other spy cases, including the Aldrich Ames case, had devastated morale. The Agency had failed to predict either that India and Pakistan were about to explode nuclear devices or that Iran and North Korea were about to test ballistic missiles capable of hitting their neighbours. During her confirmation hearings, several senators pressed her to justify the size and cost of the Central Intelligence Agency; one wondered aloud whether the United States really needed a CIA now that the Cold War was over.

She was supposed to be a mere caretaker, someone to keep the chair in the DCI's office warm for a couple of years, until Beckwith's successor could appoint his intelligence chief. But she was incapable of playing the role of caretaker and set out on a mission to make herself indispensable to whomever sat in the Oval Office after Beckwith; Republican or Democrat.

She believed she was the only person at Langley with the vision to lead the Agency through the uncertain terrain of the post-Cold War period. She had studied the history of intelligence well. She knew that sometimes it was necessary to sacrifice a few in order to ensure the survival of the many. She felt a kinship with the deception officers of the Second World War who sent men and women to their deaths in order to deceive Nazi Germany. She would never permit the Agency to be castrated. She would never allow the United States to be without an adequate intelligence service. And she would do anything to make certain *she* was the one who was running it. Which is why she had joined the Society and why she abided by its code.

At 1:00 A.M. she picked up the receiver on the secure telephone and dialled. A few seconds later she heard the pleasant, cultured voice of the Director's assistant, Daphne. Then the Director came on the line.

'You no longer need to worry about Osbourne,' she said. 'He's been reassigned, and the October case file has been effectively closed. As far as the CIA is concerned, October is dead and buried.'

'Well done,' the Director said.

'Where's the package now?'

'Bound for the Caribbean,' he said. 'It should be arriving in the States some time in the next thirty-six to forty-eight hours. And then it will be all over.'

'Excellent,' she said.

'I trust you will pass along any information that might help the package arrive at its destination on time.'

'Of course, Director.'

'I knew I could count on you. Good morning, Picasso,' the Director said, and the line went dead.

35

The *Boston Whaler* bounced over the choppy waters of the Chesapeake. The night was clear and bitterly cold; a bright three-quarter moon floated high above the eastern horizon. Delaroche had doused the running lights shortly after entering the mouth of the bay. He reached forward and pressed a button on the dash-mounted navigation unit. The GPS system automatically calculated his precise longitude and latitude; they were in the centre of the busy shipping lanes of the Chesapeake Channel.

Rebecca Wells stood next to him, clutching the wheel of the *Whaler*'s second console. Without speaking, she pointed over the prow. Ahead of them, perhaps a mile away, shone the lights of a container vessel. Delaroche turned a few degrees to port and sped toward the shallow waters of the western shore.

Delaroche had meticulously plotted his course up the Chesapeake during the long ride from Nassau to the East Coast. They had made that leg of the journey aboard a large oceangoing yacht, piloted by a pair of former SAS men from the Society. He and Rebecca stayed in adjoining staterooms. By day they studied charts of the Chesapeake, reviewed the dossiers of Michael Osbourne and Douglas Cannon, and memorized the streets of Washington. At night they went onto the aft deck and took target practice with Delaroche's Berettas. Rebecca pressed him for his name, but each time she asked, Delaroche simply shook his head and changed the subject. Out of frustration she christened him 'Pierre,' which Delaroche detested. On the last night aboard the yacht, he admitted that he had no real name, but if she felt it necessary to refer to him by something, he should be called Jean-Paul.

Delaroche was still furious about being forced to work with the woman, but the Director had been right about one thing: she was no amateur. The conflict in Northern Ireland had sharpened her skills to a fine edge. She had a superb memory and sound operational instincts. She was tall and quite strong for a woman, and after three nights of training with the Beretta, she was a more than adequate shot. Delaroche was concerned with only one thing – her idealism. He believed in nothing but his art. Zealots unnerved him. Astrid Vogel had been a believer like Rebecca once – when she was a member of West Germany's communist terrorist group, the Red Army Faction – but by the time she and Delaroche worked together she had been stripped of her ideals and was in it only for the money.

Delaroche had memorized every detail of the Chesapeake – the shoals, the rivers and bays, the flats and the headlands. All he required was a reading from his GPS unit to know exactly where he was in relation to land. He had passed Sandy Point, Cherry Point, and Windmill Point. By the time he reached Bluff Point he had grown stiff and sore with the cold. He cut the engines, and they drank hot coffee from a thermos flask.

He checked the GPS navigation unit: 38.50 degrees latitude by 76.31 degrees longitude. He knew he was approaching Curtis Point, a headland at the mouth of the West River. His destination was the next tidal river feeding into the bay from Maryland, the South River, roughly three nautical miles to the north. As he passed Saunders Point he saw the first light in the east, off the starboard side of the *Whaler*. He rounded Turkey Point and felt the gentle nudge of the tide running out of the South River.

Delaroche opened the throttle as he headed northeast up the river. He wanted to be ashore and on the road before dawn. He sped past Mayo Point and Brewer Point, Glebe Bay and Crab Creek. He passed beneath one bridge, then another. He came to a creek mouth and checked his navigation unit to make certain it was Broad Creek. The receding tide had left the creek shallower than the charts had promised; twice Delaroche jumped into the frigid water and pushed the *Whaler* off the bottom.

Finally, he reached the head of the creek. He grounded the *Whaler* in a patch of marsh grass, killed the engine, hopped overboard, and, pulling on the bowline, dragged the boat deep into the marsh.

Rebecca clambered into the forward seating compartment and took hold of a large duffel filled with supplies: clothing, money, and electronic equipment. She handed the bag to Delaroche, then stepped over the side into the sodden marsh. The car was parked on a dirt track, exactly where the Director had said it would be: a black Volvo sedan, Quebec licence plates.

Delaroche had a key. He opened the boot and tossed in the bag. He followed a series of two-lane country roads for several miles, through farmland and sunlit pastures, until he came to Route 50. He turned onto the highway and headed east toward Washington.

One hour after collecting the Volvo, they entered Washington on New York Avenue, a grimy commuter corridor stretching from the Northeast section of the city to the Maryland suburbs. Delaroche had stopped once at a roadside gas station so he and Rebecca could change into proper clothing. He crossed the city on Massachusetts Avenue and pulled into the drive of the Embassy Row hotel near Dupont Circle. There was a reservation waiting in the name of Mr and Mrs Claude Duras of Montreal.

The demands of their cover story required Delaroche and Rebecca to share a single room. They slept until the late afternoon, Rebecca in the queen-sized bed, Delaroche on the floor, with the bedspread as a mattress. He awoke suddenly at 4 P.M., startled by the surroundings, and realized he had been dreaming again of Maurice Leroux.

He ordered coffee sent to the room, which he drank while he placed several items into a blue nylon backpack: two pieces of sophisticated electronic equipment, two cellular telephones, a flashlight, several small tools, and a Beretta 9-millimetre. Rebecca emerged from the bathroom, dressed in blue jeans, tennis shoes, and a sweatshirt emblazoned with the words WASHINGTON, D.C. and an image of the White House.

'How do I look?' she asked.

'Your hair is too blonde.' Delaroche reached in the duffel bag and tossed her a baseball cap. 'Put this on.'

Delaroche telephoned downstairs and asked the valet to have the Volvo waiting. He drove west along P Street. There was a tourist map on the dashboard that Delaroche did not bother to open; the streets of Washington, like the waters of the Chesapeake, were engraved in his memory.

He crossed into Georgetown and drove along the quiet leafy streets. It was considered the most glamorous neighbourhood in Washington, with red-brick sidewalks and large Federal-style homes, but to Delaroche, whose eye was used to the canals and gabled houses of Amsterdam, it all seemed rather prosaic.

He drove west on P Street until he reached Wisconsin Avenue. He headed south on Wisconsin, accompanied by the pounding beat of rap music vibrating from the gold BMW behind him. He turned onto N Street, and the madness of Wisconsin Avenue slowly dissipated behind them.

The house was empty, just as Delaroche knew it would be. Ambassador Cannon was arriving from London the following afternoon. He was hosting a private dinner party for friends and family that evening. The next day he would take part in the conference on Northern Ireland at the White House, then attend a series of receptions in the evening hosted by the parties to the talks. It was all in the Director's dossier.

Delaroche parked around the corner from the house, on Thirty-third Street. He placed a camera around his neck and strolled the quiet block, Rebecca on his arm, pausing now and again to gaze at the large brick townhouses with light spilling from their windows. It was rather like Amsterdam, he thought, the way people kept their curtains open and allowed passers-by to gaze into their homes and assess their possessions.

He had been there before; he knew the challenges that N Street posed to a man like him. There were no cafés in which to dawdle over coffee, no shops for diversionary purchases, no squares or parks to kill time without attracting attention – just large expensive homes, with nosy neighbours and security systems.

They walked past the Osbournes' house. A black sedan was parked across the street. Seated behind the wheel was a man in a tan raincoat, reading the sports section of *The Washington Post*. So much for the Director's theory that Ambassador Cannon would be easy to kill while he was in Washington, Delaroche thought. The man hadn't even set foot in town yet, and already the house was under watch.

Delaroche paused a block away and made photographs of the home where John Kennedy had lived when he was a senator from Massachusetts. A number of Cabinet secretaries lived in Georgetown; their homes were under constant surveillance. If the official was involved in national security, such as the secretary of state or the defence secretary, their bodyguards might even have a static post in a nearby apartment. But Delaroche felt confident that Douglas Cannon's security consisted entirely of the man in the tan raincoat – at least for now.

He led Rebecca south on Thirty-first Street for half a block, until they reached an alley that ran behind the Osbournes' house. He peered into the half darkness; just as he suspected, it looked as if the back of the house was not under watch.

Delaroche handed Rebecca a cellular telephone. 'Stay here. Call if there's trouble. If I'm not back in five minutes, leave and go back to the hotel. If you don't hear from me within half an hour, contact the Director and request an extraction.'

Rebecca nodded. Delaroche turned and set out down the alley. He paused behind the Osbournes' house, then deftly scaled the fence and dropped into a well-tended garden surrounding a small swimming pool. He looked overhead and followed the lines leading from the telephone pole in the alley to the point where they attached to the house. He crossed the garden and knelt in front of the telephone switchbox at the back of the house. He unzipped the backpack and removed his tools and a flashlight. Holding the flashlight between his teeth, he loosened the screws holding the cover of the switchbox in place and studied the configuration of the lines for a moment.

There were two lines leading into the house, but Delaroche only had the equipment to tap one of them. He suspected one line was probably reserved for telephone calls, the other for a fax machine or modem. He reached inside the backpack again and withdrew a small electronic device. Attached to the Osbournes' telephone line, it would relay a high-frequency radio signal to Delaroche's cellular phone, allowing him to monitor the Osbournes' telephone calls. It took Delaroche only two minutes to install the device on the Osbournes' primary line and reattach the cover of the switchbox.

The second device would be much easier to install, since it required only a window. It was a bugging mechanism that, when attached to the exterior of a window, would detect the vibration of sound waves inside the structure and convert them back into simulated audio. Delaroche attached the sensor pad to the lower portion of a window off the main living room. It was concealed by a shrub outside and an end table inside. He buried the converter and transmitter unit in a patch of mulch in the garden.

Delaroche retraced his steps across the lawn. He tossed the backpack over the fence, then scaled it and dropped down into the alley. The two units he had just placed on the Osbournes' house had an effective range of two miles, which would allow him to monitor the Osbournes from the security of their hotel room at Dupont Circle.

Rebecca was waiting for him at the end of the alley.

'Let's go,' he said.

He took her by the hand and walked back to the Volvo.

Delaroche sat in front of a receiver the size of a shoebox,

testing the signal of the transmitter he had placed on the Osbournes' window. Rebecca was in the bathroom. He could hear the sound of water running into the basin. She had been there for more than an hour. Finally, the water stopped running and she came out, wearing a hotel bathrobe, her hair wrapped in a white towel like a sheikh. She lit one of his cigarettes and said, 'Does it work?'

'The transmitter is sending out a signal, but I won't be certain until there's someone in the house.'

'I'm hungry,' she said.

'Order some food from room service.'

'I want to go out.'

'It's better if we stay inside.'

'I've been trapped on boats for ten days. I want to go out.'

'Get dressed, and I'll take you out.'

'Close your eyes,' she said, but Delaroche stood and turned to face her. He reached out and tugged at the towel around her head. Her hair was no longer an abrasive shade of blonde; it was nearly black and shimmering with dampness. Suddenly, it was in sync with the rest of her features – her grey eyes, her luminous white skin, her oval face. He realized that she was a remarkably beautiful woman. Then he became angry; he wished he could hide in a bathroom with a bottle of elixir and emerge an hour later with his old face.

She seemed to read his thoughts.

'You have scars,' she said, tracing a finger along the bottom of his jawline. 'What happened?'

'This is not my face any longer. If you stay in this business too long a face can become a liability.'

Her finger had moved from his jawline to his cheek-bone, and she was toying with the collagen implants just beneath the skin. 'What did you look like before?'

Delaroche raised his eyebrows and pondered her question for an instant. He thought, how would anyone describe his own appearance? If he said he had been beautiful once, before Maurice Leroux destroyed his face, she might think he was a liar. He sat down at the desk and removed a piece of hotel stationery and a pencil.

'Go away for a few minutes,' he said.

She went into the bathroom again, closed the door, and switched on the hair dryer. He worked quickly, the pencil scratching over the paper. When he finished, he appraised his own features rather dispassionately, as if they belonged to a creature of his imagination.

He slipped the self-portrait beneath the bathroom door. The hair dryer stopped whining. Rebecca came out, holding Delaroche's old face in her hands. She looked at him, then at the image on the paper. She kissed the portrait and dropped it onto the floor. Then she kissed Delaroche.

'Who was she, Jean-Paul?'

'Who?'

'The woman you were thinking about while you were making love.'

'I was thinking about you.'

'Not all the time. I'm not angry, Jean-Paul. It's not as if –'

She stopped herself before she could finish her thought. Delaroche wondered what she might have said. She lay on her back, her head resting on his abdomen, her dark hair spread across his chest. Street light streamed through the open curtains and fell upon her long body. Her face was flushed and scratched from lovemaking, but the rest of her body was bone white in the lamplight. It was the skin of someone who had rarely seen the sun; Delaroche doubted she had ever set foot outside the British Isles before she had been driven into hiding.

'Was she beautiful? And don't lie to me any more.'

'Yes,' he said.

'What was her name?'

'Her name was Astrid.'

'Astrid what?'

'Astrid Vogel.'

'I remember a woman named Astrid Vogel who belonged to the Red Army Faction,' Rebecca said. 'She left Germany and went into hiding after she murdered a German police official.'

'That was my Astrid,' Delaroche said, tracing his finger along the edge of Rebecca's breast. 'But Astrid didn't kill the German policeman. I killed him. Astrid just paid the price.'

'So you're German?'

Delaroche shook his head.

'What are you then? What's your real name?'

But he ignored her question. His fingers moved from her breast to the edge of her rib cage. Rebecca's abdomen reacted involuntarily to his touch, drawing in sharply. Delaroche stroked the white skin of her stomach and the tops of her thighs. Finally, she took his hand and placed it between her legs. Her eyes closed. A gust of wind moved the curtains, and her skin prickled with goose bumps. She tried to draw the bedspread over her body but Delaroche pushed it away.

'There were things in the houseboat in Amsterdam that belonged to a woman,' she said softly, eyes closed. 'Astrid lived on that boat, didn't she.'

'Yes, she did.'

'Did you live there with her?'

'For a while.'

'Did you make love in the bed beneath the skylight?'

'Rebecca –'

'It's all right,' she said. 'You won't hurt my feelings.'

'Yes, we did.'

'What happened to her?'

'She was killed.'

'When?'

'Last year.'

Rebecca pushed away his hand and sat up. 'What happened?'

'We were working together on something here in America, and it turned out badly.'

'Who killed her?'

Delaroche hesitated for a moment; the whole thing had gone too far already. He knew he should shut it down, but for some reason he wanted to tell her more. Perhaps Vladimir was right. *A man who sees ghosts can no longer behave like a professional* . . .

'Michael Osbourne,' he said. 'Actually, his wife killed her.'

'Why?'

'Because we were sent here to kill Michael Osbourne.' He paused for a moment, his eyes flickering about her. 'Sometimes, in this business, things don't go as planned.'

'Why were you hired to kill Osbourne?'

'Because he knew too much about one of the Society's operations.'

'What operation?'

'The downing of TransAtlantic Flight 002 last year.'

'I thought it was shot down by that Arab group, the Sword of Gaza.'

'It was shot down at the behest of an American defence contractor named Mitchell Elliott. The Society made it appear as though the Sword of Gaza was involved so Elliott's company could sell a missile defence system to the American government. Osbourne suspected this, so I was hired by the Director to eliminate everyone involved in the operation, as well as Osbourne.'

'Who actually shot down the plane?'

'A Palestinian named Hassan Mahmoud.'

'How do you know?'

'Because I was there that night. Because I killed him when it was over.'

She drew away from him. Delaroche could see real fear on her face and feel the bed shaking gently with her trembling. She drew the blanket to her breast to hide her body from him. He stared at her, his face utterly expressionless.

'My God,' she said. 'You're a monster.'

'Why do you say that?'

'There were more than two hundred innocent people on that plane.'

'And what about the innocent people that your bombers killed in London and Dublin?'

'We didn't do it for money,' she snarled.

'You had a cause,' he said contemptuously.

'That's right.'

'A cause you believe is just.'

'A cause I *know* is just,' she said. 'You'll kill anyone as long as the price is right.'

'My God, but you really are a stupid woman, aren't you.'

She tried to slap him, but he caught her hand and held onto it, easily resisting her efforts to pull away.

'Why do you think the Society is willing to help you?' Delaroche said. 'Because they believe in the sacred rights of Protestants in Northern Ireland? Of course not. Because they think it will advance their own interests. Because they think that it will make them money. History has passed you by, Rebecca. The Protestants have had

317

their day in Northern Ireland, and now it's over. No amount of bombing, no amount of killing, is ever going to turn back the clock.'

'If you believe that, why are you doing this?'

'I don't believe in anything. This is what I do. I've killed in the name of every failed cause in Europe. Yours is just the latest' – he let go of her and she drew away, rubbing her hand as if it had touched something evil – 'and I hope the last.'

'I should have kept walking that day in Amsterdam.'

'You're probably right. But now you're here, and you're stuck with me, and if you do precisely as I say, you might actually survive. You'll never see Northern Ireland again, but at least you'll be alive.'

'Somehow, I doubt that,' she said. 'You're going to kill me when this is all over, aren't you?'

'No, I'm not going to kill you.'

'You probably killed Astrid Vogel, too.'

'I didn't kill Astrid, and I'm not going to kill you, Rebecca.'

He pulled away the blanket and exposed her body to the light. He held out his hand to her, but she remained still.

'Take my hand,' Delaroche said. 'I won't hurt you. I give you my word.'

Rebecca took his hand. He pulled her to him and kissed her mouth. She resisted for a moment; then she surrendered, kissing him, clawing at his skin as if she were drowning in his arms. When she guided him into her body, she suddenly went very still, staring at Delaroche with an animal straightness that unnerved him.

'I like your other face better,' she said.

'So do I.'

'When this is over, maybe we can go back to the doctor

who did this and he can make your face like it was before.'

'I'm afraid that's not possible,' he said.

She seemed to understand exactly what he was saying.

'If you're not going to kill me,' she said, 'then why did you tell me your secrets?'

'I'm not sure.'

'Who are you, Jean-Paul?'

36

WASHINGTON

The following morning Michael and Elizabeth flew from
New York to Washington, along with the children and
Maggie. They separated at National Airport. Michael
took a chauffeured government sedan to the White
House to brief National Security Adviser William Bristol
on Northern Ireland; Elizabeth, Maggie, and the children
crowded into a car-service Lincoln for the ride into
Georgetown.

Elizabeth had not been back to the large red-brick
Federal on N Street in more than a year. She loved the old
house, but climbing the curved brick steps she was
suddenly overwhelmed with bad memories. She thought
of the long struggle with her own body to have children.
She thought of the afternoon Astrid Vogel had come here
to take her hostage so the assassin called October could
murder her husband.

'Are you all right, Elizabeth?' Maggie asked.

Elizabeth wondered how long she had been standing
like that, key in hand, unable to unlock the door.

'Yes, I'm fine, Maggie. I was just thinking about something.'

The alarm chirped as she pushed back the front door.
She punched in the disarm code, and it fell silent. Michael
had turned the place into a fortress, but she would never
feel completely safe here.

She helped Maggie get the children settled, then carried
her suitcase upstairs to the bedroom. She was unzipping

the bag when the doorbell rang. She walked downstairs and peered through the peephole. Outside was a tall brown-haired man in a blue suit and tan raincoat.

'Can I help you?' she said, without opening the door.

'My name is Brad Heyworth, Mrs Osbourne. I'm the Diplomatic Security Service agent assigned to watch your house.'

Elizabeth opened the door. 'DSS? But my father doesn't arrive from London for another six hours.'

'Actually, we've been watching the house for a couple of days now, Mrs Osbourne.'

'Why?'

'After the incident in Britain, we decided it was probably best to err on the side of caution.'

'Are you alone?'

'For now, but when the ambassador arrives we'll add a second man to the detail.'

'That's reassuring,' she said. 'Would you like to come inside?'

'No, thank you, Mrs Osbourne, I need to stay out here.'

'Can I get you anything?'

'I'm just fine,' he said. 'I just wanted to let you know that we're around.'

'Thank you, Agent Heyworth.'

Elizabeth closed the door and watched as the DSS man walked down the front steps and got back in his car. She was glad he was there. She went upstairs and sat down at the desk in Michael's old study. She made a series of brief telephone calls: to Ridgewell's catering, to the valet service, to her office in New York to check messages. Then she spent another hour returning calls.

Maria, the cleaning lady, arrived at noon. Elizabeth dressed in a nylon track suit and went outside. She bounced down the front steps, waved to Brad Heyworth, and jogged down the brick sidewalk of N Street.

*

At the Embassy Row hotel, Delaroche had hung the DO NOT DISTURB sign outside the room and double-locked the door. For the past hour he had been listening to Elizabeth Osbourne: talking on the telephone, talking to her nanny and her children, talking to the DSS agent guarding the house. Delaroche now knew exactly when Douglas Cannon would arrive from London and when he would leave for the White House the next morning to attend the Northern Ireland conference. He also knew that the DSS agent parked in front of the house was named Brad Heyworth and that a second agent would join the detail after the ambassador's arrival.

He heard the arrival of a cleaning woman called Maria who spoke with a heavy Spanish accent: South American, Delaroche guessed – Peru or perhaps Bolivia. He heard Elizabeth Osbourne announce that she was going for a run and would be back in an hour. He jumped as she slammed the front door on her way out.

Five minutes later he was startled by a howling noise that sounded like the roar of a jet engine. It was so loud Delaroche had to rip the headphones from his ears. For a moment he thought some calamity had befallen the Osbournes' house. Then he realized it was only Maria, running her vacuum near the window where Delaroche had planted his microphone.

Douglas Cannon's dinner party started out as an intimate affair for eight, but in the aftermath of the Hartley Hall affair it had metamorphosed into a catered bash for fifty, with rented tables and chairs and a squad of college boys in blue jackets to park cars in the crammed streets of Georgetown. Such was the nature of celebrity in Washington. Douglas had lived and worked in the city for more than twenty years, but someone had tried to kill him, and that made him a star. The CIA and British Intelligence had contributed to the ambassador's sudden notoriety by spinning a tale of Douglas's calm under fire at Hartley Hall, even though he was safely tucked in his bed at Winfield House by the time the assault began. Douglas had willingly played along with the elaborate *ruse de guerre*. Indeed, he derived a certain adolescent delight from deceiving the barons of the Washington media.

The guests began arriving a few minutes after seven o'clock. There were two of Douglas's old friends from the Senate and a handful of congressmen. The Washington bureau chief of NBC News came, along with her husband, who was the bureau chief of CNN. Cynthia Martin came alone; Adrian Carter brought his wife, Christine. To protect Michael, who was still a clandestine member of the Agency, Carter and Cynthia said they worked on Northern Ireland issues for the State Department. Carter wanted a moment alone with Michael, so they adjourned to the garden and stood by the pool.

'How did things go with Bristol this morning?' Carter asked.

'He seemed impressed with the product,' Michael said. 'Beckwith stuck his head in the door for a minute, too.'

'Really?'

'He said he was pleased with the outcome of Operation Kettledrum and that the peace process was back on track. You're right, Adrian, he wants this thing bad.' Michael hesitated. 'So am I officially finished with Northern Ireland?'

'When the delegations leave town, we'll turn it over to Cynthia and move you back to the Middle East section.'

'If there's one constant at the Agency, it's change,' Michael said. 'But I still would like to know why Monica decided to shuffle the deck now and why she wants me off the October case.'

'As far as Monica is concerned, the October file is closed. She thinks that even if October is still alive and working he poses no threat to Americans or American interests, and therefore he does not cross the radar screen of the Center.'

'Do you agree?'

'Of course not, and I've told her as much. But she *is* the director, and ultimately she decides who we target.'

'A real man would resign in your position.'

'Some of us don't have the financial flexibility to take courageous moral stands, Michael.'

Elizabeth appeared at the french doors.

'Would you two please come inside?' she said. 'It's not as if you never get a chance to talk.'

'We'll be there in a minute,' Michael said.

'One other thing,' Adrian said, when Elizabeth had gone. 'I heard about your little portrait session with Morton Dunne in OTS the other day. What the hell was that all about?'

'A plastic surgeon named Maurice Leroux was murdered in Paris a couple of weeks ago.'

'And?'

'I was wondering if October may have changed his face.'

'And then killed the doctor who did it?'

'The thought had crossed my mind.'

'Listen, Michael – Monica has taken you off the case. I don't want any more freelancing on your part. No surfing through files, no private operations. As far as you're concerned, October is dead.'

'You're not threatening me, are you, Adrian?'

'Actually, I am.'

Delaroche removed his headphones and lit a cigarette. The large dinner party had overwhelmed his microphone, so that the only thing he heard was a constant hum, interrupted by incomprehensible snatches of conversation or occasional bursts of laughter.

He switched off the tape machine and removed his Beretta 9-millimetre from its stainless-steel carrying case. He broke down the weapon and meticulously wiped each piece with a smooth rag, while he decided how he was going to kill the ambassador and Michael Osbourne.

37

'Happy St Patrick's Day,' President James Beckwith
declared, as he stepped to the podium in the Rose Garden
the following morning. Flanking him were Irish Prime
Minister Bertie Ahern and British Foreign Secretary
Robin Cook. Behind the president were the leaders of
the province's Nationalist and Unionist political parties,
including Gerry Adams of Sinn Fein and David Trimble
of the Ulster Unionist Party, who was now effectively the
prime minister of Northern Ireland.

'We gather here today not in crisis but in celebration,'
Beckwith continued. 'We celebrate the common heritage
that binds us, and we will renew the commitment to
peaceful change in Northern Ireland.'

Douglas Cannon sat off to the side with a group of
senior White House and State Department aides who
would take part in the talks. He joined in the polite
applause.

'Last month a group of Loyalist thugs – the so-called
Ulster Freedom Brigade – tried to assassinate the American ambassador to Great Britain, my old friend and
colleague, Douglas Cannon,' Beckwith continued. 'It
was truly the last gasp by those who wish to deal with
Northern Ireland's problems with violence rather than
compromise. If anyone doubts our commitment to peace,
I ask them to consider one thing: Ambassador Douglas
Cannon is here today, and the Ulster Freedom Brigade is
but a bad memory.'

Beckwith turned, smiled at Douglas, and began to applaud. Gerry Adams, David Trimble, Bertie Ahern, and Robin Cook joined in, as did the rest of the assembled crowd.

'Now, if you'll excuse us, we have work to do,' Beckwith said.

He turned away from the podium and, with arms extended, shepherded the politicians into the Oval Office, ignoring the shouted questions of the White House press corps.

When Douglas returned to the house on N Street late that afternoon, Michael and Elizabeth were waiting for him.

'How did it go?' Michael asked.

'Better than expected. Now that the Ulster Freedom Brigade has been neutralized, Gerry Adams thinks the IRA will seriously consider decommissioning.'

'What does *decommissioning* mean?' Elizabeth asked.

'It means giving up their weapons and breaking up their terrorist cells and command structure.'

Michael said, 'The CIA estimates that the IRA alone has stockpiled a hundred tons of rifles and two and a half tons of Semtex. And then there are the Protestant terrorist groups. That's why it's so important to keep the momentum of the peace process moving in the right direction.'

'The Protestants and the Catholics have made remarkable progress in a short period of time, but the peace process could very easily collapse. And if it does, I'm afraid the violence will be unprecedented.' Douglas looked at his watch. 'Now the fun begins. The Sinn Fein reception at the Mayflower, the Ulster Unionist reception at the Four Seasons, and the British reception at the embassy.'

'What the hell is that?' Elizabeth said as they changed clothes for the receptions.

'It's a high-powered Browning automatic with a fifteen-shot clip.'

Michael slipped the gun into a shoulder holster and pulled on his suit jacket.

'Why are you carrying a gun?'

'Because it makes me feel good.'

'Daddy is going to have a DSS agent with him the entire time tonight.'

'You can never be too cautious.'

'Is there something you're not telling me?'

'I'll just feel better when your father is back in London surrounded by a bunch of marines and Special Branch detectives who can hit an assassin between the eyes at a hundred paces.'

He smoothed the front of his jacket.

'How do I look?'

'Lovely.' She pulled on her dress and turned her back to him. 'Zip me up. We're late.'

At the Embassy Row hotel, Delaroche removed his head-phones. He quickly broke down the monitors and receivers and placed them into the duffel bag. He slipped the Beretta 9-millimetre into a shoulder holster and stood in front of the mirror, inspecting his appearance. He wore a grey single-breasted business suit of American design, a white shirt, and a striped tie. Attached to his right ear was a clear plastic wire of the type used by security officers the world over.

He studied his face, staring into his own eyes, and said, 'Diplomatic security, ma'am. We have an emergency.' It was the flat American accent of the actor on the English-language tapes Delaroche had studied at sea. He repeated the phrase several more times, until he felt completely at ease.

Rebecca emerged from the bathroom. She wore a tailored two-piece suit and black stockings. Delaroche handed her a loaded Beretta and two extra clips, which she slipped into a black shoulder bag.

He had left the Volvo on Twenty-second Street, just off Massachusetts Avenue. There was a parking ticket beneath the wiper. Delaroche dropped the ticket in the gutter and climbed behind the wheel.

The limousine stopped in front of the Mayflower Hotel on Connecticut Avenue. A uniformed doorman opened the door, and Douglas, Michael, Elizabeth, and a DSS agent climbed out. They entered the hotel and walked along the ornate centre hall to the grand ballroom. Gerry Adams caught sight of Douglas as he entered the room and disentangled himself from a knot of starstruck Irish-American well-wishers.

'Thank you for coming, Ambassador Cannon,' Adams spoke with the thick accent of West Belfast. He was tall, with a full black beard and wire-rimmed spectacles. Although he appeared robust, he suffered from the lingering effects of years of imprisonment and an assassination attempt by the UVF that nearly killed him. 'You do us a great honour by joining us this evening.'

'Thank you for having us,' Douglas said politely, shaking Adams's hand. 'May I introduce my daughter, Elizabeth Osbourne, and her husband, Michael Osbourne.'

Adams looked at Michael briefly and shook his hand without enthusiasm. As he and Douglas talked about that day's session at the White House for a few moments, Elizabeth and Michael moved a few steps away to give them privacy.

Then, without warning, Gerry Adams placed a hand on Michael's shoulder and said, 'You mind if I have a wee word with you, Mr Osbourne? I'm afraid it's rather important.'

Delaroche parked at the corner of Prospect and Potomac streets in Georgetown and climbed out. Rebecca slid behind the wheel and lowered the window. Delaroche leaned down and asked, 'Any questions?'

Rebecca shook her head. Delaroche handed her an envelope.

'If something goes wrong – if something happens to me or if we get separated – go to this place. I'll come for you if I can.'

He turned away and entered a sandwich shop filled with students from Georgetown. He purchased coffee and a newspaper and sat down at a table by the window.

A moment later he saw Rebecca speed past, heading east toward downtown Washington.

'Please sit down, Mr Osbourne,' Gerry Adams said. He had led Michael into a large room adjoining the grand ballroom. His pair of ever-present bodyguards moved out of earshot. Adams poured two cups of tea. 'Milk, Mr Osbourne?'

'Thank you.'

'I have a message from your friend Seamus Devlin.'

'Seamus Devlin is not my friend,' Michael said harshly.

The bodyguards glanced at the table to make certain there was no problem. Gerry Adams waved them away.

'I know what happened that night in Belfast,' he said. 'And I know why it happened. We would never be in this position today, on the verge of a lasting peace in Northern Ireland, if it weren't for the IRA. It is a highly professional force, not to be taken lightly. Keep that in mind next time you and your British friends try to plant a tout on the inside.'

'I thought you had a message for me.'

'It's about that bitch that set up Eamonn Dillon on the Falls Road, Rebecca Wells.'

'What about her?'

'She went to Paris after the Hartley Hall affair.' Adams raised his china teacup in a mock toast and said, 'Lovely piece of work, that was, Mr Osbourne.'

Michael remained silent.

'She was living in Montparnasse with a Scottish mercenary named Roderick Campbell. According to Devlin, she and Campbell were in the market for a freelance assassin to finish the job on your father-in-law.'

Michael sat up sharply. 'How good is the source?'

'I didn't get into that kind of detail with Devlin, Mr Osbourne. But you've seen his work up close. He's not a man who goes about his business lightly.'

'Where's Rebecca Wells now?'

'She left Paris suddenly a couple of weeks ago. Devlin hasn't been able to pick up her trail again.'

'What about Roderick Campbell?'

'Gone too – permanently, I'm afraid. He was shot to death in his apartment, along with a girl.' Adams was clearly enjoying telling Michael something he didn't know. 'It probably didn't cross your sophisticated computer screens at the Counterterrorism Center.'

'Did Wells and Campbell ever manage to hire a shooter?'

'Devlin doesn't know, but I wouldn't let down the guard on the ambassador right now, if you know what I mean. It would be bad for everyone involved in the peace process if a gunman acting on behalf of the Ulster Freedom Brigade managed to kill your father-in-law at this time.' Adams set down his teacup, signalling the meeting was coming to an end. 'Devlin hopes this makes up for any hard feelings you might have about Kevin Maguire.'

'You can tell Devlin to fuck off.'

Adams smiled. 'I'll give him the message.'

Rebecca Wells sat behind the wheel of the Volvo, half a block from the front entrance of the Mayflower. She watched as Ambassador Cannon and the Osbournes emerged from the hotel, followed by the DSS agent. She started the engine, then dialled a number on her cellular phone.

'Yes.'

'They're leaving the first stop now and moving on to the second.'

The line went dead.

Rebecca dropped the Volvo into gear and slipped into the evening traffic on Connecticut Avenue.

'When did you and Gerry become such good friends?' Elizabeth asked.

'We move in similar circles.'

'What did he want?'

'He apologized for what happened to me in Belfast.'

'Did you accept?'

'Not really.'

'And that's all?'

'That's all.'

Douglas said, 'All right, time to cross the religious divide. To the Four Seasons for drinks with the Protestants.'

'You think these people will ever have receptions *together*?' Elizabeth asked.

'I wouldn't hold your breath,' Michael said.

Ninety minutes later, Rebecca Wells was parked along a

tree-lined section of Massachusetts Avenue in upper Northwest Washington. Across the street was the sprawling British embassy complex. From her vantage point she could see the forecourt of the ambassador's residence. The first guests were beginning to leave.

Rebecca opened the letter that Delaroche had given her and read it by the faint light of the streetlamps. She folded the note and placed it back in her pocket. She thought of that freezing afternoon on the beach in Norfolk, the afternoon she had left for Scotland to fetch Gavin Spencer and the guns. It was hard to imagine that it was only a month ago, so much had happened since. She remembered the strange sense of serenity that had settled over her that day, walking the flat, desolate beach. She had wanted to stay there for ever. And now this man with no past – this hired killer who made love to her as if her body were made of glass – was offering her a sanctuary by the sea.

She looked up in time to see Douglas Cannon and the Osbournes leaving the British ambassador's residence. Once again, she punched in the number on her cell phone and waited for the voice of the man she knew only as Jean-Paul.

Delaroche severed the connection with Rebecca Wells and left the sandwich shop. He walked quickly north along Potomac Street until he reached N Street. The Osbournes' house was two blocks away. He moved more slowly now, strolling along the quiet street, instinctively looking for signs of additional security.

He had to time his arrival perfectly. The DSS agent accompanying Douglas Cannon would radio his team to alert them of the ambassador's imminent arrival. If the DSS agent received no reply, he would suspect there was a problem. Which was why Delaroche was taking his time walking along N Street.

He spotted the team of DSS agents, sitting in a parked car in front of the Osbournes' house with the front windows opened. One of them, the one behind the wheel, was talking on a handheld radio. Delaroche assumed he was talking to the agent in the ambassador's limousine.

Delaroche walked to the car and stood next to the driver's side window.

'Excuse me,' he said. 'Which way is Wisconsin Avenue?'

The agent behind the wheel wordlessly pointed east.

'Thank you,' Delaroche said.

Then he reached beneath his raincoat, withdrew the silenced Beretta, and shot each of the agents several times in the chest. He opened the door and pushed the bodies down onto the seat. He closed the automatic windows, removed the keys, shut the door, and locked it.

The entire thing had taken less than thirty seconds. He tossed the car keys into the darkness and crossed the street to the Osbournes' house. He climbed the steps and rang the bell, breathing deeply to steady his nerves. A moment later he heard footsteps approaching the door.

'Who's there?'

It was the English-accented voice of Maggie, the nanny.

'Diplomatic security, ma'am,' Delaroche said. 'I'm afraid we have an emergency.'

The door opened and Maggie stood there, face perplexed. 'What's wrong?'

Delaroche stepped inside the house and closed the door. He clasped Maggie's mouth in an iron grip, smothering her scream, and pulled her face close to his. With his free hand he reached inside his suit jacket and removed the Beretta, pressing the end of the silencer into her cheek.

'I know there are children in this house, and I mean them no harm,' he whispered in his accented English. 'But if you don't do exactly as I say, I'll shoot you in the face. Do you understand me?'

Maggie nodded, eyes wide with terror.

'All right, come upstairs with me.'

The evening had gone off without incident, just as Michael had expected, but as the car sped along Massachusetts Avenue, the warning from Gerry Adams rang in his ears. If Rebecca Wells had managed to hire an assassin, it posed a new and different threat to Douglas's safety. An assassin working alone would be much more difficult to identify and stop than a member of a known paramilitary organization. Michael decided he would tell Douglas the news when they arrived home. His activities and appearances in London would have to be restricted until the threat had passed – or until Rebecca Wells could be arrested.

The car turned onto Wisconsin Avenue and they headed south into Georgetown. Elizabeth leaned her head on Michael's shoulder and closed her eyes.

Douglas laid a hand on Michael's forearm and said, 'You know, Michael, there's something I never did that I need to do now. I never thanked you.'

'What are you talking about?'

'I never thanked you for saving my life. If you hadn't taken on the case, gone into Northern Ireland and risked your life, I might very well be dead right now. Obviously, I've never had an opportunity to see you do your job before. You are a *superb* intelligence officer.'

'Thank you, Douglas. Coming from an old spook-hating liberal like you, that means a lot to me.'

'Are you going to stay on with the Agency, now that the Northern Ireland business is over?'

'If my wife promises not to divorce me,' Michael said. 'Monica Tyler wants me to take the Sword of Gaza case again. The Agency has picked up some indications the group may be planning new attacks.'

'What kind of indications?'

'Movement of known action agents, communications intercepts. That sort of thing.'

'Anything in Britain?'

'The UK is always a possibility. They like operating there.'

'I remember the Heathrow attack.'

'So do I,' Michael said.

Douglas sat back and closed his eyes as the car left Wisconsin Avenue and slipped through the quiet residential streets of Georgetown. 'When is it going to end?' he said.

'When is what going to end?'

'Terrorism. The taking of innocent life to make a political statement. When is it going to end?'

'When there are no more people in the world who feel oppressed enough to pick up a gun or a bomb. When there are no more religious or ethnic zealots. When there are no more maniacs who get their kicks by shedding blood.'

'So I guess the answer to my question is *never*. It will *never* end.'

'You're the historian. In the first century, the Zealots used terrorism to fight the Roman occupation of the Promised Land. In the twelfth century, a group of Shi'ite Muslims called the Assassins used terrorism against the Sunni leaders of Iran. It's hardly a new phenomenon.'

'And now it's come to America: the World Trade Center, Oklahoma City, Olympic Park.'

'It's cheap, it's relatively easy, and it only takes a handful of dedicated individuals. Two men named Timothy McVeigh and Terry Nichols proved that.'

'It's still incomprehensible to me,' Douglas said. 'One hundred sixty-eight people, gone in the blink of an eye.'

'All right, you two,' Elizabeth said, opening her eyes as the car braked to a halt in front of the house. 'Enough of this conversation. You're depressing me.'

Delaroche was standing on the second floor of the house, in a window overlooking N Street, when he heard the sound of a car. He parted the curtain with the silencer of the Beretta and peered down into the street. It was Cannon and the Osbournes arriving home.

He released the curtain and walked down the hall to the staircase, glancing into the master bedroom as he moved past the door. The nanny lay on the floor, her hands, feet, and mouth bound by packing tape.

Delaroche moved quickly down the stairs and stood in the darkened centre hall. It was going to be so easy, he thought – like a shooting game at a carnival – and then he would be done with it. All of it.

38

Rebecca Wells turned onto N Street and followed the limousine for two blocks, until it came to a stop. There were no spaces in front of the Osbournes' house, so the driver simply parked in the middle of the street and switched on the hazard lights. Rebecca reached into her shoulder bag and withdrew the silenced Beretta 9-millimetre.

Jean-Paul's instructions ran through her head. *I'll take care of the two men in the car and then go inside the house*, he had told her the previous night, speaking softly beneath the screaming television in their hotel room. *Wait until they're all out of the car. You kill the last DSS man, and I'll take care of the ambassador and Michael Osbourne.*

She wondered whether she had the strength to do it. And then she thought of Gavin Spencer and Kyle Blake and the men who had died at Hartley Hall, because Michael Osbourne and his father-in-law had deceived her. She checked the action on the Beretta and chambered the first round.

One of the limousine's doors opened, and the DSS agent climbed out. He walked around the back of the car and pulled open the rear door facing the Osbournes' house. Michael Osbourne came out first. He glanced around the street, his gaze settling on the Volvo for an instant before moving on. The ambassador emerged, followed by Elizabeth Osbourne.

Rebecca opened her door.

Michael turned to the DSS man and said, 'Where are the other agents?'

The DSS agent raised his hand to his mouth and murmured a few words. When he received no response he yelled, 'Get back into the car! Now!'

It was then that Rebecca Wells stepped out of the Volvo. She stood, arms braced on the roof of the car, and started firing at the DSS agent – one shot after another, just as Jean-Paul had told her.

Michael did not hear the shots, only the shattering of the limousine's rear window and the thud of the 9-millimetre rounds piercing the boot. Instead of obeying the DSS's agent's instructions to get into the car, Michael, Elizabeth, and Douglas had instinctively fallen to the pavement of N Street.

Michael suspected there was something wrong about the woman in the Volvo station wagon, but he had been too slow to seize upon the possibility that it might actually be Rebecca Wells. Now, crouching over Elizabeth and Douglas, the final seconds of the dead DSS agent's life flashed through his mind. The agent had tried to raise the other men but could not. That's because someone else has already killed them, Michael thought. Then he thought of the information Gerry Adams had given him earlier that night. Rebecca Wells had been looking for a professional assassin to kill Douglas. Her hired killer was probably somewhere close.

Michael pulled out the Browning automatic. The driver was still behind the wheel of the limousine, ducking for cover below the top of the seat. Michael grabbed Elizabeth and Douglas and said, 'Get into the car!'

Elizabeth crawled into the back seat. One of the shots struck the DSS man in the head, sending a shower of blood and brain tissue through the shattered rear window. Elizabeth looked at Michael helplessly and tried to wipe the blood from her face.

Then her eyes grew suddenly wide and she screamed, 'Michael! Behind you!'

Michael turned and saw a figure, standing high atop the curved steps leading to the entrance of the house. The man's right arm swung up and he fired twice one-handed, his silenced weapon emitting no sound, just a tongue of fire from the end of the barrel.

Even in the dim light of Georgetown, Michael knew he had seen that distinctive handling of a gun before.

The man on his front steps was October.

The first shot ricocheted off the roof of the car. The second struck Douglas in the back as he lunged into the car. He collapsed onto Elizabeth, groaning in pain.

Michael levelled his gun at October and fired several shots, driving him back into the house. On the quiet street, the high-powered Browning sounded like artillery.

'Go! Go!' he screamed at the driver. 'Get them out of here!'

The driver sat up and gunned the engine.

The last thing Michael saw was Elizabeth, screaming through the shattered rear window.

'The children, Michael!' she cried. 'The children!'

Michael dived between two parked cars where he was shielded from Rebecca Wells and October, at least for a few seconds. He peered upward toward the entrance of the house and saw October emerge. Michael aimed the Browning and fired several shots. October ducked back inside. Then, windows in the cars around him started to shatter. The woman was firing at him.

Lights had come on all along the street. Michael turned and saw Rebecca Wells, standing behind the open door of the Volvo station wagon, firing across the roof. He pivoted and thought about returning her fire. He realized that if he missed, a stray round could enter one of the neighbouring homes and kill an innocent person who had come out to see what was going on.

He aimed at his own house. He thought, please, God, let the children be upstairs in the nursery! And then he fired at October until his gun was empty.

Michael heard the first siren as he was changing his clip. Perhaps it was the gunfire, Michael thought. Or perhaps the DSS man had managed to flash an alert before he was killed. Whatever the case, Michael could now hear the wail of several approaching sirens, growing louder with each passing second.

October appeared in the doorway, waving to Rebecca.

'Go!' he yelled. 'Get away from here!'

The first police cruiser appeared on N Street.

October fired two wild shots at the car. 'Now, Rebecca! Leave!'

Michael chambered the first round of his fresh clip and fired four shots at October.

With that, Rebecca Wells climbed into the Volvo and gunned the engine, roaring past the spot where Michael had taken cover. October stepped onto the porch one last time and fired several shots in Michael's direction, then turned and ran into the house.

Michael rose and followed after him, pounding up the steps, the Browning in his outstretched hands. When he reached the doorway he peered down the darkened centre hall and saw October lift a chair and hurl it through the french doors.

October turned one last time and raised his gun. Michael heard nothing but saw the muzzle spouting fire. He leaned against the exterior of the house; on the other side of the wall he could feel the rounds crashing into the plasterwork. When the gunfire stopped, Michael stepped into the doorway and fired three more shots as October ran across the garden and scaled the fence.

Michael ran upstairs to the nursery and found the children crying in their cribs, unharmed.

'Maggie!'

He heard thumping in the master bedroom and muffled screams. He ran down the hall and turned on the lights in the bedroom. Maggie lay on the floor, bound and gagged.

'Was there just one, Maggie? Just one gunman?'

She nodded.

'I'll be right back.'

Michael charged down the stairs just as a Metropolitan Police officer entered the house, gun drawn. He levelled his weapon at Michael and yelled, 'Stop right there and drop your gun!'

'I'm Michael Osbourne, and this is my house.'

'I don't care who the fuck you are! Just drop the gun! Now!'

'Goddammit, I'm Ambassador Cannon's son-in-law and I work for the CIA! Put the fucking gun down!'

The officer kept his gun aimed at Michael's head.

'My father-in-law was hit,' Michael said. 'Both shooters have fled – a man on foot and a woman in a black Volvo station wagon. My children are upstairs with their nanny. Go help her. I'll be right back.'

'Hey, come back here!' the officer yelled, as Michael ran down the centre hall and vanished through the shattered french doors.

Delaroche did not come to Washington to get into a gunfight with Michael Osbourne. Anyone could be hit when bullets are flying around a small space, and Delaroche was unwilling to trade his life for Osbourne's.

Besides, he had hit the primary target, Ambassador Cannon, with a good shot in the back. With a little luck the wound would prove fatal. Still, he was angry about failing to kill Osbourne once again.

He stripped off the tan raincoat as he sprinted down the alley. When he reached Thirty-fourth Street he stepped directly into the path of an oncoming car, a light grey Saab with a college student behind the wheel. Delaroche raised his Beretta and aimed it through the windscreen.

'Get the fuck out of the car!'

The student climbed out with his hands raised and stepped aside. 'Take it, motherfucker. It's yours.'

'Run,' Delaroche said, waving the Beretta, and the student started running.

Delaroche climbed behind the wheel.

The college student screamed, 'Fuck you, you fucking asshole!'

Delaroche drove off. He knew he had to get out of Georgetown quickly. He raced down Thirty-fourth Street toward M Street. If he could cross the Francis Scott Key Bridge to Arlington, his chances of escape would increase dramatically. There, he could slip onto the George Washington Memorial Parkway, I–395, or I–66 and be miles from Washington in a matter of minutes.

At M Street the traffic signal turned from green to red as Delaroche approached. A sign warned NO RIGHT TURN ON RED. He considered running the light, but calmness during escapes had always served him well in the past, and he decided not to act rashly now.

He applied the brakes and came to a stop.

He looked at his wristwatch and counted the seconds.

As Michael Osbourne leapt over the fence into the alley, he heard a man shouting obscenities. A split second later he heard tyres screeching and the engine of a small car revving. By the sound of it, Michael guessed the car was heading toward M Street. He also guessed that it was October, trying to escape. He sprinted down Thirty-third Street to M Street, turned right, and kept running.

Delaroche spotted Osbourne running along M Street with a gun in his hand, scattering startled pedestrians. Delaroche slowly turned and looked straight ahead, waiting for the light to turn green.

The Beretta lay on the passenger seat. Delaroche wrapped his right hand around the grip and placed his finger across the trigger. He thought, perhaps I'll get an opportunity to fulfil the terms of the contract after all.

Osbourne arrived at the intersection. He stood in the crosswalk directly in front of the Saab, gun in hand, staring up Thirty-fourth Street. He was breathing heavily, eyes flickering back and forth.

Delaroche lifted the Beretta slowly and laid it on his lap. He considered shooting Osbourne through the windscreen but decided against it. Even if he did manage to hit Osbourne, he would be left with a damaged car for his escape. He reached out with his left hand and pressed a button on the armrest, lowering his window as the light turned green.

Several other cars had pulled up behind him, and the drivers were honking their horns, not realizing that there was a man with a gun standing in the middle of the intersection.

Delaroche sat motionless, waiting for Osbourne to make his move.

Michael stood in the intersection, heart pounding, ignoring the cacophony of car horns. He checked the faces inside every car: a forty-something suit in a light grey Saab, a pair of rich students in a red BMW, a couple of

Georgetown patricians in a rattling diesel Mercedes, a Pizza Hut delivery boy.

Everyone was honking except for the man in the Saab. Michael looked at him carefully. He was rather ugly: heavy cheeks, a blunt chin, a broad, flat nose. Michael had seen the face somewhere before but couldn't figure out where. He stared at him while the faces of his past appeared in his mind, one by one, like images on a screen, some clear and sharp, some unfocused and scratchy. Then he realized where he had seen the man before – on Morton Dunne's computer screen at OTS.

Michael aimed the Browning at October's face.

'Get out of the car! Now!'

39

The vast intersection at the base of Key Bridge is one of the most congested and chaotic in all of Washington. Traffic from the towering bridge, M Street, and the Whitehurst Freeway all converge at the same point. During the morning and evening rush hours the intersection is jammed with commuter traffic. At night, it is filled with cars streaming into the restaurants and nightclubs of Georgetown. Above it all stand the black stone steps made infamous by *The Exorcist* – sad, covered in graffiti, stinking of urine from drunken Georgetown students who consider taking a piss there a rite of passage.

None of this entered Delaroche's mind, however, as he sat behind the wheel of the Saab, staring down the barrel of Michael Osbourne's Browning automatic. When he ordered him out of the car, Delaroche pressed the accelerator to the floor and leaned down.

Michael fired several shots as the car leapt forward.

Michael dived out of the way as the Saab careered into the intersection. Delaroche sat up behind the wheel, regained control, and raced toward the entrance of Key Bridge.

Michael rolled away from the oncoming car and rose onto one knee. He took aim at the back of the Saab as it moved swiftly away from him, shutting out the blaring of car horns.

He had eight rounds left in the Browning and no backup clip.

He fired all eight shots before Delaroche could make the turn onto the bridge.

Seven tore through the boot and embedded in the rear seat.

The eighth hit the fuel tank, and the Saab exploded.

Delaroche heard the explosion and instantly felt the heat of the burning gasoline. Cars screeched to a halt around him. A young man in a Redskins sweatshirt ran to Delaroche's aid. Delaroche aimed the Beretta at his head, and the man in the sweatshirt fled toward Francis Scott Key Park.

Delaroche leapt out of the car and saw Michael Osbourne running toward him.

He raised the Beretta and fired three times.

Michael Osbourne dived behind a parked car.

Delaroche started toward Key Bridge, but a car, seemingly oblivious of the burning vehicle in the centre of the intersection, sped toward him. Delaroche leapt just before impact and tumbled over the windshield.

He lost his grip on the Beretta, and it clattered into the path of the oncoming traffic.

Delaroche looked up and saw Michael Osbourne running toward him. He stood and tried to run, but his right ankle buckled, and he collapsed onto the asphalt.

He struggled to his feet and willed himself forward. His ankle felt as though there was broken glass just beneath the skin. He managed to reach the sidewalk of Key Bridge.

A man stood there, watching the spectacle, holding the handlebars of a poor-quality mountain bike.

Delaroche punched the man in the throat and took the bike.

He climbed onto the saddle and tried to pedal, but when he exerted force with his right foot the pain made him scream. He pedalled with one leg, his left leg, while his right simply rode up and down with the rotation of the cranks.

He turned and looked over his shoulder. Michael Osbourne was running toward him. Delaroche pedalled faster, but between his broken ankle and the poor quality of the bike, Osbourne was gaining on him. Delaroche felt utterly defenceless. He had no weapon and a rattletrap bicycle for transport. To make matters worse, he was injured.

More than anything else, Delaroche felt sudden rage – rage at his father and Vladimir and everyone else at the KGB who had condemned him to a life of killing. Rage at himself for allowing the Director to force him into this assignment. Rage at himself for failing once again to kill Osbourne. He wondered how Osbourne had known it was him behind the wheel of the Saab. Had Maurice Leroux betrayed him before he killed him that night in Paris? Had the Director betrayed him? Or had he once again under-estimated the intelligence and ingenuity of the man from the CIA, the man who had sworn to destroy him. That it would all end like this – with Delaroche on a creaking bike and Osbourne chasing him on foot – was almost laugh-able. He realized that even if he managed to get away from Osbourne now, his chances of going very far were growing slimmer by the minute.

He turned and looked once more and saw that Osbourne had gained more ground. He forced himself to pedal with both legs, ignoring the pain in his ankle, while he decided what he was willing to do to get off the bridge alive.

Michael slipped the Browning back into the shoulder holster and sprinted across the bridge, pumping hard with his arms. For an instant he was transported back to the Virginia state finals of the mile. Michael had made a brilliant tactical move in the final lap to place himself in a perfect position to overtake the leader in the final hundred yards, but when they reached the home stretch he had not had the courage to endure the pain necessary to win. He had become virtually hypnotized by the other boy's back – the fluttering of his jersey in the wind, the lean muscles of his shoulders – as he pulled further and further away and broke the tape. And he remembered his father, so furious that Michael had lost that he wouldn't even console him after the race.

He had closed to within ten yards of October.

He had run nearly a mile since dashing from the house. His legs were heavy, his muscles tight from the prolonged sprint. His arms burned, and his throat tasted of rust and blood from gasping for air. He had been pursuing October for years, using all the resources and technical services the Agency had to offer, but it all came down to this, a mind-bending sprint across Key Bridge. This time he was not going to shy away from the pain. This time he was not going to be hypnotized by his opponent's back, pulling further and further away. His head leaned back, and he roared like a wounded animal, thrashing at the air with his hands as if trying to pull himself forward.

October was now just a few feet away.

Michael leapt and rode him to the ground with a heavy crash.

October landed on his back, Michael on top of him, sitting on his abdomen.

Michael punched him twice in the face, the second blow splitting the flesh high on Delaroche's cheekbone, then grabbed his throat with both hands and began to strangle him.

He had lost all sense of reason and sanity. He was squeezing October's throat, crushing his windpipe, screaming at him savagely, yet a strange calmness had come over the assassin's face. His blue eyes flickered over Michael, and a vague half smile appeared on his lips.

Michael realized October was deciding how best to kill him. He squeezed harder.

October reached up suddenly and seized Michael's hair with his left hand. He pulled Michael's head toward him and drove the thumb of his right hand into Michael's eye socket.

Michael screamed in agony and released his grip on October's throat. The assassin turned his hands to hatchets and struck Michael simultaneously twice on the temples.

Michael nearly lost consciousness. He shook his head, trying to clear his vision, then realized that he was on his back, and the assassin had slipped away from him.

Michael struggled to his feet. October was already standing, feet apart, hands near his face, eyes fastened on Michael's. He spun and delivered a vicious roundhouse kick to the side of Michael's head.

Michael stumbled from the sidewalk onto the roadbed of the bridge, directly into the path of a speeding Metro bus. The driver leaned on the horn. Michael leapt out of the way, into the arms of October.

The assassin crouched and, using Michael's momentum, lifted him over the railing.

Delaroche waited for the sound of Michael's body hitting the water more than a hundred feet below, but there was nothing. He stepped forward and looked down. Michael had managed to grab hold of the base of the railing with one hand on his way down, and now he was dangling over the water. Michael looked up, blood in his mouth, and stared at Delaroche.

The easiest thing to do would be to stomp on his hand

until he lost his grip, but for some reason the idea was abhorrent to Delaroche. He had always killed silently and swiftly, appearing from nowhere and vanishing again. Killing a man in this manner seemed somehow barbaric to him.

He leaned down and said, 'Let me go, and I will help you.'

'Fuck you,' Michael said, grimacing.

'That's not terribly wise on your part.' Delaroche reached down through the railing and took hold of Michael's left wrist. 'Reach up and take my hand.'

Michael was beginning to lose his grip on the bridge.

'You just killed my father-in-law,' he said. 'You tried to kill me and my wife. You killed Sarah.'

'I didn't kill them, Michael. Other people killed them. I was just the weapon. I'm not responsible for their deaths any more than you are responsible for the death of Astrid Vogel.'

'Who hired you?' Michael rasped.

'It doesn't matter.'

'It matters to me! Who hired you?'

But Michael's grip was beginning to weaken.

Delaroche took hold of his left arm with both hands.

Michael reached into his jacket with his right hand, withdrew the Browning, and aimed it at Delaroche's head. Delaroche held onto Michael's hand, staring at the gun. Then he smiled and said, 'Do you know the story of the frog and the scorpion crossing the Nile?'

Michael knew the parable; anyone who had ever lived or worked in the Middle East knew it. A frog and a scorpion are standing on the banks of the Nile, and the scorpion asks the frog to ferry him to the other side. The frog refuses, because he is afraid the scorpion will sting him. The scorpion assures the frog he will not sting him; to do so would be foolish, because then both of them would drown. The frog sees the logic of this statement and agrees to take the scorpion to the other side. When they reach the middle of the river, the scorpion stings the frog. 'Now we both will drown,' the frog cries as his body goes numb with the scorpion's venom. 'Why did you do that?' The scorpion smiles and says, 'Because this is the Middle East.'

'I know the story,' Michael said.

'We have been locked in this conflict for too many years. Perhaps we can help each other. Revenge is for savages, after all. I understand you were in Northern Ireland recently. Look at what revenge has done for that place.'

'What do you want?'

'I will tell you what you want to know most – who hired me to kill Douglas Cannon, who hired me to kill the conspirators in the TransAtlantic affair, who hired me to kill you because you knew too much.' He paused. 'I will also tell you about the person in your organization who is involved with these people. In exchange, you will provide me with protection and allow me access to my bank accounts.'

'I don't have the authority to make a deal like that.'

'Perhaps not the authority, but you have the *ability*.'

Michael remained silent.

Delaroche said, 'You don't want to die without knowing the truth, do you, Michael?'

'Fuck you!'

'Do we have a deal?'

'How do you know I won't have you arrested the minute you pull me up?'

'Because unfortunately, you are an honourable man, which makes you strangely ill-suited to a business like this.' Delaroche shook Michael and said, 'Do we have a deal?'

'We have a deal, you fucking bastard.'

'All right then. Drop the gun into the river and take my hand before you get us both killed.'

40

'The bullet broke several of Ambassador Cannon's ribs and collapsed his left lung,' said the doctor at George Washington University Hospital, an absurdly young-looking surgeon named Carlisle. 'But unless he suffers some serious complications, I think he's going to be all right.'

'Can I see him?' Elizabeth said.

Carlisle shook his head. 'He's in recovery now, and frankly he doesn't look great. Why don't you stay here and try to make yourself comfortable. We'll let you see him as soon as he's awake.'

The doctor went out. Elizabeth tried to sit down, but after a few minutes she was once again pacing the small private waiting room. Two Metropolitan Police officers stood guard outside the door. She wore a set of light-blue hospital scrubs, because her dress had been stained with the blood of her father and the DSS agent. Maggie and the children were in a separate room. Maggie was remarkable, Elizabeth thought. She had been threatened by an assassin and bound with packing tape, but she refused to let the nurses look after Liza and Jake. Now, Elizabeth needed just one thing. She needed to hear her husband's voice.

It had been more than an hour since Elizabeth's nightmarish escape from N Street. The police had told her what they knew. When the first units arrived, the terrorists had fled, and Michael was alive. Then he disappeared across the back garden, and no one had seen him since. Two minutes later there was gunfire on the Georgetown side of Key Bridge, and a car exploded. The car, a light grey Saab, had been stolen a moment earlier by a man with a silenced handgun. There were also reports of two men fighting on the bridge. One man dangling over the water . . . Elizabeth closed her eyes and shivered. She thought, Michael, if you're alive, please tell me.

It was eleven o'clock. She switched on the television and flipped through the channels. The story was everywhere – the local stations and all the cable news channels. No one had any news about Michael. She dug a cigarette from her bag and lit it, smoking while she paced.

A nurse came by and stuck her head round the door.

'I'm sorry, ma'am, but there's no smoking in here.'

Elizabeth looked for a place to put the cigarette.

'Let me take that, Mrs Osbourne,' the nurse said gently. 'Is there anything I can get you?'

Elizabeth shook her head.

As the nurse went out, her cellular phone rang.

She pulled a phone from her bag and switched it on.

'Hello.'

'It's me, Elizabeth. Don't say a word, just listen.'

'Michael,' she whispered.

'I'm fine,' he said. 'I haven't been hurt.'

'Thank God,' she said.

'How's Douglas?'

'He's out of surgery. The doctor thinks he's going to be all right.'

'Where are the children?'

'They're here at the hospital,' Elizabeth said. 'When am I going to see you?'

'Maybe tomorrow. I have something I need to do first. I love you, Elizabeth.'

'Michael, where are you?' she asked, but the line had already gone dead.

Rebecca Wells left the Volvo in the long-term lot at Dulles Airport and took a shuttle bus to the terminal. She dropped the keys into a trash can and went into a rest room. She entered a stall and changed clothes, trading her two-piece suit for faded jeans, a sweater, and suede cowboy boots. Finally, she pinned her hair against her head and put on a blonde wig. She looked at herself in the mirror; the transformation had taken less than five minutes. She was now Sally Burke of Los Angeles, with a passport and a California driver's licence to prove it.

She walked through the terminal to the Air Mexico counter and checked in for the late flight to Mexico City. The next seventy-two hours were going to be difficult. From Mexico, she would travel through Central and South America, changing passports and identities each day. Then she would board a plane in Buenos Aires and go back to Europe.

She sat down in the lounge at the gate and waited for the flight to be called. She tried to close her eyes, but each time she did, she saw the head of the DSS agent explode in a flash of blood.

The CNN Airport Channel was running a news bulletin on the assassination attempt.

The Ulster Freedom Brigade has just claimed responsibility for the attempted murder of Ambassador Douglas Cannon. His two assailants, a man and a woman, are still at large. Doctors at George Washington University Hospital in Washington say Cannon is in critical condition but his wounds are not life-threatening . . .

Rebecca looked away. She thought, where in God's name are you, Jean-Paul? She removed the letter he had given her four hours earlier and read it once more. *Go to this place. I'll come for you if I can.*

The flight was called. She tossed the letter into a trash can and walked to the gate.

41

'Do you have a name?'

'I use many names, but I was called Jean-Paul Delaroche for the longest, and so I think of myself as him.'

'So I'm to call you Delaroche?'

'If you wish,' Delaroche said, and pulled his lips down into a frown that was very French.

Despite the late hour, there was still a good deal of traffic on the Capital Beltway, the remnants of Washington's eternal evening rush. Michael turned onto Interstate 95 and headed north toward Baltimore. The car was a rented Ford, which Michael had collected from National Airport after fleeing Key Bridge in a taxicab. At first the driver had refused to open the door to a pair of men in suits who looked as though someone had just beaten the daylights out of them. Then Delaroche flashed a stack of twenties, and the driver said that if they wanted to go to the moon, he would get them there by morning.

Delaroche was seated in the front passenger seat, foot propped on the dashboard. He was rubbing his ankle and scowling at it, as if it had betrayed him. He carelessly lit yet another cigarette. If he was anxious or afraid, he showed no signs of it. He opened the window to release the cloud of smoke. The inside of the car suddenly stank of wet farmland.

For years after Sarah's murder, Michael had tried to picture her killer in his mind. He supposed he had imagined that he was bigger than he actually was. Indeed,

Delaroche was rather small and compact, with the tightly wound muscles of a welterweight. Michael had heard his voice once before – at Cannon Point, the night he had tried to kill him – but listening to him speak now, Michael understood that he was not one man but many. His accent drifted about the map of Europe. Sometimes it was French, sometimes German, sometimes Dutch or Greek. He never spoke like a Russian; Michael wondered if at this point he could even speak his native language.

'By the way, the gun was empty.'

Delaroche sighed heavily, as if he were bored by a tedious television programme.

'The standard-issue handgun for CIA officers is a high-powered Browning automatic with a fifteen-shot clip,' he said. 'After reloading, you fired four shots at me through the front door, three through the back door, three more through the windshield, and five into the back of the Saab.'

'If you knew the gun was empty, why didn't you just drop me from the bridge?'

'Because even if I had killed you I had almost no chance of escape. I was wounded. I had no gun, no vehicle, and no communications. You were the only weapon I had left.'

'What the fuck are you talking about?'

'I have something you want, and you have something I want. You want to know who hired me to kill you, and I want protection from my enemies so I can live in peace.'

'What makes you think I intend to live up to that bargain?'

'Men don't quit the CIA unless they have principles. And men don't come back to the CIA when their president asks them unless they believe in honour. Your honour is your weak point. Why did you choose this life anyway, Michael? Was it your father who drove you to it?'

So, Michael thought. Delaroche has spent as much time analyzing me as I have him.

'I don't think I would have made the same decision if the roles were reversed,' Michael said. 'I think I would have let you fall from the bridge and enjoyed the sight of your body floating down the river.'

'That's not something to boast about. You are virtuous, but you are also highly emotional, and that makes you easily manipulated. The KGB understood that when they placed Sarah Randolph in your path, and when they ordered me to kill her in front of your eyes.'

'Fuck you!' Michael said. He was tempted to stop the car and beat the hell out of Delaroche. Then he remembered the fight on the bridge and how easily Delaroche had nearly killed him with his bare hands.

'Michael, please slow down before you kill us both. Where are we going, by the way?'

'What happened to your face?' Michael said, ignoring Delaroche's question.

'You issued an Interpol alert, along with a computer composite of my face, so I had plastic surgery.'

'How did you learn about the alert?'

'One thing at a time, Michael.'

'Was the plastic surgeon a man named Maurice Leroux?'

'Yes,' Delaroche said. 'How did you know?'

'Because British Intelligence was aware of the fact that Leroux did work from time to time for people like you. Did you kill him?'

Delaroche said nothing.

'He didn't do you any favours,' Michael said. 'You look hideous.'

'I realize that,' Delaroche said coldly, 'and I blame you.'

'You're a murderer. I don't feel sorry for you because you had a bad experience with a plastic surgeon.'

'I'm not a murderer, I'm an assassin. There's a difference. I used to kill people for my country, but now my country no longer exists, so I kill for money.'

'That makes you a murderer in my book.'

'Are you telling me that such men don't work for your organization? You have your assassins too, Michael. So, please – don't try to claim the moral high ground.'

'Who hired you to kill Douglas Cannon?'

'Where are you taking me?'

'Somewhere safe.'

'You're not taking me to a CIA safe house, I hope?'

'Who hired you to kill Douglas Cannon?'

Delaroche looked out the window for a long time and then drew a deep breath, as if he were about to dive beneath the surface and remain there for a long time.

'Perhaps I should start from the beginning,' Delaroche said finally. He turned from the window and looked at Michael. 'Be patient and I'll tell you everything you want to know.'

Delaroche spoke as if he were reciting the story of someone else's life instead of his own. When he struggled with English, he would switch to one of the other languages he and Michael had in common: Spanish or Italian or Arabic. Not two hours before, he had coldly murdered two DSS agents, yet as far as Michael could tell he suffered no after effects from the act of killing. Michael had killed only once – a Sword of Gaza terrorist at Heathrow Airport – and he had been haunted by nightmares for weeks.

He told Michael about the man he knew only as Vladimir. They had lived in a large KGB flat in Moscow and had a pleasant *dacha* not far from the city for weekends and holidays. Delaroche was known then by his Christian name, which was Nicolai, and his patronymic, which was

Mikhailovich. He was allowed no contact with other children. He did not attend normal state schools, he did not belong to any sports clubs or Party youth organizations. He was never permitted to leave the flat or the *dacha* without Vladimir at his side. Sometimes, when Vladimir was ill or too tired, he would send an unsmiling goon named Boris to accompany the child.

Eventually, Vladimir began to teach him languages. *To have another language is to have another soul*, Vladimir would say. *And for the life that you are about to lead, Nicolai Mikhailovich, you will need many souls indeed.* Delaroche wrinkled his face like an old man and hunched his shoulders. Michael, watching him, marvelled at his ability to transform himself into someone else. When he spoke in the voice of Vladimir, he sounded like a Russian for the first time.

Sometimes a tall, dour man with Western suits and Western cigarettes would visit, Delaroche continued. He would study the young boy as a sculptor might study a work in progress. Many years later Delaroche would learn the identity of the tall man. He was Mikhail Voronstov, the head of the First Chief Directorate of the KGB – his father.

In August 1968, at the age of sixteen, he was sent to the West. He crossed into Austria from Czechoslovakia, posing as the child of Czech dissidents fleeing the Russians. He stayed in Austria for a time, then moved on to Paris, where he lived as a homeless street urchin until the Church took him in.

It was in Paris that he discovered that he could paint. Vladimir had never permitted him to pursue anything but languages and tradecraft. *There isn't time for frivolous pursuits, Nicolai Mikhailovich*, he would say. *We are racing against the clock.* He would spend afternoons drifting through the museums, studying great works. He attended art school for a time and even managed to sell a few of his works on the street.

Then the man named Mikhail Arbatov appeared, and the killing began.

'Arbatov was my control officer,' Delaroche said. 'At first I handled internal matters – dissidents, potential defectors, that sort of thing. Then I took on a different kind of mission.'

Michael ticked off a series of assassinations that he knew Delaroche had carried out: the Spanish minister in Madrid, the French police official in Paris, the BMW executive in Frankfurt, the PLO official in Tunis, the Israeli businessman in London.

'The KGB wanted to take advantage of the terrorist and nationalist movements inside the borders of the NATO alliance and its allies,' Delaroche said. 'The IRA, the Red Army Faction, the Red Brigades of Italy, the Basques in Spain, Direct Action in France, and so on. I killed on both sides of the divide, simply in order to create disorder. There were many more killings than the ones you've named, of course.'

'And when the Soviet Union collapsed?'

'Arbatov and I were set adrift.'

'So you went into private practice?'

Delaroche nodded, rubbing his ankle.

'Arbatov had excellent contacts and was a skilled negotiator. He served as my agent, entertaining offers, negotiating fees – that sort of thing. We split the proceeds of my work.'

'And then TransAtlantic came along.'

'It was the biggest single payday of my life, $1 million. But I did not shoot down that jetliner. It was that Palestinian psychopath Hassan Mahmoud who shot down the plane.'

'You just disposed of Mahmoud.'

'That's right.'

'And the body was left behind so we would conclude that the Sword of Gaza had carried out the attack.'

'Yes.'

'And then you were hired by the men who *really* shot down the jetliner to eliminate the other people involved in the operation, like Colin Yardley in London and Eric Stoltenberg in Cairo.'

'And then you.'

'Who hired you?' Michael said. 'Who hired you to kill me?'

'They call themselves the Society for International Development and Co-operation,' Delaroche began. 'They're a bunch of intelligence officers, businessmen, arms merchants, and criminals who try to influence world events in order to make money and protect their own interests.'

'I don't believe such an organization really exists.'

'They shot down the jetliner so that one of their members, an American defence contractor named Mitchell Elliott, could convince President Beckwith to build an anti-missile defence system.'

Michael had suspected that Elliott was involved in this tragedy; indeed, he had put his suspicions in writing in his report to the Agency. Still, to hear Delaroche confirm his suspicions made him feel nauseated. Sweat began running over his ribs.

'They knew you were getting too close to the truth,' Delaroche said. 'They decided it would be best if you were dead, so they hired me to kill you.'

'How did they know about my suspicions?'

'They have a source inside Langley.'

'What happened after Shelter Island?' Michael asked.

'I went to work exclusively for the Society.'

'Does the Society have a leader?'

'He's called the Director. He goes by no other name. He's an Englishman. He has a young girl named Daphne. That's all I know about him.'

'You were the one who killed Ahmed Hussein in Cairo.'

Delaroche turned suddenly and glared at Michael.

'The Society carried out the assassination at the behest of the Mossad. How did you know it was me?'

'Hussein was under Egyptian surveillance. I saw a videotape of the killing and noticed the wound on the assassin's right hand. That's when I knew you were alive and working again. That's when we issued the Interpol alert.'

'We knew about the alert immediately,' Delaroche said, staring at the back of his right hand. 'The Director has excellent contacts within the Western intelligence and security services, but he said the information on the Interpol alert came from his source at Langley.'

'Why did the Society get involved in Northern Ireland?'

'Because it thought the peace agreement in Northern Ireland was bad for business. There was a meeting of the Society's executive council last month in Mykonos. The Society decided at that meeting to kill your father-in-law and you, and I was given the assignment.'

'Was the woman in the Volvo Rebecca Wells?'

'Yes.'

'Where is she now?'

'That wasn't part of our deal, Michael.'

'Why kill me?'

'The Director has invested a great deal of money in me, and he wanted to protect his investment. He saw you as a threat.'

'Was the source from Langley at the meeting on Mykonos?'

'Everyone was on Mykonos.'

*

It was after 5 A.M. when Michael and Delaroche arrived in the village of Greenport on Long Island. They drove through the deserted streets and parked at the ferry landing. The boat lay quietly in its slip; it would not make its first trip across the Sound to Shelter Island for another hour. Michael used the public telephone next to the small clapboard shack at the terminal.

'Where the fuck are you?' Adrian Carter said. 'Everyone in town is looking for you.'

'Call me back at this number from a public phone.'

The ten-digit number he recited to Carter bore no resemblance to the actual number for the public phone. He had given Carter the number in a crude code the two men had used in the field a hundred years ago – backward, the first digit one more than the real number, the second digit two less, the third digit three more, and so on. He did not have to repeat the number. Carter, like Michael, was cursed with a perfect memory.

Michael hung up and smoked a cigarette while he waited for Carter to dress, get in his car, and drive to a public phone. The image of Carter pulling on a coat over his pyjamas made Michael smile. The telephone rang five minutes later.

'Would you mind telling me what the hell is going on?'

'I'll tell you when you get here.'

'Where are you?'

'Shelter Island.'

'What the hell are you doing there? Were you involved in that shootout on Key Bridge?'

'Just get up here on the first plane, Adrian. I need you.'

Carter hesitated a moment. 'I'll be there as soon as I can, but why do I know that this is going to suck.'

When Michael went back to the car Delaroche was gone.

366

He found him a moment later, leaning against a rusting chain-link fence, staring across the Sound toward the low, dark silhouette of Shelter Island.

'Tell me your plans,' Delaroche said.

'If you want your money and your freedom, you're going to have to sing for your supper.'

'What do you want me to do?'

'Help me destroy the source inside Langley.'

'Do you know who he is?'

'I do,' Michael said. 'And it's not a *he*. It's Monica Tyler.'

'I don't know enough to destroy Monica Tyler.'

'Yes, you do.'

Delaroche was still staring at the black water. 'Surely we could have done this somewhere else but here, Michael. Why did you bring me back to this place?' But Delaroche wasn't really expecting an answer, and Michael didn't give him one. 'I need to know one thing. I need to know how Astrid died.'

'Elizabeth killed her.'

'How?'

When Michael told him, he closed his eyes. They stood there, side by side, each clinging to the fence, as the first ferrymen began to arrive for work. A few minutes later the boat began to rumble in its slip.

'It was never personal,' Delaroche said finally. 'It was just business. Do you understand what I'm saying to you, Michael? It was just business.'

'You put me and my family through hell, and I'll never forgive you for it. But I understand. I understand everything now.'

42

When they arrived at the gate of Cannon Point, a security officer named Tom Moore stepped out of the guard shack. He was a former army ranger, with thick square shoulders and short-cropped blond hair.

'Sorry I didn't call first to let you know I was coming, Tom.'

'No problem, Mr Osbourne,' Moore said. 'We heard about the ambassador, sir. Obviously, we're all pulling for him. I just hope they catch the bastards who did it. Radio said they vanished without a trace.'

'It appears so. This is a friend of mine,' Michael said, gesturing at Delaroche. 'He'll be staying a day or two.'

'Yes, sir.'

'Come up to the house for lunch, Tom. We need to talk.'

'I don't want anything to do with it,' Adrian Carter said. 'Turn it over to Counterintelligence. Jesus, give it to the goons at the Bureau, for all I care. But just get rid of it, because it will destroy anyone who touches it.'

Carter and Michael walked along the bulkhead overlooking the Sound, heads down, hands in pockets, like a search party looking for the body. The morning was windless and cold. Carter was wearing the same bloated nylon parka that he had worn the afternoon in Central Park when he had asked Michael to come back to the Agency. He was a reformed smoker, but halfway through the story he bummed one of Michael's cigarettes and devoured it.

'She's the Director of the Central Intelligence Agency,' Michael said. 'She controls Counterintelligence. And as for the Bureau, who the hell wants to involve them? This is our affair. The Bureau will only rub our noses in it.'

'Are you forgetting that Jack the Ripper is your *only* witness?' Carter said, nodding at the house. 'You must admit he does have a bit of a credibility problem. Have you at least considered the possibility he's invented the whole thing to prevent you from arresting him?'

'He's not making it up.'

'How can you be so sure? This whole business about a secret order called the Society sounds like a bunch of bullshit to me.'

'Someone hired that man to come kill me last year because I was getting too close to the truth of the Trans-Atlantic affair. I told two people inside the Agency about my suspicions. One was you, and the other was Monica Tyler.'

'So what?'

'Why did Monica drive me from the Agency in the first place last year? Why did she remove me from the October case one week before he tried to kill Douglas? And there's something else. Delaroche said there was a meeting of the Society on Mykonos earlier this month. Monica was in Europe for a regional security conference. After the meeting she took two days of personal time and dropped out of sight.'

'Jesus Christ, Michael, I was in Europe earlier this month, too.'

'I believe it, Adrian. And so do you.'

They left the grounds of Cannon Point and walked along Shore Road on the edge of Dering Habor.

'If this becomes public it will be disastrous for the Agency.'

'I agree,' Michael said. 'It would take years to recover from a blow like this. It would destroy the Agency's reputation, in Washington and around the world, for that matter.'

'So what do you do?'

'Present her with the evidence and shut her down before she can do any more damage. She has blood on her hands, but if we do this in public the Agency will be in ruins.'

'The only way you'll ever dislodge Monica from the Seventh Floor is with dynamite.'

'I'll walk up there with a briefcase full of the stuff if I have to.'

'Why the fuck did you involve me?'

'Because you're the only one I trust. You were my controller, Adrian. You'll always be my controller.'

They stopped on a bridge spanning the mouth of a tidal creek at the foot of Dering Harbor. Beyond the bridge lay a broad plain of marsh grass and bare trees. A rather small, lean man stood in front of an easel on the bridge, painting. He wore fingerless wool gloves and a threadbare fisherman's sweater several sizes too large for him.

'Lovely,' Carter said, looking at the work. 'You're very talented.'

'Thank you,' the painter said, his English heavily accented.

Carter turned to Michael and said, 'You can't be serious.'

'Adrian Carter, I'd like you to meet Jean-Paul Delaroche. You may know him better as October.'

Tom Moore came up to the house at noon.

'You wanted to see me, Mr Osbourne?'

'Come in, Tom. There's fresh coffee in the kitchen.'

Michael poured coffee, and they sat across from each other at the small table in the kitchen.

'What can I do for you, Mr Osbourne?'

'There's going to be a meeting here this evening that I need to record, audio and visual,' Michael began. 'Can the surveillance cameras be repositioned?'

'Yes, sir,' Moore said flatly.

'Can you record on their output?'

'Yes, sir.'

Adrian Carter came into the room, followed by Delaroche.

'Do we have any audio equipment on the property?'

'No, sir. Your father-in-law wouldn't allow any microphones. He thought it would be an invasion of his privacy.' Moore's big face broke into a pleasant smile. 'He barely tolerates the cameras. Before he left for London I caught him trying to disconnect one.'

'How long would it take to get microphones and a recording deck?'

Moore shrugged. 'Couple of hours at the most.'

'Can you install them so they can't be seen?'

'The microphones are easy because they're relatively small. The cameras are the problem. They're normal security cameras, about the size of a shoebox.'

Michael swore softly.

'I have an idea, though.'

'Yeah?'

'The cameras have a fairly long lens on them. If you held the meeting in the living room, I could position cameras outside on the lawn and shoot through the windows.'

Michael smiled and said, 'You're good, Tom.'

'I did some intelligence work while I was with the Rangers. You just have to make certain the curtains stay open.'

'I can't guarantee that.'

'Worst-case scenario, you'll have the audio as backup.'

Delaroche said, 'You have any guns besides that museum piece you're carrying?'

Moore had a Smith & Wesson .38 revolver.

'I like these *museum* pieces because they don't jam,' Moore said, smacking his thick hand against the holster. 'But I might be able to lay my hands on a couple of automatics.'

'What kind?'

'Colt .45s.'

'No Glocks or Berettas?'

'Sorry,' Moore said, face perplexed.

'A Colt or two would be fine,' Carter said.

'Yes, sir,' Moore said. 'Mind telling me what this is all about?'

'Not a chance.'

Delaroche followed Michael up the stairs to the bedroom. Michael went to the closet, opened the door, and pulled down a small box from the top shelf. He opened the box and took out the Beretta.

'I believe you dropped this the last time you were here,' Michael said, handing the gun to Delaroche.

Delaroche's scarred right hand wrapped around the grip, and his finger reflexively slipped inside the trigger guard. Something about the way Delaroche handled the weapon so effortlessly made Michael feel cold.

'Where did you get this?' Delaroche asked.

'I fished it out of the water off the end of the dock.'

'Who restored it?'

'I did.'

Delaroche looked up from the gun and stared at Michael quizzically. 'Why on earth would you do that?'

'I'm not sure. I guess I wanted a reminder of what it really looked like.'

Delaroche still had a 9-millimetre clip in his pocket. He slipped it into the weapon and pulled the slider, chambering the first round.

'If you like, I suppose you could fulfil the terms of your contract at this moment.'

Delaroche smiled and handed the Beretta back to Michael.

At four o'clock that afternoon Michael entered Douglas's study and dialled Monica Tyler's office at Headquarters. Carter listened on another extension, his hand over the receiver. Monica's secretary said Director Tyler was in a senior staff meeting and couldn't be interrupted. Michael said it was an emergency and was passed on to Tweedledee or Tweedledum, Michael was never certain which was which. They kept him waiting the statutory ten minutes while Monica was pulled from the meeting.

'I know everything,' Michael said, when she finally came on the line. 'I know about the Society, and I know about the Director. I know about Mitchell Elliott and the TransAtlantic affair. And I know you tried to have me killed.'

'Michael, are you truly delusional? What on earth are you talking about?'

'I'm offering you a way out of this quietly.'

'Michael, I don't –'

'Come to my father-in-law's house on Shelter Island. Come alone – no security, no staff. Be here by 10 P.M. If you're not here by then, or if I see anything I don't like, I'll go to the Bureau and *The New York Times* and tell them everything I know.'

He hung up without waiting for her to answer.

Thirty minutes later the secure telephone rang in the study of the Director's London mansion. He was sitting in a wing chair next to the fire, feet propped on an ottoman, working his way through a stack of paperwork. Daphne slipped into the room and answered the phone.

'It's Picasso,' Daphne said. 'She says it's urgent.'

The Director took the receiver and said, 'Yes, Picasso?'

Monica Tyler calmly told him about the call she had just received from Michael Osbourne.

'I suspect October is the source of his information,' the Director said. 'If that's true, it would seem to me that Osbourne has a rather weak case. October knows very little about the overall structure of our organization, and he is hardly a credible witness. He is a man who kills for money – a man without morality and without loyalty.'

'I agree, Director, but I don't think we should simply dismiss the threat.'

'I'm not suggesting that.'

'Do you have the resources to eliminate them?'

'Not on such short notice.'

'And if I simply arrest October?'

'Then he and Osbourne will tell their story to the world.'

'I'm open to suggestions.'

'Do you know how to play poker?' the Director asked.

'Figuratively or literally?'

'A little of both, actually.'

'I believe I understand your point.'

'Listen to what Osbourne has to say and evaluate your options. I know I don't need to remind you that you swore an oath of allegiance to the Society. Your first concern is upholding that oath.'

'I understand, Director.'

'Perhaps you will be presented with an opportunity to resolve the matter yourself.'

'I've never done that sort of thing, Director.'

'It's not so difficult, Picasso. I'll wait to hear from you.'

He hung up the telephone and looked at Daphne.

'Begin calling the members of the executive council and the division chiefs. I need to speak to each of them urgently. I'm afraid we may be forced to close down shop for a while.'

Monica Tyler hung up the telephone and stared out of her window at the Potomac. She walked across the room and stopped in front of a Rembrandt, a landscape she had purchased at auction in New York for a small fortune. Her eyes ran over the painting now: the clouds, the light spilling from the cottage, the horseless trap in the grass of the meadow. She took hold of the frame, and pulled. The Rembrandt swung back on its hinges, revealing a small wall safe.

Her fingers worked the tumblers automatically, eyes barely looking at the numbers; a few seconds later the safe was open. She began removing items: an envelope containing $100,000 in cash, three false passports in different names from different countries, credit cards corresponding to the names.

Then she removed one final item, a Browning automatic.

Perhaps you will be presented with an opportunity to resolve the matter yourself.

She changed clothes, exchanging the tailored Chanel for a pair of jeans and a sweater. She placed the items from the safe into a large black leather handbag. Then she packed a small overnight bag with a change of clothes.

She pulled the handbag over her shoulder and reached inside, wrapping her hand around the grip of the Browning; she had been trained by the Agency to handle a gun. A member of her security detail was waiting outside in the hall.

'Good afternoon, Director Tyler.'

'Good afternoon, Ted.'

'Back to headquarters, Director?'

'The helipad, actually.'

'The helipad? No one told us anything about –'

'It's all right, Ted,' she said calmly. 'It's a private matter.'

The security man looked at her carefully. 'Is there something wrong, Director Tyler?'

'No, Ted, everything's going to be just fine.'

43

SHELTER ISLAND, NEW YORK

Michael maintained a tense vigil on the lawn of Cannon Point. He was drinking Adrian Carter's vile coffee and smoking his own vile cigarettes, pacing the frozen grass with a pair of Douglas's bird-watching binoculars around his neck. God, but it was a cold night, he thought. He looked once more at the western sky, the direction Monica would come, but there was only a spray of wet stars, scattered over the black carpet of space, and a sliver of moon, white as exposed bone.

Michael looked at his watch – 9:58 P.M. Monica's never on time, he thought. 'Monica will be ten minutes late for her own funeral,' Carter once cracked, while cooling his heels in Monica's dreary anteroom. *Maybe she won't come*, Michael thought, *or maybe I just hope she won't*. Maybe Adrian had been right. Maybe he should just forget about the whole thing, leave the Agency – for good, this time – and stay on Shelter Island with Elizabeth and the children. *And what? Live the rest of my life looking over my shoulder, waiting for Monica and her friends to send another assassin, another Delaroche?*

He checked the time once more. It was his father's old watch: German-made, big as a silver dollar, waterproof, dustproof, shockproof, childproof, faintly luminous. Perfect for a spy. It was the only one of his father's possessions Michael had taken after he died. He even kept the lousy retractable band that left a puckered brickwork pattern on the skin of his wrist. Sometimes he would look at the watch and think of his father – in Moscow, or Rome, or Vienna, or Beirut – waiting for an agent. He wondered what his father would think of all this. *He never told me what he was thinking then*, Michael thought. *Why should now be any different?*

He heard a thumping sound that could have been a distant helicopter, but it was only the nightclub across the water in Greenport – the house band gearing up for yet another dreadful set. Michael thought of his motley operational team. Delaroche, his enemy, his living proof of Monica's treachery, waiting to be wheeled onto the stage and wheeled off again. Tom Moore, parked in front of his monitors in the guest cottage, about to get the shock of his life. Adrian Carter, pacing behind him, chain-smoking Michael's cigarettes, wishing he were anywhere else.

Michael heard the thump of the helicopter long before he could see it. For an instant he thought there might be two, or three, or even four. Instinctively, he reached for the Colt automatic that Tom Moore had given him, but after a moment he saw the lights of a single helicopter approaching over Nassau Point and Great Hog Neck, and he realized it was only the night wind playing tricks on his ears.

He thought of the morning, two months earlier, when the helicopter bearing President James Beckwith had made the same journey to Shelter Island, setting off the chain of events that had led him to this place.

The images played out in his mind as the helicopter drew nearer.

Adrian Carter on the levee of the reservoir in Central Park, seducing Michael into coming back.

Kevin Maguire strapped to a chair, and Seamus Devlin

smiling over him. *I didn't kill Kevin Maguire, Michael. You killed him.*

Preston McDaniels being crushed beneath the wheels of the Misery Line train.

Delaroche, smiling over the rail of Key Bridge. *Do you know the story of the frog and the scorpion crossing the Nile?*

Sometimes intelligence work is like that, his father used to say – like chaos theory. A breath of wind disturbs the surface of a pond, moving a reed of grass, which sends a dragonfly to flight, which startles a frog, and so on and so on, until, ten thousand miles away and many weeks later, a typhoon destroys an island in the Philippines.

The helicopter swept low over Southold Bay. Michael looked at his father's wristwatch: one minute past ten. The helicopter descended over Shelter Island Sound and Dering Harbor, then set down on the broad lawn of Cannon Point. The engines shut down, and the rotor gradually stopped twisting. The door opened, and a small staircase unfolded to the ground. Monica climbed out, a black bag over her shoulder, and marched resolutely toward the house.

'Let's get this nonsense over with,' she said, brushing past Michael. 'I'm a very busy woman.'

Monica Tyler was not a pacer, but she was pacing now. She toured Douglas Cannon's living room like a politician inspecting a trailer park after a tornado – calm, stoic, empathetic, but careful not to step in anything foul. She paused from time to time, now frowning at the floral slipcover on the couch, now grimacing at the rustic throw rug in front of the fire.

'You have cameras somewhere, don't you, Michael,'

she said, making a statement rather than asking a question. 'And microphones.' She continued her restless journey around the room. 'You don't mind if I close these curtains, do you, Michael? You see, I've been through that little course at the farm too. I may not be an experienced field man like you, but I know a little something about the clandestine arts.' She made a vast show of closing the curtains. 'There,' she said. 'That's much better.'

She sat down, a reluctant, arrogant witness taking her place at the dock. The log fire began to spit. She crossed one leg over the other, resting her long hands on the faded denim of her jeans, and settled a frozen gaze on Michael. The prosaic surroundings had stolen her physical intimidation. There was no gold pen to wield like a stiletto, no glossy secretary to interrupt a meeting that had unexpectedly turned unpleasant, no Tweedledum and Tweedledee, watchful as Dobermans, clutching their leather folders and secure cell phones.

Delaroche entered the room. He was smoking a cigarette. Monica glared at him with disdain, for tobacco, like personal disloyalty, was among her many pet peeves.

'This man is called Jean-Paul Delaroche,' Michael said. 'Do you know who he is?'

'I suspect he is a former KGB assassin code-named October who now works as an international contract killer.'

'Do you know why he's here?'

'Probably because he nearly killed your father-in-law last night in Georgetown, despite our best efforts to stop him.'

'What game are you playing, Monica?' Michael asked sharply.

'I was about to ask you the same question.'

'I know everything,' he said, calmer now.

'Believe me, Michael, you don't know everything. In fact, you know next to nothing. You see, your little escapade has severely jeopardized one of the most important operations currently being conducted by the Central Intelligence Agency.'

The room had gone silent, except for the fire, which was spitting again, crackling like small arms. Outside, the wind was moving the leafless trees, and one was scratching against the side of the house. A truck grumbled along Shore Road, and somewhere a dog was barking.

'If you want the rest, you have to shut down your microphones,' Monica said.

Michael remained motionless. Monica reached for her handbag, as if getting up to leave.

'All right,' Michael said. He stood, walked to Douglas's desk, and opened a drawer. Inside was a microphone, about the size of a finger. Michael held it up for Monica to see.

'Disconnect it,' she said.

He pulled the microphone from its cable.

'Now the backup,' she said. 'You're too paranoid to do something like this without a backup.'

Michael walked to the bookshelves, removed a volume of Proust, and pulled out the second microphone.

'Kill it,' Monica said.

Delaroche looked at Michael. 'She has a gun in the handbag.'

Michael walked over to the chair where Monica Tyler was seated, reached inside the bag, and pulled out the Browning.

'Since when do CIA directors carry weapons?'

'When they feel threatened,' Monica said.

Michael set the safety and tossed the Browning to Delaroche.

'All right, Monica, let's get started.'

Adrian Carter was a worrier by nature, which made him strangely ill-suited to the business of sending agents into the field and waiting for them to come out again. He had endured many tense vigils concerning Michael Osbourne over the years. He remembered the two endless nights he had spent in Beirut in 1985, waiting for Michael to return from a meeting with an agent in the Bekaa Valley. Carter had feared Michael had been taken hostage or killed. He was about to give up when Michael stumbled into Beirut, covered in dust and smelling of goats.

Still, nothing compared to the uneasiness Carter felt now, as he listened to his agent confronting the Director of Central Intelligence. When she demanded that Michael disable the first microphone, Carter was not terribly worried – there were two in the room, and an experienced field man like Michael would never give up his ace in the hole.

Then he heard Monica demand disconnection of the second, followed by thumping and scratching as Michael dug it from the bookshelf. When the feed from the room fell silent, he did the only thing a good agent-runner can do.

He lit another of Michael's cigarettes, and he waited.

'A short time after I was appointed DCI, I was approached by a man who referred to himself only as the Director.' She spoke like an exhausted mother, reluctantly telling a fairy tale to a child who refuses to go to bed. 'He asked me if I would be willing to join an elite club, a group of international intelligence officers, financiers, and businessmen dedicated to the preservation of global security. I suspected something was amiss, so I reported the incident to Counterintelligence as a potential recruitment by a hostile organization. CI thought it might be operationally productive if we danced with the Director, and I agreed. I sought approval from the president himself to begin the operation. I met with the man called the Director three more times, twice in Northern Europe and once in the Mediterranean. At the end of the third meeting, we came to terms, and I joined the Society.

'The Society has very long tentacles. It is involved in covert operations on a global scale. I immediately began collecting intelligence on membership and operations. Some intelligence was laundered through the Agency, and we took countermeasures. Sometimes, we deemed it was necessary to allow Society operations to continue, because disrupting them could jeopardize my position inside the hierarchy of the organization.'

Michael watched her as she spoke. She was calm and collected and utterly lucid, as though she were reading a prepared speech to a gathering of shareholders. He was in awe of her; she was a remarkable liar.

'Who's the Director?' Michael asked.

'I don't know, and I suspect Delaroche doesn't know either.'

'Did you know he had been hired to kill my father-in-law?'

'Of course, Michael,' she said, narrowing her eyes scornfully.

'Then what was that song and dance in the executive dining room about? Why did you remove me from the case?'

'Because the Director asked me to,' she said flatly, then added, 'Let me explain. He thought it would be easier for Delaroche to carry out the assignment if you were no longer in charge of the case. So I removed you and quietly took steps to ensure your father-in-law's safety. Unfortunately, those steps were not successful.'

'If that was the case, why was he unprotected in Washington?'

'Because the Director assured me that Delaroche would not operate on American soil.'

'Why didn't you tell me?'

'Because we didn't want you to do anything rash that might jeopardize the security of the operation. The goal was to draw Delaroche into the open so he could be eliminated – taken off the market, as it were. We didn't want you to frighten him away by locking your father inside a vault and throwing away the key.'

Michael looked at Delaroche, who was shaking his head.

'She's lying,' he said. 'The Director arranged everything for me here – transportation, weapons, everything. He specifically decided to carry out the assassination in Washington because he knew the ambassador would be more vulnerable here than in London. It was timed to coincide with the Northern Ireland conference to increase the impact on the peace process.' He paused a moment, eyes moving from Michael to Monica and back again. 'She's very good, but she's lying.'

Monica ignored him, looking at Michael.

'This is why we didn't want Delaroche to be taken into custody, Michael. Because he would lie. Because he would fabricate. He would say anything to save his own skin. And the problem is, you believe him. We wanted him eliminated, because if he was arrested, we suspected he might pull a stunt like this.'

'It's not a stunt,' Delaroche said. 'It's the truth.'

'You should have played your part better, Michael. You should have just taken your revenge for Sarah Randolph and killed him. But now you've created quite a mess – for the Agency and for yourself.'

Monica stood up, signalling that the meeting had come to an end.

Michael said, 'If you insist on playing it this way, you leave me no other choice but to go to Counterintelligence and the Bureau with my suspicions about you. You'll spend the next two years going through the Agency equivalent of Chinese water torture. Then the Senate will want a piece of you. Your legal bills alone will bankrupt you. You'll never work in government again, and no one on Wall Street will touch you with a barge pole. You'll be destroyed, Monica.'

'You don't have enough proof, and no one will believe you.'

'The son-in-law of Ambassador Douglas Cannon alleges that the director of the Central Intelligence Agency was involved in the attempt to assassinate him. That's a helluva story. There's not a reporter in Washington who wouldn't jump all over it.'

'And you'll be prosecuted for leaking Agency secrets.'

'I'll take my chances.'

Adrian Carter stepped into the room. Monica looked at him; then her eyes settled back on Michael.

'A witch hunt will destroy the Agency, Michael. You should know that. Your father was caught up in the Angleton mole hunt, wasn't he? It almost ruined his career. Is this your way of taking revenge on the Agency for your father? Or are you still resentful of me because I had the gall to suspend you once?'

'You're not in any position to piss me off right now, Monica.'

'So what do I have to do to prevent you from making this reckless allegation against me?'

'You're going to resign at the appropriate time. And until

385

then, you're going to do exactly as Adrian and I say. And you're going to help me put the Society out of business.'

'God, but you're a naive fool. Putting the Society out of business is impossible. The only way to control them is to be part of them.' She looked at Delaroche. 'What do you plan to do with *him*?'

Michael said, 'I'll handle Delaroche.'

Michael reached into his coat pocket and withdrew a cassette tape.

'I made this last night, along with a few duplicates,' he said. 'It contains a full accounting of your role in the Society, the TransAtlantic affair, and the attempt to kill my father-in-law. I'm going to set up a trip wire. If any harm comes to Adrian, Delaroche, or me, copies of this tape will be sent to *The New York Times* and the FBI.'

Michael placed the tape back in his pocket.

'It's your move, Monica.'

'I've given six years of my life to the Agency,' she said. 'I've done everything in my power to ensure its survival and to protect it from men like you – dinosaurs who lack the vision to see that the Agency has a role in this new world of ours. The game has passed you by, Michael, and you're too stupid to even notice.'

'You've used the Agency as a personal plaything to advance your own interests, and now I'm taking it back.'

She pulled her bag over her shoulder, turned, and walked out.

'It's your move, Monica,' Michael repeated, but she simply kept walking. A moment later they heard the whine of the helicopter engine coming to life again. Michael stepped onto the veranda in time to see Monica's chopper lift from the lawn and disappear over the waters of the Sound.

They spent the rest of that day waiting. Carter stood

on the veranda, field glasses around his neck, staring toward the Sound like a border guard on the Berlin Wall. Michael circled the house, marching along stony beaches and through the woods, searching for signs of an enemy buildup. All the while Delaroche just watched them, a slightly bemused bystander to the wreck he had caused.

Carter stayed in touch with Headquarters. Had anyone heard from Monica? he would ask innocently at the conclusion of each conversation. The answers grew more intriguing as the day progressed. Monica's cancelled all meetings. Monica's holed up in her office. Monica's not taking calls. Monica's gone underground. Monica's refusing food and drink. Michael and Carter debated the significance of the reports, as spies are prone to do. Was she drawing up the terms of surrender or preparing a counterattack?

In the afternoon Carter went into the village for food. Delaroche cooked omelettes for them, propped on a stool, because he couldn't stand long on his swollen ankle. They drank one bottle of wine, then another. Delaroche provided the entertainment. For two hours he lectured: training, tradecraft, assignments, cover identities, weaponry, and tactics. He told them nothing they could ever use against him, but he seemed to take pleasure from even the slightest unburdening of secrets. He said nothing of Sarah Randolph or Astrid Vogel or the night a year earlier at Cannon Point, when he and Michael had shot each other. He remained very still as he spoke, hands folded on the table, left hand covering the right in order to hide the puckered scar that had led Michael to him.

Carter asked the questions, because Michael was already somewhere else. Oh, he was listening, Carter thought – Michael, the human Dictaphone, capable of monitoring three conversations and reciting each of them back to you a week later – but a corner of his mind was turning over another problem. Finally, Carter switched to Russian, a language Michael did not speak, and the two men finished their conversation in private.

At dusk, Michael and Delaroche walked. Michael the former track star had wrapped Delaroche's ankle in heavy white tape. Carter remained behind in the house; it would be like eavesdropping on quarrelling lovers, and he wanted no part of it. Still, he could not resist the urge to step onto the veranda and watch them. He was not a voyeur, just a control officer, looking out for his agent and old friend.

They walked along the bulkhead toward the dock, Delaroche limping slightly. As the light grew weaker, Carter could not tell one from the other, so similar were the two men in height and build. He realized then that in many ways they were two halves of the same man. Each possessed traits present, but successfully repressed, in the other. If not for birthright, the haphazard roulette wheel of time and place, each might very well have walked the opposite path: Jean-Paul Delaroche, virtuous intelligence officer; Michael Osbourne, assassin.

After a long time – an hour, Carter guessed, because uncharacteristically he had neglected to record the time the conversation began – Michael and Delaroche started back toward the house.

They paused at Michael's rental car and faced each other over the hood. Carter still could not tell which was which. One seemed to be speaking with intensity, the other lazily kicking at the ground with the toe of his shoe. When the conversation ended, the one who had been kicking the ground held out his hand over the hood of the car, but the other refused to take it.

Delaroche withdrew his hand and climbed into the car.

He drove through the security gate and sped into the darkness along Shore Road. Michael Osbourne walked slowly up to the house.

APRIL

44

Ambassador Douglas Cannon was released from George Washington University Hospital on an unusually hot morning in the second week of April. Overnight it had rained, but by mid-morning the puddles were blazing beneath a fierce sunlight. Only a small company of reporters and cameramen waited outside in the drive, for Washington's media suffer from a sort of collective attention deficit syndrome, and no one was really interested in watching an old man leaving the hospital. Still, Douglas managed to 'make news,' as they say in the trade, when he loudly demanded to walk rather than ride out in the obligatory wheelchair – so loudly, in fact, that he could be heard by the reporters outside. 'I was shot in the back, goddammit, not the legs,' Cannon rumbled. His remarks were reported that night on the evening news, much to the ambassador's delight.

He stayed at the house on N Street in Georgetown for the first two weeks of his recovery, then went home to his beloved Cannon Point. A small crowd of well-wishers waved and shouted as Douglas's car passed through Shelter Island Heights. He remained at Cannon Point for the remainder of the spring. The security guards accompanied him as he walked the stony tide line of Upper Beach and the footpaths of Mashomack reserve. By June he felt strong enough to go for a sail aboard *Athena*.

Uncharacteristically, he surrendered the helm to Michael, but he barked orders and criticized his son-in-law's seamanship so forcefully that Michael threatened to throw him overboard off Plum Island.

Old friends urged Douglas to resign his post in London; even President Beckwith thought it would be best. But at the end of June, he returned to London and settled into his office at Grosvenor Square. On July 4, Independence Day, he made a special appearance before Parliament, then travelled to Belfast, where he received a hero's welcome.

To coincide with his visit, the British and American intelligence and security services released the findings of their joint investigation into the Ulster Freedom Brigade's attempt to kill Cannon in Washington. The report concluded that there were two terrorists involved, a woman named Rebecca Wells, who was also involved in the Hartley Hall affair, and an unidentified man who apparently was a professional assassin hired by the group.

Despite a worldwide search, both terrorists remained at large.

Within hours of Cannon's visit to Northern Ireland, a large car bomb exploded outside a market near the corner of the Whiterock Road and the Falls Road. Five people died and another sixteen were injured. The Ulster Freedom Brigade claimed responsibility. That night a fringe Republican group calling itself the Irish Liberation Cell avenged the attack by setting off a massive truck bomb that flattened much of central Portadown. The group promised to continue its attacks until the Good Friday peace accords were dead.

For many weeks the endless corridors at Langley crackled with rumours of a shakeup on the Seventh Floor. Monica was leaving, according to one rumour. She was staying for ever, according to another. Monica had fallen out of favour with the president. Monica was about to become secretary of state. The most popular rumour among her detractors was the story that she had suffered a nervous breakdown. That she had become delusional. That in a fit of psychotic rage she had tried to smash her precious mahogany office furniture to splinters.

Inevitably, the pervasive rumours about Monica reached the ears of *The Washington Post*. The newspaper's intelligence correspondent chose to discard the more salacious things he had heard, but in a lengthy front-page piece he *did* report that Monica had lost the confidence of the Agency's rank and file, the barons of the intelligence community, and even the president himself. That afternoon, during a photo opportunity with schoolchildren in the Rose Garden, President Beckwith said that Monica Tyler retained his 'full and complete confidence.' Translated from Washington-speak into plain English, the remark meant that Monica Tyler was being measured for the drop.

She was besieged with interview requests. *Meet the Press* wanted her. Ted Koppel telephoned personally to invite her on *Nightline*. A booker from the staff of *Larry King Live* actually tried to talk her way past the guards at the front gate. Monica turned them all away. Instead, she released a written statement saying that she served at the pleasure of the president, and if the president wanted her to remain she would.

But the damage was already done. Winter descended on the Seventh Floor. Doors remained tightly closed. Paper stopped flowing. Paralysis was setting in. Monica was cut off, said the rumour mill. Monica was less accessible than ever. Monica was finished. Tweedledee and Tweedledum were rarely seen; when they did appear, they moved about the halls like skittish grey wolves. Something had to be done, said the rumours. Things couldn't go on this way.

Finally, in July, Monica summoned the staff to the auditorium and announced that she was resigning, effective September 1. She was making the announcement early so that President Beckwith – whom she admired deeply and had been honoured to serve – would have ample time to choose a suitable successor. In the meantime there would be changes in the senior staff. Adrian Carter would be the new executive director. Cynthia Martin would take Carter's place as chief of the Counterterrorism Center. And Michael Osbourne would be the new deputy director for operations.

In the autumn, Monica dropped from sight. Her old firm wanted her back, but Monica said she needed some time to herself before returning to the grind of Wall Street. She began to travel; reports of her whereabouts regularly reached Carter and Michael on the Seventh Floor at Langley. Monica was always alone, according to watch reports. No friends, no family, no lovers, no dogs – no suspicious contacts of any kind. She had been seen in Buenos Aires. She had been spotted in Paris. She had gone on safari in South Africa. She went scuba diving in the Red Sea, much to the surprise of everyone at Headquarters, since no one there had ever unearthed the fact that she was an expert diver. In late November a surveillance artist from the CIA's Vienna Station photographed Monica seated alone in a chilly café in the Stephansplatz.

That same night Monica Tyler was walking back to her hotel after dinner, through a narrow pedestrian passageway in the shadow of St Stephan's Cathedral, when a man appeared before her. He was average in height, compact in build, and light on his feet. Something about the way he moved, the determined rhythm of his gait, set off alarm bells in her head.

Monica glanced over her shoulder and realized she was alone. She stopped walking, turned around, and started back toward the square. The man, now behind her, only quickened his pace. Monica did not run – she realized it would be pointless – she just closed her eyes and kept walking.

The man drew closer, but nothing happened. She stopped and spun round to challenge him. As she turned the man removed a gun from the inside of his jacket. A long, slender silencer was fitted into the end of the barrel.

'Dear God, no,' she said, but the man's arm swung up and he fired rapidly three times.

Monica Tyler fell backward, staring upward at the spires of the cathedral. She listened to the sound of her killer walking away, felt her own blood leaking from her body onto the cold cobblestones.

Then the spires of St Stephan's turned to water and she died.

In Georgetown, Elizabeth Osbourne heard the telephone ringing. Now that Michael was the deputy director, phone calls at four in the morning were not uncommon. She had an important meeting with a client in the morning – she had transferred to the firm's Washington office when Michael was promoted – and she needed to sleep. She closed her eyes and tried not to listen to Michael murmuring in the dark.

'Anything important?' she asked, when she heard him replace the receiver.

'Monica Tyler was murdered tonight in Vienna.'

'Murdered? What happened?'

'She was shot to death.'

'Who would want to kill Monica Tyler?'

'Monica had a lot of enemies.'

'Are you going in?'

'No,' he said. 'I'll deal with it in the morning.'

She closed her eyes and tried to sleep, but it was no good. There was something in Michael's voice that disturbed her. *Monica had a lot of enemies.* Including you, Michael, she thought.

Some time before dawn he left their bed. Elizabeth got up and went downstairs. She found him in the living room, standing before the french doors, staring into the half-lit garden.

'Michael,' she said softly, 'are you all right?'

'I'm fine,' he said, without turning around.

'Is there something you want to talk about?'

'No, Elizabeth,' he said. 'I just needed to think.'

'Michael, if there's –'

'I said I can't talk about it, Elizabeth. So please drop it.'

He turned away from the french doors and walked past her without speaking.

Elizabeth saw that his face was the colour of ash.

The Society for International Development and Co-operation convened its annual summer conference in a lakeside château, high in the mountains of New Zealand's South Island. The site had been chosen long in advance, and the frozen lake and dense fogs of the New Zealand winter proved a befitting allegory for the Society's dreadful state following Picasso's demise. The Director's background at MI6 had prepared him for the occasional blown operation, but nothing at the Intelligence Service could compare with the global folding of the tents that occurred in the hours after Picasso's unveiling. Overnight, all operations ceased. Plans for new undertakings were quietly scrapped. Communication fell silent. Money stopped flowing. The Director sealed himself in his mansion in St John's Wood with only Daphne for company and did what any good operations man does after a right royal cock-up – he assessed the damage. And when he felt the time was right, he quietly set about stitching together the scattered remnants of his secret order.

The conference on South Island was supposed to be a sort of coming-out party. But the Society's rehabilitation was halting at best. Two members of the executive committee did not even bother to attend. One tried to send a proxy, a suggestion the Director found laughable. Shortly after convening the meeting, the Director, in a rare fit of pique, moved to expel them both. The motion passed on a voice vote, which Daphne dutifully recorded on her steno pad.

'Item number two on the agenda is the passing of Picasso,' the Director said, then gently cleared his throat. 'Her death came as a terrible shock to you all, I'm sure, but at least she's no longer in a position to do the Society any harm.'

'I congratulate you for dealing with the problem so professionally,' said Rodin.

'But you don't understand,' the Director said. 'Her death truly *did* come as a shock, because the Society had absolutely nothing to do with it.'

'But what about October? He is still alive, is he not?'

'I would assume that to be the case, I'm not certain. Perhaps the CIA has hidden him. Perhaps Michael Osbourne killed him and covered it up. The only thing I can say for certain is that all our attempts to locate him have failed.'

'Perhaps I could be of assistance,' said Monet, the chief of operations for Israel's Mossad. 'Our men have proved themselves capable of finding fugitives in the past. Finding a man like October shouldn't prove too terribly difficult.'

But the Director slowly shook his head. 'No,' he said. 'Even if October is still alive, I doubt he'll ever be a problem to us in the future. In my opinion, it's best to let the matter drop.'

The Director looked down and shuffled his papers.

'Which brings me to the third item on our agenda, the situation in the former Yugoslavia. The Kosovo Liberation Front would like our help. Gentlemen, we're back in business.'

EPILOGUE

LISBON
BRÉLÉS, FRANCE

Jean-Paul Delaroche had taken a small flat in a sagging amber apartment house overlooking the harbour in Lisbon. He had been to Lisbon just once, and only briefly, and the change in setting gave new life to his work. Indeed, he experienced his most productive period in many years. He worked diligently from morning until mid-afternoon, producing fine works of the churches and the squares and the boats along the waterfront. The owner of an eminent Lisbon gallery saw him painting one afternoon and enthusiastically offered to show his work. Delaroche accepted his card with his paint-smudged fingers and said he would think about it.

At night he went hunting. He stood on his balcony and looked for signs of surveillance. He walked for hours, trying to draw them into the open. He went cycling in the countryside and dared them to follow. He bugged his own flat to see if anyone was entering while he was away. On the last day of November he accepted the fact that he was not being watched.

That evening he left his flat and walked to a good café for dinner.

For the first time in thirty years he left his gun behind.

In December, he rented a Fiat sedan and drove to France. He had left Brélés, the old fishing village on the Breton coast, more than a year ago and had not set foot there since. He arrived at midday, the day after setting out from Lisbon, having spent one night in Biarritz.

He parked in town and went walking. No one recognized him. At the *boulangerie*, Mademoiselle Trevaunce served him his bread with barely a *bonjour*. Mademoiselle Plauché from the *charcuterie* used to flirt with him shamelessly; now she joylessly carved his ham and his wedge of goat cheese and sent him on his way.

Delaroche went to the café where the old men passed afternoons. He asked if any of them had seen an Irishwoman around the village: black hair, good hips, pretty. 'There's an Irishwoman living in the old cottage on the point,' said Didier, the crimson-faced owner of the general store. 'Where the madman used to live – *le Solitaire*.'

When Delaroche pretended not to know what he meant by the last remark, Didier just laughed and gave Delaroche directions to the cottage. Then he asked if Delaroche wanted to join them for some wine and olives. Delaroche just shook his head and said, '*Non, merci*.'

Delaroche drove along the coast road and parked about two hundred yards from the cottage, in a lay-by overlooking the water. He saw smoke rising from the chimney, only to be sliced away by the wind. He just sat there, picking at the bread and the cheese, smoking, watching the cottage and the waves beating against the rocks. Once, he caught a glimpse of her raven hair, passing before an open window.

He thought of the last thing Michael Osbourne had said to him that night before they parted on Shelter Island. *She deserves worse*, he had said. *She deserves to die*. Osbourne was too decent a man – too virtuous – to condemn Monica to death, but Delaroche believed he knew what was in

Osbourne's heart at that moment. It was a small price to repay Osbourne for giving him his freedom. Actually, he rather enjoyed it; she was one of the most offensive people he had ever met. And there was one more thing – she had seen his face.

Rebecca stepped onto the terrace, arms folded beneath her breasts, gazing at the setting sun. Delaroche thought, does she want to see me? Or does she want me to stay away so she can put the entire business behind her? The easiest thing would be to turn around and forget about her. Go back to Lisbon and his work. Take up the gallery owner on his offer to show the paintings.

He started the engine. Even the distant sound made her turn suddenly and reach beneath her sweater. It was the hiding, Delaroche thought. She's jumping at noises, reaching for guns. He knew the feeling too well.

Rebecca stared at the car for a long time, and after a while her mouth lifted into something like a smile. Then she turned away and looked out to sea again and waited for him to come to her. Delaroche dropped the car into gear and started down the road toward the cottage.

ACKNOWLEDGEMENTS

While *The Marching Season* is a work of fiction, it obviously deals with real events in Northern Ireland, past and present. Because the conflict involves the English and the Irish, there is no shortage of great writing on the subject from which to draw. Indeed, I consulted dozens of non-fiction books while preparing this manuscript. The great works by Martin Dillon – including *The Shankill Butchers* and *The Dirty War* – were especially helpful, as were standards such as *The Troubles* by Tim Pat Coogan and *The Provisional IRA* by Patrick Bishop and Eamonn Mallie. Trying to catch history in the act can be a tricky proposition, but the World Wide Web and the phenomenon of on-line journalism made my task easier. Each morning, I was able to consult newspapers in London, Belfast, and Dublin to see what was happening on the ground in the Province. I wish to commend Martin Fletcher of *The Times* of London and the entire Northern Ireland crew of the BBC for their outstanding coverage of a remarkable year.

I interviewed several current and former CIA officers for this book and its predecessor, *The Mark of the Assassin*. I wish to thank the dedicated officers of the CIA's Counter-terrorism Center and Northern Ireland team. They patiently answered as many of my questions as they could and gave me some valuable insights into the way they go about their job.

Ion Trewin of Weidenfeld & Nicolson in London served as my travelling companion in Ulster and permitted me to set up shop in his Highgate study. He also offered some superb suggestions on how to improve the manuscript, as did his assistant, Rachel Leyshon.

As always, a heartfelt thanks to everyone at ICM and to the remarkable team at Random House and Ballantine.

And finally, none of this would be possible without the friendship, support, and enthusiasm of three extraordinary people: my agent, Esther Newberg; my brilliant editor, Daniel Menaker; and my publisher, Ann Godoff. You are the best.